MW01505546

THE MAJESTIC IMPOSTOR

TANYA BIRD

For Rhiannon. Sorry for your loss x

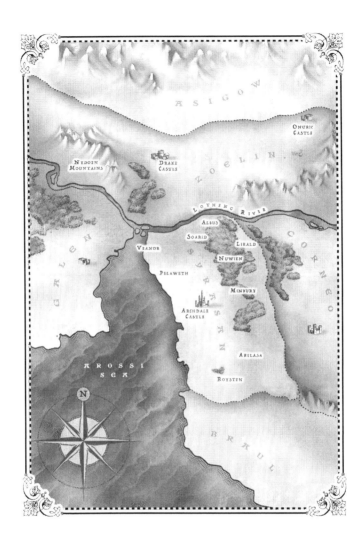

PROLOGUE

*A*ldara thought she was familiar with pain—that was until labour tore through her like a starved animal. 'I can't do it,' she sobbed. She had remained brave for hours, breathing through the increasing pressure and tightening that pulled across her front. But then the nausea had arrived, rolling over her with each contraction. Her nightdress clung to her like a second skin.

'I need to get you on your back so I can take a look,' Dahlia said.

Aldara was on her side with her legs pulled up, gripping the edge of the bed like it was the only thing keeping her together. Even the thought of having to move brought fresh tears. 'I can't. I'm sorry, but I can't move.'

Dahlia glanced out the window. Kadmus had gone to fetch Byrgus's daughter, Iris, who had agreed to help deliver the baby when the midwife had refused.

'I'm going to be sick,' Aldara said.

Dahlia held the pail up next to the bed, but nothing came. She put it down again and looked to the window.

'Maybe she's not coming either,' Aldara said, her body stiffening with the arrival of the next contraction. '*Aaaargh… ahhh…*'

Dahlia's hands twisted in front of her. 'The contractions are coming closer together.' She pressed her palm against her brow. 'If you had told Prince Tyron about the pregnancy, he would have ensured a midwife attend the birth.'

Aldara closed her eyes. They had been having the same conversation for months—Dahlia insisting she tell Tyron, and Aldara insisting he was doing enough and they could manage without burdening him further. She had planned to tell him after his marriage to Princess Tasia of Zoelin. Telling him prior might jeopardise the plans he had put in place to ensure Syrasan's alliance with Zoelin remained strong without the Companion trade. What would his family say of his illegitimate child? What would King Jayr of Zoelin make of the bastard born to his sister's betrothed? She told herself the secret protected him. One more month and the princess would be of age. No more excuses. No more nurturing hope.

Her reasons were not all noble. A childish part of her kept hoping he would show up one day and she could say the words to his face, see the change in him at hearing the news. Of course, he would have come immediately had she simply asked to see him, but she did not want to ask. She wanted him to come of his own choice—and come for her, not the infant who trapped him.

Months had slipped past. Too many months. She knew he would feel deceived by her long silence. Now the baby was here, and he would be hearing of it after the event. The thought pressed down on her until the next contraction crashed over her body. '*Aaaaaah… I can't do it. I can't… aaaargh.*'

Dahlia lifted Aldara's nightdress and peered as best she

could at what was now the crowning head. 'You do not have a choice. The baby is coming right now.'

Aldara did not even register her mother's words. Her mind had shut everything out, her body heaving with its own impulses.

The sound of horses out front made Dahlia rush to the window. 'Iris is here. Thank God.'

Another heave of her body and a sound resembling a roar tore from her throat.

Iris rushed in and went straight to Aldara, lifting her nightdress and positioning her legs so she could gauge her progress. 'Good girl. You are doing great. Almost there. One more push and the head will be out.'

Dahlia brought a basin of water and some soap to Iris. The woman scrubbed her hands while keeping her eyes on Aldara.

'Mother,' Kadmus called from the doorway.

'Not now, Kadmus,' Dahlia snapped, putting the water down and passing Iris a towel. 'You need to wait outside with your father.'

Aldara opened her eyes for a moment and looked at her brother. He had removed his straw hat, and his face was covered in dust from the dry roads. She took in his expression and saw that something was wrong. Her eyes closed again and nausea swelled in her as the familiar pain began in her back and clawed along her sides until the pressure between her legs made her cry out once more.

Kadmus stepped back from the door and joined Isadore outside.

Iris was back beside Aldara, holding one of her hands, saying soothing words her mother could not find.

'Good girl. You know what to do. Keep pushing now.'

Her tone was firm and loud. It was just what Aldara needed.

'There's the head,' Dahlia said, her hand covering her mouth. 'You are almost there.'

Aldara was past the point of fear and pleading; she had crossed over into primal and fierce. When the next contraction came, she gritted her teeth and pushed.

'Good girl,' Iris said when the baby landed in her hands. She wiped at the nose and mouth with the clean towel Dahlia had handed to her. A delicate cry filled the small house.

'It's a boy,' Iris said, looking across at Aldara and smiling. 'With ten fingers and ten toes.'

'Praise God,' Dahlia said.

Aldara lifted her head. Her entire body was still trembling, and pieces of hair clung to her face and neck. 'I want to hold him,' she said, shifting onto her back and reaching for him.

'Let Iris clean him up first,' Dahlia replied.

'That's quite all right,' Iris said, wrapping the baby and handing him to his mother. 'There is plenty of time for that later.'

Aldara's hands shook as she took the weight of him and pressed him to her chest. So small. So helpless. His dark eyes gazed up at her for a moment.

'I've never seen a newborn so alert,' Iris said, sitting by Aldara's feet. 'Look at him taking you in.'

Dahlia seemed to be anchored to the floor by the window. 'He's healthy, then?'

Iris glanced at her. 'Certainly seems that way.'

'I should tell your father and brother it is a boy. They are waiting for the news,' Dahlia said, fleeing the room.

Aldara's eyes remained on her son. Ten fingers, ten toes—and Tyron's long lashes.

'What name will you give him?' Iris asked, gazing down at the boy.

Aldara pressed her lips to his warm, damp head and breathed him in. 'Mako.'

Iris raised her eyebrows. 'I've never heard it before.'

'It's Galen.'

Iris stood and pressed down gently on Aldara's stomach. 'What does it mean?'

'Prince's son.'

Iris stopped and glanced at her. Aldara's eyes remained on Mako. Before either of them could say another word, Dahlia walked in, the smile gone from her eyes. Her shoulders were limp and her gaze on the ground. Aldara looked up and felt her insides still as she took in her mother.

'What's wrong?' she asked. 'Kadmus had that same look on his face a moment ago.' She held her son closer. 'Is it something to do with the baby?' Her eyes shifted to Iris.

It seemed Iris was also waiting for an answer.

Dahlia clasped her hands in front of her and then released them again. 'It is the king,' she said. 'He is dead.'

Nobody spoke for a moment. Mako let out a small cry, and Aldara jumped at the noise. The cry grew louder.

'Kadmus heard the news in the village when he went for the midwife.'

'When?' Aldara whispered. 'When did he die?'

Her mother's eyes closed for a moment. 'Early this morning.'

Aldara looked at the window where the sun was now low in the west. They had lost their king. Tyron had lost his father. No, Tyron had lost his father on the same day his son had taken his first breath. The realisation made her cold. But not as cold as her next thought. 'Pandarus is king,' she said aloud.

Dahlia glanced down at the baby pressed against her daughter's chest. 'Yes.'

And what would King Pandarus do when he learned of

5

his illegitimate nephew? To what lengths would he go to ensure King Jayr did not hear of Tyron's bastard son?

Aldara ran a finger across Mako's brow. Now she *had* to keep the secret. She would make sure no one found out until after Tyron had married the princess.

CHAPTER 1

*T*yron was walking down the south-wing corridor towards the throne room when Leksi fell into step beside him. He looked across at his friend's matching expression. Being summoned at the same time was never a good thing. 'You too?'

Leksi nodded. 'What do you think?'

Tyron glanced behind to ensure they were alone. 'I think a few days spent in the company of King Jayr of Zoelin is never a good thing for our king.'

Leksi looked across at him. 'Just be thankful you are let off all the social duties. My head feels as though it is splitting in two.'

A smile spread across Tyron's face. 'I'm not "let off". I'm forbidden to attend—there's a difference.'

That was not entirely true. Whenever King Jayr was staying at Archdale Castle, Tyron found a way to be away or busy. King Pandarus was happy with the arrangement as he struggled to repair the relationship between the two kingdoms. Too much change in a short period had a way of scaring people. King Jayr had only just stopped sulking about the end of the trade agreement when King Zenas had passed away, further delaying his plans.

Tyron's gaze shifted to Leksi, who was not looking his usual sharp self. 'You might be obliged to attend the gatherings, but the excessive drink is your own choice.'

'It was a bad choice—I see that now. Would you show more compassion if I told you I was trying to keep up with your sister?'

'No.' He shook his head. 'I take it she was in fine form last night?'

Leksi thought for a moment. 'She certainly kept King Jayr entertained. Am I the only one who sees similarities between them?'

'You are not the only one.'

'He is the first man who has kept her attention for an entire evening.'

'What about you?'

Leksi tilted his head. 'Besides me. Perhaps she has finally found a new muse.'

Tyron winced at the thought. 'Then I must have a word with her if the two of you are representative of her taste in men.'

Leksi pretended to be offended. He was about to reply when King Jayr and his entourage of guards and advisors turned the corner and came walking towards them.

'There was no need for your brother to send a welcome party,' Leksi said.

Tyron resisted the urge to turn around and walk in the opposite direction. 'I thought they had already left,' Tyron said beneath his breath.

'You thought or hoped?' Leksi replied, finding a smile as King Jayr came to a stop in front of them, his gaze fixed on Tyron.

The king rubbed at his beard, sections of it clean-shaven to display the ink beneath, while waiting for the men to bow in front of him. Tyron obliged, his eyes going to Grandor Pollux, who stood on the king's left. The advisor, who wore a vest that revealed more of his torso than it covered, nodded a greeting, and Tyron returned the gesture. It was not uncommon for Zoelin men to have muscle on display, but every time Tyron saw the man he was reminded of Aldara, the memories fresh as though the brutality had taken place a few days ago rather than years. Seeing the man displaying his strength in that way fuelled his anger. He tried to remember how long it had been since he had seen her now. He did the math while they stood in awkward silence. Seventeen months. Seventeen months since he had pulled her from the icy waters of the Lotheng River. Seventeen months of remembering, of trying to forget. It had not helped when his father had passed suddenly—grief had pounded down on him like stone. He had finally glimpsed the king he remembered from his youth—strong, proud and fiercely protective of his people. But the pressure of ruling is hard on the big of heart, and one night, his father's just gave up.

'If you had remained hidden for a little longer, you would have missed us completely,' Jayr said, regarding him. 'We are on our way to the stables.'

They made no secret of the fact that they did not like one another.

'King Pandarus wanted to see me, disrupting my plan to do just that.'

A smirk formed on Jayr's face. 'Until next time, Prince Tyron.'

'Your Majesty,' Tyron said, bowing again.

Jayr went to leave and then stopped. 'And good luck,' he said, a mischievous glint in his eyes.

Tyron said nothing in reply, not wanting to reveal that he

did not know what he was referring to. Satisfied, King Jayr continued past him, his men a moving border around him.

Leksi waited for the men to turn the corner before speaking. 'What do you think that was about?'

Tyron resumed walking, eyes ahead. 'The fact that he requested an audience with both of us usually means one thing.'

Leksi pretended to think on the topic. 'He has confirmed a date for your wedding?'

Tyron glanced at him, suppressing a smile. 'No. He wants us to fight someone.'

'God, I hope it's King Jayr.'

'You and me both, but I doubt he would announce it to King Jayr first.'

'One would hope his advisors would advise against that. Though they never cease to surprise me.'

Pandarus had selected new advisors after his coronation, putting an end to what he had termed 'old ideas' and 'outdated strategies'. The problem was that Pandarus's forward thinking was anything but sound, and the men he had chosen seemed to say yes to everything.

As they rounded the corner, they almost ran into Queen Salome, who appeared to have just left the throne room. The men bowed and looked down at the small girl buried in the skirt of her dress. Tyron crouched down in front of her.

'How is Princess Tai this morning?'

The young princess peeked out and smiled at him.

'I just took her to visit her father,' Salome said, encouraging the child to step forward. 'Visitation seems to be by appointment of late.'

The queen's disappointment was not lost on Tyron. 'He should have some more time now that King Jayr has departed.'

'One would think. I suspect he will make more time for his family when I give him a son,' she said, resting a hopeful hand on her bump.

Tyron knew she only spoke with such honesty in front of him. She would not dare say such a thing in front of Princess Cora or Queen Mother Eldoris, even if it was the truth.

'We're about to see him,' Leksi said. 'How is his mood?'

Salome looked at him. 'For his daughter? Distracted and short. He was eager to be rid of us, as I suspect he is waiting to see you,' she said, looking at Tyron.

'Did he mention the wedding?' Leksi asked, a smile flickering.

Salome glanced at him. 'The poor girl is surely an old maid by now.'

'Very funny,' Tyron said. 'Need I remind you both that we recently lost our king, and a wedding would not have been appropriate.'

'That was eight months ago,' Leksi said.

Tyron reached out and touched Tai's nose before standing. 'Sorry, I did not realise my grief had an expiry. I told our king I would marry the princess and I will.'

'Hopefully while she can still bear children,' Leksi said, enjoying himself.

Tyron bowed before Salome. 'If you will excuse us, Your Majesty, we must get going.'

'Good luck in there,' Salome said, taking her daughter's hand and leading her past them.

Leksi exhaled and looked at Tyron. 'Are you ready?'

Tyron shook his head. 'No.' He stepped up to the door and the guard swung it open, moving inside to announce their arrival.

Every one of Pandarus's bad decisions over the previous few years suddenly made more sense. Tyron had always known the alliance with Zoelin was a strategy of intimidation, but as it turned out, it was not for Syrasan's protection from Corneo, but rather Syrasan's domination of Corneo.

Tyron sat across from his brother, his king, who was waiting for him to say something other than what his expression clearly stated. 'You want to *take* Corneo?'

Pandarus nodded, eyes shifting to Leksi for a moment to gauge his reaction. 'Eventually, yes. But first we take the West. There is work to be done there first in convincing them to trust a new king.'

'Yes,' Tyron said. 'Taking over their lands and killing the men who stand in our way will not help things.'

Pandarus shifted in his chair. 'Lord Belen has control of the West and most of Corneo's grain supply. King Nilos takes everything, to the point where Lord Belen struggles to feed his own men. I believe his loyalties can be swayed.'

'You think he will be loyal to you when we storm in and take control of his home?'

'He will not have a choice.' Pandarus looked at Leksi. 'You are very quiet. What do you say on the matter?'

Leksi had a knack for not displaying his opinions on his face. 'I will go where you send me, Your Majesty. I will fight alongside your brother as I have always done.'

'We will lose men,' Tyron said. 'Lord Belen's men are skilled fighters. Even the serfs and labourers are trained as archers and swordsmen.'

Pandarus nodded. 'Yes. I go into this with all of the facts.'

Tyron studied his brother. 'I am trying to figure out why you are doing this. You will finish with more mouths to feed.'

'I will finish with twice the army.'

Leksi cleared his throat. 'Will the Zoelin army be fighting with us?'

Pandarus glanced down at his hands. 'Not this time, but we can win without them.'

Tyron's eyebrows shot up. 'Not this time?'

'King Jayr agreed to keep Corneo out of Syrasan. This is a very different fight.'

Tyron knew Jayr's refusal was more likely due to the annulment of the Companion trade and the delayed marriage to the king's sister.

Pandarus lay a hand flat on the table and looked down at it. 'Under my reign, our army will be twice as strong, and King Jayr will have no choice but to fight alongside us.'

'Is that what this is about?' Tyron asked. 'You want to prove yourself to King Jayr.'

Pandarus's dark eyes went to Tyron. 'Careful, brother. Father may have overlooked your insubordination, but you have a new king now.'

Tyron's gaze fell to the table between them. 'When do we leave?'

'Two weeks,' Pandarus replied, standing up.

Tyron and Leksi also stood, bowing.

'I will prepare our men,' Tyron said.

Pandarus sniffed and nodded. 'And when it is done, it is time for you to marry Princess Tasia of Zoelin. We need to ensure the Zoelin army is standing with us when we take Masville Castle.'

There it was, the inevitable mention of the wedding.

Tyron swallowed. 'Of course.'

As they were leaving, Pandarus turned and asked, 'Can you win? With your mind in opposition, can you win?'

Tyron stopped and turned to his brother. 'I serve you until my death. If you want the West, we will take the West, Your Majesty.'

Pandarus nodded and watched them leave the room, the doors swinging open and then closing behind them. Only when they were outside did Tyron dare to look at Leksi. His friend's expression mirrored his own.

'So it begins,' Leksi said.

Tyron's eyes closed. 'So it begins.'

CHAPTER 2

*A*ldara woke and felt around next to her. When she realised Mako was not there, her eyes snapped open and she sat up, searching for him. Her gaze went to the figure by the window. Kadmus stood with Mako asleep in his arms, swaying and humming a tune Aldara did not recognise. He glanced at her, saying nothing for fear of waking his nephew.

'Thank you,' she whispered, appreciating the extra few minutes of sleep. The room was still dark, which was no surprise. Mako was always first awake but would happily doze off again as long as it was in someone's arms.

Kadmus nodded in her direction and resumed humming.

She felt so grateful for her brother during those moments. Between Kadmus and Isadore, Mako was never short a father. Of course, none of them replaced Tyron.

Guilt washed over her as she thought of him. He deserved to know he had a son, deserved the choice to see him and be a part of his life. She had every intention of telling him after the wedding—the wedding that had been delayed by King Zenas's death and then Pandarus's coronation. It felt like it might never happen.

'You are spoiling him,' Dahlia said, stepping off the ladder from the loft and brushing down her dress. 'The boy needs to sleep in a bed. His own bed,' she added, glancing at Aldara.

'The weather will turn cold soon, and he will need the warmth of his mother,' Aldara replied, still watching Kadmus and Mako.

'Not for a few more months,' Dahlia said. She walked over to Kadmus, checking on the infant before heading over to the pot on the stove and peering inside.

There was enough food. The garden was still supplying vegetables, and Tyron continued to send some supplies directly to the farm a few times each month. No letters, only food. Each time a crate arrived, Aldara would write a letter of thanks and never hand it over, because every word that did not form part of the statement 'you have a son' felt like deceit. Then she would remind herself that there was a reason they did not write letters. Words inhibited what they were trying to do—build a life independent of the other.

Mako opened his eyes and looked about, smiling when he saw Aldara sitting up on the bed—a familiar smile that made her throat close. Kadmus carried him over and handed him to her before going to take a seat at the table. She nursed him while the others waited for the food to heat.

'I saw Leo helping you yesterday,' Dahlia said, eyes on the pot. 'He is being very generous with his time.'

Kadmus poured a cup of water and smiled into it as he drank.

'Isn't a bit early in the morning for this?' Aldara said, not looking up.

Dahlia crossed her arms. 'Am I not allowed to make observations?'

Aldara glanced over at Kadmus, who knew better than to speak up on the topic. She did not want to start an argument.

'Yes. He is being very generous with his time. He is a good friend.'

Leo was Iris's son. He had a knack for showing up whenever Aldara was out working in the paddocks with Mako kicking about in the nearby grass. He was a year older than Aldara and one of the few people who did not look down on her situation and contribute to the scandal. Quite the opposite, actually. He had shown little interest in Aldara when they were children, but since her return, he seemed to be seeing her through new eyes. Normally she would discourage the unwanted attention, but she did not want to discourage the playful interaction between Leo and her son. Their connection was heart-warming, and she did not have many friends.

'I do not see him helping Kadmus,' Dahlia said.

Isadore descended the ladder, tucking his shirt into his trousers and stretching his stiffened neck. 'Leave her be,' he said. 'Aldara has enough to worry about for now without you trying to marry her off.'

Dahlia tutted. 'Not too many men are prepared to take on a wife with a child. She cannot afford to be fussy.'

'Thank you for reminding me of my dismal prospects,' Aldara said, fixing her nightdress and facing Mako to her. He smiled at her as she kissed his face.

'Perhaps he has heard about the food we are receiving,' Kadmus said. 'That would make more sense.'

'Maybe you should spread the word,' Aldara said, not looking at him. 'Might help you find a wife.'

Dahlia lifted the pot from the stove and carried it to the table where Isadore had just taken a seat. 'All right, all right. Eat something, and then off to work.'

Aldara walked over to her father and handed Mako to him so she could change her clothes. Isadore placed a hand on her arm to stop her.

'I bought some ink yesterday.'

She blinked and looked down at his hand. 'All right.'

He frowned at her. 'So you can write to your friend.'

She smiled at him. 'Thank you.'

Kadmus, who did not miss a thing, spoke up. 'Ink is not the issue. Aldara does not write because she is a terrible liar.'

'That's not true. I write.'

Kadmus tilted his head, challenging her. 'Really? How many letters since Hali returned to Syrasan?'

'Four.'

'And how many has she written?'

Aldara swallowed. 'More than four.'

'Every month,' Kadmus said, turning his attention to the food being placed in front of him. 'She writes you every month asking when she can come visit.'

Aldara turned, her father's hand sliding away as she walked away. Hali also did not know about Mako, as Aldara was worried the news would find its way to Archdale. There were only so many letters she could fill with farm-related news without raising suspicion. She preferred to appear busy than fill letters with lies.

As she slipped into her dress, she listened to the banter behind her in hope that it would distract her from self-loathing.

THE FOLLOWING AFTERNOON, Kadmus and Isadore went into Roysten to get supplies, leaving the women behind to complete the chores. Aldara was in the barn milking when Artemus began to bark. She stilled and listened as a wagon came to a stop in front of the house. Mako, who was in a wrap against her back, began kicking his legs with excitement.

'Should we see who is here?' Aldara asked, inspecting the pail to see if there was enough milk. She stood and gave the goat a pat, untying the rope from the collar, and walked towards the barn door with Mako squealing behind her. She opened the small door, eyes on the pail where the milk slushed about, careful not to spill, and then closed the door behind her before looking over at the house.

Standing with her mother were Hali, Sapphira and Stamitos. Dahlia's apron had been removed and she glanced nervously towards the barn. Three pairs of eyes followed her gaze and settled on them. The pail dropped from Aldara's hand and the milk painted the dirt white before seeping into the dry earth. Hali took a few steps towards her and then, noticing the baby strapped to her back, stopped. Dahlia wrung her hands in front of her as she watched the exchange. The rolling pail came to a stop against Aldara's ankle. Even from that distance Aldara could see their minds ticking over, trying to process the image in front of them.

Hali resumed walking. It was more of a march. When she was just a few yards from Aldara, eyes fixed on the infant, she said, 'You have a *baby*?'

Aldara could not find any words as her friend approached, not slowing down at all. When Hali reached her, she wrapped her arms around them both. It took Aldara a moment to get her arms to move, but they eventually found their way around her friend. Her eyes closed.

A sob escaped Hali. She pulled back to look at them both. 'Is it… yours?'

Aldara blinked and tears ran down her cheeks. She could not lie. 'Yes.'

Hali went to work loosening the wrap so she could free Mako. Aldara stood still, her body resigned to what was happening

'Well, I suppose this explains your silence since my

return.' She pulled the infant into her arms, a smile spreading across her face. 'Hello,' she cooed. 'What's your name?'

Aldara glanced over to where Sapphira and Stamitos stood motionless. 'His name is Mako.' She bit down on her lower lip. 'I'm sorry. I meant to write—'

Hali laughed. 'You did write. To tell me about the harvest and the chickens and the beans. Nothing about the fact that you had a *baby*.'

Aldara glanced down at her hands. 'I'm sorry. I was going to tell you—'

'When? When he was grown-up? What were you thinking, keeping such a thing from me?'

She had been thinking only of Mako.

'What are you doing here?' Aldara asked, her eyes welling again. Hali pulled her in and squeezed her so tightly she could hardly breathe through it.

'What do you think I'm doing here?' she said, beginning to cry. 'You should have told me.'

Aldara stared at Stamitos, who still had not moved towards them. 'I couldn't. I haven't told the father.'

Hali pulled back and stared at her in horror. 'Why not? How does he not know?' She looked down, thinking. 'Who *is* the father?'

Aldara swallowed. 'Tyron,' she whispered, more tears escaping.

Hali looked down at the infant in her arms, his tiny hands were exploring her face. 'What do you mean? That's impossible. Sapphira told me you haven't seen him since you returned home.'

'I haven't.' She could see Hali doing the math.

'I don't understand.'

Mako reached out for his mother, and Aldara took him and placed him on her hip. 'The last time I saw Tyron was at Lord Yuri's manor.'

Hali shook her head. 'That was ages ago.'

'That was seventeen months ago.'

Hali stared at Mako. 'Aldara, why have you not told Prince Tyron that he has a son?'

More tears escaped her. 'It's complicated.'

Hali looked at her. 'Well, it's about to get more complicated. Are you ready to explain to Prince Stamitos why you have a child with his brother's green eyes?'

Aldara shook her head. 'No.'

Hali turned to look at Stamitos and Sapphira, who were now walking towards them. 'You better get ready.'

ALDARA HAD NEVER SEEN Stamitos mad. His tense silence unsettled her. He watched Mako from across the room inside the small house, careful never to meet her eyes. It took that dark mood to finally see the similarities between him and Tyron.

'Would you like to hold your nephew?' Aldara asked him.

He shook his head and shifted his feet, not even managing a reply.

'What news do you have from Archdale?' Aldara directed the question at Sapphira, who had barely said two words since arriving.

Sapphira brushed her cropped hair back from her face and smiled weakly. 'All the Companions remain there, except for Ella. I believe she was sent to a manor south of Veanor.'

'Ella?'

'I just realised you probably never met her.'

'King Zenas's Companion,' Hali offered.

'Of course,' Aldara said, looking down. 'I'm surprised Pandarus kept Fedora on as mentor.'

'King Pandarus,' Stamitos said.

Aldara looked at him. He had always ignored titles in the past. 'Forgive me, my lord.'

The formality embarrassed him and he looked out the door.

They were all standing because there were not enough chairs for everyone to sit. The heat from the stove was stifling as Dahlia stood in front of it preparing a meal for her silent visitors.

'So,' Aldara said, trying again. 'What brings you all this far south?'

Stamitos's eyes returned to her. 'The girls were worried about you because you were not responding to their letters.'

Aldara glanced at her mother, who continued to stir the pot while listening for her response. 'Well, now you know why.'

Stamitos stepped past Aldara. 'I'm going to get some air,' he said, striding out of the house.

Sapphira went to go after him and Aldara held a hand up to stop her. 'I'll go,' she said, handing Mako to Hali. She stepped out into the blinding heat, feeling the eyes on them from the small window. 'Stamitos, wait.'

He did not slow down. 'It was a long journey. I just need to stretch my legs.'

She broke into a run and came around in front of him. 'Whatever you need to say, you can say it. It's all right. It's me.'

He stopped short of running into her, his contorted face reminding her of Kadmus when he was upset with her. 'I don't trust myself to speak.'

Her eyes searched his face. 'I was going to tell him after the wedding—'

'Yes, you said that.' His gaze went to the grazing sheep behind her.

She exhaled. 'Then your father died… Pandarus became king…'

'*King* Pandarus.'

She looked at her feet. 'King Pandarus.'

He looked at her then, but his expression was guarded. 'What exactly are you afraid of?'

'I'm not sure if you remember, but Pandarus does not like me very much.'

His expression softened and he folded his arms in front of him. 'There is something you should know.'

She waited.

'Tyron is about to leave Archdale. He is going east, to fight.'

Aldara felt her heart slow. 'I was not aware of any trouble in the East.'

'Pandarus has an army of men ready to cross the border. Tyron will lead them.'

She shook her head, trying to understand. 'Why?'

'There is a manor in Wripis that controls most of Corneo's food supply. They are going to take control of it.'

She closed her eyes for a moment as she realised why Pandarus would do such a thing. 'Does he want the throne? Does King Pandarus want Masville Castle?'

Stamitos watched her for a moment. 'Is that really so surprising?'

'I suppose not. It cannot possibly end well for anybody.'

'No.'

Aldara studied him. 'Why? Why is he doing it?'

Stamitos shook his head, wanting for a better answer. 'For all the reasons you imagine Pandarus would. He wants more.'

'Do you mean *King* Pandarus?' she asked, making an effort to keep her face serious.

A smile crept across Stamitos's face as he realised how

ridiculous he had been with her earlier. 'He is my brother. If anyone is allowed to disrespect him, it is me.'

Her eyes shone at him. 'That's fair.' She hesitated for a moment. 'Will they win in Wripis?'

His expression turned serious again. 'Lord Belen has skilled men who will fight well.'

'Will King Nilos send men?'

Stamitos unfolded his arms. 'Eventually, but by the time they arrive, the manor will be secured.'

Aldara thought for a moment. 'What about the support King Jayr promised? Will the Zoelin army fight alongside Tyron?'

Stamitos shook his head. 'Not this time.'

'He will no doubt help later once he has established if he is on the winning side.' She glanced down at her toes. 'You might not believe me, but I was trying to protect Tyron and our son. I have seen first-hand the lengths our king and his so-called allies will go to in order to protect their interests.' She looked up at Stamitos to read his reaction. 'I kept thinking, what is one illegitimate child to these men and their agendas?'

Stamitos's face filled with pity. 'Do you honestly think Tyron would let anything happen to either of you?'

She closed her eyes. 'No. He would die first,' she said, opening her eyes again and looking at him.

He nodded and inhaled. 'And do you expect me to keep your secret?'

'I don't expect anything. I only ask that you consider things from the king's perspective. If you could just wait until after the wedding.' She pressed her lips together, her gaze moving to the sheep. 'Is the wedding still going ahead?' She was thankful she could not see his face.

'Yes. It will take place when Tyron returns.'

She nodded. 'If you could just wait until then, my son won't seem like such a threat.'

'Lie, you mean?'

She did not reply.

He held out his hands. 'If he does not return from Corneo, he will never know. Can you live with that?'

She pressed her palms against her temples. 'I can barely live with myself now. But then I think about Pandarus finding out, and the power he has, and what that might mean for all of us.'

'I will not say anything for now, but I really hope you do.'

The sun was sinking in the west when the wagon pulled away from the farmhouse. Hali's head poked out from the window, her hand relentlessly waving, pausing only to wipe at tears. At least this time they got to say goodbye, and Hali was returning to Lord Yuri's manor where she would be loved and fussed over. Aldara knew Lord Yuri was not the kind of man to be deterred by gossip and scandal; he would be far too content to take much notice. Hali had said in one of her letters that his sons said little on the matter. Perhaps seeing their father happy was enough to silence any objections.

Sapphira and Stamitos reached a hand through the window as the wagon turned onto the road, and Aldara could not help but feel envious of the life they had managed to build together, despite everything and everyone that was against them.

A low whinny came from a nearby paddock where the horses were grazing. Aldara looked over to see Otus waiting to be acknowledged. She occasionally rode the old warhorse, indulging in the memories it brought back. She did not want to forget.

Aldara glanced back to see her mother standing in the doorway, her apron already tied around her. They looked at one another for a moment before Dahlia turned and walked back inside. Aldara was about to follow her when she saw Leo striding across the grass towards her, hat pushed back on his sandy hair and a broad smile on his face. And there it was—that feeling of forcing a smile while remembering looking at Tyron and being unable to help it. The feeling of guilt and disappointment because she knew this kind man fell so very short of her prince.

Mako was asleep in the house, and the last thing she felt like was being alone with Leo. She raised a heavy hand, a greeting that did not require words. She should have been pleased by his interest; after all, her prospects were so very dismal. It was possible this man was interested in building a life with her and was capable of loving her son, without any lures of wealth. It was what Tyron would want for her.

She looked away for a moment. What was it he had said the last time she had seen him?

'I'm not sure there is life after you.'

CHAPTER 3

*A*ldara balanced the wood on the chopping block and raised the axe. She brought it down with force and the wood split apart, the pieces tumbling to the ground. She reached for another large log, not bothering to stack the smaller pieces forming a mountain around the block. Down came the axe. She stopped only to wipe at the sweat forming on her brow. That was what she did when anxiety coiled within her—she worked through the fog of it.

'Kadmus can do that,' Dahlia said, coming to a stop a short distance away.

Aldara did not look up. 'Kadmus does enough.'

Dahlia glanced at the house where the men were. They were eating their evening meal, Isadore letting Mako take what he wanted from his bowl.

'You have not told me what Prince Stamitos said yesterday.'

Aldara brought the axe down again and then let the head of it rest at her feet. She was breathing hard. 'You can probably guess from his silence. He was angry at me, believes I have deceived people by keeping silent.'

Dahlia's mouth was pinched in that way that indicated she had an opinion on the subject.

'This is the part where you tell me you agree with him,' Aldara said, waiting.

'All right. I agree with him,' Dahlia said. 'You should have told him as soon as the pregnancy was confirmed. He would have taken care of you both, provided for you.'

Aldara bent, picked up a log and placed it on the block. 'He already provides for us. How much more are you hoping for?'

Dahlia folded her arms in front of her. 'I know you think I don't understand your situation, but you are wrong.'

The axe came down and a piece of wood flew to the side, landing at Dahlia's feet.

'Really?' Aldara asked, letting the axe drop to the ground. 'Did you share an illegitimate child with a prince?'

Dahlia lifted her chin. 'No. I shared an illegitimate child with the king.'

The words drifted between them. Aldara studied her mother, trying to figure out if she was capable of such a lie.

'What do you mean?' The question came out as a whisper.

Dahlia glanced once at the house and then took a step towards her. 'Perhaps I should have told you some time ago. The events have always felt rather private.'

Aldara shook her head. 'What events? What are you talking about?'

A flood of breath came from Dahlia. 'I was the king's Companion for a short period. It was a long time ago.'

Questions fought for space inside Aldara's head. 'What king?'

A flock of birds passed overhead, their cries going unnoticed.

'King Zenas, of course.'

Aldara stared, trying to sort the information in her mind.

She slumped down on the chopping block, her gaze fixed on her mother. 'I think you are going to have to start at the beginning.'

Dahlia shoved the piece of wood away from her foot. 'All right, but not here. Kadmus knows nothing of this. I don't want him hearing it this way.'

Aldara stood on shaky legs and turned from the house. 'Let's go for a walk.'

They walked side by side, long after the sun had burned through the hills, replaced by the songs of insects at dusk. It was the first time Dahlia had let Aldara in—the first time Aldara had seen who her mother was before the life she resented so openly.

Like many in the South, Dahlia had grown up hungry. Her father had been a cottar, one of the lowest peasant occupations. Her mother had been a drunk. Dahlia had been the youngest of four. Her eldest brother had left to be a foot soldier and never returned, the next went to work one day and never came back, and her sister had gone to work as a maid in a noble household—later she was found working in a brothel. But God had blessed Dahlia with beauty and a sharp mind. During her thirteenth year, she had discovered that both could be used to her advantage. She would stroll through crowded markets, colliding with men of noble birth and smiling apologetically. Later the men would discover the coin pouches missing from their pockets, but none of them would suspect the golden-haired girl with grey eyes who had peered up at them through youthful lashes.

In her sixteenth year, an offer of marriage was made to her father by a clothier who, ironically, she had stolen from a few times. Her father had said yes. She had been called into the room to stand in front of the plain, awkward man, trying to imagine a life with him. They agreed on a date while she stood silent next to her father.

The next day she had gone to the marketplace, strolling between the tables holding a basket filled with items she had not paid for. The vendors seemed friendlier that day, happy even. When she asked one man the reason for his good mood, he had replied that the king would be passing through the next day. Dahlia had picked up a jar of preserved carrots as he spoke. He had looked north, in the direction from which the king would come, and she had slipped the jar into her basket, covering it with the small loaf of bread as she followed his gaze, reflecting his excitement with her vibrant smile.

The next day she had put on her best dress, paid for by stolen coin and made by the very clothier she was deceiving, and walked north for two hours. Her gaze was fixed on the road ahead as she waited for the king to pass. She carried a stolen jar of wine, a gift for her king. When the royal wagon came into view, led by guards in royal dress made from fabric you could not buy in the South, she had stepped out into the middle of the road and curtsied.

'Move aside,' the guards had shouted at her.

But she simply stood and waited for them to stop. She was far too pretty to trample. 'I have a gift for His Majesty,' she had told them.

The king had taken the gift from her, listened to her, watched her. A few days later he had made an offer to her father that she come live at Archdale as his Companion. The clothier was never mentioned again.

The young and besotted king had not cared to wait for her to be refined by a mentor. He had rushed her to his bed, and a few weeks later Dahlia had discovered she was pregnant. All of her plans had come crashing down around her. As soon as her mentor realised, she was pulled from her bed in the middle of the night and sent away. At first, she had rejected the support he offered her, but it was either consent or return to the South in disgrace. Instead, she accepted the offer of a few acres of viable land outside of Roysten.

With women not permitted to own land, she was also forced to accept the hand of one of the king's serfs, Isadore, who was prepared to marry her, manage the land and raise the child as his own. When the baby was born dead, Dahlia begged Isadore to say nothing of the child's death for fear the king would take the land from her. But Isadore was an honest man, and he had insisted she write to the king of his son's death. King Zenas surprised her by sending the papers for the land along with his deepest condolences.

'He made mistakes, but he was a good man,' Dahlia said, finishing her story.

Aldara had tears running down her cheeks, not only for the hardships her mother had endured but for her newfound ability to finally share them. Dahlia made no move to comfort her, her past having robbed her of that ability.

'Father has told me for years that I look just like you at this age. How is it King Zenas did not recognise something in me?'

Dahlia shrugged, eyes on the horizon. 'It was a long time ago. He only knew me a few weeks, and then I was gone. It was the lust of a young king, nothing more.' She looked at Aldara then. 'What is between you and the prince is something else. It's not something I ever planned for. I just wanted a better life for you... the life I had for a fleeting moment.'

Aldara blinked and more tears escaped. 'Had you given me a choice, I would have chosen this life.'

Dahlia turned her face away. 'This is not a life. It is a sentence.'

'You're wrong,' Aldara said. 'You are seeing only through your eyes. I loved my life before Archdale. I would have been happy living this way.'

'Would have?'

She brushed at the tears. 'Before I met him. Now it all feels hollow.'

Dahlia wrapped her arms about her. The air had long ago gone cold. 'Tell him. If he is half the man his father was, it will be all right.'

Aldara looked at her mother, eyes pleading. 'I cannot control what happens once the news is out there.'

Dahlia shook her head. 'Let Prince Tyron worry about that. Trust his reaction. Your part will be done.'

A stiff breeze blew as they turned towards the house.

Aldara wiped at her face with both hands. 'I'll write to him tonight.'

CHAPTER 4

*E*ldoris did not like being summoned to the throne room like she was one of Pandarus's men. He seemed to be spending more and more time in there of late, holding secret meetings and making plans that would have his late father shaking his head with disappointment. Now he was sending Tyron off to fight a dirty war against people who were already up against their own king while trying to survive famine.

Yes, she knew far more of the politics than Pandarus would care to admit.

She arrived at the throne room and the doors swung open in front of her.

'The queen mother, Your Majesty,' the guard said.

Pandarus was standing behind a chair, reading. He looked up from the letter and waved her in.

She glanced at the poor-quality parchment in his hand. 'My dear son, you are free to visit me at any time. Actually, it might do you good to leave this room on occasion.'

He held the letter up as she came to a stop in front of him.

'Did you know about this?' he asked, thrusting it towards her.

She narrowed her eyes and gave him a disapproving glance before taking it from him. As she read the words, her stomach tightened. 'Where did you get this?'

'One of my men intercepted it.' He stepped away from her and began to pace.

She looked at him, confused. 'One of your men? Has Tyron not seen it?'

'No.'

She shook her head as she comprehended this. 'Why are you intercepting Tyron's private correspondence?'

Pandarus stopped and turned to her. '*That* is your first question after learning that Tyron has a bastard son?'

She flinched at the word. 'Pandarus, please. It is not the infant's fault he was born out of wedlock. And she is not the first Companion to birth a child of royal blood.' She could hardly believe the words coming from her mouth.

Pandarus resumed pacing. 'It never ends with this girl. I thought we were finally rid of her, but she continues to have her claws in him.' He shook his head. 'He cannot be burdened with this now. We must keep it from him until the time is right.'

Eldoris was taken aback by this. 'Tyron has a right to know.'

'He will,' Pandarus snapped. 'I will give him the letter once the West is ours.'

Eldoris watched him. The decision to move in on Corneo was bold for a young ruler, and it was weighing on him. 'I suggest you set a date for the wedding before this news reaches King Jayr. We both know what that man is capable of.'

'Yes. Now is not the time to lose allies.'

She wanted to say that perhaps he should have waited to make his move on Corneo, but did not dare.

'This is what comes of delays.'

She could see Pandarus was getting more and more worked up. 'They were not delays at our end—they were matters of propriety. Tyron could not very well have a wedding celebration so soon after losing his father and king.'

Pandarus gripped the back of the chair and leaned on it.

She hated seeing him in over his head. 'Tell me what is on your mind. I know you have advisors, but I am your mother.'

He exhaled and looked at her. 'Perhaps Tyron should not know of this until after the wedding.'

A sinking feeling came over her. 'Pandarus, he needs to be told.'

'Can I trust him to fulfil his obligations after learning this?'

She did not mean to hesitate before answering. 'Tyron is a man of his word, like his father.'

He tapped his fingers on the chair as he watched her.

She cleared her throat before speaking. 'I understand you not wanting him distracted before a fight. Let Tyron take the West, but then you must tell him. If you wait until after the wedding, it will be viewed as deceitful rather than thoughtful.'

Pandarus pushed off the chair and walked over to her, taking the letter from her hands. 'Say nothing of this to anyone until I say otherwise. Understand?'

She curtsied before her son. 'As you wish.'

ELDORIS WALKED in circles in the solar. She was doing the math, trying to figure out if Tyron had continued to see the girl after he had sworn to his father he would stay away. The marriage to Princess Tasia was their only hold on the alliance after abandoning the Companion trade agreement. They had King Jayr to thank for that. His removal of the girl without using the appropriate channels, and without the consent of her parents, meant all blame fell to him. Tyron had been right—King Jayr was not going to risk facing Asigow without allies. His self-preservation instincts had seen him agree to the new rules.

She stopped walking after a few simple sums confirmed that the child could have been conceived during their fleeting reunion seventeen months earlier. No herbs would have been given to the girl during her captivity, and Eldoris knew well enough that it only took one careless instant to tear apart lives. The sensible part of her reprimanded her son and resented the girl for not seeking a physician to take care of the problem, but the mother part of her felt sick at even thinking such a thing. This was Tyron's son—and her grandson. The boy had been conceived by two people who loved each other. How many children of noble birth could lay claim to that?

'For goodness' sake, Mother. You are going to wear holes in the rug,' Cora said, her book snapping shut. 'What on earth did Pandarus say to you that has you this worked up?'

Eldoris stopped and looked at her daughter, whose dark eyes were taking her in. She was far from trustworthy, but was at least proving herself capable of loyalty at times. 'I gave my word to Pandarus that I would not speak of it to anyone,' she said, turning away.

Cora shrugged and placed the book on the small table by her armchair. Her bracelet made a chiming noise as it slid along her wrist. 'Suit yourself.' She lifted her chin. 'Though I wonder,' she began, with all the marks of a dramatic performance, 'if it has anything to do with the big argument between Stamitos and Sapphira upon returning from their journey south.'

Eldoris exhaled and took the bait. 'What argument?' Stamitos and Sapphira never fought, despite her daughter-in-law's impossible nature.

A satisfied smile flickered on Cora's face. 'They too have a secret. Something to do with Tyron. Stamitos wants to tell him, but Sapphira believes it is not his place. Would you like to trade further information?'

Eldoris frowned. 'Honestly, Cora, how many maids have you corrupted into becoming one of your spies?' While she outwardly displayed disapproval, inwardly she was piecing together the new information. Was it possible Stamitos knew of the child? Not only possible, but likely. Sapphira and Aldara were friends, after all, and it would not have been unreasonable for Sapphira to suggest they visit the former Companion while touring in the South.

She closed her eyes. That explained the timing of the letter to Tyron. She had been found out.

When she opened her eyes, she saw Cora leaned back in her chair, hands spread across the velvet-covered arms.

'They are connected,' Cora said. 'Your secret and my secret are the same, aren't they?'

Eldoris inhaled. 'You do not have a secret. All you have is a fight between a married couple, and they are as common as the people reporting to you.' She walked past her daughter towards the door. 'Now if you will excuse me, I need some air.'

Cora laughed behind her.

'You mean you are going to speak with Stamitos.'

Eldoris stiffened but continued walking. 'Yes. And I will make sure no maids are lingering nearby.'

❧

Sapphira tried to flee when Eldoris confronted them in the great hall, but one glance from the queen mother held her in place.

'This feels like it is between the two of you,' Sapphira said, her pleading eyes on Stamitos.

Stamitos crossed his arms and smiled. 'I get the distinct impression my mother would like to speak with you also.'

'Stay where you are,' Eldoris said to her. She looked across at the servant laying out the food on the table. 'Leave us.'

When they were alone, Eldoris looked straight at Sapphira. 'Did you visit Aldara during your recent tour in the South?' Her tone made it clear she was in no mood for games.

Sapphira glanced at Stamitos, who was looking at his feet. 'Yes, we did.'

She waited for more. 'And?'

Sapphira looked at Stamitos once again but he would not raise his eyes. 'And it was a very pleasant visit.'

Eldoris shook her head and looked at her son. 'Stamitos, look at me when I am speaking to you.'

He looked up with eyes of a young boy caught doing something wrong. 'Sorry, I thought you were speaking to Sapphira.'

'King Pandarus intercepted a letter from Aldara to Prince Tyron. I am wondering if you know what that letter might have entailed.'

Stamitos's eyebrows shot up. 'Pandarus *intercepted* a letter addressed to Tyron?'

'Let us stay on topic,' she replied, despite that having been her first question earlier. 'What did you discover during your visit?'

'The family had a successful harvest,' Sapphira offered.

Eldoris's gaze shifted to her and she fell silent. 'Stamitos, what did you discover during your visit with Aldara?'

He glanced apologetically at Sapphira, who was all but shaking her head at him. 'She has a son.'

She leaned closer to him. 'You mean Tyron's son.'

The three of them were quiet for a moment.

'She was trying to protect the boy,' Sapphira said, breaking the silence. 'She felt it would be best for everyone to share the news after the wedding—'

'Yes,' Eldoris snapped. 'I read the letter with her explanation.'

'Well it is out now,' Stamitos said, sounding relieved. 'I am glad I did not have to be the one to spill it to Tyron.'

Eldoris had to force the words out. 'Tyron is about to go into battle. The king has asked that nothing be said to him until his return.'

'That's not his decision,' Sapphira said, unable to stop herself.

Eldoris blinked and looked at her. 'Your king has made his wishes clear. I suggest you continue as you were, knowing nothing on the matter. Do you understand?'

Stamitos shifted his weight from one foot to another, nodding. Sapphira said nothing.

'It might not be the most ethically sound decision, but it does ensure Tyron is in a strong state of mind for what is ahead. Pandarus will tell Tyron after he has secured the manor.'

Sapphira continued to shake her head. 'Or he might die never knowing the truth.'

Eldoris flinched and Stamitos cast Sapphira a look that made her avert her eyes.

'You have been in my family for five minutes,' Eldoris said. 'I have known my children their entire lives. Tyron needs a clear head to win this fight.'

Sapphira bit down on her bottom lip before looking back at the queen mother. 'I understand. It's just that… Aldara will wonder at Tyron's lack of response.'

Eldoris eyes shone a little brighter. 'My son's well-being is more important than her feelings right now, don't you agree?'

'We understand,' Stamitos said, speaking for both of them.

Eldoris's eyes remained on Sapphira for a fraction longer to ensure she understood. 'Enjoy your meal,' she said before turning and walking away from them.

CHAPTER 5

*I*t was an uncomfortable send-off. Tyron's family stood in the solar, looking everywhere but at one another. They were readying themselves for the first battle since King Zenas's passing. Tyron wondered at their inability to meet his gaze.

'Where is Queen Salome?' he asked.

'Unwell,' Pandarus said.

Just one word.

'Pregnancy is hard on her,' Eldoris added. 'I am afraid it is no better this time around.'

'Pregnancy is hard on every woman,' Cora said, all but rolling her eyes.

They fell silent again.

'Anyone would think I was not coming back here,' Tyron said, trying to stifle the awkwardness. 'How mournful you all look.'

His mother smiled a stiff sort of smile. 'Of course you are coming back. Everyone is just a bit nervous.'

Tyron glanced at the door where Pero and Leksi were waiting on the other side for him. In a few months, Pero would come of age and fight alongside him—an unnerving thought, not because of his lack of skill but rather his preference to stay up at night writing sonnets. For now, he would remain at the back, watching the horror of war from a safe distance. 'I will send word when we have secured the manor.'

Pandarus nodded, more nervous than he cared to admit. A few grey hairs had appeared around his temples, his new responsibilities ageing him beyond his twenty-eight years.

'And I will send more men to dispatch along the supply area. We cannot predict when or how King Nilos will respond.'

'We'll be ready,' Tyron replied. But the sentiment sounded empty.

His mother stepped up to him, taking hold of his face and kissing his left cheek. 'Keep safe. And keep your men safe.'

Stamitos stepped up and gripped Tyron's shoulder. 'Leksi will take care of him, like he always does,' he said, before embracing his brother briefly.

'Why do you all assume I need him to win?' He looked over at Sapphira, who seemed unable to raise her eyes to him. Before he could say anything to her, Cora spoke up.

'You might not need him to win, but you need him to stay alive.'

She was wearing a silk dress in Syrasan red, the one way she could show support. When she did not move towards him, he walked over to her and brushed his lips on her cheek.

'Would it kill you to wish me luck?'

'I would hope you are crossing into Corneo armed with more than luck.'

'He is armed with the Syrasan army,' Pandarus said. 'Many of the men have been through years of vigorous training.'

Tyron said nothing of the other men, the foot soldiers, many who could barely handle the weapons given to them.

Instead, he turned to Pandarus and bowed, the rest of his family watching, everything necessary had been said and nothing more. A fuss would indicate weakness, and they needed to make a display of their strength.

Tyron glanced once at Sapphira, who still refused to look at him, then turned away. The doors swung open and he exited, Leksi falling into step beside him and Pero following behind.

When the doors shut behind them, Leksi spoke. 'Did Cora send any parting sentiments?'

Tyron looked at him. 'No.'

'She must be feeling my departure deeply if she could not even find words.'

Tyron shook his head, refusing to smile.

'The men wait in Minbury for you,' Leksi said, moving on to more serious matters.

Tyron glanced out of the large window in the corridor as they passed it. 'Good. We'll stay there tonight. Tomorrow we'll cross with rested horses.'

They turned the corner and continued towards the front entrance of the castle. The morning sun cast an eerie glow through the open doors.

'Do you feel ready?' Leksi asked, not looking at him.

Tyron squinted as they stepped out into the sunlight and descended the stone steps. A passing servant stopped and bowed as Tyron passed. Whenever he thought about being ready to fight, to die, his mind drifted to Aldara. It was not fear of death that plagued him, but the fear of leaving her behind—again. 'I am as ready as I will ever be.'

Leksi kept his eyes ahead. 'We come out alive, as we always do.'

Tyron nodded. 'Don't fret, I have your back.'

Leksi laughed. 'Your words soothe me.'

Tyron turned his face up to the sky. His gaze shifted

south, following the endless blue all the way to Aldara. How would she react to his death? Would grief twist like a knife through her middle, like the day the Zoelin men had taken her from him? Of course it would, for despite the passing of time, nothing was lost between them.

Yes, he would come out alive. If only to spare her the anguish of his death.

CHAPTER 6

One hundred and twelve knights on horseback and two hundred and forty-seven foot soldiers. Long-bowmen, archers, crossbowmen and peasants with halberdiers who would be the first to die. They moved in two lines through Corneon forest, weapons in hand and eyes fixed on the trees in front of them where death lurked.

Tyron's gaze moved across the shadows and turned to the sky whenever a bird took flight. His dark mare walked with her tail lifted and ears shifting, listening. Boiled leather wrapped the horse's face, chest and rump. The armour would protect her from superficial wounds, but that was all.

The men on foot in front of Tyron swung their weapons through the foliage to clear a path for the horses that followed behind. Leksi was beside him, covered with chain-mail armour and marked with the royal *S*. His dark eyes peered out from beneath his helm, glancing at Tyron before returning forwards.

'Arrows incoming!' came a voice nearby.

Tyron lifted his shield as they rained down around them.

'Ready your bows!' he shouted as his horse's front legs lifted off the ground.

'Nock!' Leksi shouted next to him. Men burst from the trees, running towards them. 'Mark! Draw! Loose!'

Tyron lowered his shield and watched as the Corneon men twisted and fell to the forest floor with arrows protruding from vulnerable body parts. He looked farther along the line where the archers had not succeeded in stopping them, watching as the men collided in a clash of swords and roar of battle cry.

He turned his horse and lay his heels into its sides. Drawing his sword, he brought it down on the men marked with a golden *C*. They writhed beneath the blows of his sword as he took them down in one brutal swing, maintaining a pace that brought the advantage of surprise. His own footmen fell alongside them, their inexperience and lack of skill evident.

Another line of men emerged from enemy trees, shouting cries of battle behind shields intended to amplify the sound.

'Ready your bows!' Leksi shouted, his horse coming to a skidding halt next to Tyron. 'Nock! Mark! Draw! Loose!'

Arrows pierced the enemy at close proximity. Tyron kicked his horse and it lurched forwards, enabling him to slay the remaining men before they had a chance to regroup. He pushed the mare harder, weaving between the stray, bewildered men into the belly of the enemy. An arrow pierced the chest of the mare and her front legs stopped working mid-stride. Tyron saw it and braced for the fall. The horse ploughed face-first into the forest debris. Tyron leapt from her back as she rolled before stopping still, eyes wide, reflecting the horror around them.

Men descended on Tyron, swords swinging and shields raised against him. He closed his mind and manoeuvred around the enemy swords with skill, chest heaving with the effort of each movement while his own swords blocked the blows. When he knocked a blade from an enemy hand, he swooped to claim it, driving it through the stomachs and necks of the men circling him while fending off their attempts to do the same.

He lost himself to it, no longer counting men but sensing them—their movement, position, vulnerability. Only when he felt the sting of a sword against his side did he return to himself. Then he could smell the blood and see the fear in the eyes of the young men who died at his hand. It was him or them. It should have been an easy choice.

One Corneon man was not young, not vulnerable. He came at Tyron with experienced hands and eyes that had seen it all before. Tyron watched as the man's relentless sword knocked the weapon in his left hand to the ground. There was no opportunity to get it, so he gripped the hilt of his remaining sword with both hands and raised it just in time to block a blow to his neck.

For a moment, Tyron considered the idea that this man might be a better swordsman than him, that the soldier might end his life and live the remainder of his days a hero. As they watched one another through the slits in their helms, Tyron felt at peace with the idea—until an arrow pierced his opponent's neck. He stilled as more arrows hissed around him, taking down the remaining men, their golden Cs pressed against the dirt.

When the arrows stopped, he turned, searching for the next blade, but what he found was a circle of death around him. His own men arrived, trampling the bodies as they tore past him before disappearing into the trees.

Panting hard, his eyes returned to the soldier who would no longer be a hero. He wanted to remember his face.

'Tyron,' Leksi called.

Tyron turned to Leksi approaching on horseback, hand

extended for him. He reached for it and pulled himself up behind the saddle. Leksi's horse danced beneath them as it waited for instructions.

'Ready to finish?' Leksi asked. His helm was gone, and blood ran from his brow.

Tyron took the bow from Leksi's back and grabbed a handful of arrows from the quiver hanging at his side. 'Don't slow until we are on the other side of their army.'

Leksi nodded, his sword in hand, painted with enemy blood. 'We're taking the manor?'

'Yes, we're taking the manor.'

Leksi glanced down at Tyron's side, where blood oozed through his armour. 'All right,' he said, eyes returning forwards. 'Let's take the West.'

THE EIGHTEEN-HUNDRED ACRES produced enough grain to feed the entire west of Corneo; however, King Nilos controlled the supply, which meant that a large portion went to Masville Castle, and the rest was distributed to noble households all over Corneo. While Tyron knew taking control of the grain would render the results Pandarus wanted, the power they now held over the hungry did not sit well with him. People would pledge loyalty to Syrasan's new king or starve, because there was nowhere for the hungry to go.

Tyron's men marched Lord Belen from the house down to the lawn where the prince waited with Leksi. Some of Lord Belen's men lay dead around them, many more hidden among the trees where they had fallen earlier. Tyron observed the lord as he took in the scene around him, his eyes heavy with it.

'I ask that no harm comes to my family,' he said, unafraid.

Tyron took in his dishevelled appearance and plain clothes usually reserved for men of a lower rank. His weapons had been taken from him.

'I admire your decision to surrender the manor and prevent more lives being wasted. No further harm will come to any member of your family, your men, serfs or servants, as long as they pose no threat.'

Belen's eyes moved over Tyron, taking in his blood-soaked clothing. 'You fought alongside your men?'

Tyron could tell he was trying to assess his character. 'Of course.'

Belen nodded. 'I suppose you want my grain. Everyone wants the grain.'

Tyron glanced at Leksi, who remained next to him, hand on the hilt of his sword, a neutral expression on his blood-crusted face. 'We are not here for the grain.'

Belen did not look convinced. 'Why are you here? My land? My house that has belonged to my family for more than two hundred years?'

Tyron did not reply straight away, interested in what conclusions the lord would draw without prompts.

'We knew the moment your father died that the young king would go looking for more.'

Tyron had known it also but could not very well admit it.

Belen exhaled, his anger evaporating into despair. 'If you are not planning on killing us, where do you expect us to go?'

Tyron looked west to gauge the time. He had already sent a messenger to Pandarus, but it would be some time until Stamitos arrived. 'Pledge your loyalty to King Pandarus, to Syrasan, and you and your family can remain here, keep a hold of your land.'

Belen studied him. 'I have a king.'

Tyron nodded. 'I understand—I am asking you to commit treason. That is why I will give you a choice. Pledge your loyalty to Syrasan, or take your family, and all those loyal to King Nilos, and flee east.' He paused. 'Your king will no doubt reward your loyalty to him.'

Belen exhaled, and Tyron caught something in his expression confirming his suspicion that King Nilos would do no such thing.

'You will not find too many loyal to King Nilos in the West. They are loyal to me.'

Pandarus's information had been correct—for once.

'Why is that?' Leksi asked, speaking up for the first time.

Belen shifted his feet. 'Because at the end of every harvest, King Nilos sends men to rape my land. He takes whatever he wants, paying less than the cost of producing it. I am left with barely enough to survive on.' He paused for a moment. 'Last year we were forced to *buy* grain for four times the amount we were paid.'

The wound on Tyron's side throbbed. He glanced down at it. 'I see.'

Belen noticed. 'That will need to be stitched up,' he said, nodding towards it. 'We have a physician that can take a look at it.'

There was sincerity in his tone.

'That won't be necessary. We have a physician tending the wounded.'

Belen nodded and looked away, thinking. 'It is the men.'

Tyron narrowed his eyes. 'What is?'

'King Pandarus wants to grow his army, take the Corneon throne perhaps.'

Tyron blinked. 'I think we are a long way off that.' At least he hoped that was true.

'You have powerful allies that ensure Syrasan is untouchable. Galen in the East, Zoelin in the North. With Corneo under Syrasan rule, there will be no one left to fight.'

A weak smile appeared on Tyron's face. 'I wish that were true, but in my experience, there is always someone to fight.'

A moment of understanding passed between them.

'I would like some time to speak to my family, to my men,' Belen replied, eyes on the ground between them. 'I understand your terms. They are reasonable given the circumstances, but it is difficult for me to pledge loyalty to a king responsible for the dead around us.'

Tyron would have been suspicious of any other answer. 'You have until the morning. You are free to remain in the house while you make your decision, but all weapons must be surrendered. If one of your men so much as holds a butter knife to one of my own, the offer will disappear. Do we understand one another, Lord Belen?'

Belen nodded slowly. 'Yes.' He gave a small bow before turning away.

Tyron watched as two Syrasan guards followed him back into the house where his family waited for him. Only when Lord Belen was out of sight did he turn to Leksi. 'Have every able-bodied man help identify and bury the dead.'

Leksi was still looking away at the spot where Lord Belen had disappeared. 'What do you suppose Pandarus would say of your rather civil approach?'

'As long as he gets what he wants, he will not care about the methods used.'

Leksi folded his arms across his chest. 'Pandarus would have made the man pledge his loyalty on the spot and cut his throat when he refused.'

Tyron knew his brother well enough to know that was true. 'Then we would have been looking over our shoulders the whole time we were here, waiting for retaliation. Loyalty cannot be forced. It has to be his choice or we will not be able to trust it.'

'Oh, I agree. I'm just not sure King Pandarus will.'

'Let me worry about Pandarus.' He looked about at the bodies, noticing the smell. 'Stamitos will bring more men, and horses.'

'Shame about your mare.'

Tyron nodded.

'You're not tempted to pull Otus out of retirement?'

The suggestion made Tyron look down. He had given the gelding to Aldara, and the mention of the horse reminded him of her. 'No. He has earned his quiet farm life.'

'I'll organise the men,' Leksi said, turning.

Tyron nodded, remaining where he was, breathing away the demons that scraped at his mind. There was no time to come undone, and definitely no time to think about her. He always made sure there was no time. If he paused long enough and let her back in, he might find himself standing in front of her, tearing her life apart once again because there was a selfish part of him that still wanted her at any cost.

He inhaled deeply. It was time to bury the dead.

CHAPTER 7

The following morning, the sun appeared like a bloodstain on the horizon. Tyron stood outside of his tent, washed and dressed, watching the sky change colour. He rubbed at his tired eyes. After being stitched and bandaged, his wound had throbbed through the night, keeping him awake. Not true—his thoughts had kept him awake.

The sound of Leksi relieving himself made him turn around.

'Would it kill you to do that away from the tents?'

Leksi finished and turned to him. 'I should be using the garderobe in the manor, but you decided to be courteous *after* killing his men.'

Tyron smiled despite himself. 'Lord Belen does not need more reasons to resent us.' He had suggested they set up camp with the rest of the men and leave the family to discuss the choice given them. 'Perhaps you'll stop crying when you see this.' He gestured to the crate of fruits and breads that had been delivered by a servant that morning. 'Lord Belen sent food.'

'Great. Does this mean he will bend the knee?'

Tyron glanced at the manor. A few servants had emerged outdoors, casting wary glances in the direction of the camp-site as they went about their chores. 'How many dead?'

'Forty-two Syrasan men. Almost twice that number of Corneon men.'

Tyron nodded. 'We certainly have our work cut out for us.'

'That means living in tents for a while, I assume.'

Tyron nodded. 'Yes, that means living in tents for a while.'

'I was afraid of that.' Leksi pulled a small bag of sage and salt crystals from his pocket and used a cloth to rub it over his teeth. He was one of the few men who bothered with oral hygiene during war. He noticed Tyron watching him. 'Lord Belen has two daughters.'

Tyron's eyebrows went up. 'And?'

'I'm just sharing information with you.'

'Great, now let me share some. Both daughters are off limits.'

Leksi spat the paste onto the grass. 'You'll change your mind once Lord Belen pledges his loyalty.'

'Lord Belen might change his mind if you violate his daughters.'

'You offend me.'

Tyron noticed Lord Belen striding towards them. Alone, which was a good sign. 'Have one of Lord Belen's men eat some of the food before sharing it among the men.' He wanted to ensure nothing had been poisoned. Even if he trusted Belen, he knew little of those who served him.

Leksi followed his gaze to Belen and nodded before picking up the crate and walking off towards the other tents.

Tyron's arms remained loose at his sides as he waited for Lord Belen to reach him. 'Good morning.'

Belen stopped a short distance from him and bowed.

'Good morning, my lord.' He stood and looked over at the men who were beginning to emerge from their tents.

Tyron decided to skip any pleasantries. 'Did you and your family reach a decision?'

Belen turned and studied him for a moment. 'I appreciate your men keeping away from the house overnight.'

'As I said, the house is yours unless you decide otherwise.'

'I see you have men positioned on the south boundary.'

'I have men positioned all along the boundary. We are expecting a visit from King Nilos at some point.' Tyron watched Belen's reaction to this news. He did not seem surprised. 'Will you be staying at the manor, Lord Belen? Will you pledge your loyalty to King Pandarus, or will you be travelling east with your family today?'

Belen looked around at the landmarks his family had spent centuries building. 'I'll be honest. I don't think much of King Pandarus. He has a reputation for brutality, and his alliance with King Jayr makes me nervous.'

It made Tyron nervous as well.

'But I like you,' Belen continued. 'I have heard nothing but good things about you since you came of age. Now I have seen first-hand how you treat your men, and even how you treat your enemies. Your actions are fair, your loyalties clear. I respect that you fight with your men instead of hiding behind walls.'

Tyron suspected he was referring to King Nilos's two sons, neither of whom had seen battle. He looked over to where Leksi stood with the food, fending off hungry men, relieved it was safe for consumption. 'I appreciate the kind words, but I am eager to hear your decision. If King Nilos's army shows up, I need to know if you will be fighting along-side us or against us.'

'I have not sent any messages to King Nilos, but that is not to say he is not aware of the situation. I imagine he has spies planted in my household. That's just the way of things.' Lord Belen frowned before continuing. 'You could kill me if you wanted, and you could kill any man who tried to stop you or refused to join you. There would be no issues of trust then, and the house would be yours to do with as you please.'

'Where would it end? What of your wife and daughters? There are already enough children without fathers after yesterday. This feels far more civil, don't you agree?'

'Yes, but I can't help but wonder why. I wonder what it is you want. King Pandarus wants my men to fight. Is that what you want?'

Tyron looked over at the big house. 'I would like to see you and your family remain in the home that your ancestors built. I would like you to continue to produce grain—grain that will distributed a little more... fairly. I would like to have your men fight alongside my own in hope that the growth of our army reduces our reliance on allies serving their own needs.'

Belen regarded him. 'Such as your new Zoelin friends?'

Tyron said nothing.

Belen looked about at the tents covering his lawn. 'I would like to pledge my loyalty to you, to serve under you. And as your loyalty is to your king, mine will be also. I trust you will keep your word, that my family will continue to live here freely, as we have always done, and that my men and their families will be protected the same as your own.'

Tyron watched him, thoughtful. 'You understand that you will be expected to fight against your own king when the time comes?'

Belen met his gaze. 'My loyalty is to the West. This new arrangement benefits them most of all. King Nilos has starved us for long enough.'

'I must ask something. If I had come to you and had this

56

conversation a few days ago, what would your response have been?'

Belen blinked. 'Are you wondering whether our men died for nothing? Wondering if perhaps we could have come to an agreement without a fight?'

'I suppose I am.'

Belen smiled. 'A man's true identity is revealed during war. It was your conduct as my enemy that has brought us to this point.' He paused. 'Would I have pledged my loyalty had you simply asked? We both know the answer to that.'

Tyron nodded. Before he could respond, one of his men came running up to them.

'Forgive me the interruption, my lord. Prince Stamitos has just arrived.'

Tyron turned to see a group of riders trotting towards them, a Syrasan flag on display as Stamitos took in his surroundings.

'Am I to expect more tents?' Belen asked, glancing at Tyron.

Tyron nodded. 'I'm afraid so. Come, I will introduce you.'

Tyron and Stamitos strolled along the tree line, away from the men and the noise. The sound of shovel on earth reached them from the north where men were still burying the dead.

'The men seem in rather good spirits,' Stamitos said. 'Anyone would think it was an easy win for you.'

Tyron's eyes were on his feet. 'Not easy. Uncomplicated at best.' He wiped his brow with his hand, the sun already hot on them.

Stamitos glanced in the direction of the tents. 'You and Lord Belen seem to be on good terms.'

'We want the same thing.' Tyron stretched the tension from his neck. 'King Nilos has made things easy for us.'

'It's one thing to resent your own king. Something else to pledge loyalty to another.'

A smile flickered on Tyron's face. 'He cannot stand up to King Nilos without our support. It is a good arrangement for everyone.'

Stamitos stopped walking and looked at him.

'What is it?' Tyron asked, taking in his worried expression. 'Is all well at Archdale?'

'Yes.'

Tyron emitted an uncomfortable laugh. 'Then why do you look like you are about to deliver bad news.'

His brother sucked in a breath, head already shaking before the words had even been spoken. 'It's not bad news as such.' He hesitated. 'A letter came for you.'

Tyron's gaze fell to Stamitos's hand. 'Where is it?'

'Pandarus has it.'

He was silent for a moment. 'Why does Pandarus have it?'

Stamitos reached up and rubbed at his neck. 'Because he plans on giving it to you at a later date.'

Tyron narrowed his eyes. 'And you disagree?' Silence. 'Brother, why does Pandarus have a letter addressed to me, and why does he not want me to read it yet?'

'He wants you focused on the war.'

'I am focused on the war. Who is the letter from?'

Stamitos hesitated again. 'Aldara.'

Every possible thought ran through his mind at the same time. 'What does she say in the letter?'

'I have not read it.'

Tyron's hands went into his hair. 'But you must know of its content if you are bringing it up.'

'I have an idea of the main points.'

Tyron released his hair and his hands went to his sides. 'And?'

He watched his brother struggle against the wishes of his king.

'I believe she was writing to tell you of her son.'

Tyron turned away from the words. 'Her son,' he repeated. 'I was not aware that she had a... I did not know she had married.'

'She is not married.'

Tyron turned back to his brother. 'You are going to have to explain everything before I lose my mind trying to figure out what is going on.'

'The boy... he is yours.'

Tyron's arms went heavy and he stopped breathing for a moment. 'What do you mean he is mine? That's not possible.' But even as he said the words, he was piecing the information together. 'How old is he?'

'Almost at the end of his first year.'

Tyron's eyes widened. 'And how do you know this without having read the letter?'

Stamitos's cheeks reddened. 'Because I met him during our tour in the South. Sapphira wanted to visit Aldara. Hali was in Arelasa and asked to join us—'

'What a grand reunion. And you didn't think to tell me?' Tyron began walking away. 'You have known all this time and did not tell *me*?'

Stamitos caught up with him. 'I wanted to, but she asked me not to. Then Mother forbade me from saying anything—'

'Our mother knew also?'

Stamitos rolled his eyes. 'Pandarus also forbade her from saying anything.'

'That's horseshit.'

Stamitos was searching for words that might help the situation.

'Aldara was going to tell you after your wedding so the boy would not pose a threat. You know how mothers are, always trying to protect their children.'

Tyron just shook his head.

'She had planned to tell you, but then Pandarus became king... She was afraid for both of you.'

Tyron did the math in his mind. 'Months later. Pandarus became king *months* later. She would have known she was with child before then.' A fire had lit inside of him. 'She did not trust *me* with the news, after everything that has happened.'

'Stop for a moment.'

Tyron swung around.

Stamitos exhaled calmly. 'To be fair, she has good reasons for not trusting those in power.'

'Is that what Sapphira said?'

'Yes, actually, but she's right.'

Tyron rested his hands on his hips, shaking his head. 'Do you know what gets me? She wrote to tell me only after she had been found out.'

Stamitos's face filled with pity. 'She was going to tell you after the wedding. Think of the potential damage if King Jayr finds out.'

'Yes, by all means, keep the secret—but not from *me*.'

'She was trying to protect you also.'

Tyron closed his eyes, knowing Stamitos was right. So why did he feel like he wanted to punch a tree? 'I should have known you would listen to Sapphira instead of doing the right thing.' He barely knew what he was saying.

'Really? You are blaming my wife for protecting her friend and *your* son?'

'*I* can protect my son!'

Stamitos raised his hand to quieten him. 'The entire camp is going to know if you keep this up.'

Tyron glanced at the tents before resuming walking. He had no idea where he was going.

Stamitos kept up. 'His name is Mako. At the risk of sounding rather feminine, he has your eyes.'

Tyron slowed his pace. 'Mako? It sounds like a Galen name.'

'It is. Translates to "prince's son".'

Tyron stopped walking and his fingers returned to his hair, gripping tightly. Other feelings competed for room with the anger. 'How did she seem? When you saw her, how did she seem?'

'Surprised.' Stamitos smiled. 'She didn't know we were coming.'

Tyron nodded. 'How long ago did she send the letter?'

Stamitos thought for a moment. 'About a week before your departure.'

He released his hair. 'She will be wondering why I have not responded.'

'She knows you were leaving to fight.' He watched Tyron for a moment. 'Perhaps that is why she felt compelled to tell you.'

'In case I died? She didn't want it on her conscience.' He was surprised at his own malice.

'Maybe she wanted to keep you alive.'

Tyron stiffened and closed his eyes for a moment. 'I need to go to her.' He turned and marched towards his tent.

Stamitos's eyebrows shot up. 'What? Now? You cannot leave now.' He ran to catch up. 'Tyron, we are in the middle of a war.'

Tyron did not slow. 'I will ride overnight. I can be back here in two days. You and Leksi can handle things until then.'

'Me? I have one hand. I doubt Leksi will even let you leave.'

Tyron shook his head. 'Leksi does not have a choice. And

no one expects you to fight. Just keep the men in line and away from the house.'

'And if King Nilos shows up with his army?'

'He won't, not that quickly.'

'Tyron, you cannot leave. What about Lord Belen?'

'You can trust him.'

'Oh really? Did he bend the knee?'

Tyron rolled his eyes. 'Have him bend the knee if it will make you feel better.'

'Having you here would make me feel better.'

Tyron stopped and placed his hands on his brother's shoulders. 'You are more than capable of leading these men. Please. I need to see her, see my son. The war is not going anywhere.'

'If Pandarus finds out—'

'I'll be back in a few days.'

Stamitos's face was filled with doubt. 'Two days.'

Tyron squeezed his shoulders before releasing them. 'Tell Leksi I am going alone. It is best if I am discreet.'

'Two days,' Stamitos said again.

Tyron turned around, breaking into a run. 'Two days,' he called behind him.

CHAPTER 8

*H*e rode overnight, stopping once at Lord Xerxes's manor in the east of Syrasan for a fresh horse. The gelding was handed over without question, a groom taking his worn-out horse off to the stables for a rest and feed, ready to be collected when Tyron returned.

It was mid-morning when he turned off the road into Roysten and walked his horse across the uneven earth towards the old farmhouse. His pulse quickened as he thought about what he would say to her, say to him. He had difficulty planning words because he could not predict his reaction at seeing her, or laying eyes on his son for the first time.

Dahlia came out of the house, hand across her eyes trying to identify him under the harsh light. He knew the moment she recognised him because her hands went behind her back to untie her apron. Even from that distance, he recognised the flash of panic in her eyes.

'My lord,' she said when he reached her, dropping the apron inside the door behind her and lowering into a curtsy.

Tyron stopped his horse a few feet from the house and

dismounted. 'Good morning,' he replied, his gaze moving past her. 'I apologise for the intrusion.'

Dahlia shook her head. 'Not at all. You just took me by surprise, as I had heard you and your men were in Corneo.' She tried to smile.

'We are. That is, I will be returning there soon.'

Her eyes flicked sideways to the paddocks. 'What can I do for you, my lord?'

The house was silent behind her. Empty, perhaps. 'I was hoping to speak with Aldara.' He did not want to say anything more to her mother. 'Is she here?'

Dahlia turned and looked between the house and the barn, to the empty fields where the barley crop had stood a few weeks before. Now it was just dirt.

'She left an hour ago to check the boundary fences along the forest line.'

He nodded. 'Is she alone?' For some reason, he could not ask directly about the child.

Dahlia watched him for a moment before answering. 'Not alone, my lord.'

Tyron remounted and turned his horse in the direction of the forest.

'I can go and collect her, if you would prefer? You are welcome to wait inside.'

'That won't be necessary,' he replied, already moving. 'I am sure I can find my way.'

Dahlia pressed her lips into a flat line. 'Head towards the trees on the far side of the paddocks,' she said, gesturing.

He nodded once and kicked his horse into a trot, disappearing between the house and barn and travelling along the edge of the barren fields that would remain that way until the rain arrived. Once he was a good distance from the house, he slowed his horse to a walk, his gaze shifting around the paddocks, searching for her, feeling for her. The forest came into view and he followed the fence, preparing himself for what he would soon see.

He heard her before he saw her, a laugh reaching him. The sound made him pull up his horse and listen. It came again, but there was another noise accompanying it—the squeal of a child, the same squeal Princess Tai made when he threw her into the air and caught her. The sound of happiness.

Tyron swung his leg over the gelding and dropped onto the grass. He tethered the horse to the fence and bent down to slip between the fence posts. Walking under the cover of trees, he followed the laughter that rang around him like a bell. And then he stopped, his dark form blending with the shadows.

Aldara stood thirty yards away, bronzed and smiling, a different girl to the one he had dragged from the freezing Lotheng River all those months back. She wore a short-sleeved cotton dress the same colour as the open sky that framed her, and her feet were bare.

Tyron's gaze shifted to the lanky man standing next to her, then to the infant he was holding, whose face was flushed from laughter. The man tipped the baby gently upside down and a squeal followed. Aldara's face lit up at the sound and she bent down over the infant, tucking her golden hair behind her ears as the laughter increased. The man had the biggest smile of all, and Tyron could not blame him. Look at all he had within arm's reach.

When they were all upright again, he passed the child to Aldara, who kissed the baby's face the intrusive way a mother does. Tyron's eyes burned at the sight. The image of them together wrung the air from his lungs. Happiness and anger tore through him. He was not sure how that was possible. Perhaps because everything was as it should be, and yet nothing was.

The man reached up and ran his thumb across the baby's cheek before resting his hand briefly on Aldara's arm. Tyron watched her face change. The laughter fell away even though the smile remained. He had seen that expression before, at social gatherings she had been forced to attend as a Companion. She was still following Fedora's rules: never show your discomfort or pull away.

Guilt clawed at his insides when he realised he felt relieved by her reaction. Had he really thought he could watch her with another man and feel anything other than blinding possessiveness? What was it she had said to him the day he had walked away? *I'm yours until death, even if I'm not with you.*

He stepped back from the tree he stood behind, deeper into the shadows, and then turned and walked away. When he reached his horse, he mounted and headed back to the house, not stopping to bid farewell to Dahlia, who stepped outside when she saw him approaching. He cantered back down the dirt track and turned onto the road that would take him east.

Aldara walked Loda towards the barn, one hand holding the reins, the other pressing Mako to her. As she neared the house, she saw her mother striding towards her, squinting against the bright sun and mouth set with worry. Aldara turned towards her, moving away from the barn.

'What's wrong?' she called, when she was close enough to be heard.

Dahlia was all but running to close the distance between them. 'Did you speak with him?'

'Who?'

'Prince Tyron,' Dahlia replied, already getting her answer.

Aldara's felt cold at hearing his name. 'What are you talking about?' she asked, looking about.

'He was here. He went looking for you. Did you really not see him?'

Her heart was pounding now. 'How long ago did he leave?'

Dahlia thought for a moment. 'Fifteen minutes. Perhaps more. He left without a word, rode straight past me. I assumed it was because it did not go well with you.'

Aldara pushed Loda forwards and handed Mako down to her mother. 'I need to find him.'

Dahlia took the infant and glanced at her daughter's feet. 'You are not wearing any shoes.'

Aldara had already turned the mare away from them. She kicked Loda into a canter and headed for Byrgus's farm. If she was fast, she could cut through the paddocks and the forest at the back of his property and catch up with Tyron. She picked up speed, pounding towards the fences and leaping over them without slowing. Leo was still making his way back to his house and turned to watch her gallop past him.

'Aldara!' he called, but she did not slow.

Her heels went into the mare's sides as she weaved through the orchard. Once clear of the apple trees, she leapt over the final fence and disappeared into the trees on the other side. She knew every track and fallen log in that forest, navigating with ease, pushing the mare faster at every opportunity. On the other side of those trees was the road that would lead her to Tyron. He had a long journey ahead of him, so she hoped he was travelling at a far more sensible speed than she was.

Ducking to avoid a low branch, she cleared a thick trunk that lay across the track carved out from hooves and boars. The road came into sight and she burst through the trees, descending the slope to the road in a few strides before almost colliding with another horse. The frightened horse came to a skidding halt and Loda leapt sideways to avoid a collision. Aldara turned to face the rider and saw Tyron, eyes wide, staring at her. She tried to calm the mare dancing beneath her.

'Easy, girl,' she said, eyes remaining on Tyron.

He continued to watch her while she swallowed down the tears that were threatening to escape, despite no words having been exchanged.

'Where are you going?' she asked.

He slowly shook his head, eyes moving over her. 'Where is your saddle?'

She looked down. 'With my shoes. Where are you going?' she asked again.

'Back to Corneo.' He glanced east as if she might see the destination for herself. 'We have hold of the West.'

'Congratulations.' It was a hollow sentiment. 'You received my letter?' Loda had finally stilled, so she loosened her grip on the reins.

No, Pandarus had the letter, but he could not tell her that. 'It arrived at Archdale before I left' was all he said.

She studied him, trying to read him but finding herself unable to. 'Why are you leaving?'

He looked away. 'I saw the two of you. You seemed so happy. It didn't feel right to intrude.'

'Intrude?' She knew by his expression that he had likely seen the *three* of them and knew how it must have appeared. 'Leo is our neighbour. He has been very kind in helping us out with the harvest.' He said nothing. 'And other chores that are difficult with a baby—'

'You don't need to explain yourself to me.'

'Please,' she said, waiting for him to look at her. 'Come

and meet your son before you leave. That is why you came, isn't it?'

He looked at her, wounded and unsure. 'All right.' He glanced at the road behind him. 'Should we take the road? Like normal people?'

'Yes.' She tried to smile. 'We will take the road.'

He turned his horse, and she pushed Loda up next to him so the horses were side by side. He widened the gap between them.

'Where are you staying in Corneo?' she asked.

His hands rested on the saddle. 'A manor in Wripis.'

She thought for a moment. 'Is Leksi with you?'

He glanced across at her. 'Yes.'

'I'm glad.'

They plodded past the trees and paddocks, unsure what words they should speak next.

'You look well,' Tyron said after a long silence.

She turned to him, taking in his dark hair, cut short like any other soldier. 'You look like you need a long sleep. Perhaps you can rest before your return.'

'That's not a good idea.' His reply came fast.

She studied his rigid posture. 'So you will meet your son and then leave?' She paused. 'And then what?'

With his eyes forwards, he replied, 'Then I try to stay alive, and you continue as you were—happy, just as I witnessed earlier.'

She moved her horse closer to his, and this time he did not move away.

TYRON STOOD with Mako in his arms amid the grazing horses. He had left his sword behind, along with the inquisitive stares of Aldara's family. He had not wanted his first moments with his son to be experienced under their watchful eye, so they had taken a walk together. Aldara stood a few paces from them, watching as Mako continued to touch the stubble on his face. The only time Tyron's gaze shifted from him was when she spoke.

'I don't know why, but I expected you to appear… awkward with him.'

'Thanks a lot.'

'Perhaps "inexperienced" would have been a better choice of word.'

He glanced at her. She had a hand on her brow like a shield against the sun. Her lips were pressed together the way they did when she was nervous.

'I've had a lot of practice with my niece, Princess Tai.'

He looked back at Mako and pretended to nip his fingers. The boy squealed and then laughed, looking at his mother to gauge her reaction. Aldara smiled at him before looking down.

'Of course. How old is the princess now?'

'Almost two years.'

Otus lowered his head and began to nibble at the grass again.

'Would you like to sit for a while?' she asked.

He glanced back at the house, some distance behind them. 'All right.'

They sat in the grass and Mako reached for his mother. Aldara reluctantly took him from Tyron, standing him up while supporting the weight of him. He bounced up and down, feigning control over his legs.

'Is he close to walking?'

Aldara shook her head. 'He was a late crawler, so I don't think he will be walking anytime soon. Mother blames me.' Noticing his frown, she added, 'I tend to carry him around a lot.'

Watching them together, Tyron did not doubt it. 'He doesn't look like you.'

'Because he looks like *you*.' A hint of a smile formed. 'Normally questions are raised about the father, not the mother.'

'How can I be certain he is in fact yours?'

A full smile spread across her face. 'I have two witnesses who saw the whole thing.'

'Yes, but can I trust the word of a midwife?'

Her smile fell away. 'There was no midwife as such. My mother and neighbour helped with the delivery.'

Tyron glanced in the direction of Byrgus's farm. 'The neighbour you were with earlier?'

She tilted her head in a way that suggested he should know better. 'Of course not. His mother, Iris, arrived just in time. She has a lot of experience, but not a lot of children left to show for it.'

'Why no midwife?'

Aldara kept her gaze on Mako, sensing his disapproval. 'She was busy.'

Tyron felt his teeth press together. 'You mean she would not come.'

She glanced at him and shrugged. 'I didn't need her in the end.'

'Women die giving birth. Had I known you were with child, I would have sent someone to stay with you while you were lying in.'

She burst out laughing at that. 'Lying in is something noble women do prior to birth.'

The sound of her laughter distracted him. He was quiet for a moment. 'And what do peasant women do?'

She sat Mako on her lap and looked at him. 'Work.'

He shook his head. 'I would have sent someone to help with the work.' His eyes travelled again to the neighbouring farm. 'Though it seems you already had help.'

Aldara's eyes shone at him.

'What?'

'Nothing.' She shrugged. 'It's just that you only glimpsed the man at a distance and already you dislike him.'

He was jealous and had no doubt she could see it. 'My eyes work fine from that distance. You forget, I know the minds of men better than you do. I saw enough.'

She pressed her lips together to stop from smiling. 'And you forget that Fedora was my teacher for a number of years. I know something about men also.'

'I don't forget any of it.'

Her expression fell. 'I didn't mean it like that.'

He looked away from her. Mako was leaning forwards now and dropped onto his hands and knees before crawling over to him. Tyron waited for his son to reach him before picking him up and sitting him on his leg.

'You are angry at me.'

'I'm not angry,' he lied.

She exhaled. 'I had always planned to tell you after the wedding. I have heard nothing of a date—'

'The wedding is still going ahead.' It came out more abrupt than he had intended. 'There was a mourning period, and now this business in Corneo…'

She shook her head. 'You don't have to explain. I just wanted to make sure you understood my reasons, but I suppose you read it all in the letter.'

He decided it was not the time to tell her Pandarus had intercepted the letter and that the entire family likely knew of the boy. 'You were pregnant before Pandarus took the throne. You should have told me then.'

He saw guilt in her eyes when she looked at him. Her gaze fell to Mako, who was watching the horses.

'I was waiting.'

'For what?'

She looked pained by her thoughts. 'For you to come.'

'I would have, had I known.'

She shook her head. 'Not for Mako.' She was struggling with the words. 'I was waiting for you to come… for me.'

He stared at her, unblinking. 'Aldara, why were you waiting for me to come here?'

She could not look at him. 'You told me you were praying for one more miracle.'

He felt his throat tighten. 'And you told me you could not return to Archdale, that you did not belong there, that you would not survive that life.' He wanted her to look at him and confirm this. 'Did you not?'

Her eyes welled up, but she did not cry. 'Yes.'

He was silent for a moment. 'What miracle were you waiting for?' He wanted to know what other possibility she imagined for them.

'It was childish. I see that now. You are right, of course. I should have told you when I knew for sure.'

He wanted a different answer but just nodded in agreement.

'Mako was born the day your father passed,' she said, looking up at him.

He looked at his son. When he could not think of a response, he said, 'Pandarus knows.'

Aldara went still. 'Oh.'

His gaze returned to her. 'You must know I would never let anything happen to either of you.'

There was sadness in her eyes. 'I know you would do anything for us, but neither of us knows if it would be enough.'

He drew a breath. 'Pandarus wants this information buried as much as we do.'

She nodded. 'That's good to know.'

He exhaled hard. 'That came out wrong. I just need you to trust me. You still trust me, don't you?'

'Until my death,' she replied without hesitation. They looked at one another for a moment, and then she swallowed. 'What happens now?'

He watched her, feeling the same pain he saw in her face. 'What do you want to happen?'

'We don't get what we want. We get only fleeting moments, like this one.'

He could not stop himself from reaching up and touching her. The tips of his fingers ran across her right cheek until her face filled his hand, her skin familiar beneath it. Her head fit perfectly. She leaned in to him, turning so her lips brushed his palm. His entire body reacted. He withdrew his hand and stood up, settling Mako comfortably against him before offering his free hand to her. She looked up at him, lips parted and breath shallow. Her gaze fell to the extended hand, and she reached up and took it. His much larger hand swallowed hers as he pulled her to her feet with barely any effort. She stepped back from him, no longer looking at him. Mako began to cry for her.

'He wants his mother,' Tyron said, holding him out for her.

'He's probably hungry.' She glanced up at him. 'There are no wet nurses on the farm.'

He smiled and looked down.

'Can you do something for me?'

Anything she asked, he would do it. 'What is it?'

'Don't go just yet. Let me take care of Mako so I can say goodbye without him clawing at my dress.'

He was fighting off a similar urge to his son. 'Of course.'

They walked back to the house and found Kadmus outside chopping wood for the stove. Tyron waited outside with him, answering questions about what was happening in

Corneo, while Aldara slipped inside to tend to Mako. Twenty minutes later, she reappeared with a much happier Mako in her arms.

Tyron took him from her and let his son explore his face once again. 'You take care of your mother,' Tyron said. He pressed his lips against Mako's soft hair before holding him out for Aldara to take.

'I'll take him,' Kadmus said, grabbing the boy and swinging him up in the air. The squeals could still be heard after they had gone inside.

Aldara and Tyron stood alone, listening.

'How does the new horse compare to Otus?' Aldara asked, gesturing to the gelding tethered by the trough.

They turned and walked towards the horse, pieces of loose hay blowing about their feet.

'This is not my horse.' He did not mention the fact that his new mare had been killed by an arrow aimed at him.

They stopped next to the horse and it turned its head to smell Aldara. Tyron watched as she stroked its head and murmured words to it. He thought about how it might feel to have those words spoken against his bare skin. He had to turn away.

She stopped and looked at him, an inquisitive expression on her face.

He forced a smile, but it faded quickly.

'Thank you for coming,' she said. 'I know the news must have come as a shock. I thought you might be angry at me.'

'Who says I'm not angry at you?'

She looked at him, trying to gauge whether he was serious.

'Well, then I thank you for your forgiveness.'

'That's awfully presumptuous of you.'

His eyes were smiling even if his mouth did not move.

She curtsied, and when she rose, she seemed to be waiting for him to say something—or do something.

'I would like to come back and visit Mako before I am wed.'

She averted her eyes. 'He would love that. He seems to understand who you are.' She hesitated. 'Please take care of yourself in Corneo. If anything were to happen—'

'Nothing will happen,' he assured her. 'Not if you continue to pray for me.' He smiled then.

'You know me so well.'

He reached out and then dropped his hand back to his side. 'Write if you need anything. I hope the food is helpful.'

She glanced behind at the house. 'It is, thank you.'

'It will continue to arrive, for as long as you need it.'

'Until you are wed?'

He frowned and saw she regretted her question. 'How could you ask that?'

'I'm sorry.' She looked away. 'I really am very appreciative. I don't know why I said that.'

Tyron knew. Pain made you say things you did not mean.

'Safe travels, my lord.' She spun and walked towards the house, eyes down.

He took a step after her. 'Aldara.'

She turned and looked at him.

'I will continue to pray for one more miracle. Until I draw my last breath.'

He should have just let her walk away, because her face went into her hands, and then he was moving towards her. She looked up and started walking towards him; then she broke into a run, and his own pace quickened. As she reached him, she sprang into his arms, and he caught her like a child. He was overcome with familiarity as her legs went around him. His entire body pulsed with the feel of her. When her lips met his, he opened his mouth, desperate to taste her. No doubt her family was watching out of the window, but it was too late to care about that. She pressed against him, one arm tightening around his neck while the other slid into his hair, taking hold of it.

'The barn,' she whispered into his open mouth.

She did not need to tell him; his feet were already moving in that direction. He really hoped her father was not in there working, because he was about to see his daughter consumed by a man who had completely lost control.

CHAPTER 9

Tyron's back slammed against the back of the small door. He reached behind for the latch, his mouth remaining on her the entire time. It was dark inside with all the doors closed and no lanterns burning. Narrow streams of sunlight filtered through the gaps in the walls, casting lines of light across their bodies.

Aldara released her grip on him, sliding down his body until her feet were on the ground. He watched as she pulled her dress over her head, his breath catching. She kept going, slipping her undergarments down and letting them drop to her feet. Still fully dressed, he let his gaze fall to her breasts and continue down, swallowing thickly.

She was the one who went to him, taking his hands and placing them on her. Her eyes closed at the feel of them on her bare skin. When her head tilted back, he withdrew his hands, and she opened her eyes to look at him. She recognised the expression on his face—a combination of resignation and helplessness. They knew when it was over, they would each have given another part of themselves, but neither of them had the strength to stop what was about to happen.

'I know' was all she said.

His eyes closed as she reached for him, removing his belt and pulling at the tunic shielding him. He helped her, eyes opening to watch her. All that remained was his shirt, like a white flag on his body. He tugged it over his head, and her eyes travelled down to the bandage wrapped around his ribs. He had said nothing of being injured.

'It's nothing,' he said, reading her mind.

When their eyes met, she saw there was no pain, only hunger equal to her own. She stepped forwards until her bare skin was on his, and surrendered.

In the late afternoon, Aldara looked down at Tyron, asleep on top of one of the horse blankets they had thrown across the hay. She knew once he fell asleep it was difficult to wake him; she remembered that about him.

His exhaustion was evident in the slackness of jaw and dark circles around his eyes. What had he been thinking, leaving the manor the day after he had fought so hard to take it? Her eyes went again to the bandage around his middle. A red bloodstain showed where the injury lay beneath it. She stood and picked up the side of the blanket where she had been, placing it gently over his naked body. He did not stir.

Aldara walked into the house to find her family seated at the table, eating their evening meal. They stopped eating and looked at her, though her father's eyes returned quickly to his food. Kadmus leaned back in his chair and crossed his arms, a playful expression on his face that made her cheeks burn. Mako was seated on Dahlia's lap and immediately reached out for Aldara.

'Where is Prince Tyron?' Dahlia asked.

Aldara walked over and took Mako from her, careful not to look at anyone else.

'He is asleep in the barn. He rode overnight and is exhausted.'

Kadmus coughed and Isadore continued to study his food, shredding meat from a chicken bone with the care one would take with a painting.

'The sheep and horses need to go in for the night.'

'I'll do it,' Aldara replied, kissing Mako's head.

'And they need feeding—'

'I'll do it, Mother. I'll take care of everything.' She looked up briefly. 'I need some bandages.'

Dahlia stared at her for a moment before getting up from the table. She rummaged around, finding the scraps of boiled material, while Aldara nursed Mako on the bed.

'Will the prince be staying the night?' Dahlia asked, taking Mako from her and handing over the clean bandages.

'I don't think so. He has to get back.' Her voice came out like a whisper. She glanced once at Kadmus, who was half frowning, half smiling. 'Can you take care of Mako for me until I return?'

Dahlia nodded. 'Wait,' she said, walking over to the table. She handed Mako to Isadore and picked up Aldara's plate, putting some chicken, beans and barley bread onto it before handing it to her daughter. 'He must keep his strength up. Especially if he is injured.'

Aldara looked at the food and then at her mother, whose eyes remained on the plate. 'Thank you.'

Another nod.

When Aldara arrived at the barn, she saw that Tyron had not moved. She placed the food and bandages out of reach of the chickens and grabbed some halters for the horses, glancing at Tyron before leaving the barn.

The horses had already made their way to the bottom of the paddock, knowing a feed awaited them. Aldara attached the halters and led them to the barn, placing them in the two stalls, Loda and Otus always together. She fed them, gave them fresh water, and then went to feed the chickens and goat. Afterwards, she began the long walk to find the sheep, whistling for Artemus, who was still keeping guard of them. She barely had to do anything once Artemus knew it was time to bring them in. Walking behind the flock, she watched the dog work, keeping enough distance so as not to panic them. When they arrived at the barn, the sliding door began to open. Tyron appeared, wearing only his trousers and boots. She struggled to look at him.

'It's too heavy for you,' he said when she came to stand next to him.

She smiled. 'No it isn't.' Her eyes went to his bandaged chest. 'But it's much too heavy for you.'

They watched the sheep run past into the barn before Tyron closed the door behind them. Aldara went to fetch some water and watched him drink and wash. When he was done, she retrieved the food from its hiding spot and sat down on the blanket with him. She could always tell when he was hungry by the way he eyed the food.

'Have you eaten?' he asked, looking up at her.

'Yes, go ahead. You need your strength.'

He did not move. 'You are lying. You were always a terrible liar. I'm not eating unless you do.'

Reluctantly, she reached for a small piece of bread and ate it slowly. He barely chewed, swallowing the food in whole chunks. Suddenly he stopped eating and pushed the plate towards her.

'You eat the rest,' he said, pointing to the piece of chicken and handful of beans.

'I'm really not very hungry.'

He just looked at her until she relented and ate.

Once she had finished, she took the plate away and washed her hands, returning to him with the clean bandages.

She carefully untied the soiled one and began to unwrap it. She studied the neatly stitched finger-length cut before carefully washing the area around the wound. He sat still for her, all except a stray finger that traced her thigh as she wrapped the new bandages around him, her hair brushing against his bare chest every time she reached behind him. Once finished, she went to dispose of the others and wash her hands again.

When she returned, she looked everywhere but at him.

'Why can't you look at me?'

She forced her eyes up to meet his. 'I don't know. Perhaps because you are leaving soon.'

He pulled her onto his lap and brushed her hair to one side so he could kiss her neck. 'That is exactly why you should be looking at me.' His hands were wandering beneath her dress. 'What was it you said earlier? "We don't get what we want. We get fleeting moments, like this one."'

Her eyes closed so she could savour the warmth of him. 'How do you suppose we spend our final moments together?'

He laid her on the blanket and covered her mouth with his.

～

'Tyron.'

He felt the word whispered against his ear, but sleep kept a hold of him.

'Tyron.'

It was her, so he opened his eyes, searching for her face. There it was, inches from his in the dark. He had fallen asleep again.

'Sorry,' he said. 'How long have I been asleep?' He sat up and saw that she was dressed with a shawl wrapped around her.

'An hour. I thought you needed it.'

He did need it, but he also needed to get going if he was to keep his promise to Stamitos. 'Stop getting dressed. It's inconvenient.' He saw the flash of her teeth in the dark.

'Get dressed,' she said, handing him his clothes.

'I was about to tell you to *un*dress.'

She seemed to be waiting for him, so he did as he was told, eyeing his boots in her hands.

'Are you really that keen to be rid of me?'

She suppressed a smile and held the boots out for him. 'Come.'

'Where?'

She tugged on his arm. 'A quick ride together before you leave.'

He looked around, trying to gauge the time. 'It's dark.'

'Yes.' She was pulling him to move faster. 'Just like the first time we rode together.'

He followed her to one of the stalls, lit up by lantern light, and saw that Loda and Otus were bridled. 'Where are the saddles?'

She smiled again and stepped up to Loda, springing onto the mare's back, gripping with her legs until she was upright. 'It's all right. You are old and injured, so you can use the stool.' She gestured to the stool by the door.

He looked back at her. 'That's very generous of you to offer a stool in place of a saddle.'

'You're very welcome.'

She watched as he patted Otus before mounting him for the first time in two years.

Once outside, Aldara cantered off into the darkness, leaving Tyron no choice but to follow. She did not slow until they reached the gate that opened into the forest. Once through, they walked their horses side by side.

Tyron glanced across at her, wanting to know where they were going.

'Just a few minutes,' she said, eyes ahead. 'Then I promise I'll take you back.'

He smiled to himself, praying that the inner child living inside of her would remain forever.

'We used to play soldiers here when we were young.'

He looked around at the dense trees. 'When you were young? Or last week?'

She laughed at that. 'Before Archdale, I'll have you know.'

He moved his horse closer to hers, and as he reached for her, she turned Loda sharply and the mare bumped gently against his horse. His hand dropped.

'I see. This really is like the first time we rode together. You can stop pretending you are all grown up now.'

She pushed Loda into a trot, and he watched as she turned left and slipped between the trees. He stayed on the track, or at least what he thought was a track. After a few moments, he stopped and listened for her. Not a sound.

'Are you going to jump out of the trees and scare me?' Silence. 'You may be disappointed by my reaction.' He exhaled and looked around. That was when he noticed Loda tethered to a tree behind him. He turned his horse and walked back, looking around for Aldara. 'Very clever. Can we go back now?'

Again he listened for her but heard nothing. He was about to dismount and go search for her when he felt the tip of a blade pressed into his back. He went still, and for just the briefest moment, he considered the possibility that it was someone other than Aldara.

'You are going to have to be a bit sharper, my lord, if you want to survive the coming war.'

He turned to see her standing next to Otus's rump, a long stick in hand. He felt relieved at the sight of her, shaken by the sensation of not knowing where she was in a dark forest.

'Thankfully, my enemies do not tend to sneak up from behind, you big cheat.'

She lowered the stick and shrugged. 'My game, my rules.' As she walked past him, he knocked the stick from her hand with his foot. She stopped and looked up at him. 'That doesn't count. I already won.'

He reached down and took hold of her arm, pulling her closer. 'Ride with me.'

She thought for a moment. 'I should probably confess something. I also use the stool to mount Otus. He is much taller than Loda.'

He lifted her off the ground. 'You don't need a stool when I am here.'

'You're injured. Put me down.'

He was already placing her in his lap. 'That's much better.' He kicked Otus forwards so they could get Loda.

'You'll tear your stitches.'

He laughed as he bent to untie the mare. 'Goodness, you sound like my mother.'

'I choose to take that as a compliment.'

'And I reserve the right to uphold the meaning intended.' He kissed the top of her head.

They walked slowly back, Aldara tucked in front of him, her head resting against his chest. He soaked up the feel of her pressed against him and the smell of her hair. The thought of leaving was like a fresh wound in his side.

When they arrived at the barn, he reluctantly lowered her to the ground and then slid down next to her. The horses went back into their stall, their bridles removed. They stood watching them for a moment, like they had many times before.

'A lot of our time together is spent saying goodbye,' Aldara said. 'I wish we could skip that part, but it would be rather strange to have you ride off without a word, I suppose.'

He looked at her, no longer able to touch her if he intended to leave. 'I will come back before the wedding.'

She nodded, and he immediately wished he had not mentioned the event.

They left the barn and walked over to where his horse was tethered. A soft glow came from the house, the stove still burning and providing light for sewing and weaving. Tyron untied his horse and turned to Aldara.

'My water flask,' he said. 'It was probably taken inside to be refilled. Do you mind?'

She looked at him for a long moment before replying. 'Of course not.'

He watched her walk away, her eyes on her feet until she reached the door. The moment she stepped inside, he mounted his horse and rode off down the track towards the road. He wanted to save her more unnecessary pain.

He did not look back because their moment was over. It was time to return to Corneo and prepare to fight.

CHAPTER 10

Tyron stopped at Lord Xerxes's manor to collect his horse and return the one loaned to him. The sleeping household erupted into action in the dead of night, with Lord Xerxes ordering his men about and waking the cook in case Tyron should want some food.

'That is very kind of you, but unnecessary. I will eat when I arrive at the manor.'

'Will you not stay and rest a while?' Lord Xerxes asked as they watched a groom saddle the bewildered horse.

'I'm afraid I am needed in Corneo as soon as possible. It was a risk leaving my men at such a critical time.'

Lord Xerxes nodded. 'Yes, it must have been of some importance.'

Tyron nodded, saying nothing more as the horse was brought to him. He mounted and gathered the reins.

'I imagine you are bracing for an attack.'

Tyron glanced at him. 'We are prepared.'

Lord Xerxes bowed. 'May God watch over you and your men, my lord.'

'Thank you for opening your home. I hope when we next meet, it is at a far more sensible hour of the day.'

Tyron rode hard, crossing the border just before sunrise. He stayed off the roads, removing all Syrasan markings in case he encountered anyone. The news of their win would be starting to filter outside of the manor, and there would always be some who would not accept the new way of things, even if Lord Belen told them to. He could not blame them for their divided loyalties; King Nilos's rule was all they had ever known.

He reached the woods two hours south of the manor and slowed to a walk amid oaks that had owned the land for hundreds of years. There was a distinct lack of animals in the forest, likely due to overhunting. The hungry had a way of finding food, but what to do when the food was gone?

Birds took flight overhead, and Tyron looked up to watch the startled flock take to the sky. He wondered if he was the source of their fear and looked about. Intuition made him reach for his sword, his hand resting there as he kicked his horse into a canter. The last thing he needed was an unnecessary encounter with an angry boar, or worse.

He watched the ears of his horse twitch, listening for something he could not hear. Clicking his tongue, he sped up, leaning forwards to encourage the gelding to go faster. The horse came skidding to a halt when another burst from the trees in front of them. Tyron drew his sword, taking in the guard's uniform marked with a *C*. He would know within seconds if the rider was a threat.

A sword flashed, giving Tyron his answer. Two additional horses joined from either side and a hammer came swinging towards him. He raised his sword, blocking the blow as the other rider reached for him. He hit the man in the face with the hilt of his weapon before swinging back in the direction of the man with the hammer. The guard in front of him watched, relaxed in the saddle, not yet needed. Judging by his clothing, he was higher in rank than the others. A bow rested against his back, which told Tyron they were not there to kill him—they were there to capture him.

Three armed men. He had fought with worse odds.

The immaculately dressed guard returned his sword to its sheath and retrieved a length of rope.

That is optimistic, Tyron thought.

The prince reached for the dagger strapped to his calf and flung it, striking the man's arm so the rope dropped from his hand. Two hammers swung at Tyron from either side. One blow would render him unconscious. He ducked, leaning back so his shoulders brushed the rump of his horse. The hammers collided above him. Before they could try again, Tyron thrust his sword up, knocking the hammer from the hand to his right before returning upright.

As he turned to the rider on his left, weapon ready, a chain dropped down his face, a fourth rider behind him. He slipped his free hand beneath it before it could tighten around his neck and pulled down hard, turning just in time to see the hammer come at him.

THE FIRST THING Tyron was aware of was his pounding head. Blood crusted his left eye, and when he opened it, he could see the ground rushing beneath him. Nausea rose up, or was it down? It took him a moment to figure out he was bound and draped across a horse. The sound of him being sick drew the attention of the other men.

'Welcome back,' came a voice to his left. The words were smooth and articulate, a voice belonging to someone of noble birth.

Tyron turned his head, counting the same four riders

from earlier, now surrounding him. The rider in front had hold of his horse. He tried to look up at the man who had spoken. 'Who are you?' he asked, blinking away dizziness.

'I am Sir Proteus, loyal servant to King Nilos of Corneo.' He glanced down at Tyron, his expression slick. 'You really should not wander around in the woods alone.'

Tyron closed his eyes as he fought against rising sickness. The name was familiar. It was possible he had met the man during his travels to Corneo some years back. 'Do you know who I am, Sir Proteus?' He heard the horse move closer.

'Prince Tyron of Syrasan, sometimes referred to as the Prince of Mercy among your own people. You are a long way from home, my lord, and your shiny reputation will do you no favours here.'

The man opposite laughed. Tyron opened his eyes to look, but everything was spinning. He glimpsed his sword hanging from Proteus's saddle, in sight, out of reach. Intentionally, no doubt.

Tyron was sick on the ground once again and the man on the other side of him pulled him upright. His feet were bound, so he was forced to sit sideways in the saddle, gripping the front to stop from falling off.

'You'll be feeling that knock for a few days,' the man said, moving his horse away.

'Do not try anything foolish,' warned Proteus. 'Any heroic displays are wasted on me.'

Tyron did not have the stomach to try anything. He was struggling to remember what had happened while trying to figure out where he was. He looked up to gauge the direction they were travelling, but the blinding sun made him look down again. East, maybe. His tongue moved in his mouth as he searched for his flask that was no longer there. 'Might I have some water?'

Proteus ignored him. A flask of water was thrust before

his face from the other side. Tyron's gaze travelled up the extended arm to the man's face. 'Thank you,' he said, taking the flask between his tied hands. There were no trees for shade, and the heat pressed down on them. 'Where are you taking me?' he asked between drinks.

'To meet our king,' Proteus replied, eyes ahead.

Tyron focused on him as best he could. He did seem familiar. 'Have we met? The last time I was in Corneo, perhaps?' His eyes went to the arm he had struck with the dagger earlier. It had been wrapped and was resting on the front of the saddle.

'I met you before that,' Proteus replied. 'Across the battle-field a few times.'

'Obviously not on the battlefield if we are both here to speak of it.'

Proteus turned to him. 'I cannot help but wonder what you were doing riding about, unescorted, on land belonging to King Nilos.'

Tyron struggled to form coherent thoughts. 'Liaising with the friendly locals.'

The men laughed, but not Proteus. He did not seem capable of it. Instead, he just looked at Tyron.

'We had men along the southern border from the moment you crossed into Corneo. We are not as clueless as your king would lead you to believe.' He watched Tyron's face for any reaction to his words. 'And we watched you cross into Syrasan two days ago.'

Tyron frowned. 'Why let me cross?'

Proteus narrowed his eyes. 'You left your men the day after taking the manor, travelling in daylight, alone. You could have crossed safely into the North where your own men were positioned, but you were going south in quite a rush, were you not? So much of a rush that you were careless with your own life. I will admit, I was curious to see what or who you would return with. And so we waited, knowing you would not leave your men for long.'

'I am sorry to disappoint you by returning empty-handed.'

Proteus smiled for the first time. 'Do I look disappointed? We had an army of men ready to move, and now we have everything we need right here with us. What better gift for our king than the Crown Prince of Syrasan himself?'

Tyron faced forwards and held the water out for the guard to take back.

'Hood him,' Proteus said with an even tone.

Tyron looked back, taking in the man's smug expression.

And then everything went black.

THE ARTIST'S impression of King Nilos outside of Archdale's church had been wrong. The sleek man from the painting was far more robust than he remembered. Whatever food shortages Corneo was experiencing, they did not extend to their king. The entire chicken carcass on the plate in front of him was proof enough.

Tyron was on his knees before him, eyes adjusting to the light after having his head covered for the last few hours of their journey. Two guards held him in position, in case he decided to flee while bound, surrounded by Corneon guards, with no weapons and no way out. Much better to hear the king out before deciding to die.

'You have probably heard that I am a man of my word,' King Nilos said, picking up his cup and taking a long drink of wine. The liquid stained his mouth and beard, and he did not wipe it away.

Tyron had actually heard quite the opposite from Lord

Belen but thought it not the best time to say so. There was a speech coming, and he had no choice but to listen.

'It has come to my attention that Lord Belen not only lost the fight against you, but has since continued to cooperate with your demands. I do not know what you call that in Syrasan, but in Corneo, we call it treason. It is a crime punishable by death.'

Tyron resisted the urge to roll his eyes at the patronising speech.

'When my father...'

It was going to be a long one.

He took the opportunity to examine the throne room, its expensive furnishings and elaborate rugs conveniently positioned either side of his knees. Looking about, he realised he seemed to be kneeling on the only exposed stone in the entire room. His eyes flicked to the guards either side of him, holding him in place.

'You have made things much easier for me,' Nilos continued. 'Now it becomes a simple exchange.'

Tyron's gaze returned to the king. 'Let me guess, me for the West?'

Nilos pushed the large plate away and leaned back in his chair, the buttons on his tunic straining. 'You will be free to leave once every Syrasan man has fled across the border, or lies dead on Corneon soil.'

Tyron studied him for a moment. 'And what of Lord Belen and the men loyal to him?'

Nilos shook his head. 'Lord Belen is like a dog. Feed him, show him a little attention, and he will follow you anywhere.'

Tyron did not have a response.

'I shall send a messenger. Let's get this done quickly, shall we?'

The plan was flawed. 'While it might sound like a solid plan, Your Majesty, you may be overestimating my value. I can tell you with a great amount of certainty that King Pandarus will not evacuate the West, not even for me.'

King Nilos watched him for a moment. 'I met the two of you a few years ago, back when King Pandarus was managing relations and you were forced to manage them on his behalf. I am not surprised by your response.' He shifted in his chair, trying to find a more comfortable position. 'But your mother is Galen, and Galen women do not let people kill their children. I am confident your men will leave my land, and you will depart here with your head attached and tail between your legs.'

'And what if King Pandarus does not agree?'

Nilos picked at the food in his teeth with a fingernail. 'Then you will be beheaded and your men killed. Get the same result whether your brother puts his pride aside or not.' He waved his hand. 'Take him away.' A final glance at Tyron. 'And send the messenger.'

CHAPTER 11

*D*ust made its way through the open window of the wagon, forcing Eldoris to hold a handkerchief over her nose and mouth. The roads were so dry and cracked, one would think snow in the cold season an impossibility. Her tired eyes closed, and she let the sway of the wagon shake the worries from her.

She tried to remember the last time she had travelled south. Her children had been young, Stamitos round-faced and full of laughter and energy. All her children had been safe.

She opened her eyes, the dust lit up in front of her face. She thought of Tyron chained in a cell, and that was enough to make them close again, her lips pressing together to contain the emotion.

She lowered the handkerchief. 'How much longer?'

A guard rode up beside the window, leaning down so she could see him. 'About an hour at our current pace, Your Grace.'

She nodded and raised the handkerchief again.

Aside from the two guards on horseback and the driver, she was travelling alone, to the objection of her ladies, her daughter and even her king, her eldest son, who could barely look at her. When Pandarus had told her the news of Tyron's capture, she had predicted the words that would follow. He would not submit to King Nilos's demands in order to get his brother released. Those were the hard decisions men in power made. And they were not easy to digest.

She rarely cried in front of her children, but she had cried that day. Pandarus had stiffened in front of her, unsure what to say, how to act, what to do or make of the mess before him. After a long silence, he had tried to comfort her with words, telling her that with the support of Lord Belen and the Zoelin army, they would take Masville Castle and get Tyron back. What he did not say was that King Jayr's support was dependent on the marriage of Tyron to the Zoelin princess, and that could not happen with her son imprisoned. If the alliance with Zoelin was flaky before, it was hollow now.

As the wagon pulled off the road onto a narrow, uneven track, Eldoris gripped the door to steady herself and looked out of the window at the small farmhouse. The entire dwelling was the size of her bedchamber. She blinked against the fresh cloud of dust, her gaze shifting to the barn that had been rebuilt after Zoelin guards had burned it to the ground.

A woman stepped out of the house, squinting against the harsh sun. She turned and rushed back inside, returning a few moments later wearing a different dress, her fingers smoothing down loose strands of hair. The wagon stopped in front of her and the driver hurried down to open the door. Eldoris took hold of the offered hand and stepped down. There was something familiar about the woman standing in front of the door, perhaps her resemblance to Aldara. The woman dropped into a curtsy.

'Your Grace.' Dahlia rose and folded her hands in front of her. 'What an unexpected honour.'

Eldoris took in the faded dress, callused hands and laced boots one would expect to see on a labourer. 'I apologise for showing up uninvited. I was hoping to speak with Aldara. Is she here?'

Before Dahlia could answer, Aldara stepped out of the house, Mako on her hip, clutching handfuls of his mother's dress. Eldoris's breath caught as she looked at him. He looked just like Tyron as a baby.

'I will be inside if you need anything,' Dahlia said, curt-sying and disappearing into the house.

Aldara gave a small curtsy and then looked around, trying to find words. 'I apologise if I seem unwelcoming, Your Grace. I am just a bit surprised to see you here.'

Eldoris's eyes remained on the boy. 'May I?'

Aldara hesitated before walking over and handing Mako to her. His large eyes took in his elaborately dressed grand-mother before taking hold of the necklace around her neck.

'Gentle, Mako,' Aldara said.

'It is all right,' Eldoris said, smiling down at him. 'My chil-dren were the same. I gave up wearing jewels around them.'

'I am afraid such things are a novelty around here.'

Eldoris looked at Aldara, eyes moving over her. She knew about the food Tyron sent the family and said nothing of it to anyone.

'Does Prince Tyron know you are here... visiting?' Aldara's eyes shifted to the mounted guards next to the wagon.

Eldoris could see the girl trying to figure out her inten-tions. She probably feared the child would be taken from her. She handed Mako back to Aldara to ease her mind. The mother wrapped her arms around the boy, his head resting against her collarbone.

'No,' Eldoris replied. 'Tyron does not know I am here.' She watched fingers tighten on the child. 'Tyron was taken prisoner a week ago. He is being held at Masville Castle in Corneo.' Watching Aldara's face, she could see how her own would have appeared when the king had shared the news with her. 'He was last seen by Lord Xerxes when he stopped there for his horse. He crossed the border too far south. Did not stand a chance on his own.' When Aldara said nothing, she continued. 'As you can imagine, it is a difficult time for my family. A difficult time for me.' She turned her face away for a moment. There was no way she would let herself cry.

'Prisoner?' Aldara said, her face collapsing.

Eldoris turned back to her. 'Yes. He is alive for now. King Pandarus is hopeful.' The words stuck.

'King Pandarus is hopeful?' Aldara's head shook. 'Is anyone else hopeful?'

Eldoris swallowed hard. Seeing her own fears mirrored was difficult. 'We are all hopeful,' she lied. 'What other option is there?'

'What does King Nilos want in exchange for his life?'

'He wants us to give up our hold on the West.'

Aldara eyes searched the queen mother's face. 'Will he do it?'

Eldoris lowered her gaze.

Mako began to cry, so Aldara bounced him and stroked his head. 'What is King Pandarus doing to get him out?'

It was a bold question, but not surprising. If only Eldoris had an answer.

'He has a plan, does he not?' There was a plea in Aldara's tone.

Eldoris studied the girl. 'It is a complex situation, and there are a lot of aspects to consider.'

Tears fell down Aldara's face. 'What about you? Do *you* have a plan?'

Eldoris's mind had not stopped since hearing the news. 'Nothing that Pandarus would approve of.'

'What about something Pandarus would not approve of?'

The conversation was treasonous, and she should have put an end to it. 'Nothing viable yet.'

'What can I do to help?'

'You cannot help. Not with this.'

Aldara pressed her lips against Mako's head and quietened. 'Why did you come here?'

Eldoris watched the infant relax beneath his mother's affection. It was all so simple at that age. 'I thought you would want to know. It was not something I could write in a letter. I am certain Tyron would want you to hear it from me rather than via rumour.' She hesitated. 'And… I thought you might know something we did not.'

A sob escaped Aldara, and Mako looked up to watch the tears fall. 'He came here. That is why he was travelling alone.' A sharp intake of air. 'This is why I did not want to tell him. I knew it would not end well. It never does.'

Eldoris could not pretend she had not placed blame on Aldara for a brief period, but she had seen sense soon after. 'Yes, we are aware that he came here. It was his decision to travel alone to meet his son.' She paused. 'It was our decision not to give him your letter, to keep it from him. And then it was Stamitos's decision to tell him when he did. I cannot blame him. It is not easy to betray the people you love.'

She could tell by Aldara's face that she did not know about the last part.

'He… Prince Tyron did not receive my letter?'

Eldoris was finding the heat stifling. 'King Pandarus thought it best we wait, so as not to distract him.'

Aldara closed her eyes as the pieces fell into place. 'I see. It seems we all betrayed him.'

'I am surprised Tyron said nothing of how he learned the news.'

Aldara shook her head. 'I suppose he did not want to validate my lack of trust.'

Eldoris's gaze fell to the ground between them. She considered leaving but did not wish to leave on bad terms. She was trying to decide on a course of action when Aldara brushed away her tears and straightened herself.

'Would you like to come inside and eat with us, Your Grace?'

Eldoris glanced behind her at the wagon. She had not intended to stay, and she was certainly not one for entering the houses of strangers and eating food with commoners who could not afford to feed others. But then her eyes returned to Mako. 'Thank you. That would be lovely.'

Aldara held Mako out to her, as if understanding her need to hold him at that moment. She pressed the boy against her and followed Aldara into the house.

THE THOUGHT of Tyron imprisoned consumed Aldara. She imagined every aspect from the lack of clean water to all the different ways he might be executed if Pandarus failed him. What would happen in the cold season? She remembered well the hacking coughs of the men in the tower at Drake Castle once the snow had arrived and the temperature plummeted.

Two weeks after Eldoris visited, Aldara's milk dried up. As Mako had only just had his first birthday, Iris suggested some herbs—but nothing worked. Dahlia blamed stress. Blamed her, perhaps. Isadore held up the chubby boy and said there was enough of him to survive the winter, then winked at her. Kadmus just smiled and said it was because Mako preferred to eat the same food as them. Nothing eased her guilt.

Eldoris had promised to update her if there was any news. No letters came, and her imagination soared. She dragged herself around the farm, completing chores without any memory of doing them. At night she lay awake watching Mako sleep, unable to follow him. She wondered how Tyron had coped with crushing anxiety while she had been in Zoelin. Then she realised the answer—he had not coped at all. She turned and faced the other way, hoping the visual break from her son, who looked very much like his father, would help her mind. She stared at the cot sitting against the wall that Isadore had made. It sat empty, just like her.

Four weeks after receiving the news, Aldara thought she might lose her mind while waiting to hear something. She was thinking about writing a letter to the queen mother when a wagon pulled up at the front of the house around noon.

'Who haven't we had visit us from Archdale yet?' Kadmus asked, peering out the window. 'I really hope it is Princess Cora.'

'I wouldn't hold your breath,' Aldara replied, coming up next to him to look. 'It's not a royal wagon.'

Mako was playing on the floor, and she swooped to kiss him before stepping outside. She waited as the driver opened the door, trying to hazard a guess at who it might be. When Hali stepped out, Aldara felt herself tear up. They looked at one another and Hali let out a huge breath, her face filled with pity.

'I knew I needed to worry,' Hali said as Aldara came towards her. 'Look at you. When was the last time you slept?'

When Aldara was close, she opened her arms and

wrapped them around her friend. 'Thank you,' she whispered into Hali's hair.

'This is what sisters do.' Hali pulled back and brushed at her cheeks. 'I only have a few hours. I am on my way to Arelasa to visit with my family.'

'Once again, this is very much out of the way.'

'I know, so start talking.' She threaded her arm through Aldara's and they strolled away from the house. 'Lord Yuri has been in contact with Leksi. Did you know that Pandarus's plan to take Masville Castle is dependent on the support of the Zoelin army?'

Aldara nodded. 'Yes.'

'And did you know King Jayr is not sending any men?'

'Tyron is betrothed to his sister. One would think that would be enough reason to help.'

'There cannot be a wedding if Tyron is…' She did not finish.

Aldara stopped walking. 'What? Dead?' She swiped away the loose hair blowing across her face.

Hali bit down on her lip. 'I was going to say imprisoned.'

Aldara stared at Hali while she thought. 'I need to get him out of there.'

Hali's mouth fell open. '*You* need to do nothing except leave this to the king and his army of trained men. Lord Yuri says there will be a negotiation.'

Aldara shook her head. 'Pandarus does not negotiate—it's beneath him.'

'Even if that is true, there is nothing you can do to help. Your Companion skills will not be of much use in this situation.'

The breeze stilled and Aldara's eyes burned as she considered those words.

'What? I know that look. What is going on in that head of yours?'

'Nothing,' Aldara replied, looking away. 'I was just thinking about what you said.'

Hali narrowed her eyes. 'Which part?'

Aldara tried to blink away the thoughts taking shape in her mind. 'About Companions. I was just thinking about how the tradition began in Corneo.'

Hali crossed her arms in front of her. 'So?'

'So… the royal men have Companions.'

'So?' Hali waited for a response and then her expression fell. 'Oh no you don't. Don't even think about it.'

'Think about what?'

She waved a finger in front of Aldara's face. 'I know you. You are capable of some crazy things, but this'—her finger circled Aldara's face—'this is insane.'

'What are you talking about?'

Hali's head shook furiously. 'Oh, are you going to make me say it? The two of you are as crazy as each other.'

Aldara almost laughed. 'You may have to say it as I'm lost.'

Hali took a step back from her as if she were suddenly contagious. 'No. Absolutely not.'

There was nothing she could hide from her friend. They had learned years ago how to communicate without the need for words. Aldara took a step towards her. 'It was just a thought.'

'I knew it,' Hali said, taking another step back. 'There cannot be much difference between a Syrasan Companion and a Corneon Companion, am I right? You could just slip across the border and win the affections of King Nilos. Is that it?'

Aldara thought of her mother all those years ago, thrusting herself in front of the king, getting his attention and stealing his heart during their first meeting. 'I cannot leave Mako.' As soon as she said it, she could not think of a reason why outside of the fact that she was his mother. After all, he was weaned, amid a family that loved and cared for him as much as she did. But she was his mother. What sort of mother left their child to get into bed with the enemy?

'Aldara.'

'What?'

'You are still thinking about it.'

Aldara looked down. 'My goodness, Hali, they are just thoughts. I would never do anything reckless.'

'Like the time you defended my father at the tournament?'

Aldara did not raise her eyes.

'Did you think my father would not tell me? You were lucky Tyron came and stopped you from being lashed.'

Yes, he had come for her, because he would do anything to ensure she was safe. She wondered if she was capable of the same.

Hali reached out and took her hands, forcing Aldara to look at her again. 'Promise me you will not do anything foolish.'

Aldara opened her mouth, but no words came.

Hali practically shook her. 'You chose this life, your family. You are free and safe with people who love you.' When Aldara did not reply, she added, 'Tyron wants you here. He wants you safe. So just be patient, please. Wait.'

'Wait for what? His death?' Aldara looked down at their hands. 'This life… my life… it does not work without him.'

Hali groaned. 'When you were imprisoned in Zoelin, Tyron did not rush across the border and get everyone killed. He waited. He made a plan and implemented it with the help of his family and friends. You cannot be impulsive in these situations, because people's lives are at stake.'

Aldara gave a small smile. 'Look at you, all grown up.'

Hali ran her thumbs across the tops of Aldara's hands. 'I

learned a thing or two during my time at Onuric. I know what can happen to a woman at the hands of a powerful man.' Her expression softened. 'Before I go, I want you to promise me you will not do anything impulsive or foolish.'

Aldara exhaled and squeezed Hali's hands. 'I promise.'

CHAPTER 12

*S*ix weeks.

He had been imprisoned for six weeks, and no letters arrived for her.

Was he hungry? Plagued by thirst? She wondered if perhaps he would refuse the food offered, preferring to control the circumstances of his death. Maybe they were denying him what he needed to survive because they needed something from him, something he could not give. Something he did not want to give.

Aldara remembered well the thirst she had felt, waiting in the trees away from the flowing Lotheng River. How her tongue had swelled in her mouth, how it had been all she could think about. Her thirst, and him.

She reached out and picked up the cup of water from the table, studying it before bringing it to her mouth. It was clean and cool against her throat. She savoured the sensation.

'Are you all right?' her father asked her.

Her eyes went to him. They were all seated around the table, eating the evening meal, some of the ingredients provided by Tyron while he likely went without. She placed the cup down, her gaze shifting to Mako perched on Isadore's lap, holding a spoon in one hand which he dipped into Isadore's bowl, licking the fatty liquid off it before dipping it again. The other hand clutched a piece of bread that he had forgotten about. When she did not respond, Kadmus stopped eating and looked up. Her mother put her spoon down, but her gaze remained on the table in front of her. Perhaps she sensed what was coming.

'I have an idea,' Aldara said, unsure who to look at. 'There might be a way I can help get Prince Tyron out of Masville Castle.'

Kadmus leaned back, watching her.

Isadore glanced at Dahlia who did not look up. 'What idea would that be?'

Mako hummed as his tongue ran over the spoon that did not fit into his mouth. He would be fine, she told herself. She waited for her mother to look up.

'King Nilos holds the Corneo flag tournament at the end of the warm season.' She tried to bring strength into her voice. 'He believes it lifts the spirits of his people going into harder times.'

Kadmus laughed at this. 'Hoping they might forget their hunger after a day of fun?'

Isadore shot Kadmus a glance that silenced him.

'Many of the common people attend in hope of getting an audience with the king and princes. They try to sell their valuables in time for the cold season, as they do here in Syrasan.'

Kadmus narrowed his eyes. 'So you want to sell King Nilos a few sheep?'

'Let her finish,' Dahlia said, speaking up for the first time.

Aldara had a drink of water, her mouth dry from the thoughts she was about to say aloud. She placed the cup back down on the table and decided to say the words to her mother.

'And Companions. Fathers present their daughters to be sold as Companions.'

Her mother seemed to understand perfectly. When Aldara worked up the courage to look at her father, she could see he was confused.

'Help an old man out and explain it plainly.'

She still could not look at Kadmus. 'If King Nilos was to take a new Companion, or perhaps one of his sons, she would go to Masville Castle where Prince Tyron is being held.'

A harsh laugh escaped Kadmus. 'You expect a Corneon Companion to help a Syrasan prince escape? You better than anyone should know how ridiculous that idea is.'

'I think what Aldara is saying is that the Corneon Companion would in fact be Syrasan,' said Dahlia.

Aldara nodded and looked between the thoughtful faces.

'That is even more ridiculous,' Kadmus said in a way that suggested the conversation was over.

Aldara had expected a dismissive reaction from him. 'Why is it ridiculous?'

He rolled his eyes. 'So many reasons. You expect a Syrasan Companion to pass as a Corneon peasant? They would have to be starved and put to work for a few months for that to be convincing. Their full figures and porcelain complexions would immediately raise suspicions. The only other option is to send an actual peasant. Good luck finding someone with a convincing Corneon accent who is willing to hang for their prince.'

Aldara glanced at her father, who was trying to concentrate on the conversation. 'You are right,' she said, looking back to Kadmus. 'A Companion from Archdale would raise suspicion, as would any woman of noble birth. I have no doubt there are desperate fathers among the poor willing to hand over their daughters for the right price, but there would not be enough time to prepare a girl from scratch.'

Kadmus crossed his arms. 'Then what are you suggesting?'

'A common woman who could transform into the ideal Companion of any man, one who had spent years training for such a role. Of course, I would need to work on my Corneon accent.'

Isadore turned Mako to the window, perhaps so he would not witness his mother's insanity.

Kadmus stood, his chair scraping against the floor. 'You cannot be serious.'

The sharp tone made her jump. She looked across at her father, waiting for him to say something, but his eyes were on Mako.

'It has been six weeks,' she said. 'King Pandarus is not going to withdraw his men.' She swallowed. 'Tyron will die in that place.'

Kadmus turned to Dahlia. 'Please tell me this is not another one of your plans to get Aldara into bed with royalty?'

'That's enough,' Isadore said, eyes on his son. 'Either sit down and finish the conversation calmly or leave so the rest of us can.'

Mako let out a small cry, squirming amid the tension. Aldara reached across the table and took him from her father. He nestled in against her chest, noticing the bread in his hand and returning to it with enthusiasm.

Kadmus took a deep breath and sank back into his chair. 'Did Hali put this idea into your head when she visited here?'

'No.'

Kadmus shook his head as he thought. 'Absolutely not. The fact that we are even having this conversation is ridiculous. I mean, what exactly is your plan? Hope you are not shot down crossing the border and then parade yourself at the tournament?'

It was not actually a question so Aldara did not reply. She let him go.

'Say that King Nilos does notice you amid the crowd of daughters being pushed in front of him, and say he likes what he sees. Then what? You think you can just go to Masville and stroll down to Prince Tyron's cell? Do you think the guards will then praise your dedication and let you both leave?'

'Kadmus—' Isadore said.

'It's all right,' Aldara said. Her eyes were closed, her lips pressed against Mako's head. 'He is angry and just needs to finish his tantrum.'

Kadmus leaned towards her. 'You are insane! You have a son, for God's sake.'

The words stabbed her but she had been expecting that. She opened her eyes and looked at him. 'I would form a plan with the help and support of the queen mother.'

'So this is her idea?'

'No.'

Kadmus shot from his chair, this time tipping it backwards. 'She does not care about you! Do you really trust her with your life?'

Mako began to wail, the bread falling from his hand. Isadore stood up, but before he could say anything, Kadmus got in first.

'Don't bother. I'm leaving.' He strode out of the house, his feet crunching against the dirt as he headed for the barn. Everyone was silent for a moment while Aldara tended to Mako, cutting him another piece of bread and slathering it with butter. He took it from her but did not eat it, his hand wrapped around it while she soothed him.

'Your brother makes some good points,' Dahlia said, staring across at her. 'What you are thinking of doing carries risk even with a well-thought-out plan. You would be trusting people who do not value your life.'

Aldara nodded and turned to her father. 'I think the idea is worth discussing. I can write to the queen mother and see what she says. If the idea cannot work, or carries too much risk, I will let it go.'

Isadore looked at Dahlia and took in a lungful of air before exhaling. 'She's more like you than you care to admit.'

Dahlia's gaze returned to the table. 'Yes, more and more every day. Bold and foolish.' She looked at Aldara. 'Write to the queen mother if you wish. At the very least, your letter will demonstrate your loyalty to the crown. Nothing bad can come from that alone.'

Aldara glanced at the door Kadmus had exited. Something bad already had.

A LETTER ARRIVED, not via the priest at the church but delivered directly into Aldara's hands. She ran her thumb over the royal seal before setting Mako down in the dirt so she could read it without him tearing it from her. He took a few wobbly steps before dropping onto his hands and knees. Soon he would be walking—a baby no longer.

The messenger let his horse drink from the trough while waiting for her to read it. She glanced over at him before breaking the seal and unfolding it.

DEAR ALDARA,

Thank you for your letter. I was hoping to have good news to share by now, but the nature of the situation prevents either side from moving in any meaningful direction.

Your suggestion is dangerous, and yet the only viable option we have at this point outside of attacking Masville Castle, which would likely see Tyron used as a pawn. As the person with the most to lose, the decision to explore this option further is yours to make. If you decide to proceed, you will be required to come to Archdale as soon as possible to prepare. The plan will require the combined efforts of many here at the castle if it is to be successful. Please give your answer to the messenger along with details of your travel plans should you wish to go ahead.

Rest assured, you will be under my jurisdiction and protection within these walls.

Sincerely,
   Eldoris

The letter went slack and Aldara's hand fell to her side. Her eyes went to Mako, who had crawled a great distance away before trying once again to get to his feet. She pushed down the panic rising at the thought of leaving him. The possibility of not returning to him made her insides ache. He stumbled forwards into the dirt. He never cried when he fell. His face determined, he pushed off his hands and tried again. Finally, on unsteady feet, he turned his body to show his mother his dirty hands. All of his clothes were filthy as well.

'It's all right,' she called to him. 'We will wash them later.'

Mako pointed behind her and she turned to see Kadmus walking towards her, his face beaded with sweat. His sleeves were rolled up in an attempt to cool himself.

'What does it say?' he asked, stopping a few feet from her.

She glanced down at the letter. 'The queen mother has invited me to Archdale. It seems they are out of options.'

He shook his head and looked away. 'Of course she would invite you. She knows you are the only one foolish enough to volunteer.'

The constant hostility was tiring, but she knew his anger stemmed from his protectiveness of her. There was no shortcut through it. She would likely be the same if the situation were reversed. 'I'm going to accept the offer and go to Archdale.'

'Go to Corneo, you mean? You will be selling yourself to strangers again.'

Her expression was helpless. 'I cannot leave him in that place.'

He nodded. 'And what about Mako?'

She turned to her son. 'He will come with me to Archdale. Then he will return here when I leave.'

Kadmus looked sceptical. 'The queen mother agreed to that?'

The messenger pulled his horse away from the trough and walked towards them.

'The queen mother will accept my terms.'

'I'm coming with you,' he said. 'At least for a few days until we know the plan.'

Relief welled inside her. He might not have agreed with her decision, but he would not abandon her for it. 'Thank you.'

He did not reply, just turned and walked back to the barn. Aldara's gaze shifted to the house where her mother stood in the doorway. They watched one another for a moment before Dahlia turned away and slipped back inside the house. Aldara looked back at the waiting messenger, his face red and dripping. He waited for her response.

'Tell the queen mother that I will be arriving at Archdale tomorrow, and that my son and brother will be travelling with me.' The words were choking her. 'And tell her... tell her we are going to get Prince Tyron out.'

CHAPTER 13

A lantern cast soft light over Pandarus, who sat in a chair watching the flame shift behind the glass. Eldoris felt a crushing sadness at the sight of her firstborn son possessed by his dark thoughts. Even with all the power he had inherited, he could not figure a way out of their situation.

'It is late,' Eldoris said from the doorway. 'You must try to get some sleep.'

Pandarus looked up, seemingly surprised to see her standing there despite the guard announcing her arrival a few moments earlier. 'You are one to talk.'

She walked over and slipped into the chair next to him, holding out the letter she had received from Aldara an hour earlier. 'This just came.'

Pandarus looked at the folded parchment in her hand before taking it from her and unfolding it. He read it and placed it on the table without comment, eyes returning to the flame.

'I have assured her she will be safe here. That protection extends to her son and brother.'

Pandarus's head moved up and down in a thoughtful nod. 'Why does this feel like a warning? Is that what you think of me? That I would harm a child?'

'Of course not.' But the truth was she did not know what he was capable of. She knew that he had once handed the girl over to Zoelin guests without Tyron's knowledge. She knew Aldara's recovery had taken months. While she could not blame Pandarus for the actions of the men, she suspected the decision to give her to them had been malicious.

'There is no point worrying about King Jayr finding out. It will not make much difference now.'

'Is there any word from him?'

Pandarus shook his head. 'Not a word.'

Eldoris closed her eyes. 'His silence on the matter will not be forgotten.'

'He does not owe us anything.'

'I must disagree.'

Pandarus looked at her. 'No Companion trade, no wedding. What did you think was going to happen?'

'They are still betrothed. If he wants a wedding, he must agree to fight with us when the time comes.'

Pandarus turned away, his tired eyes blinking against the light. 'Instead of responding with an army of men, we are sending one girl.'

'Never underestimate what a woman with enough motivation can achieve.'

'We have one foolish girl motivated by love. It is hardly inspiring.' Pandarus leaned back in his chair. 'She will never make it out of that place. You do realise that, don't you?'

'I have to think differently, because the thought of that little boy growing up without a mother or father is despairing.'

Light danced on the table in front of them. Pandarus's expression was solemn.

'I cannot withdraw our men now.'

Eldoris looked across at him. 'Yes, I know that.'

'And you hate me for it.'

'No.' She felt a lot of things, but not hate. 'But I desperately want my son back.'

When Pandarus turned his face to her, she saw the same broken boy from fourteen years earlier, the one filled with self-doubt after realising his fighting skills were not improving at the same speed as his younger brother.

'I would never wish him dead.'

She swallowed and leaned forwards, placing her hand over his. 'Of course not. You forget that I know you—your mind and heart. I helped to shape it.'

'You must be very disappointed,' he said, withdrawing his hand from beneath hers.

She straightened, eyes remaining on him. 'Ruling a kingdom is no easy feat.' She tried to find honest words for him. 'You are leading us in a new direction, and I am afraid of what it might cost us.'

They were silent for a moment.

'Queen Salome has taken to her chambers,' Eldoris said. 'Soon there will be new life at Archdale.'

'Let us pray for an heir this time.'

Eldoris studied her son. 'Why not go and visit your wife before you retire? It may be a few weeks before the baby arrives. It can be very lonely shut away from everyone.'

Pandarus exhaled. 'Yes, I know the feeling.'

She stood, preparing to leave. He remained sitting, not looking at her.

'The load will feel much lighter when your brother returns to us.'

He did not reply.

Eldoris turned away. She would have to keep hope for both of them.

When she arrived at her bedchamber, she waved away the maid and kneeled next to the bed, palms pressed together and face down. 'Oh mighty, loving God, please watch over my son and return him to me.'

It was all she managed to get out before collapsing against the bed, her body heaving. Every suppressed emotion erupted, the quilt beneath her face becoming a wet mess from open-mouthed tears.

Return him to me.

ahlia had said little on the subject, for once leaving the decision to Aldara. Whatever her opinion, she did not share it with her daughter. Isadore, on the other hand, had been unable to keep quiet on the subject.

'Stay here, with us. With your son.'

Aldara could barely look at him. 'I can't. I'm sorry.'

'Am I supposed to let you go into a dangerous situation where I might not see you again?'

It was as if the reality had finally sunk in for him. She did not have an answer for him.

'I know you love him. I would not be much of a father if I did not ask at least once.'

He did not ask again.

They left the farm before sunrise, allowing time for frequent breaks. Mako was wrapped to Aldara's front, happy to be part of the journey after waving goodbye to his grandparents, who had waved back, faces resigned. Her guilt was heavy, and knowing she would soon say goodbye to her son did not help.

Mako rode with Kadmus for the last part of the journey.

He beamed with importance sitting in front of his uncle in the saddle, Kadmus's arm secured around him. Kadmus had filled his pockets with bread, and every time Mako began to grizzle, he reached in and handed him a small piece.

'Barley will sprout from his ears if you keep that up,' Aldara said, shaking her head.

He glanced across at her. 'Would you rather listen to your son cry?'

There was something in his tone. When she looked at him, she realised that while he had chosen to accompany her, watch out for her, he was nowhere near forgiving her. 'He will be all right.' she said quietly. 'I am coming back.'

'You don't know that.'

No, she did not know that. They finished the journey in silence.

When the trees thinned and the walls of Archdale rose in front of them, Aldara stopped Loda to give herself a chance to process the view and the feelings surging inside of her. Every memory pulled at her. All she could do was wrap her arms about her middle and feel them.

'Are you all right?' Kadmus asked.

She released her arms and tried to straighten. 'Yes. Let's go.'

They approached the portcullis where two guards were waiting to question them. Aldara stopped in front of them, clearing fear from her throat.

'My name is Aldara. The queen mother is expecting me.'

'And who might you be?' he asked Kadmus.

'I am her brother.'

'You can wait here,' the guard replied.

Aldara swung Loda around to face them. 'No. They come in with me or we turn back, leaving you to explain to the queen mother why we left.'

The guard studied her for a moment before signalling

behind him. The portcullis came to life, the noise and movement holding Mako's attention. The guard waved them through.

'Go ahead of me,' she said, not taking any chances.

Kadmus looked at her for a moment and then rode past her, not speaking. His eyes returned to the guards as he passed beneath the gaping wall.

Aldara hesitated. She had promised herself she would never return, and there she was, entering of her own will. For Tyron, she would follow. She pushed Loda forwards.

'This way,' said a guard on the other side.

He walked ahead of them, leading them to the stables where a groom rushed out to take the horses. Aldara recognised the boy, a little older now. He had been at the stables the day she had left. His eyes rested on her briefly as she dismounted. Loda gave a low whinny as she took in the familiar surroundings. Aldara patted her neck before the groom walked her away, and then she went over to take Mako from Kadmus, propping him on her hip while she waited for her brother to join her on the ground. He looked more nervous than she was, eyes roaming the yard and peering into stalls filled with Syrasan's finest horses.

'Are you ready?' she asked, her lips pressing together.

A long whistle came from him as his horse was led away. 'This is your death wish. Are *you* ready?'

She stared at him. 'I appreciate you being here, but I also need you onside. Now more than ever.'

He rocked on his feet, trying to get blood circulating after a long time spent in the saddle. 'After you.'

A GUARD ANNOUNCED their arrival and the three of them stepped into the solar, their peasant clothes contrasting the elaborately decorated room. Aldara glanced down at her plain dress and then at Kadmus's tunic with the missing buttons. Mako wore tights and a linen shirt, his green eyes shining at Eldoris. A smile spread across her face at the sight of him.

'Come in,' Eldoris said when they hesitated in the doorway.

Kadmus glanced at Aldara before following her into the room. He bowed before Eldoris, taking in the furnishings, the books and the silver trays holding refreshments as he rose.

'Please, sit.'

'Thank you, but we have been sitting for hours,' Aldara said.

Eldoris nodded. 'Of course.' She remained standing also. 'May I?' she said, gesturing to Mako.

Aldara handed the boy to her, Kadmus's gaze following his nephew.

'Thank you all for coming. I have met with the king and a number of advisors on how we should proceed.' She brushed the hair away from Mako's eyes before looking at Aldara. 'Both your brother and son are welcome to stay here with you until your departure.'

Kadmus cleared his throat. 'I am needed back on the farm.'

'And the child?' Eldoris asked, her tone hopeful.

'He will stay with Aldara until the tournament. I will come and collect him before she leaves.'

Aldara's eyes were on her son. 'When will that be? Has King Nilos set a date for the tournament? I was not entirely sure it would go ahead given all that is happening.'

Eldoris gave her a tight smile. 'It is during difficult times that people most need to embrace their traditions. King Nilos will use the event as an opportunity to reassure his people and keep hold of their confidence.' She paused to give Aldara time to absorb her words. 'The tournament will be held two weeks from today.'

Aldara met her gaze and nodded.

'You are free to change your mind at any time over the course of the next few weeks, right up until you cross that border. Then you will no longer be under my jurisdiction. Do you understand?'

'Yes.'

Kadmus looked away.

'And there is something else I need to make clear,' Eldoris continued.

Aldara waited.

'We are putting plans in place to control as many aspects as we can, but we have no influencers at Masville Castle. We can prepare you, but once you are inside those walls, you will need to rely on your instinct and sharp mind. Do you understand what I am saying?'

Aldara glanced at Kadmus whose eyes burned at her. 'Yes. You can help get me into Masville Castle, help me navigate their world, but you cannot get me out. I will have to make it up as I go.'

Eldoris looked visibly relieved that she understood.

'We will make sure you go to Masville with the best chance of success, but I am afraid the rest will be up to you.'

'Are you sure about this?' Kadmus asked. 'We can leave right now—that is what she said.'

Aldara just looked at him. Her answer had not changed. 'I cannot leave him in that place.'

He shook his head, unable to understand her logic.

'Where do we begin?' Aldara asked, turning back to Eldoris.

Eldoris bent and placed the boy on the floor so he could crawl about. To her surprise, he stood and took a few unsteady steps. 'He's walking.' She could not stop her smile. 'How quickly they grow.'

All eyes were on the boy.

'Yes,' Aldara whispered.

'We have three months,' Eldoris said. 'New Companions are mentored for a three-month period before they are introduced. You will have three months to implement a plan, and if it is not possible to get him out safely, you will return without him.'

'What does that mean?' Kadmus asked, stepping forwards. 'Being introduced?'

Eldoris gaze shifted to him. 'Women are mentored and prepared for three months before they socialise or lay with members of the royal family. It is not only a matter of refinement and education, as some diseases are more widespread among the poor in Corneo. Three months is a safe amount of time for any symptoms to present, and also for herbs to become effective.'

'Herbs for what?' Kadmus asked.

Eldoris glanced at Aldara, surprised by the question.

'Herbs to prevent pregnancy.'

Everyone looked at Mako. Aldara had not been given herbs when she had been imprisoned at Drake Castle because there had been no need. He was the proof that it only took one time.

'The man who buys you will likely still spend time with you during those three months, though he should do the honourable thing for that period. It will be more of a... courtship, for lack of a better word. Three months should be enough time.'

'Wait a minute,' Kadmus said, appearing agitated. 'We are sending Aldara over there *hoping* these men are honourable? What is she to do if they don't want to wait?'

Eldoris was saved from having to answer when the door opened and a guard entered.

'Fedora, Your Majesty.'

'Send her in.'

Aldara looked at Kadmus, eyebrows raised, and then at the doorway. Her former mentor stepped into the room and curtsied before the queen mother.

'Your Majesty.' She rose and turned to Aldara, back straight. Her honey skin was polished and flawless, her dark eyes bright, a feature attributed to her Zoelin heritage. 'Welcome back to Archdale, Aldara.'

There was something resembling amusement in her eyes. Previously, it would have been unheard of for a queen to invite a Companion into a room. But the two women standing before Eldoris were going to help bring back her son, so she had no choice but to put propriety aside.

'Are you ready for this?' Fedora asked. Her gaze shifted to the infant who now sat at Aldara's feet.

Aldara swallowed. 'Not really, my lady.'

Fedora nodded, understanding. 'Let us get to work, then.'

CHAPTER 15

*A*ldara knew how to be a Companion. What she did not know was how to fight, manipulate, seduce, and speak with a Corneon accent. And there was no time to ease into the lessons.

'Say it again,' Fedora said, pacing in front of her.

It was day one.

Aldara watched her mouth move. 'May I please have the bread?'

Fedora shook her head. 'Soften the "d" when you say bread.'

'I did soften it.'

Astra, who was watching them in the main room of the Companion quarters, laughed, visibly enjoying Fedora's pummelling.

'*Bread*,' Astra said slowly.

'*Bread*,' Aldara repeated. 'Does it not sound the same as when I say it?'

'No,' Astra said, tilting her head, an amused expression on her face. 'You sound like a common girl from the south of

Syrasan.' She was better at everything, always had been. And was happy to point out the fact.

Aldara had been surprised to discover she was still Pandarus's Companion. She imagined the king wanting something fresh to go with his new status and suspected he was simply too busy building his empire.

'Your accent will give you away,' Fedora said. She stopped walking and turned to Aldara. Her long silk skirt had a part that extended to the top of her thigh, and her long leg flashed briefly.

Aldara sighed. 'Can I not just say I am from Corneo's west? There cannot be much difference the closer they are to the border.'

'Not right now you cannot. Unless you want to be beheaded at the tournament as a traitor.'

Aldara bit down on her lip. Yes, such a suggestion might be problematic with the West being occupied by Syrasan and all.

'May I please have the bread?' Fedora said, clapping her hands to gain Aldara's attention.

Aldara drew in a breath.

ON DAY TWO, Aldara's eyes travelled down Sapphira's toned arm to where she held six arrows in her draw hand. 'What are you doing?'

Sapphira kept her eyes forward. 'Taking you to a new level of archery.'

'What's wrong with my current level where I hold my arrows in my bow hand?'

Sapphira smiled. 'This way requires more skill, but you will be able to release arrows in a faster sequence.'

Aldara pressed her lips together and glanced behind her at the castle. 'Why do I feel like I am being prepared for war?'

Sapphira released the first arrow, and with a flick of her hand, another replaced it. Six arrows in under eight seconds.

'Who taught you that?'

'Stamitos,' she said, smiling. 'It was a verbal lesson,' she added. The smile on her face faded when she saw Aldara's tense expression. 'You need to be prepared to fight for your life should it come to that. It probably won't, but wouldn't you rather be ready for any outcome?' She brushed some loose hair from her face. She had kept it short, despite being encouraged to grow it by the ladies who tended her.

Aldara shook her head. 'I'm scared to death, you know.'

'We're all afraid of death,' Sapphira replied, shrugging.

She shook her head. 'Not of dying—of failing. What if I cannot get him out? What if I cannot get myself out and Mako has to grow up without a mother?'

Sapphira looked at her with sympathy. 'Eldoris said you're free to leave. No one would judge you for changing your mind.'

Aldara licked her parched lips. 'I would judge me.' She shook away the fear closing around her. 'This is the only plan they have, and it might work.'

Sapphira stepped up to her and handed her the bow. 'Then come here and stop wasting time.'

DAY THREE.

'Where is Mako?' Aldara asked, glancing at the window to gauge the time. It was late afternoon.

Fedora was seated, watching Panthea and Aldara go through the lesson. She exhaled. 'He is with the queen mother. You are too distracted when he is around.'

Aldara missed him, but she could not expect her mentor to understand. Fedora made no secret of the fact that she was not maternal. Or perhaps she had trained herself not to be.

'Focus,' Panthea said, stepping closer to her. The noble Companion was enjoying the change in her routine. 'It is our first introduction, and my eyes have remained on you a fraction longer than what is deemed appropriate. You have established that I am attracted to you. Now what?'

These were not new lessons. The techniques had been used during her time as a Companion at Archdale, but never had she depended on them so much. 'The most important technique is purposeful eye contact,' she began. 'One second only, then look away.'

'Why do we look away?'

'Because we are ladies caught in a moment of desire. It demonstrates good morals to appear like we are fighting them.'

Panthea nodded and glanced at Fedora. 'Now what?'

'Use my hands. Touch myself and objects around me.'

'Examples?' Fedora said, standing up and walking over.

Aldara looked at her. 'My collarbone, hair, my bare arm. Run a finger along the rim of a cup and down the stand.'

'But do not touch him, no matter how much he wants you to,' Panthea said. 'What else?'

'Body language and proximity.'

Fedora waved a hand to keep her talking.

'Show flesh, lean in, stand close without making contact.'

'Anything else?' Fedora said, watching her.

Aldara thought. She found herself reflecting on the ways Tyron read her, the way she drew his eyes without meaning to. How many times had he whispered into her hair, 'Do you realise the effect you have on me?' She swallowed. 'Lips,' she said, her voice thick.

Fedora raised her brows and waited.

'Smile because I cannot help it. Part my lips when I become breathless with need. Bite down on them when trying to control my impulses.'

A smile spread across Panthea's face. 'Our little girl really has grown up.'

ON DAY FOUR, Aldara stood in the butts with Stamitos and Sapphira under a clear sky and gentle sun. She studied the wooden sword in her hand. It was heavier than she would have guessed. 'I cannot believe Fedora allowed this as part of the curriculum.'

Stamitos stood across from her, holding a wooden sword also. 'Even she knows there are some situations you cannot flirt your way out of.'

Aldara watched him as he began to circle her. 'Shouldn't Sapphira be teaching me? I feel quite disadvantaged against a man who has trained his entire life.'

He stopped moving and held up his arm with the missing hand. '*You* feel disadvantaged?' He began moving again. 'Besides, who do you think taught Sapphira?'

'He's pretty good with one hand,' she said. 'Even for a boy.'

Aldara smiled and Stamitos shook his head.

'Ready?' he asked Aldara.

'For what? Are you just going to start? You haven't taught me anything yet.'

He smiled at her. 'This is the fastest way to learn.'

He raised his sword and brought it down towards her head. She immediately raised her own and blocked the slow blow, her heartbeat quickening.

'Good. Let's begin.'

ON DAY FIVE, Aldara walked with Fedora along the castle wall. The mentor had suggested they take some air after a long morning brushing up on Corneon history. The other Companions had offered to care for Mako, enjoying the novelty of a child in their quarters.

'You are tired,' Fedora said, squinting against the high sun. 'I would normally suggest you take a few hours off, but there is so little time.'

Aldara watched a man come towards them, a sack of grain over his shoulder. He nodded as he passed them. 'I am fine. I am probably getting more rest here than I would have on the farm.'

'I suppose tiredness comes with being a mother with no governess.' She did not sound overly sympathetic.

'Yes.'

Fedora slowed her pace. 'Let's talk about the mentor.'

Aldara glanced at her. 'The Corneon mentor?'

Fedora nodded. 'We have been gathering as much information as we can. Lord Belen and his men are proving to be very helpful.'

'And Lord Belen is trustworthy?'

Fedora's gaze fell to her briefly. 'I was surprised also, but it seems there is bad blood between him and King Nilos.'

'Lucky for us.'

They fell silent as they passed a maid with a basket of laundry.

'It will be helpful to know her story. Understanding her history may help you to cultivate a relationship with her.'

Aldara had spent so much time focused on gaining the attention of the royal men that she had forgotten about gaining the approval of the women she might soon be living with. 'All right. What do you know about her?'

They turned the corner and continued along the gravel path.

'Her name is Petra. She had a typical beginning for that part of the world, presented to King Nilos at a flag tournament in her sixteenth year. He made a generous offer and her parents accepted. She has been at Masville Castle for eight years.'

'How long was she a Companion before mentoring?'

They slowed their pace again.

'Four years.'

'A mentor in her twentieth year?' Aldara turned her head to Fedora. 'That seems rather young.'

'It is. There are reports that the girl became pregnant a number of times during those four years. While each incident was handled with discretion, each procedure carried more risk.'

The memory of Idalia made Aldara shudder.

'Because the king was attached to the girl, he kept her there as a mentor. She trained under the previous mentor for a few years before finally replacing her.'

Aldara stared down at her feet. 'I am surprised she remained at Masville at all. Her presence must have been torturous to the king.'

Fedora stopped walking and Aldara next to her.

'It was. The king's attachment prevented him from letting her go. I imagine he tried to keep physical distance for a period, but Petra soon became pregnant again. That time she refused to let a midwife take care of the matter, only telling the king after it was too late to terminate the pregnancy. Still, he did not send her away.'

Aldara's hands went to her stomach. 'She had the child? At Masville?'

There was distress in Fedora's expression. 'Yes, but the child was taken from her soon after it was born.'

Aldara clenched the fabric around her navel. 'King Nilos took her child away?'

'Everything I tell you is hearsay. This is what we were told.'

They continued walking towards the courtyard where maids were gathered hanging bed linen in the sun, their conversations whispered between the sheets. The pair walked around the edge to avoid the hanging laundry.

'The story paints a dismal picture of King Nilos,' Aldara said. 'The fact that he did not have the decency to send them away together so the child could remain with its mother...'

Fedora stiffened next to her.

'You must move past that. I tell you this to make you aware of the feelings the king may still carry for the woman mentoring you, and the resentment she may hold for him which may work in your favour.' She was all business with no space for pity.

'How many Companions are there?' She watched Fedora relax next to her with the shift in conversation.

'Two. The eldest prince, Felipe, took a new Companion a few months ago. She was only recently introduced. The tournament will be her first public gathering. The youngest prince, Kyril, came of age the previous year and selected his first Companion at last year's tournament. He is rumoured to be quite smitten with his choice so will likely not be an option for you. King Nilos, on the other hand, has a history of taking a new Companion, only to send her away a few months after she is introduced.'

Aldara nodded. 'Not surprising if he is still besotted with the mentor.'

'Prince Felipe seems to be following in his father's footsteps, frequently taking new Companions and immediately growing bored of them.'

It reminded Aldara of Pandarus. 'If selected, it sounds as if I will only have a few months before I am disposed of anyway.'

Fedora frowned at her. 'If selected? It is your role to ensure one of the men makes an offer for you. Win the tournament. Get his attention. And keep it.'

Aldara stopped walking and turned to her. 'Win the tournament?' She thought she had not heard correctly.

Fedora's expression did not change. 'You will potentially be competing for attention against hundreds of women. The winner of the tournament gets a private audience with Prince Felipe, or even the king himself.'

'Are women allowed to enter?'

Fedora blinked. 'No, but they are not allowed to enter the Syrasan tournament either. It did not stop you then, and it cannot stop you now.'

Aldara felt the colour leave her face.

ON DAY SIX, Aldara rode out of the castle with Stamitos, leaving Mako in Sapphira's care. Clouds had gathered in the sky for the first time in weeks, hinting that the eternal sunshine they had grown accustomed to would not last. She drew in a deep breath and glanced around as the portcullis was lowered behind them, locking her son inside.

Stamitos looked across at her, taking in her worried expression. 'He is quite safe with Sapphira, even if they do spend the afternoon playing with weapons.'

Aldara tried to relax in the saddle. 'I know.'

'It will be good practice for her.'

Aldara looked at him. 'Good *practice* for her?' Her eyes narrowed. 'Is there a reason why she needs to practice?'

He nodded. 'I suspect she is with child, though I suspect she is also in denial, despite my explaining to her a number of times how babies come to be.'

A smile broke across Aldara's face. 'Stamitos, that is

wonderful news. I am surprised she has not said anything to me.'

'I'm not. Sapphira views pregnancy as a weakness, as though her physical body has failed her strong mindset. Despite her reluctance, she will be a wonderful mother, assuming our children survive childhood.'

She laughed. 'Yes, I have an image of them running about with swords in their hands from the moment they are able to grip a weapon.'

'Sapphira tells me she walked at nine months.'

Aldara shook her head. 'That does not surprise me. Anything to improve her aim.' She exhaled, allowing her mind to slow for a moment. 'Where are we going?'

They turned off the road, arriving at an open field marked with flags.

'No number of coy smiles and teeth flashing guarantees you an audience with King Nilos of Corneo, but winning the tournament will.'

She stared at the marked field in front of her, an uneasy feeling returning. 'Whose idea was this? We cannot predict the quality of the competitors, these men who have spent years training for the event.'

'No, but we know what you can do with *no* training. You can win. Your mare is fit, responds well to you, and is fast.'

Aldara shook her head. 'I leave in eight days.'

He kicked his horse into a canter. 'Then we better get started. Tell me everything you remember.'

She hesitated before following after him. 'Fifteen flags, each numbered. They must be retrieved sequentially and one at a time to the barrel next to the timekeeper. The horse and rider must move around the flag as they collect it. If the rider comes off the horse, they are disqualified. If the rider drops a flag, they are disqualified. If a rider misses the barrel, they are disqualified. The rider with the fastest time, according to the timekeeper, wins.'

Stamitos glanced about at the numbered flags and then turned to her, smiling. 'I guess I am timekeeper.'

Later that day, they walked their horses back to the castle just as the sun was setting. Loda's head hung close to the ground, her neck crusted with dried sweat. When they reached the stables, two grooms took the horses off to be washed, watered and fed. Aldara was happy to let someone else do it for once. Her legs were unsteady beneath her, and her hands ached despite the glove Stamitos had given her to prevent blisters. She was forced to stop halfway up the steps to the castle to rest. When Stamitos went to help her, she waved him off.

'You go ahead and check that my son is still alive.'

'We'll go easier tomorrow,' he said, suppressing a smile.

'Go ahead, laugh. Just know I will be telling Tyron about your unspeakable training methods.'

'He will thank me when he is out.'

She looked up at Stamitos, the smiles on their faces wavering. He turned and walked ahead, remarking to the guard at the door that she might be a while.

When Aldara reached the guest chamber, she was about to open the door when she saw that it was slightly ajar. Voices reached her from inside. She went still, listening. Mako's familiar laugh came pouring through the gap in the door, making her smile.

She peered through the crack, expecting to see Sapphira with her son. Instead she saw Princess Cora sitting in the chair by the window with Mako in her lap. She was holding a book, her arms wrapping him, describing the images she was pointing to in a tone that one reserved for children. The story she was telling was nothing to do with the book she was holding; it was a made-up story, a fairy tale perhaps.

Blood pounded in Aldara's ears. She would never have permitted Mako to be left alone with the princess, and yet, without an audience, she witnessed Cora as she had never seen her before—warm. She held the boy close, her lips above his right ear. His small hands rested comfortably on her arms, moving with her whenever she turned a page.

Aldara pushed the door so it swung open. She stepped inside and watched as Cora shut down in front of her, closing the book and lifting Mako off her. She placed him on the ground and stepped back from him.

'Sapphira is not feeling well,' she said, taking another step away from Mako. 'I offered to watch until you returned, not realising you would be gone so long.'

Aldara watched her, unblinking, unsure how to respond. The Cora in front of her now was the one she remembered well—cold and distant. 'Thank you,' she managed.

Cora picked up the book and glanced once at Mako before gliding past Aldara and out of the room. When she was gone, Aldara stepped backwards until her back was against the door and continued to walk until it clicked shut behind her. She let out a breath, not realising she had been holding it, and placed a hand over her pounding heart.

Mako took a few steps towards her, smiling, and pointed at the door. 'Aunt.'

ON DAY SEVEN, Aldara sat opposite Eldoris in the solar. Mako played on the floor with some small wooden toys Sapphira had given him. Every now and then, he would hold one of them up to show them, and they would stop their conversation to acknowledge whatever was in his hand. Satisfied by the attention, he would then return to playing.

The queen mother wanted to talk to her about the needs

of powerful men. Whatever Aldara thought she knew was apparently not enough. The ability to read a man's wishes was just the beginning.

'You need to be in control. You have the power to shape those wishes and alter their behaviour. There is skill in doing all this without raising suspicion. Understand?'

'Yes.' But she would struggle to implement it.

'It does not matter how much you know about them, as there are some things you cannot possibly know until you are alone with them. Observe how he interacts with other people, who he respects, who he does not. This tells you a lot about a man. Discover what he desires, but more importantly, why? And do it all with discretion. When you truly know him, then you will know the best way forward.'

Aldara rubbed the skirt of her dress between her fingers. She was fidgeting—failing already.

'Do not doubt yourself, Aldara. You see through people. I discovered that about you simply by watching you with my sons. Tyron knew that about you. He is the same.'

His name hung in the air between them.

'You are telling me that these skills will shift the power, that by playing these games I will gain some form of control. I need to know how that translates into getting Tyron out.'

Eldoris watched her. 'You are doubting yourself.'

Aldara let go of her dress and leaned forwards. 'I am afraid you have too much faith in my abilities.'

The queen mother shook her head, her eyes heavy. 'No one can teach you what you are asking for. There are too many variables. You need to take the tools you have and figure it out when you arrive. I cannot guide you on who to trust, but only help you to figure that out for yourself. I do not know King Nilos, but I have known many men in his position, what they tend to want, what pushes them away.'

Aldara brought her palm to her forehead. 'Now is probably a bad time to mention that I am not like the other Companions. These… skills… do not come naturally to me.'

'Of course not. I suspect that is why my son loves you.'

Aldara sat back in her chair.

'Do you want to know why you are the best person to go?'

Aldara waited.

'Because when you are inside that castle, with the knowledge that Tyron is possibly in chains beneath the floors you walk on, you will find a way to get to him. It is what you do for the people you love.' Her eyes welled up. 'And the men who stand between the two of you will be nothing but instruments you play and put aside when it is time to play another.'

Aldara took a shuddering breath, knowing it was the truth. What were a few powerful men in comparison to what she felt?

ON DAY EIGHT, Stamitos introduced Aldara to knives and daggers. She spent time handling them and practising various grips. One would travel with her to Corneo, strapped to her inner thigh.

'Start with an outwards position,' Stamitos began. 'Blade pointing up, thumb on top and fingers underneath. Now slip your index finger to the front, above your thumb.'

Aldara looked down at her hand, copying the motion.

'Now flip the knife down, like this, and grab it with your thumb. Put the other three fingers behind it again. This is really important as it will enable you to move from an outwards position to a chambered position, powerfully and efficiently.'

She practiced the switch. 'Ah, I see. So I change

depending on whether I want to drive the knife through someone's stomach or my own heart.' She smiled.

He smiled back, laughter in his eyes. 'Now you are getting it.'

That evening Aldara soaked her aching body in a tub of hot water. Even with all the labour she did on the farm, she seemed to have woken up muscles that had never been used. She was looking around the guest chamber at the expensive drapes and large bed she shared with Mako, feeling like a trespasser, when a maid came in carrying a tray of food. Aldara sat up in the water, looking past her. She had been expecting Eldoris to bring Mako. 'Where is my son?' she asked.

'I have not seen him,' the maid said, laying the food out on the small table and then disappearing from the room.

Aldara climbed out of the tub, got dressed, and attempted to eat something on the tray, though she found she was having difficulty swallowing the food. She had sent word to the queen mother as soon as she had returned to her rooms and could not think of any reason they would be delayed.

She had just decided to go and search for him when a knock came at the door. Rushing to open it, she found Eldoris standing there, holding Mako's hand.

Aldara dropped to her knees and pulled him into her arms. Only then did she realise she was shaking.

'Mako insisted on walking the whole way,' Eldoris said. 'It took us a little longer than expected.'

Aldara's eyes closed tightly as she hugged the boy to her. 'I was worried.' She stood up, placing Mako on her hip. The boy wrapped his chubby arms around her.

Eldoris looked taken aback. 'He was hungry so we ate together before coming here. Next time I can send a messenger, if you would prefer?'

Aldara could not look at her.

'You must know that you can trust me with him,' she added.

Aldara looked at her. 'Of course. It is just that I have given up so much and he is all I have now. If anything were to happen to him…' She could not finish.

'I understand. I am sorry for causing you worry.'

Aldara studied her for a moment. 'I must ask, what does King Pandarus say of Tyron having a son?'

Eldoris blinked, thinking for a moment. 'Very little.'

'I cannot imagine he is very happy about it.'

'People are seldom happy when it comes to children born out of wedlock. That is the world we live in.'

'I am happy,' Aldara replied, looking down.

Eldoris's cheeks flushed. 'Of course you are. You are his mother.' She looked at Aldara for a moment. 'Get some rest.'

Aldara nodded. 'Thank you for caring for him today.' She turned around.

'Aldara.'

She turned back and waited.

'I too am happy that this amazing little boy came to be.' Her gaze fell to Mako. 'Do not ever think otherwise.'

ON DAY NINE, Aldara got pummelled. She had risen early and met Stamitos at the butts to fight with swords. He wanted her to get used to the weight of the real thing so she would not be any more disadvantaged if the need arose to use one. He had the good sense to use blunt swords so she did not accidentally disembowel him during their session.

When she was thoroughly exhausted, they left the castle once again for more tournament practice, hoping to improve her time.

'Four minutes thirty-nine seconds,' Stamitos said. 'Your fastest time yet.'

'But will it be fast enough?'

Stamitos gave her a reassuring smile. 'You will find out in a few days, won't you?'

'I guess so.'

They made their way back to the stables, and when Aldara dismounted, her legs collapsed beneath her.

'I'm all right,' she said, as Stamitos and one of the grooms helped her to her feet. 'Just a bit wobbly.'

He did not look convinced. 'I hope this is the end of your day. You need to rest or you will never make it to the tournament.'

'Actually, I have a dress fitting.'

He frowned down at her. 'I will take you where you need to go.'

They walked slowly to the north wing, and Stamitos watched her disappear into the Companions' quarters before leaving her. When she arrived at the dressing room, Fedora looked her up and down, her face pinched with concern.

'Are you all right? Your legs are trembling.'

Aldara did not look down at them. 'A long session in the saddle, my lady.' She looked across to where Astra stood holding up a blue cotton dress.

'This will not make you feel any better,' Astra said, glancing down at the dress with distaste. 'This is your rather ugly garment for the tournament.'

Fedora took it from her hands and held it up for Aldara to see properly. 'It is entirely appropriate given you will be attending as a Corneon peasant.'

Aldara studied the simple one-shouldered gown with the flowing skirt. 'It will be good to ride in. Nice and loose.' She reached out and touched it. 'And light.'

'I have seen potato sacks with more appeal,' Astra replied.

Fedora gave her a stern glance. 'We are working on a mask that will make up for the plainness of the gown.' She held it out for Aldara to take. 'Try it on for the seamstress, but then you must go and rest. You cannot afford to get sick now.'

She did not have any energy left to argue.

DAY TEN. Poisons. It was a far cry from the usual lessons of a Companion. One of the castle's physicians sat across the table in the main room of the Companions' quarters. Violeta sat next to Aldara, taking notes, visibly displeased by the task of scribe. The physician looked equally as displeased, gazing about the room as though promiscuous women might descend on him at any moment.

He retrieved a linen bag from inside his tunic and released the drawstring. Inside were three corked jars, each the size of a finger. He set them carefully on the table between them.

'Atropa belladonna,' he began, pointing to the first. 'This one is produced from the root of the plant, making it rather toxic. A few drops will not kill an adult, but might kill a child. Symptoms include blurred vision, loss of balance, slurred speech, hallucinations, delirium and convulsions. A small amount will make a man quite sick without killing him. And it works fast.' When he was certain Aldara was keeping up, he moved his finger to the next jar. 'Next we have conium maculatum. If ingested, it will cause paralysis of various body systems, including the respiratory system. The victim's mind will be aware of what is happening right up until death.'

Aldara glanced at Violeta, who continued to write, seemingly unaffected by what she was taking down.

'Finally we have chondrodendron tomentosum,' the physician went on. 'Again, causes paralysis in the same way as the previous, but the heart may continue to beat for longer after the victim is paralysed.' He looked again at Aldara. Her eyes remained on the jars. 'It can also be used on the tips of arrows and darts. It is not always possible to gain access to a victim's food or drink.'

Aldara stared down at it, not breathing. Victim. She wished he would stop using that word. The thought of a person being her victim was too much. 'How am I meant to get these into Masville Castle?' she said to no one in particular.

'They will be strapped to the inside of your leg,' Violeta replied.

Aldara turned to her, taking in her relaxed expression at the mention of smuggling poisons into a castle. They would be travelling next to her dagger. 'There are a lot of things being strapped to my body. I just hope I can walk under the weight of it all.'

The physician shifted in his chair.

'Once inside, find a place to hide everything,' Violeta continued. 'Separately, if you can. That way if something is discovered by one of the women, you still have supplies.'

Aldara exhaled and her gaze dropped to the poisons. 'I look forward to talking my way out of that one.'

Day eleven.

Three days before the flag tournament.

Eldoris came to her chamber in the morning, knocking lightly before stepping inside. Her hair was pulled tight on top of her head, a ruby necklace wrapped around her throat. She spotted Mako peering out of the large window, a piece of cold chicken in his hand, and smiled.

Aldara, who had already finished her morning meal, lay down her cup of steaming tea and stood to curtsy. 'Your Majesty.'

'He loves the height, has no fear of it.'

Aldara turned to look at her son. 'Yes, he is not afraid of anything, it seems. He is the only child I know who laughs when knocked over by a stray sheep.' Her eyes returned to Eldoris and she saw that her smile had disappeared. 'Is something the matter?'

Eldoris hesitated. 'He wants to see you.'

'Who?'

'King Pandarus.'

Aldara glanced again at Mako. 'Oh. About anything in particular?'

Eldoris clasped her hands in from of her. 'He did not say.' She paused. 'Would you like me to accompany you?'

She shook her head. 'From what I have learned about powerful men, that would give the impression I am afraid.' She tried to smile.

'We cannot have that,' Eldoris replied, eyes bright.

'But thank you for the offer.' She pretended that she was not nervous at the thought of facing him alone. 'Could you take care of Mako for me?'

Eldoris's gaze returned to the boy. 'Why not take him with you? Let Mako meet his uncle and king.' She paused. 'It is easy to dismiss blood you have not met. Let Pandarus see the child who looks just like his brother.'

Aldara wanted to object, but the man was his uncle, whether Pandarus wanted to acknowledge it or not. 'All right, I will take him.'

Later that morning, Aldara stood outside of the throne room with Mako in her arms, trying to remember the last time she had laid eyes on Pandarus. Two years. And yet when the doors swung open and she saw him standing there, she might have guessed ten. The crown he wore, no doubt as a reminder to her, did little to hide the frown lines on his face, or the splashes of grey hair.

'Aldara, Your Majesty,' the guard said.

Pandarus nodded and watched her enter, assessing her in the way he always did.

Mako's legs squeezed her waist as she curtsied, his arms wound tightly around her neck. When she rose, he peeked out from beneath her chin, taking in Pandarus's serious expression before burying his face again.

'Good morning, Your Majesty.'

He said nothing for a moment, continuing to study her. When the silence became too much, he looked down at the boy. 'So, this is the boy Tyron gallantly rode off to meet.'

His physical ageing was not matched with maturity.

'This is Mako.' She turned him around so the king could see him properly. 'Prince Tyron's son.'

Pandarus folded his arms. 'As you are aware, the church does not recognise children born out of wedlock.'

'With all due respect, Your Majesty, the church does not have to. I am not seeking their approval.'

Pandarus's gaze swept the boy, who was trying to turn so he could cling once again to his mother. 'He is afraid of me, perhaps.'

'He does not know you.' *Not like I do*, she thought. She watched as a flicker of recognition moved over the king's face.

'I see my brother in him,' Pandarus said, seeming disappointed by the fact. He sat on the edge of the table, forgetting propriety in her presence, or not caring about it. 'The flag tournament is in three days.' He watched for reaction to his words. 'I told them that fourteen days would not be long enough to prepare you.'

For once they agreed on something, but she would never admit that to him. 'Fourteen days is all we had, so we have made the best of it.'

He regarded her for the longest moment. 'Are you truly prepared to die for him? There is a very good chance neither of you will leave that place. And even if you do, can you live with the cost?'

'You need not worry. My son will be fine.'

'I am not talking about your son. I am talking about climbing into bed with our enemy to save your prince.'

She turned Mako back around and his limbs enveloped her once again.

'These men are not Tyron,' he continued when she said nothing. 'How many of them do you suppose wait to bed the women they own?'

She lifted her chin. 'That is for me to worry about, is it not?'

He leaned forwards. 'And how will you explain your lack of virtue?'

She reminded herself to breathe. 'Perhaps I will tell the truth, that two Zoelin men took it from me against my will.'

He returned upright and then looked away. 'You leave for Wripis in two days. You will spend the night at the manor so your horse is fresh for the tournament.' He waved his hand. 'That is all.'

She did not move. 'If the plan does not work, if I fail to get him out, what happens next?'

His eyes returned to her, darker than before. 'If you fail, then you are both as good as dead. You will not care what happens next.'

She curtsied. 'Your Majesty,' she said, turning to leave.

When she reached the door, he called out to her. She

turned around, taking in his pained expression. There was something raw in it that made her fingers loosen on Mako.

'I had someone draw up a map of Masville Castle with details of what I remember from my visit there a few years back. It will not be entirely accurate, but I suggest you study it before you go.'

It was not much of an olive branch, more of a twig, but it showed he wanted her to succeed. She watched him for a moment before bowing her head. 'Thank you, Your Majesty.'

DAY TWELVE BEGAN down in the butts. The cool morning air was a reminder that the warm season could not last. Stamitos was showing her how to predict an opponent's actions from their body language and movements.

'Should I be worried by how much fighting-related training is happening?' Aldara asked, stepping back when Stamitos lunged for her.

Sapphira was standing back, watching them. 'No one is expecting you to go into battle. We just want to ensure that if someone comes at you with a sword, you know how to get out of the way.'

'That is very comforting. Should I be expecting people to come at me with swords?'

Aldara watched as Stamitos's left heel slid right, indicating that his right foot was about to come forwards. She lunged left, avoiding his hand.

'Good,' Stamitos said. 'Don't forget to keep your body weight even on your feet. If you are resting on your heels, you might fall backwards if they make contact. Once you are on the ground—'

'They win.'

'How grim you are. I was going to say they have the advantage.'

Sapphira walked towards Aldara. 'That's when you fight dirty. Do whatever you need to get back on your feet and run for your life.'

Stamitos placed his hand over his crotch and exhaled. 'Sapphira can take it from here. I don't have the stomach for it.' He walked off and collected the flask of water lying in the grass.

Sapphira took hold of her shoulders and waited for Aldara to look at her. 'I want you to promise me something.'

Aldara studied her expression for a moment. 'Let me hear what it is first before I commit.'

Sapphira kept a firm grip on her. 'I want you to promise me that you will stay sharp and level-headed at all times, but if the need arises for you to fight, you will fight with every ounce of remaining strength in order to stay alive.'

Aldara glanced over at Stamitos. 'Sounds like a reasonable request.'

'That is not a promise.'

Aldara felt her shoulders being squeezed. 'All right,' she laughed. 'I promise to fight with every ounce of my strength to stay alive.'

'Good.' Sapphira released her grip. 'Now you need to go and see Fedora. The girls are going to take care of your… grooming.'

Aldara winced. 'Yes, Rhea warned me about a Corneon hair-removal technique using hot beeswax.'

'Walking away now,' Stamitos called out, hands going over his ears.

A smile spread across Sapphira's face.

～

ON DAY THIRTEEN, Kadmus waited outside the castle in the shadows cast by the tall walls. Aldara exited on horseback with six guards, armed and immediately suspicious of their surroundings. Mako sat in the saddle in front of her, pointing and exclaiming at every new sight. When he spotted Kadmus, his face lit up. He turned to Aldara, showing her that his uncle stood waiting for them. She bent down and kissed his happy face. He ignored the affection, his full attention elsewhere.

The guards stopped a few feet away and waited for her to hand the child to Kadmus. Mako went to him, arms outstretched.

'Hello,' Kadmus whispered, kissing the boy's cheek. 'Did you miss your uncle?'

Aldara smiled but she felt as though she had handed her heart over to him. Every doubt surged within her.

Kadmus looked up, reading her expression. 'It's not too late to change your mind. You have not crossed that border yet.'

Aldara went to speak, but a strong breeze blew from the west, lifting the fabric of her dress and pulling it in the opposite direction—east, to Corneo. Her eyes closed for a moment as she waited for the air to still. 'Take care of him until I get back,' she said, opening her eyes.

He shook his head, disapproval etched into his face. 'Make sure you come home.'

She smiled, barely. Then, looking down at Mako, she said, 'See you soon.'

He was too absorbed with his uncle to take much notice of her.

She could not have imagined how hard it would be to ride away from her son. She felt a deep aching, dulled only by the torrent of guilt. But every time she went over it in her head, she came to the same conclusion—she could not let Tyron die in that place without trying.

Turning Loda away from them, her insides tearing, she joined the guards whose sole purpose was to get Aldara safely to Wripis. She turned once, relieved to find Mako content in her brother's arms, waving as though she would soon return. Her eyes moved up and met with Kadmus's. He did not smile, did not wave. The only way for her to earn his forgiveness was to return. Maybe then he would be able to look at her with light in his eyes once again.

They rode east to Corneo, where a Corneon man she had never met would take her into the belly of the enemy and sell her to a stranger for the second time in her life. If all went to plan, if she caught their attention, if just one liked what he saw, if she could *make* him like it, then she would be sleeping under the same roof as Tyron. She would find a way to get him out. That was how she was able to ride away from her son, with the wind pulling her east to Tyron.

Keep praying for your miracles, she thought. *I'm coming.*

CHAPTER 16

*B*eing locked inside a dungeon seemed almost laughable at first. Tyron felt like a cliché. He was safe from death for now, only because King Nilos was hopeful of a better outcome, despite Tyron telling him that Pandarus would not surrender the West for the life of his brother. Then what would become of that life? King Nilos would end it, make an example of him. Pandarus, driven by guilt and pride, would retaliate, sending men to Masville Castle where they would be met by his head on a spike at the gates.

Too much time alone with his thoughts was making him dramatic, depressed. Insane, perhaps.

He sat on the straw mattress on the floor, studying the familiar marks on the walls made from the prisoners before him. Names, maybe. Some phrases written in Braul, messages perhaps, or thoughts driven by hunger. In theory he should have known what it said, as he had learned to speak Braul as a child, when the relationship had mattered, when there was something to be gained from it other than more mouths wanting food. He had not spoken a word of it since.

His gaze moved up the same corroding stone walls stained with water, a dismal sign for the cold season ahead, before stopping at the small hole twenty feet above him, posing as a window. It cast a circle of dull light into one corner of the cell. He often sat beneath that circle, aware of what happened to men starved of sunlight. While no heat made it through, he was comforted by the light shifting across him as he moved beneath it. He strongly suspected that the only thing to make it through would be freezing air and perpetual darkness in the cold season. Perhaps the snow would cover it completely and he would feel what it was like to be buried.

He recalled his arrival there, descending twenty-four steps into darkness. He had counted them, counted everything, needing to remember, to feel in control. He had passed five additional cells, three of them occupied. There were no cells past his, only walls to hold him. The only people he saw now were the guards who came to empty the chamber pot and deliver water, a potato, and some grey slush in a bowl that resembled gruel. He had once asked a guard for a change of clothes, only to be met with silence and a dismissive shake of the head. At least they brought food. They could not have him dying on them yet.

The thought had crossed his mind, more than once, to jump the guard who walked into his cell, take his weapon, cut his throat, and then make his way up the twenty-four stairs. What stopped him was the number of people who would die at his hand before someone finally shot an arrow through his heart. It was a better way to die than the way they had planned—knowing and waiting.

He could handle dying during a fight, had been preparing

for such an end his entire life. Soon he would learn his sentence; perhaps that would be the time for bold acts. It was not a matter of escape, as there was nowhere for him to escape to. It was about control. If death was inevitable, he wanted to die on his terms. The difficult part was not acting prematurely, risking his life before he knew for certain it would end. And things were not that bad. A glance at the shackles attached to the wall on the other side was a good reminder that they could be much worse. He could survive the confines of a cell, but not the confines of shackles. He had seen what it could do to men with healthy minds—and his mind was far from healthy.

One question plagued him. Would Aldara forgive his death? He closed his eyes for a moment so he might see her with their son, walking together through summer grass. Yes, Mako would likely be walking now, his fingers gripping Aldara's. If he tried hard enough, he could imagine his own fingers threaded through hers, pulling her along, turning his head whenever she spoke or laughed. Did she know where he was? He hoped not. He preferred the image of her smiling and barefoot, face upturned to the sun.

He pushed off the bed and crawled over to the corner where the light hit, pretending he could feel heat from it. His hand found the small stone he used to make his own markings on the wall, a counting of days in case his mind failed him. There were fifty-four marks. *Scrape.* Fifty-five. Lucky for him there was no space for self-pity in the small cell. He stood and began to pace, as he did most days, to ensure his muscles did not wither. Afterwards, he would lie on his stomach, pushing his body up with his arms, finding comfort in exertion. He had seen strong men reduced to bones after long periods of confinement, and he could not afford to be one of them. When the time came, he would need to be able to hold a sword and withstand a blow from one.

And that time would soon come.

CHAPTER 17

They crossed the Corneon border around noon, the guards a moving barrier around Aldara. It seemed they were not taking any chances despite the high number of Syrasan men securing the area. The woods thinned and they stepped out from the cover of trees, crossing an open plain, its grasses scorched by the sun. She tried to imagine crops growing there, but the soil seemed to have given up.

The guards' eyes roamed the open space, seemingly bracing for something. Aldara tried not to imagine the possibilities as they cantered beneath a veil of dust. Finally, they reached another forest, the trees bringing welcomed shade but no comfort for the guards who remained alert. She wondered if Tyron had disappeared beneath the same ageing branches. If one of Syrasan's most skilled fighters could not make it through unscathed, then caution was justified.

'How much farther to the manor?'

A startled hare scampered in front of the horses and the guards drew their swords. The sound of six blades leaving their sheaths made her breath catch. The horses moved closer together, trapping her as the men searched the trees around them. When the guards finally put their weapons away, she did not ask any more questions.

It was mid-afternoon when the manor came into sight. No high walls, just open lawns sprawled with tents of heavy linen, tents that would not withstand rain when the cold season arrived.

When Aldara spotted Leksi waiting for them, relief washed over her. He looked handsome in his red uniform, despite his unkempt hair and dishevelled appearance. He smiled at her, but it did not reach his eyes. She wondered what he thought of the plan they were about to implement.

After dismounting, she turned to him, attempting to appear brave. 'Sir Leksi.'

He bowed his head. 'Aldara.'

He turned and she fell into step with him, taking in her surroundings, the manor stripped of its Corneon markings, flags of red now blowing at its highest points. She turned to watch Loda being led away by a groom.

'They will take good care of the mare. She will have plenty of time to rest before tomorrow's tournament.'

She nodded and faced forwards again.

'You realise Tyron is going to have me hanged when he learns I helped implement this plan?'

She knew it was probably true. 'Do not fear. I will speak up on your behalf.'

Leksi stopped outside a large tent, turning to her. 'Are you absolutely sure you want to do this? I'm only going to ask you this once. After that, we move forwards as planned, your life at risk, your son an orphan if it should all go wrong.'

She felt her insides clench at the mention of her son. While she was no less afraid, she had worked too hard to turn back now. 'He will die if we do nothing. I believe I can do this, get him out.'

He looked around at the other tents. 'You have three months. After that, you leave, without him if you have to.'

'Three months,' she repeated.

He walked into the tent and she followed. He gestured to the small stool.

'Thank you, but I'll stand after such a long ride.'

He nodded. 'Are you ready to hear the plan?'

She glanced once through the flap of the tent where the soldiers moved about performing duties. 'I am ready.'

'Your father's name is Quinn. He will escort you to the flag tournament and facilitate your sale should an offer be made.'

When the offer was made, she thought. She could not afford to think otherwise. 'Is Quinn Corneon?'

'Yes, a potato farmer from Thovaria in the North and a long-time friend of Lord Belen's. You can trust him. People that far north don't generally attend the tournament, so the risk of him being recognised is low.'

She nodded, absorbing the information. 'A potato farmer from Thovaria.'

'Tho-va-ri-a,' he said slowly. 'It is very important you get the pronunciation right.'

Another nod. 'Thovaria. And my name?'

'Medea. The eldest of his three daughters. You have two younger sisters: Oya, aged twelve, and Pax, aged fifteen.'

'And how old am I supposed to be?'

'Seventeen.' Seeing the doubt on her face, he added, 'We had to shave a few years to not raise suspicion about the fact that you are unmarried. A farmer with three daughters would normally marry off the eldest as soon as she came of age.'

She knew that was true. 'Medea, aged seventeen.'

'Lord Belen has some other people who are prepared to help. There is a young man from a family east of here who

157

supplies straw to Masville Castle once a week. He can get messages in and out of the castle.'

'How will I get the messages from him?'

Leksi smiled at the brilliance of what he was about to say. 'He knows a ditcher at the castle who will deliver the letter. He would retrieve correspondence from the cart and pass them along to Velma, a young laundry maid who happens to be sweet on the boy. She has agreed to pass on the letters under the pretence that they are from your father simply wanting to check on his daughter.'

'Velma,' she repeated.

'She will find you when she has a letter for you, so do not raise suspicion by seeking her out.' He paused to ensure she was following. 'When you have a plan in place, send word. We will have horses waiting one hour north of the castle, on foot, to take you the rest of the way. You will need to allow about three days for the letter to reach us. And keep the letters minimal on details. Avoid using names unless absolutely necessary.'

She nodded, feeling panicked by the onslaught of information. 'I see. Brief letters and no last-minute plans.'

'If you do, you will need to find your own way to the manor. Be aware that Corneon guards patrol the area between Wripis and Ituco, so make sure Tyron is not wearing anything with Syrasan markings.' He watched her for a moment. 'Do you have any questions?'

She was trying to arrange her thoughts.

'I imagine Fedora has prepared you for your time inside, but if you need a male perspective on anything…'

She saw the first glimpse of the Leksi she knew. 'I think I have your sort figured out.'

He smiled properly for the first time. 'The flag tournament is held in—'

'Chelia. A three-hour ride south-east of here. The tournament begins at noon, and competitors must register at the stables prior to the event.'

Leksi nodded. 'Lord Belen has offered you a room in the house this evening. Much safer than a tent surrounded by men who have not sighted a female for a number of weeks.'

'Thank you.'

Leksi gestured towards the entrance of the tent and they stepped outside. He escorted her all the way to the front of the large house. 'If you have any questions, or need anything, send a messenger. Otherwise, I will see you in the morning.'

'With my new father.'

'With your new father.'

She inhaled and let the air rush from her lungs. 'In a few months this will all be over. Tyron will be free, and I will be with my son.'

'That is the plan,' he replied, not looking at her.

The door opened and a servant looked Aldara up and down before saying, 'Lord Belen is expecting you.' He stepped back so she could enter.

Aldara glanced once at Leksi before walking through the door.

'Medea,' Leksi called to her. She immediately turned. 'Well done. From now on, use only that name.'

She nodded, watching him until the door closed between them.

THE MORNING OF THE TOURNAMENT, Aldara could not eat. The maid who had brought her food tried to encourage her to eat something, but Aldara's stomach turned at the thought. The girl left the tray on the small table by the bed and went to stand by Aldara as she stared down at the blue dress laid out on her bed.

'It's rather plain for the occasion,' commented the maid.

Aldara bent to pick up the package next to it and unwrapped the mask Fedora and the other women had made. Between the layers of linen was one of the most elaborate pieces she had ever seen. The leather mask was dyed purple and painted with gold, its edges trimmed with elegant stitching. One side of it extended above the face, wrapping the hair. Purple feathers sprouted from an orange silk flower.

'It's beautiful,' said the maid.

It was the first time Aldara had seen it, and she had to agree.

The maid picked up the blue silk flowers sitting loose beside it. 'I suppose these are to go in your hair?'

Aldara studied them. 'I suppose so.' She reached down and unwrapped the other package containing blue jewelled slippers. They were light and flexible, designed to stay on without the need for stirrups. Fedora had done well.

Once Aldara was dressed, the maid collected all of her things and packed them into the bag. 'Will you be taking your belongings with you?'

Aldara shook her head. Arriving with a packed bag would be rather presumptuous. 'They can be sent to Sir Leksi's tent so they do not clutter the house while I am gone.'

The maid picked the bag up and left her alone in the room. Aldara took a shaky breath and sat on the bed, lifting the skirt of her dress and strapping the dagger and poisons to her thigh. She had never considered herself a Companion even when she was one, but now she needed to find the Companion inside of her, the one Fedora had spent years trying to mould, the one she had glimpsed briefly at Archdale but never managed to hold on to. She would need to be fierce, alluring, and bold beneath the gazes and hands of men—do whatever was necessary to get herself and Tyron out of Masville Castle alive. She stood and glanced at the window where the angle of the sun reflected her image back to her. She held the mask in front of her face, her grey-painted eyes burning through the holes. *They will take notice today*, she told herself.

The maid returned to tell her that her horse was saddled and waiting outside. Aldara removed the mask and followed her downstairs. Leksi was standing with Lord Belen, who she had met the night before, and another man who she could only assume was her new father, Quinn. He smiled at her, revealing a missing tooth. She did not have it in her to smile back.

'This is Quinn,' Leksi said. 'He will escort you to the tournament.'

Aldara nodded in his direction.

'You need not be afraid,' Lord Belen said. 'He may look frightful, but he is harmless and not intimidated by people of superior birth.'

'Listen to you. Superior birth?' Quinn looked back at Aldara, eyes rolling. 'There's nothin' superior about this one, let me assure you,' he said, gesturing to Lord Belen.

The banter helped Aldara to relax. She turned to face Lord Belen. 'Thank you for your hospitality, my lord.'

He bowed his head. 'You are welcome anytime. We shall see you back here soon with Prince Tyron.'

'Yes.' She turned to Leksi, who could not disguise the concern on his face. 'Wish me luck.'

'Follow the plan and be smart. Send word if you run into trouble.'

She tried to smile but the action failed. Turning away from them, she walked over and mounted Loda, dismissing the groom when he tried to assist. She tried to find some parting words while she waited for Quinn to mount his horse, but nothing came, so she turned Loda south and rode away. When Quinn trotted up next to her, she could still feel the others watching her.

Quinn looked across at her. 'It's a very brave thing you are doing for your prince.'

She did not look at him. 'I'll be honest, I'm not feeling overly brave at this moment.'

He faced forwards. 'You know, you'll be the first woman to ever compete in a flag tournament.'

She exhaled. 'I'll be the first woman to compete in a *Corneon* flag tournament. I raced in Syrasan a few years back.'

His eyes widened with surprise. 'Yeah? And how did it go?'

She glanced across at him. 'Actually, rather well.'

They rode the next few hours in silence, mostly because Aldara was struggling to follow any conversation. Her mind had splintered with nerves and she was having difficulty expelling them.

When they arrived in the village of Chelia, its roads lined with the poor trying to sell whatever they had to those passing by them, she had to stop and dismount. She walked away from the road and leaned over, retching. Nothing came up because she had not eaten anything. She straightened, touching her forehead and above her lip where sweat had gathered. Her breathing deepened as she tried to pull herself together. Quinn, who had been waiting with the horses, held out a flask of water. She took it from him and had a few small sips while trying not to meet his gaze. When she was done, he offered her an apple.

'I bought it from the young girl over there. She needed the coin, you needed the food. Everyone wins.'

Aldara glanced at the small girl, maybe six years old, a small basket in front of her filled with some apples and a few blackberries. She held tightly to the coin Quinn had just given her.

162

'You need to eat if you are going to win this thing,' he said, hand still extended towards her.

She looked down at the apple and took it. 'Thank you.'

They walked side by side down the busy road, their horses trailing behind. People moved around them, many heading in the same direction, towards the thrill and excitement of the tournament. Aldara stopped to retrieve her mask, which she had carefully secured to the saddle. She brushed the feathers out with her fingers before putting it on, careful not to disturb the blue flowers weaved through her hair.

'Ready?' Quinn asked.

She ignored the tremble in her legs. 'Ready.'

CHAPTER 18

*A*ldara soon realised the flag tournament was a much larger and more elaborate affair in Corneo than at home. Unsurprising given the event was birthed in Corneo long before the kingdom was divided. The king of the newly formed kingdom of Syrasan had wanted his people to remain connected to their heritage while adjusting to a new ruler and way of life.

The field was not some makeshift, roped-off area. It was an immaculate lawn with permanent fencing and large berfroises that remained in place year-round. She looked about, taking in all the details from the tall horse sculptures at the entrance to the long stables on the far side of the field. It was safe for her to stare in awe, as much of the crowd was doing the same.

'The royal family is not here yet. We should get you registered with the timekeeper,' Quinn said, leading them through the crowd.

Aldara adjusted her mask. 'All right.'

They remained on foot, their horses trailing behind them, passing in front of the berfroises where noble guests stood in small groups, brass cups in hand. The men wore tunics in yellow and gold, the women silk dresses in many colours and masks encrusted with citrine, garnet, sapphire and topaz. Aldara had spent so much time envisioning Corneo's poor that she had forgotten about the nobility who never went without, even when the rest of the kingdom was wilting with starvation. She tried not to stare, not wanting to draw attention from the wrong people, but the men noticed her anyway, perhaps because she was not pinched with starvation but rather glowing in comparison. While her simple gown labelled her as a peasant, her polished skin and full face were anything but common.

'That's a good sign,' Quinn said, gesturing to the men watching her.

She continued walking, not looking in their direction again.

They followed the boundary fence all the way to the stables where the men gathered, inspecting the expensive horses that would compete in the event. They stopped a short distance away from the hustle, watching for a moment. Men in worn tunics and high boots shouted across the backs of horses at one another.

'There are no women in there,' Aldara said, resisting the urge to chew her lip.

Quinn turned to her, his bushy brows raised so high that his forehead was striped with deep burrows of skin. 'Of course there are no women. Women do not compete. Women do not buy the horses. Women do not—'

'I get it,' she said, raising a hand to silence him. 'I understand.' She walked forwards, tugging gently on Loda's rein so the mare would follow. Only when they approached the entrance did she notice the man sitting behind a wooden table holding a quill, listening hard to the man across from him. The timekeeper. 'There he is,' she said, nodding in his direction.

Before Quinn could respond, a broad-chested man stepped in front of Aldara, a hand raised in front of him.

'That's far enough,' he said, looking only at her.

She stared up at the large man who narrowed his eyes. 'I need to register for the tournament.' She smiled at him. 'I am just on my way to the timekeeper.'

He did not smile back. '*You* are competing?'

'Faster than any man here,' Quinn said next to her, his tone light.

The guard ignored him and moved his eyes over Aldara's small frame. 'You?' he repeated.

'Yes.' Her smile widened, revealing her teeth.

'Look around you. There are no women here. Now get.' He gestured sharply with his hand.

Aldara thought about the dagger and poisons strapped to her leg and how she might use them on him. As tempting as it was, she suspected there was a far easier way to get around the big man who wanted women to know their place. She reached out and placed her hand on the guard's wrist, then turned to Quinn. 'Perhaps my father could register on my behalf and I could wait out here with you. You are right,' she said, turning back to him. 'It is not appropriate for me to go in. Would that be all right with you?' She made sure she asked his permission, like a good girl.

He glanced down at the small hand on his wrist. He was a tough man, but a man first, and the touch of a pretty female weakened his resolve. He exhaled. 'He can try, but the time-keeper has the final say.'

Aldara looked at Quinn, hopeful.

'Leave it to me, daughter,' he said to her. 'Let your father sort you out. You wait here with this fine gentleman. He'll keep the men away in my absence.'

Aldara turned her face up to the guard. 'Is that all right with you?' she asked, gazing up at him as though he were her saviour.

He glanced again at the hand on his sleeve before nodding. Only then did she withdraw, remaining close to him, giving the impression that she needed his protection. The guard tried to ignore her, but she could see the change in his breath from having her stand so close.

She peered past him to where Quinn was having an animated conversation with the timekeeper, smiling the whole time. The timekeeper nodded and put his quill to paper, taking down the name given him. Relief surged through her and she took a step back from the guard.

When Quinn rejoined them, he gave a look that confirmed his success. 'Let's go.'

Aldara smiled up at the guard a final time. 'Thank you.'

He nodded curtly and looked away.

Only when they were some distance from the stables did Aldara speak. 'I am surprised the timekeeper did not make a fuss about my gender.'

'Well, I did not make a fuss about it.'

She looked across at him. 'What do you mean? You did tell him I was woman, did you not?'

'It was too noisy for a detailed conversation.'

She stopped walking. 'Quinn, he is going to figure it out when I step out onto the field.'

'At least you will be on the field.' He glanced at Loda. 'He assigned a stall for your horse, but I figured you didn't want to leave her there.'

She shook her head. 'No.'

'There are thirty-four riders registered so far.'

Her eyes widened. 'Thirty-four? How many more is he expecting?'

'There are normally forty-odd registrations.' He looked

around to make sure no one was listening before asking the next question. 'How many competitors do they have in your corner of the world?'

She thought back to the year she had attended and remained for the entire event. 'Around fifteen.'

He smiled and whispered, 'Well, you're not in Syrasan anymore.'

She squinted beneath her mask. 'No.'

He gave a deep laugh. 'Cheer up. You don't need to win to get the attention of these men. They'll notice you when you are the only rider in a frock.'

'That is very comforting.'

Another laugh from him. 'I can see you are not one to be reckoned with by the way you played that guard back there. Though if you were really my daughter, I'd tan your hide for that sort of behaviour.'

There was something about his unfiltered manners that made her warm to him. 'Let's find some shade.'

They waited beneath a tall oak, Aldara making an effort not to fidget or frown, distracting herself by watching the children playing nearby. Her mind went to Mako. She did not think she had room for any more emotions and was surprised when longing hit sharply. She thought about how much her son would enjoy playing with the other children— how she was robbing him of the opportunity to have a sibling like she had, with Leo perhaps, because she was stuck in this eternal hole of Tyron.

A royal wagon pulled up in front of the berfroises. The crowd moved out of the way, then turned to see who was inside. Queen Lachina stepped out, alone. Her only daughter had died at age twelve from smallpox during a tour in the South of Corneo. Aldara watched her step up into the royal berfrois where four chairs waited. The queen glanced once at the noble guests, her expression hidden by a green lace-covered mask tied at the back of her head with thick ribbon. Her silk dress was a few shades lighter and covered her arms and neck. Aldara guessed her to be around forty, but it was difficult to tell with the mask and jewels and layers of expensive fabric. She took a seat and raised her hand to the people below.

'Here they come,' Quinn said.

Aldara followed his line of sight to the main entrance where King Nilos entered at a trot, flanked by his two sons and a spray of guards. Two men rode in front with flags of gold marked with a *C*. She did not know what she had been expecting, but the large red-faced man did not seem to match whatever image she had conjured. She watched him closely, the way he dismounted his horse and tossed the reins at the waiting groom, hitting him in the face. The way he walked past the waiting serfs, desperate to speak to him. The way he sat next to his wife without glancing in her direction. She wondered what pleased a man like that, one spoiled by life and disconnected from his people. What would a man like that want in a Companion? The only way to tell would be to get in front of him, feel his eyes on her, watch where they travelled. What would he say to a woman so beneath him?

She turned back to the two princes. 'Which one is Prince Kyril? It's difficult to gauge age when they are masked.'

'On the left,' Quinn said, keeping his voice low and not gesturing.

The prince acknowledged the groom with a nod as he handed him the reins. Finally, a glimpse of good manners. Even with his mask in place, she could see that his brother, Prince Felipe, was a handsome man with his square jaw, straight nose and strong physique. The women in the crowd seemed to be gravitating towards him. She watched them move away, stepping up into the berfrois, once again ignoring the serfs waiting for an audience.

'Is it not custom to at least acknowledge the men waiting to speak with them?'

Quinn snorted. 'What for? So they can get stuck listening to their complaints? Every year is the same: Where will the food come from? The king does not have an answer.'

The princes went between the noble guests, patting the backs of the lords and nodding at their wives. The men bowed and the women swept into practised curtsies. Prince Kyril, his long, sandy hair held in place by his mask, was looking for someone. Aldara knew when he spotted them because he straightened, a broad smile spreading across his face. He made his way over to where a woman stood, unchaperoned, at the back of the berfrois. His Companion. Her dark brown hair was swept up high. A gold chain ran along the top of her head, connecting with the sleek carved mask. Her dress was a fusion of coloured silk and cream lace, butterflies made from fabric dotting the flowing skirt, the top a simple bodice with no sleeves at all. Scandalous by Syrasan standards.

After a few moments observing them, she realised that Prince Kyril would not be looking at anyone but his Companion that day. She was down to two men.

She found Prince Felipe standing with a round-faced, petite girl with lips painted red. Her honey-coloured hair was tucked low and secured with a large yellow flower a shade lighter than her mask. Her dress was made from a stiff fabric and cut sharply around her figure. White teeth flashed as she spoke to the prince, but he seemed distracted. Aldara took in his turned-away feet and unsmiling mouth. He brushed a finger over his nose before excusing himself. She watched the woman, trying to gauge her reaction to the rather brief conversation. She was staring off after the prince, her mouth pinched. Soon another gentleman came to stand by her, and the immediate transformation in her manner confirmed to Aldara that she was the other Companion.

'Prince Felipe does not seem overly taken with his Companion.'

Quinn squinted in hope of improving his vision over that distance. 'He just arrived. How can you tell?'

She could tell.

A horn sounded, deep and long from the centre of the field where the timekeeper now stood on a narrow platform. On the ground next to him sat another man on a stool, quill in his hand and a metal object by his feet she did not recognise.

'Why are there two men?'

'The one seated will write down the times recorded on the mechanical clock.'

She frowned. 'Mechanical clock? What does the time-keeper do if he does not keep time?'

Quinn shrugged. 'He signals the times recorded and gets to feel important standing on his piece of wood for a few hours before returning to his ordinary life where no one takes notice of him.'

Aldara suppressed a smile. The process was more sophisticated than in her kingdom, where one man was entrusted with precise counting. She was waiting for the first rider to enter the field when she noticed everyone turn towards the berfroises.

Seeing her confusion, Quinn said, 'The king always gives a speech before the tournament gets going.'

Aldara looked over to where King Nilos stood behind the barrier, waiting for quiet. Then came an eerie silence, broken only by the occasional cry of a child or whinny from a distant horse.

'People of Corneo, noble guests,' the king boomed. 'Every year we gather here to celebrate the best of our kingdom: the skilled men, the finest horses, the prettiest women…'

Laughter came from the crowd.

'Today is the day we show our gratitude for our way of life and celebrate all that is great about Corneo.' He paused. 'Many of you are aware of what has taken place in the West, the betrayal of our own, submitting to the whims of a king barely weaned from the breast of his mother.'

Another laugh.

'The West will soon be free of these lice, and the betrayal not forgotten. Syrasan may have taken some land, but I have taken the king's brother. Prince Tyron, supposedly one of Syrasan's best swordsmen, rots in my dungeon while we drink here today. King Pandarus will withdraw his men, or the next time he sees his brother, it will be only his severed head.'

Cheers erupted.

Aldara's gaze shifted to a clapping Quinn, who gave her a look that suggested she needed to applaud the sentiment of Tyron's death. A bad taste filled her mouth as her hands came together in a stiff slap.

'Let the tournament begin!' the king shouted, arms outstretched.

A horn sounded and the first rider entered the field, the applause increasing.

'You keep your head about you now,' Quinn said, eyes forwards.

The noise around her made her nerves soar. When she imagined riding out to stunned silence, her mouth dried. In order to collect her mind, she needed to close off the noise—close off everything.

The tournament began and she forced herself to watch, edging closer to the boundary fence with each rider, studying their techniques and strategies. Loda stirred behind her as one of the horses thundered past them, legs outstretched and breathing strained. Aldara stepped back and held onto the mare, needing the balance as much as the horse needed reassurance.

Quinn looked at her, eyebrows raised in question. 'You're not losing your nerve, are you?'

She shook her head, afraid speech would betray her. The timekeeper's arm went up in the air, indicating the fastest recorded time.

'Even faster than the one before,' Quinn said, releasing a long whistle. 'Four minutes twenty-six seconds,' he said, reading the timekeeper's hand signals. 'They've really brought it this year.' He turned to her again. 'What is your fastest time, by the way?'

She was still gripping Loda's bridle. 'Four minutes thirty-nine seconds,' she breathed out.

A genuine look of concern came over Quinn's face. 'How do you plan on shaving thirteen seconds off your time?'

She did not have a plan at all. 'Let's hope the breeze is blowing in a favourable direction.'

It took just under three hours to get through the first thirty-three riders. When the thirty-fourth horse entered the field, Aldara turned to Loda and began, with trembling hands, to unfasten the girth of the saddle.

A look of horror came over Quinn's face. 'What in God's name are you doing?'

'Getting ready,' she replied. 'I'm next.'

He stepped closer to her. 'Which is why you should be checking the girth and getting on your horse, not unsaddling.'

She glanced up at him before placing the saddle and blanket at his feet. 'Less weight' was all she said.

Quinn crossed his arms and narrowed his eyes. 'I did not agree to come here and watch you kill yourself.'

'Lower your voice, *Father*,' she whispered.

Rider thirty-four galloped past and they turned to watch him. When Quinn looked back at her, she saw his concern was beyond the role he was playing.

'It's all right. I won without a saddle last time,' she said, trying to ease his mind. 'Don't let anyone steal it.' She patted his arm and then sprang onto the mare's back, fixing her dress so her legs were modestly covered. 'Wish me luck.'

He shook his head and stepped back so Loda could pass him. 'Go on then, show us what you can do without a saddle.'

She nodded and pushed Loda into a walk, keeping to the fence line. She felt more eyes on her as she passed the berfroises and braved a look to see if any of them belonged to royal men. No such luck. They were all deep in conversation, taking advantage of the break between riders.

The first horn sounded and a rumble of excitement came over the crowd again. Aldara paused at the gap in the fence and exhaled all the way, eyes on her hands which were now visibly shaking. Another deep breath.

'Let's go,' she said to Loda, pushing her into a trot. They made their way across the field towards the timekeeper. The cheers faded to a few isolated claps, likely belonging to people who had not yet caught sight of her. She told herself it was fine; she had expected that reaction. At least it was not laughter. When she reached the two men in the centre of the field, confused and gaping, she smiled. The man with the quill glanced down at the list of names in front of him.

'Medea,' Aldara offered, helping him out.

The timekeeper stepped off the platform and snatched the parchment from the other man's hands. Aldara saw the disappointment when he spotted her name.

'I thought the name sounded feminine,' he said, turning his hardened face up to her.

She continued to smile. 'And you were correct.' Thankfully, her hands had stopped shaking just in time. 'Shall we begin?'

The timekeeper shook his head. 'Women are not permitted to enter.'

She frowned at him, appearing genuinely surprised. 'I was not aware of that rule. Is it written somewhere?'

He narrowed his eyes. 'I can write it down if you like.'

She glanced at the royal berfrois where she discovered everyone watching. At least she had managed to get their attention.

'You need to leave the field,' the timekeeper said, waving her away with a hand.

She did not move, instead glancing again at the berfrois where Prince Felipe had gotten to his feet, hand over his brow trying to see what was happening. If she continued to hold up the tournament, he would be forced to intervene.

'I would like to know the logic behind your decision,' Aldara said, turning back to the timekeeper.

His face reddened at her request. 'I do not owe you an explanation. Now remove yourself before I have the guards remove you.'

Prince Felipe was now making his way down the steps of the berfrois. Once on the ground, he broke into a jog towards them. At the fence, he grabbed hold and swung his legs over in one easy leap. The nearby women squealed with surprised delight at his agile display, turning to one another and conversing as he jogged away. As he got closer, he fixed his gaze on Aldara, seemingly annoyed. He came to a stop in front of her horse.

'What is going on here?'

She kept her face neutral. 'There seems to be a problem with my registration, my lord.'

He frowned, eyes moving over her. '*Your* registration?'

She had his attention. 'Yes. Apparently there is a rule.'

He folded his arms, an amused expression on his face. 'And what rule would that be?'

She held his gaze. 'That women are not permitted to compete.'

A smile tugged at the corners of his mouth.

'I have never heard of that rule,' she continued. 'My father, who has attended the tournament since childhood, has also never mentioned it.'

Prince Felipe looked down, seeing that she was bareback. 'It is common knowledge more than a rule. I am surprised your father permitted you to register.'

There was definite amusement in his eyes. 'My father gave up trying to teach me the rules some years back.' It was a bold statement that could have easily worked against her with a man of his status. But she had a feeling he was intrigued by her insubordination, so she took a chance and watched the light come to his eyes.

'Do you really think you can beat the men before you?'

She glanced at the timekeeper, whose mouth was hanging open, ready to protest. 'I would like to try, my lord.'

The prince was silent for a moment. She did not smile because he did not want another smiling girl; it was her tenacity that held his attention.

'Let her race,' the prince said, eyes remaining on her.

The timekeeper's expression fell. 'But my lord—'

'Let her race,' Felipe said again, an edge to his tone.

There was something in his manner that reminded her of Pandarus. She looked away for the first time.

The timekeeper nodded and handed the paper back to the

other man, who was watching Aldara with suspicion. 'As you wish, my lord.'

Prince Felipe's gaze dropped. 'Where is your saddle?'

'My father has it. The less weight, the faster I go.'

He laughed at that. 'Is your father ready to collect your broken body when you fall, or should I have my own men at the ready?'

'Just one man, my lord. I'm not that heavy.'

He bowed before her, and when he rose, the light danced in his eyes. 'Perhaps I will come and collect you myself.'

Her eyes remained on his. She definitely had his attention now. 'So if I fall, I am gallantly carried off the field by the Crown Prince of Corneo. And what if I win?'

Another smile, wider that time. 'Just try to stay on the horse.'

She bowed her head as he turned and strode away, back towards the berfrois, the food, the wealth, the stench of greed. Her heart beat hard in her chest with delayed shock. All eyes were on her now, the men curious, the women perplexed.

Once Felipe was seated, the timekeeper raised his horn to his lips. Loda went rigid beneath Aldara as she gathered the reins and took a handful of mane along with them. She leaned forwards, her eyes on the first flag. The horn sounded and Loda lunged forwards with the slightest change in pressure to her sides. The confused crowd had fallen silent. She blocked them out.

One flag at a time, just like we practiced.

The pounding of Loda's hooves combined with the pounding in her ears. Aldara leaned down and took hold of the first flag, moving her outside leg back and pushing Loda hard around the tight turn. The mare responded with each shift in her weight, the bridle obsolete. They galloped back to the empty barrel and Aldara speared the long pole into it while Loda's hind legs slid in a semicircle as she turned. Aldara's eyes were on the next flag, her heels pressing into the mare's sides, and Loda's ears were turned, listening.

'Come on,' Aldara whispered.

Retrieve the flag, return it, repeat.

Fifteen flags.

One flag at a time.

When she passed along the fence, she spotted Quinn out of the corner of her eye, her saddle by his feet, watching. She did not look at him for fear of what his expression might give away. No glances at the timekeeper either. She did not need to see his arm, limp at his side. Eyes on the next flag, eyes on the barrel. She had nothing more to give, going as hard and as fast as she could, taking every turn with calculated precision. She could feel sweat running beneath her leather mask. Blinking against it, she tried to clear her vision before giving up and tearing the mask from her face. It fell to the grass behind them.

Two more flags.

She could have sworn she glimpsed the timekeeper's arm up when she hurled the second-to-last flag into the barrel. The thought alone distracted her, causing Loda to go wider than was necessary. She made up for the delay with more speed. 'Ha!' she shouted, the mare lengthening her stride, her hind legs tucking beneath her as they galloped towards the final flag. Her arm outstretched, torso flush against Loda's neck, she snatched the final flag, pulling on the inside rein. Loda's body tilted towards the ground as she turned.

For the final gallop to the barrel, she did something she rarely did with Loda: she dug her heels in—hard. The mare emitted a grunt and her head lowered, her stride lengthening one last time. The drum rumbled with the force of the last flag being thrown in, and Loda, caught up in the excitement, galloped towards the fence on the other side, where families watched with expressions varying between awe and disapproval. Aldara sat upright and pulled on the reins to slow her, forced to turn the mare to the left to avoid colliding with the fence. Her eyes went to the timekeeper, whose raised arm seemed to have a bend in the elbow as though fighting to keep it up.

She had the fastest time for the day, but there were more riders to follow. Braving a glance at the royal berfrois, she saw that King Nilos was watching her with interest. Win or lose, she now had his attention.

Her hand went to Loda's neck, praising the mare's efforts. 'Thank you, girl.'

She exited the field and walked back along the fence. This time when she passed in front of the berfroises, all eyes were on her. She bowed her head at King Nilos before facing forwards again. When she reached Quinn, she slipped from Loda's back and grabbed hold of him for balance.

'Easy does it,' he said, holding her up.

She let go and straightened herself. 'Is he still looking at me,' she whispered.

'Who?' Quinn looked at the royal berfrois.

She stepped away, not wanting to appear as spent as she felt. 'King Nilos.'

He turned back to her, a smile spreading across his face. 'No, but Prince Felipe is.'

Aldara brushed at the skirt of her dress, which was covered in horse hair. 'Too bad he already has a Companion,' she replied.

'I don't expect that will stop him if he sets his sights on you.'

Aldara looked at him, remembering that Pandarus often had more than one Companion at a time, despite the fact that the tradition had always been one.

Four more riders followed her, none of them fast enough.

She knew in the first thirty seconds of the final rider that he would not beat her time. Quinn shook his head next to her.

'You are actually going to win this thing.'

She said nothing. The whole thing was too much—the race, the win, the performance in front of the men. Panic rose at the realisation that she would soon have an audience with a member of the royal family.

'You get us in front of the king and leave the rest to this potato hustler,' Quinn said, turning to her. The smile fell from his face. 'You're not going to be sick again, are you?'

She hoped not, because the final rider had passed the timekeeper and he signalled one of the slowest times of the day. People around them turned and looked at her. A few of them began to clap while others simply stared, unsure of what reaction was appropriate. The timekeeper looked lost out in the middle of the field on his platform, liaising with the other man, no doubt looking for errors in the recorded times so as to not have to declare her the winner.

Before any formal announcement was made, a guard approached them, his expression serious.

'Prince Felipe has requested an audience with you both.'

Aldara looked back at Quinn, who was fitting the saddle back on Loda.

'You heard the man,' he said. 'Let's not keep his lordship waiting.'

They followed the guard, Aldara holding tight to Loda's rein, back to the royal berfrois where Prince Felipe stood, hands resting on the barrier. The timekeeper had been brought before him also and eyed her warily. She stopped in front of the prince and curtsied, and when she looked up at him, she saw the same light in his eyes she had seen earlier. She had made an impression.

'My lord.' It sounded like a question. Quinn came to stand by her, the way a protective father would.

Felipe shook his head as he tried to figure a way forwards. 'What is your name?'

'Medea, my lord. This is my father, Quinn,' she said, gesturing to the beaming man next to her.

'It's an honour, my lord,' Quinn said, giving a bow bordering on theatrical.

Felipe's eyes returned to Aldara. 'Medea,' he repeated, trying out the name. He took in her dress and barely painted face. 'Medea, your time was the fastest recorded this day.'

She blinked. 'You seem surprised.'

He laughed at that. 'I *am* surprised.'

Her eyes went past him to his family, who watched her with interest—except for the queen, who stared out at the field.

'Is that your way of congratulating me, my lord?'

He tilted his head, attempting to read her. 'No, actually. I am afraid I must disqualify you.' There was no apology in his tone. 'As you must realise, we cannot hand the title over to a woman.'

Quinn went to speak and she silenced him with a glance. She would have loved to dispute the decision also, but she already had what she needed. Her eyes went again to the king, who seemed content letting his son handle the matter.

'You should be grateful I let you compete at all,' Felipe continued, sounding more and more like Pandarus.

'Why did you, my lord?'

He shook his head. 'I suppose I wanted to see if you could finish.'

'There is not much my Medea cannot finish, my lord,' Quinn said. 'She is a force to be reckoned with since coming of age last year.'

Not only had they shaved off a few years, they had also shaved off a child.

'Where are you from, Medea of seventeen?'

'Thovaria, my lord,' she replied, her pronunciation perfect. 'Our family has a potato farm there.'

'You travelled a long way for the tournament.' The prince glanced over his shoulder at his father. 'Do you enjoy being the daughter of a potato farmer?'

That was the moment she knew he was going to offer her a very different life.

'No girl in her right mind grows up with dreams of being a potato farmer,' Quinn answered. There was humour in his tone. 'It won't be for much longer if the men in our village have their way.'

Felipe raised an eyebrow in question. 'Oh?'

'They're always sniffing about the farm,' Quinn said, putting an arm around Aldara.

'Are they indeed?'

Nausea returned to Aldara in violent waves. She could not afford to vomit in front of the royal family, so she remained silent, swallowing down the overwhelming sensation.

Felipe thought for a moment and nodded. 'We must continue with the ceremony, but do not leave the tournament without seeing me first.'

'We would not want to miss the ceremony,' Quinn said, laughing.

Prince Felipe turned to the timekeeper, who had been silently watching. His expression was visibly more relaxed.

'The title will go to the man with the fastest time.'

'Yes, my lord,' said the timekeeper, bowing and then glancing triumphantly at Aldara before striding away.

Felipe looked at her once more. 'I will come and find you shortly.'

She curtsied and turned away, following Quinn back to the shade.

'Your face is awfully pale,' Quinn said, his voice low. 'I

thought you might be happier. Everything is going to plan.'
He removed his tunic and laid it on the grass, gesturing for
her to sit.

'Thank you,' she said, taking a seat.

He kneeled in front of her and offered the flask of water.
'I'm afraid it's too late for cold feet.'

She took the flask, eyes on him as she drank. 'I know,' she
said, handing it back to him.

She was about to be sold for the second time in her life.

CHAPTER 19

*T*welve pieces of gold. That was her worth. She later discovered that ten pieces was standard. Prince Felipe had paid Quinn twelve, likely hustled by the savvy farmer who got to keep the gold as payment for the part he played. Quinn left with Loda, assuring her that he would return the mare to the manor where she would wait for Aldara to return. He had said goodbye in a way fitting of a father before leaving her, casting a concerned look in her direction as he disappeared from sight. Aldara suspected the concern was genuine.

She travelled to Masville Castle in a cart filled with servants. They stared at her as she climbed in and took a seat on a hessian sack stuffed with straw and continued to stare at her for the rest of the journey. Aldara turned her face away, looking out at the bare paddocks and crumbling houses where people stood with drawn faces and stooped heads, watching her with the same blank expression the servants were.

The castle rose on the horizon, reaching out of the thinning trees. When they arrived at the high wall, they waited as the portcullis went up. Aldara took mental notes of every detail and was surprised to discover a second gate. The cart stopped once more, the portcullis behind them lowering, momentarily caging them in. Her eyes travelled along the walls, discovering holes, men visible through them. She marvelled at the cleverness of the space, one that trapped unwanted visitors and allowed archers to shoot at them while remaining protected behind a wall.

She felt relief when the gate in front of them began to move, cart lurching forwards once more. The sound of it closing behind her made her hands clammy. She looked around the courtyard, alive with people unloading carts and shouting instructions. Tilting her face up to take in the castle's sharp rooftops, she closed her eyes, feeling for Tyron. Surely if his heart was beating inside these walls, she would hear it.

'Move,' came a voice beside her.

She opened her eyes to find one of the servants glaring down. The cart had come to a stop and the other passengers were waiting for her to move out of their way.

'Sorry.' She jumped down and stepped to the side so they could pass. She looked about, wondering whether she should follow them inside or wait for someone to collect her.

'Medea?'

Aldara turned to see a woman standing in the doorway, light brown hair braided to one side and sad blue eyes. She wore an embroidered dress that showed off her figure. Her chin was raised, hands folded in front of her. 'Are you the mentor?'

The woman nodded. 'My name is Petra, but you will address me as "my lady".'

Aldara exhaled, once again trapped in that world. At least she had come willingly this time. 'Yes, my lady.'

Petra regarded her for a moment, as if trying to decide

something. Her overall demeanour was far less threatening than her previous mentor's.

'Follow me.'

Aldara watched her turn and walk away. She hesitated, sucked in a lungful of air, exhaled slowly, and followed after her.

∼

IT WAS NOT the introduction Aldara had predicted, yet it was no surprise.

'That's enough,' Petra said, her tone sharp. 'Calista, go and bathe.' Her eyes dared the girl to say one more word.

Calista's eyes returned to Aldara. 'What is the point? Prince Felipe is never going to request me now that *she* is here.'

Aldara continued to stare at the floor. It seemed Felipe's Companion also possessed the ability to read men. She had watched their exchange at the flag tournament—and she was not happy. Aldara knew there was no point in trying to convince her otherwise, because her fears were valid.

Calista's face was streaked with dark paint and contorted by fury. Her hair had come loose and hung about her face. Aldara looked up, meeting her eyes but saying nothing as the girl turned and marched from the room, hands curled into fists.

'How very unbecoming,' said Prince Kyril's Companion, clearing her throat. 'My name is Nyla.'

She smiled at Aldara as though the outburst a moment earlier had not happened at all. She could afford to smile because it was not her position being threatened by a new arrival. There was kindness in her eyes, which helped Aldara to relax.

'Medea.'

'I was going to send you off to bathe, but I think perhaps we will wait for Calista to finish,' Petra said, glancing at the doorway.

'That was a very bold way to gain the attention of the king today,' Nyla said, stepping closer. 'How did you know it would work?'

Aldara waited for Petra to pull her into line, but the dark circles around her eyes suggested she did not have the energy to close the conversation down. 'I was not riding to gain the attention of the king,' she lied. 'I was riding to win.'

Nyla shook her head, confused. 'Why?'

'For the same reason others do.'

Nyla glanced at Petra. 'You mean the men?'

'Yes.'

She laughed and it was exactly the kind of laugh Fedora would approve of—refined and feminine. 'That is the funniest thing I have ever heard.' She touched a finger to her brow. 'Let me guess, you have only brothers, all older than you.'

Aldara shook her head. 'I am the eldest of three daughters.'

'Oh.'

'I think that is enough questions for now, Nyla,' Petra said. She studied Aldara for a moment before looking away. 'Come, I will show you around.'

There was nothing Aldara had not seen before: a main room with a fireplace, a dressing room, a bathing room and a shared bedchamber. One difference was there was no curtained-off section for Petra—she slept alongside the others.

'Leave us, please,' Petra said to Nyla, who had been following along for the tour.

The taken-aback Companion excused herself and left them alone in the dressing room where garments hung wall to wall, rows of colourful shoes beneath them. On the far side of the room sat a dressing table with mirrored glass behind it.

'Do you understand what you are doing here?' Petra asked, studying Aldara.

Aldara looked back at her. 'I understand what a Companion is, if that is what you are asking.'

'Do you?' There was something chilling in her tone. 'Does your father understand that he has handed you over for good? That once King Nilos tires of you, which he will, you will be sold to the highest bidder?'

Three months, Aldara reminded herself, ignoring the falling sensation inside. 'Yes.'

Petra reached out and tucked in a dress that was poking out from the clean line of garments. 'You will attend church at least twice a week. There are two sermons each day. As the queen usually attends in the afternoon, Companions attend in the morning. When you attend will depend on what else is happening. Lessons also tend to be in the mornings when the girls are freshest. Like the others, you will learn history and languages, along with various art forms. I will work with you privately in the afternoons on refinement of your social skills, as the other women are more advanced and their time can be better spent developing their talents.' She paused. 'Do you play any musical instruments? Sing? Or dance, perhaps?'

Here we go, thought Aldara, remembering how miserably she had failed at all forms of arts. 'I dance a little.'

Petra nodded. 'We shall see what can be done with that. Nyla is a very gifted singer.'

Aldara suspected Nyla was gifted at most things. 'And Calista?'

Petra stilled. 'She was only recently introduced, but she is competent with the flute.' She glanced at the door before speaking again. 'You will be given herbs to drink. These herbs will prevent pregnancy once you are introduced. In a few days' time, once you have settled in, a midwife will come and check you.'

She had been worried about that possibility. 'Check me for what?'

'Check that you are virtuous and free of disease.'

Aldara's gaze went to the dresses. 'I should probably let you know in advance that I am not… intact.' The words caught in her throat when she said them. When she looked over to gauge Petra's reaction, she did not seem surprised.

'Is the king aware of the fact?'

'No one asked me.' She attempted to smile. 'I imagine it would be quite an uncomfortable conversation between strangers.'

Petra was not smiling. 'Now it is a conversation I must have. The king may reject you if he suspects promiscuous behaviour—'

'I am not promiscuous, my lady.'

'Your actions suggest otherwise.'

'I was not given a choice.'

Something flickered in Petra's eyes. 'I see. You will have to forgive my scepticism. I have been doing this a long time.' She paused. 'Let us wait and see what the midwife says, shall we?'

Aldara nodded, glad to be done with the topic. At least she had not been forced to lie. While the memory of her first time with a man had faded over the years, washed away by Tyron, she would never forget the two men who had taken so much from her that night.

'Medea,' Petra said loudly.

Aldara jumped. She could not afford to be unresponsive to her new name.

Petra's gaze seemed to go straight through her. 'You can go and bathe now.'

Aldara glanced at the doorway where Calista stood, wrapped in a robe, a guarded expression on her face. 'Yes, my lady,' she said, her gaze going once again to the floor.

But first she would have to find a hiding place for the dagger and poisons still strapped to her leg.

～

DURING HER FIRST week at Masville, Aldara was not permitted to leave the Companions' quarters. She attended lessons with the other women and ate the food given her. She did a few basic chores, tasks one would assign to a young child, like clearing the table, or stripping one's bed when the linen needed washing. At night she lay in her bed, feeling Calista's eyes on her, going over Pandarus's rough sketch of the castle in her mind—which did not include a dungeon because he had not seen it during his time in Corneo. In the mornings she woke tired, bringing questions from Petra who assumed she was missing home and brought her various herbs to help her sleep. Whenever she felt overwhelmed, she thought of Mako, but not for too long as thoughts of him brought a tightness to her chest that prevented her from functioning. Instead, she thought of Tyron, lying awake underground, unaware that she was nearby, and that she belonged to the man who held him prisoner.

At the end of that first week, the midwife came, asked her to remove her clothes, to raise her arms, take out her hair, lie on the bed, raise her knees. Aldara stared at the roof and fought the urge to kick. Once finished, the midwife left to speak with Petra, and Aldara sat on the bed with a robe pulled tightly about her, wanting a bath.

A short while later, Petra returned and stood near the bed. 'The midwife found scars conducive with childbirth or assault. Tell me which it is so I can decide on how we should proceed.' Her tone was practical, as if they were discussing a recipe for bread.

What answer to give? 'Both,' she whispered.

Petra's eyes did not move from her. She was thinking. 'Where is the child?' The question came out of her like a release of breath.

Aldara swallowed, wanting to choose another answer. 'Safe.'

The mentor's mouth pressed into a tight line. She looked like she was about to say something, but turned instead and walked out of the room.

Aldara let her head drop to the pillow and buried her face.

IT WAS her eighth day of confinement, and Petra had taken the other women away to practice their music so as not to disturb Aldara who remained behind, copying a section of a book onto a piece of parchment. The only thing harder than learning to write was pretending to learn to write. She had to remember to let the ink pool in places and keep the letters uneven because farmers in the North most certainly did not read or write.

She hated being confined indoors, and the frustration was building into panic. How was she meant to achieve anything trapped in a room?

She had just dipped her quill into the ink when Petra returned alone. Aldara jumped when she appeared next to her.

'You scared me, my lady,' she said, standing. 'You have very quiet footsteps.'

Just like Fedora.

Petra's expression was serious. 'I wanted to let you know,

before the others return, that the midwife's finding reported to King Nilos suggested you had minor scarring conducive with assault.'

Aldara waited for her to say something else, but she was done. 'You said nothing of… the child?'

'I thought it best not to.'

Aldara searched her face for an explanation. 'And what did His Majesty say in reply to your report?'

'Very little. I imagine the information will be passed along to Prince Felipe, who may have more of an opinion on the matter.'

Aldara hesitated. 'King Nilos does not want me as a Companion, does he?'

'We shall find out soon enough.'

Aldara's gaze fell to Petra's arms, folded delicately in front of her, a red handprint visible around her right wrist. Petra unfolded her arms and let them drop to her sides. When Aldara looked up, she saw the subject was not open for discussion. Petra reached out her left hand and ran a finger along the crooked words she had copied.

'Please remain patient and we shall see what unfolds.'

As she went to pass her, Aldara called, 'My lady.'

She stopped walking and turned, eyebrows raised in question.

'Thank you for not mentioning the child.'

Petra nodded, fatigue weighing down her eyelids. 'Why further complicate things?'

Aldara watched her walk away, her eyes returning to the ring around Petra's wrist until she disappeared around the corner.

CHAPTER 20

*D*uring her second week at Masville, Aldara was seated in the dressing room, brushing out her hair, when a maid rushed into the room. Aldara went still, watching as the girl looked about, checking that no one else was there.

'Medea?'

Aldara's heart quickened. 'Yes?'

The maid pulled a piece of parchment from the sleeve of her dress and held it out. It had been folded so many times it was as thick as it was wide. Aldara took it and shoved it into the pocket of her dress while the girl turned and fled.

'Thank you, Velma,' Aldara called to her back before she disappeared through the door.

Aldara went immediately to the garderobe at the end of the corridor, as it was the only place she was assured privacy.

A

Excellent news. Well done. Your mare is with me. Be smart and stay safe.

L

THAT WAS IT. A few words that said very little and yet brought so much comfort and reassurance. She exhaled and tore the letter into small pieces before dropping them down the chute. She would have preferred to burn it, but could not risk holding onto it while waiting for an opportunity. She washed her hands and stepped back out into the corridor. As she rounded the corner to the Companions' quarters, she stopped walking. There stood Prince Felipe, leaning against the wall with his arms crossed, his leg bouncing in a manner that suggested his patience was wearing thin.

She resumed walking, eyes on him. 'My lord,' she called as she approached. 'Does Petra know you are waiting out here?' She stopped in front of him and curtsied. 'Has she gone to get Calista?'

He pushed off the wall, his eyes moving over her. 'Actually she has gone to find you.'

'Me?' She glanced at the doorway.

He cleared his throat. 'My father wanted me to check on you, see if you have settled in.'

She regarded him for a moment. 'His Majesty sent you?'

'Yes.' A smile flickered. 'So have you? Settled in?'

Her eyes went intentionally to his lips. 'I am still adjusting to being indoors all the time.'

He smiled at that. 'You potato farmers love the outdoors.'

She smiled back, despite his patronising tone. 'Yes, we potato farmers do.'

Petra came out of the door and looked visibly relieved to see her standing there. 'Medea, I was just looking for you.' There was an edge to her tone that Aldara suspected would be sharper if the prince were not standing between them.

'I believe you are going to have to keep a close eye on this one,' Felipe said.

'His Majesty sent Prince Felipe to check on me,' Aldara told her. 'Isn't that thoughtful?'

Petra smiled at the prince. 'Very. Though I am always happy to report to him directly.' Something in her expression suggested otherwise.

'I don't mind,' replied Felipe. 'I thought I might take Medea for a turn about the castle, show her around.'

Aldara had to keep herself in check as she did not want to appear too eager. 'I would love that. I have not seen much outside of these rooms.'

'A tour, then?'

She nodded, thoughts of Tyron filling her head. 'An excellent suggestion.'

Petra looked between them, her expression giving nothing away. 'Enjoy the air.'

They went downstairs, past the armoury and laundry, exiting a small door. Aldara's breath hitched as she stepped out into the sun. It felt glorious on her bare arms. But she could not relax and enjoy it, because as they walked along the east wall of the castle, Felipe pointing at landmarks and explaining them to her as though she lacked any intelligence at all, her eyes went to the servants and guards, counting them, studying their behaviour and the attention they paid to their surroundings. All the while, she emitted sounds of interest, encouraging Felipe to continue.

'It's all very impressive,' she said, noting the change in his posture when she said that, as if he had built it with his own hands. 'I'm fascinated by the idea that so much of the castle is below ground. What secret rooms lie beneath us, my lord? The wine cellar, perhaps? The dungeon?'

He laughed. 'I should not be surprised by your fascination

with underground rooms and dungeons. It seems you are drawn to danger.'

'You seem to have me figured out.' Moving closer to him, she asked, 'Will the dungeon be part of the tour?'

There was amusement in his eyes. 'The dungeon is along the west wall beneath the buttery, and it is no place for a lovely creature like yourself.' He stopped walking and turned to her.

She mirrored him, already dreading whatever he would say and her reaction to it.

'I want to let you in on a secret.'

'All right.'

'I asked my father to purchase you.'

She maintained eye contact. 'I can't say that I'm surprised by your revelation, as I am yet to speak with your father.' She paused. 'He must trust your judgement.'

'When I saw you on that horse, wearing that mask...' He reached up and pushed a piece of hair away from her eye, and she fought against her urge to step back from him.

'You liked the mask?'

'A masked woman is my undoing.'

Aldara frowned. 'It is no wonder, then, that you enjoy attending the flag tournament.'

His fingertips were on her cheek then. 'I am often disappointed when the mask comes off, but not with you. When you stood before me, your raw beauty on display, I had to own you.'

'Oh?' Her feet really wanted to move. 'And what of your Companion?'

His hand fell away. 'You will not have to worry about her for much longer.'

They resumed walking, and Aldara did not ask any more questions. She already knew the answers, and feeling responsible for Calista's exile was too much.

When they reached the north wall, she relaxed at the sight of maids and servants moving about, completing chores and chatting between themselves. It reminded her of Archdale, and she was surprised to find herself comforted by such a thought. But soon they turned the corner, stepping into a blanket of shadows. The air smelled of human waste, but she did not care, because she knew Tyron was close. Her stride lengthened, feeling him somewhere beneath her. She stopped when she saw barred holes along the bottom of the wall.

'Are they windows?'

Felipe glanced down and scoffed. 'A generous description. More like air holes for the prisoners.'

Come on, feet, move. But she was anchored to the earth covering him. When Felipe stopped to look at her, she asked, 'Tell me about the prisoners.'

His eyes shone at her. She could tell he liked her dark side, the one she had created just for him.

'They are no different to the criminals in your village.'

She tilted her face up to him. 'I am afraid that we cannot lay claim to ever holding a Syrasan prince.'

He stepped forwards, took her hand, and placed it on his arm before walking on, saying nothing more on the subject.

Aldara walked at his side, counting the number of holes they passed. Six. She had no idea how she was walking away from him, knowing that if she ran to those dark holes, calling his name into each one, one would answer her.

'You are shivering,' Felipe said, looking down at her in surprise.

'It is cold in the shadows.'

He placed his free hand over hers and they stepped out of the darkness, arriving at the south entrance of the castle. She felt as though she were being pulled back by an imaginary hand.

When a servant came into sight, Felipe released her hand

and stepped away from her, propriety preventing him from walking about the castle with another Companion on his arm. They went through the main door and made their way back to her quarters. When they arrived, Felipe turned to her, his eyes moving over her face.

'I am not one for walks—except with you.'

She watched him. 'That is the outside of the castle done. Perhaps next time you can show me the inside. I hear you have some fine paintings on display.'

'Do you paint?'

She recalled the painting she had given Tyron, the brown mess of oils that hung in his bedchamber. How many times had they laid there, their stomachs hurting from laughter, taking turns critiquing it in Fedora's voice? She could still feel his body shaking beneath her head, begging her to stop. 'No, but I admire those with skill.'

His eyes were on her lips, and she knew exactly what he was thinking. He leaned towards her and then stopped himself. 'Until next time.'

She curtsied and turned away, her expression falling as soon as he could no longer see her face. Pausing at the door to collect herself, she listened as the prince's footsteps faded behind her. She was barely through the door when Calista lurched at her, pushing her into the wall.

'You whore!' she shouted, coming at Aldara with a raised hand.

Aldara blocked the blow with her arm, and when Calista went to strike with her other hand, she blocked that one also.

'How dare you!' Calista screamed, her frustration fuelling her rage.

Aldara ducked down and slipped past her, calmly backing away. She did not want to fight someone already in a world of pain.

'What on earth is going on?' Petra said, stepping through

the doorway at the other end of the room. She looked between the two of them, taking in Aldara's calm expression and then Calista's wild eyes.

'I saw her!' Calista said, her eyes welling. 'Walking with Prince Felipe, her arm through his. She planned this entire thing. Came for him, knowing he already had me!'

Watching Calista fall apart in front of her was one of the most painful things she had ever witnessed—and it was her fault.

'That's quite enough,' Petra said, walking over to Calista. 'Calm yourself at once.'

Calista was panting, and a heavy sob came from her. 'I gave up everything to come here. I was supposed to be married, and I gave it all up. And for what? To be replaced at the first opportunity.'

I'm sorry, Aldara wanted to say.

'Who will want me now?' Her hands went over her face, fingers digging in.

No one said anything, not even Petra, who should have closed the conversation down. The anger had left Calista, replaced with something much sadder. Aldara only looked at her feet, unable to watch anymore.

I'm sorry.

The sobs subsided and Calista left the room. No one went after her. What comfort could they possibly offer?

That evening, after Nyla left to spend the night with Prince Kyril, Aldara laid awake in her bed, listening to Calista's soft, sleepy breaths across from her. Every time she thought sleep a possibility, her eyes would snap open, guilt and fear pounding inside of her chest.

A few hours before dawn, she gave up the fight for sleep and was about to fetch some water when she heard Petra whispering. Aldara went still, listening and watching through the dark. She could make out Petra's form, kneeling by

Calista's bed. She was telling her to wake up. The two of them left the room, and a few moments later, soft weeping reached Aldara through the open door. She pressed her eyes shut, remaining that way for hours.

Only once the room had lightened did Aldara find the courage to sit up and look around at the empty beds.

CHAPTER 21

Three weeks after arriving at Masville Castle, Aldara wrote Leksi a letter asking if he could send someone to check on her son. She knew it was a big ask, but the separation from him was choking her. She made sure to update Leksi of her progress—or lack thereof—telling herself there was only so much she could do under Petra's watchful eye. She wondered how on earth she was going to free Tyron from a dungeon she had no access to. And then what? It was her responsibility to come up with a plan, but all she could see was walls and guards, people and things in her way.

She took the letter with her to the laundry when she dropped off the dirty bed linen, slipping it into the maid's hand as she sat the basket down. Velma took it without a word, stuffing it into her pocket before continuing with her work. As Aldara was leaving, she noticed a guard's tunic lying next to a pile of towels.

'Do the guards not launder their own uniforms?'

Velma glanced across at the tunic. 'They most certainly do. Occasionally we will sew on a button or two, but only for the men with no wife to do it for them.'

'I see.' Aldara smiled and left the women to their work.

Petra said little of Calista's departure other than she would not be returning. Aldara did not ask questions, did not want to know the details, did not want to feed her own guilt. She just attended her lessons and did as she was told, which seemed to keep everyone happy. And life moved forwards—without Calista.

Aldara often found Petra watching her, as if trying to figure her out, perhaps wondering if she felt the same grief at being separated from her child.

Yes.

Petra taught Aldara how to dance and sing. And then no more singing. The mentor was on the same dead-end road Fedora had travelled down, trying to find something spectacular to offer to the men who had paid twelve pieces of gold.

'The only thing I do well is work and ride,' Aldara said apologetically.

Petra just nodded absently, moving on to the next thing.

Aldara had not seen Prince Felipe since Calista's departure, and while she was grateful for the space, she also needed him in order to move about the castle. Since Felipe decided when she left her quarters, she remained hidden away, like the daggers and poisons she had brought with her.

It was exactly one month after her arrival when Prince Felipe showed up at the Companions' quarters, asking for her.

'My lord.' She noted his confident stance and smug smile. 'I was afraid you had forgotten about me.'

He leaned in when he spoke to her. 'I thought you might want to finish the tour.'

Yes, she most definitely wanted to finish the tour. She forced a smile. 'I thought you would never ask.'

He stepped back from her and they walked down the long corridor with its glass windows casting light at their feet, side by side, only stopping or speaking once they had arrived at whatever Prince Felipe wanted to show her. She glimpsed the buttery behind him and some narrow stairs to her right that burrowed down under the ground.

Aldara felt her mouth go dry as she stared into it. 'What is down there?'

He crossed his arms. 'You wanted a dungeon, I give you a dungeon.'

She turned to him, trying to read his expression. 'Are we going in?'

'You want to go *in*?' He laughed. 'Are you not afraid?'

'Not when I am with you.' She hoped she sounded convincing.

A smile lingered and his eyes travelled down to her lips. 'Are you sure about this?'

She lifted her head. 'I think I can handle a few badly behaved men.'

He took hold of her cheek. There was a roughness in his manner that surprised her. She made an effort not to stiffen beneath his touch. Tyron was so close, but Felipe was closer —much too close. She readied herself, because if he kissed her, she would need to kiss him back, just a few yards from Tyron.

A guard climbed the steps towards them and Felipe released his grip on her.

'My lord,' the man said, glancing at Aldara. 'Is there some-thing I can help you with?'

Felipe nodded. 'Give the prisoners a warning to be on their best behaviour. I will be bringing the lady down for a tour of the dungeon.'

The guard frowned and looked again at Aldara. 'A tour, my lord? Of… the dungeon?' He glanced behind him.

Felipe looked at Aldara, waiting for her to confirm her wishes.

'I am ready when you are, my lord.' She felt a tremble take over her body. Soon she would lay eyes on him.

The guard shifted his weight from one foot to another. 'Give me a moment, my lord.' He turned and descended the steps. When he got to the bottom, he removed the crossbar and walked inside.

Blood pounded in her ears at the sound of steel hitting iron. 'What is he doing?'

Felipe gazed down the long hole. 'He is just reminding them of their manners. It has been a long time since they will have seen a woman like you.'

She faced him. 'A woman like me?'

He leaned close to her ear. 'A beautiful woman, hand-crafted by God.'

The feel of his breath made her stomach knot. Luckily, the guard came back up the steps, stopping halfway and nodding in their direction. 'Whenever you are ready, my lord.'

It was not until they reached the bottom, and the dark corridor stretched out in front of them, that Aldara realised Tyron might not be able to hide his own shock, or control his reaction in front of the prince. Perhaps he would think his mind was playing tricks on him once again. What she was about to do was brutal.

Her eyes wandered to the ring of keys hanging by the door. Below them was a ledge where the mace sat next to a lantern, a jar of water and a wooden cup. The guard moved aside to let them pass, and Felipe grabbed the mace and signalled for Aldara to follow him into the cool walkway, a solid wall on one side and cells lining the other. Aldara followed him, her hands damp with nerves. The first two cells were empty, nothing but mould-covered mattresses and dark corners. In the third cell a man stood, hands clutching the bars. One strike of the mace against the iron had him stepping back.

'There are six cells,' Felipe said. 'Prisoners range from petty thieves to murderers.'

And Tyron.

In the fourth cell, an older man lay on a mattress, eyes staring at the wall opposite. He did not even glance in their direction.

'What are they fed?' Aldara asked, looking at the untouched grey muck next to the man.

Felipe walked slowly so she could look about. 'Nothing appetising.'

Aldara winced behind him. 'How long have these men been here?'

The fifth cell held a boy close to her own age. He stood back from the bars, arms crossed and starved eyes following her.

'It varies depending on the prisoner. Some of these men have been here a few weeks, awaiting their sentence.'

They passed the fifth cell where a large man lay asleep on the mattress, his limbs hanging over the edges. There were six cells in all, and they had now passed five of them.

'Then there is our Syrasan prince,' Felipe said, stopping in front of the next cell. 'He has been here much longer.'

Aldara stopped next to him, a ringing sound in her ears. A man sat on the mattress with his knees pulled up and wrists resting on them. His eyes were open, staring at the hole above him where light filtered through, casting an eerie glow. She barely recognised him beneath the facial hair. Had Felipe asked her something? She hoped not because she had stopped listening.

'And how long will he be here?' she thought she asked.

Tyron's head turned at the sound of her voice and his green

eyes locked on hers. His body went rigid, as if he were about to move, but the smallest shake of her head stopped him. She turned her attention to Felipe, who was watching Tyron.

'Until we get what we want,' Felipe replied. 'Isn't that right, Prince Tyron?'

～

HIS BURNING EYES went to Felipe, but he did not answer him. It was safer if he did not speak. He blinked hard, hoping she would disappear, that his mind was just being cruel like it had many times before. His gaze returned to her. She stood still as she conversed with the prince, looking so small next to him. She was not dressed in peasant attire like the last time he had seen her, but as something more—something he could not fathom.

What was she doing with that man?

He did not know whether to drink in the vision of her or cover his eyes against it. A strange energy coursed through him. He suspected that if he ran to the bars, he might have the strength to separate them.

Perhaps it was his imagination, but he could have sworn she moved closer to that man. What was happening? He had finally lost his mind and there was no coming back this time.

'And… what is it you want?' she asked Felipe, standing much too close.

When the prince looked at her, there was something in his expression that made Tyron want to get to his feet and reach through those bars for him.

'It is rather simple, Medea.' He reached up and touched her hair. 'I just want what is mine.'

Medea. He had called her Medea. Then he touched her. And she let him.

'Have you seen enough?' Felipe asked her. 'I can show you inside one of the empty cells if you like?'

She smiled up at him. *Smiled.*

'And risk you locking the door behind me? I think I have seen enough.'

The prisoner in the third cell called out to Felipe, demanding something. While the prince was distracted, Aldara's eyes returned to Tyron, moving over him. The only thing that stopped Tyron from getting to his feet and going to her was the possibility of putting her in further danger.

'Let's get you out of here,' Felipe said, gesturing for her to walk in front of him.

What have you done? Tyron's mind raced with possibilities.

The guard had stepped into the corridor, shouting at the prisoner to be quiet. Tyron watched Aldara flinch at the noise as she turned to walk away. He saw it then, for the first time since laying eyes on her. Fear.

Aldara did not look at him again. She was smart enough to know she could not hide herself that well.

The prince walked behind her, his gaze at a height that made Tyron's fists clench a little tighter.

And then she was gone.

Only when the heavy door creaked closed and locked in place did he get to his feet, hands going into his hair, gripping it tightly. He went to the bars and pressed his forehead against them, testing their strength while trying to make sense of what was happening. He had coped until that point, with only himself to worry about. To include her, to let her in, to worry about her to the point of insanity would break him. Now he would be forced to strangle the first man who came within arm's reach, take his weapon, and storm the castle, killing every living thing that stood between them. Surely she knew that, that her coming to Masville would strip him of his ability to act rationally.

He paced along the bars like a penned dog, teeth pressing together and eyes closed as he tried to organise his thoughts. She had done this, heard of what had happened, waited, hopeful of a resolution. He knew how it felt to wait, the helplessness. So she had made a plan to get him out, left her son, her home, her safe place, because doing nothing was not an option. He knew that, but was still so angry at her, and angry at himself for getting captured and forcing her to act so stupidly.

Tyron took a deep, ragged breath and sank to the ground, his back against the bars.

Half an hour after Aldara had left, he was sitting in the same spot, staring at the wall opposite, when he heard a tapping noise, like something hitting the floor. His eyes went to a tiny cream dot in the far corner. He stood and walked over to it, scooping it up and exploring it with his fingers. It was a long ribbon of parchment, torn from a larger piece. When he unfolded it, he saw that it was a note in Aldara's handwriting.

I AM GETTING YOU OUT. *Do nothing but trust me.*

HE SCREWED it up until it was as dense as a pebble in his hand and shoved it into the pocket of his trousers before turning his face up to the window.

'Damn it.'

CHAPTER 22

When Aldara arrived back at the rooms, she was surprised to find Nyla seated in an armchair in front of the unlit fireplace with a book open in her lap.

'Where have you been?' Nyla asked, looking up.

She had returned with Prince Felipe half an hour earlier, but after searching the rooms and discovering no one was there, she had seized the opportunity to write Tyron a short note. Moving fast, hands shaking with the fear of being caught, she had run to the table and written a few words along the bottom of a piece of parchment she had been writing on earlier that morning. Tearing it off and blowing furiously, willing the ink to dry faster, she had gone to the door and peered outside, ensuring the corridor was clear before leaving. She had then gone outside and made her way to the west wall, tossing the note through the last window, into the pit beneath her feet where Tyron would be frantic, pacing and unforgiving.

'With Prince Felipe' was all she said, taking the seat opposite her. With only two Companions, there was no competition for prime positions. 'What are you reading?'

Nyla held it up so she could see the cover.

'A Tale of Deceit,' Aldara read aloud.

Nyla dropped the book back onto her lap but continued to look at Aldara.

'What's the matter?' Aldara asked, trying to read her expression.

Nyla shook her head. 'You read rather well for someone who has been learning for just a few weeks.'

Aldara kept her face neutral. 'Well, I have excellent teachers. How long did it take you before you could read difficult books like that one?'

'I have been here a year, but I read slowly in comparison to someone like Petra who has been reading for years.' She pushed her long brown hair back from her eyes. 'Prince Kyril does not care much for books. He prefers songs.'

Aldara smiled at her. 'Songs sung by you?'

'Of course.'

There was a naivety about her that reminded Aldara of Hali. 'Prince Kyril could not keep his eyes off you at the tournament. How did the two of you meet?'

Nyla leaned back in her chair, welcoming the memory. 'At the tournament a year ago. It was the first year I had attended. My family is from Nedola, on the coast. It was an extravagant trip for a potter and his family.'

'Your father was a potter?'

Nyla glanced at the door. 'We are not meant to discuss our previous life.' She looked back down at her book.

Aldara leaned back in her own chair. They had the same rules at Masville as they did at Archdale. 'Of course. I suppose it will take me a while to get used to the rules.' She paused. 'Is Petra quite strict with their enforcement?'

'That all depends on her mood,' Nyla said, raising her eyes again.

Aldara frowned. 'What do you mean by that?'

She glanced again at the door. 'There are days where she will tear through you for mispronouncing a word, and then there are days when she does not have it in her to do anything at all.' She lowered her voice and leaned forwards in her chair. 'There was one day she did not get out of bed even once. The king requested an audience and she did not even *try* to get up.'

'Was she ill?'

Nyla shook her head. 'The king sent a physician to examine her, and he found nothing physically wrong with her.' She settled back. 'The next day she got up and carried on like nothing had happened.'

Aldara thought of Tyron, who had suffered in the same way. 'Perhaps she just needed a day of rest.' She looked at the dead fireplace.

'Or perhaps she did not want to meet with the king,' Nyla said, pressing her lips together after the words escaped her.

Aldara studied her for a moment, watching the conflict play out on her face. 'Why would she not want to meet with the king?'

Nyla hesitated. 'Because King Nilos has an… odd obsession with her.' Her voice had dropped to a whisper. 'He still beds her despite her position. It is the worst-kept secret in the castle. She is likely with him right now.'

Aldara felt like there was a weight pressing down on her chest. 'And does she welcome his… affections?'

Nyla shook her head and resumed reading. 'Not from what I have observed.'

It was likely that Nyla did not know about the son they shared, the child that had been taken from his grieving mother. She could not blame Petra for rejecting the man responsible.

Before another word could be spoken, Petra walked in, looking frail and slightly dishevelled. She said nothing as she passed the girls and disappeared through the other door, emerging only when the evening meal arrived. Her hair was damp, and she had put on a long-sleeve dress despite the rare balmy temperature for that time of year. The reason became evident when Petra reached for a piece for bread. The sleeve of her dress slid up her arm as she extended it, revealing purple bruising on her wrist.

'What happened to your arm?' Aldara asked, not taking her eyes from it.

Petra withdrew her hand and placed it in her lap. 'That is none of your business.' Her expression matched her cold tone. 'Eat your food and remember your place,' she added, quieter this time.

Nyla looked between them and then at her plate.

Aldara slid the bread across the table so it was in front of Petra. 'Yes, my lady.'

CHAPTER 23

*I*f she was to have any success escaping, Aldara needed to venture farther than the garderobe. So during her second month at Masville Castle, when she was walking with Prince Felipe, his arm brushing against hers, she raised the topic with him.

'It would be nice to bring a book outdoors and feel the sun on my skin before the cold season arrives.'

It had been seven days since she had seen Tyron, and the only thing progressing was her comprehension of Braul, a language that had not been taught at Archdale.

Prince Felipe looked across at her. 'I will have a word to Petra, though I am not sure you should be wandering about outdoors without a chaperone.'

She looked up at him. 'Why not? There are more guards than servants at Masville.'

He stopped walking and took hold of her arm. 'Exactly. And they will all be looking at you.'

She tried to hide her surprise at the comment hinting at jealousy and struggled to think of an appropriate response. 'I imagine the guards have far more important things to do.'

His grip on her arm tightened, just enough to wipe the smile from her face.

'I thought you would know better of men after being raped in your village. That is what you claimed, was it not?'

Aldara could no longer hide the shock on her face. She glanced down at his fingers gripping her arm. 'My lord, you are hurting me.'

He let go of her arm but neither of them moved. 'It is all right. I do not blame you for what happened.'

She took in his expression and body language, which contradicted his words. 'Why *would* you blame me?'

He tilted his head as if it were a ridiculous question. 'Come on now. You know how women are, leading a man on and then making a fuss when he follows through on her wishes.'

She lowered her eyes. It was the first time she could not make herself look at him. 'You think women make a fuss about… rape?'

He took hold of her shoulders, gentle this time. 'I am simply saying that the term is thrown around.' He was quiet for a moment before adding, 'I do hope the culprit was caught and the punishment just.'

The answer was no. She had been a Companion doing her role. And yet it had taken her weeks to recover from the injuries she sustained at the hands of the Zoelin men she had been handed to.

She raised her eyes to him. 'Yes. Thank you for your concern.'

But there was no concern, just an empty sentiment. As she looked at him, her stomach curled with the realisation that he intended to kiss her. She was forced to stand there as he brought his thin lips to hers, parting his mouth just enough for her to taste onion on his breath. She closed her eyes, keeping her body soft but letting her mind go wherever it needed to so she would not pull back from him. When he finally released her, he ran his thumb over her lips, his eyes hungry. She took a step back, pretending to catch her breath while trying very hard not to wipe at her mouth.

'Come. I will return you to your quarters before I am undone by you.'

She smiled and took his arm. 'A very responsible suggestion, my lord.'

They walked together, Felipe talking and Aldara trying to process her feelings of repulsion at what had taken place between them.

That afternoon, Petra told her that she was free to do her reading outdoors if she wished to. At least something good had come of her morning with Felipe. Aldara collected a book, and as she was passing through the main room, she grabbed a bread roll and a piece of salted pork from the table where they had just eaten and put it in her pocket. She walked outside, heading west along the castle wall until the six holes came into sight. She pulled out the roll and pork and made a hole in the bread so she could stuff the meat inside. As she reached the final window, she crouched to brush invisible grass off her shoe and simultaneously pushed the roll between the bars.

Leaving him was difficult. The temptation to call to him, hear his voice, a cough, anything, was painfully overwhelming. But with her expression neutral, she left, walking a full circle back to the east side of the castle where there were trees for shade and the air did not smell of human waste. She sat down, leaning against the trunk of a tree of a tall oak, pretending to read.

She studied the guards and servants, observing their routines. She watched the men on the north wall, counting them, noting the weapons they carried and the attention they paid to their surroundings. There were really only two ways out of Masville: over the wall or through the entrance where they could become trapped between the two portcullises and shot down by invisible men while unable to defend themselves.

She turned a page of her book before letting her eyes return to the wall where guards wandered between the turrets, often in pairs. From what she could see, there were only ever four men keeping watch at one time. She guessed the situation was similar on each wall, but she was going to need to know for sure before attempting anything.

When the air cooled and the sun had disappeared behind the castle, offering light to Tyron on the other side, she got up and made her way back to the small door. As she passed the laundry, Velma appeared in the doorway and called to her. She stopped and looked at the laundry maid.

'I have some mending for you to take up,' Velma said, indicating for Aldara to come into the laundry.

Aldara followed, passing another maid who was heating an iron on the stove. When they reached the far side of the room, Velma handed her a basket with some garments in it, lifting the top one to reveal a letter underneath. Aldara took the basket. 'Thank you.'

The maid nodded. 'I have to get the linen inside before it gets damp.' She stepped past Aldara and exited the room.

Aldara's eyes went to the table where the folded laundry sat in neat piles. At the end was a guard's tunic, no doubt waiting for a button to be sewed on. She looked at the other maid, still busy at the stove, and walked towards the door, slipping the tunic into the basket and snatching a pillow cover off the top of the linen pile as she passed the table. Someone was going to get into trouble for misplacing it, but she tried not to think about that, as there was only so much guilt she could carry at one time.

On her way back, Aldara stopped at the garderobe to read the letter.

A

Your son is in good health. Focus and be patient with the process. I have complete faith in you.

L

ALDARA HELD the letter to her chest for a moment before tearing it up and watching the pieces float down into the dark hole. After washing her hands, she stuffed the tunic into the pillow cover she had stolen and hid it beneath the garments. Picking up the basket, she made her way back to the Companions' quarters.

As there was no one in the main room when she arrived, she went straight through to the bedchamber to hide the tunic beneath her bed. When she entered the room, the first thing she noticed was that the linens had been stripped, a task she had always been responsible for herself. Her heart quickened and she dropped the basket on the ground, immediately going in search of the dagger she kept tucked inside the bottom sheet of her bed. It was not there. She got down on her hands and knees and began feeling around underneath in case it had dropped down.

'Are you looking for this?'

Aldara looked up to see Petra standing in the doorway, holding her dagger. She felt the blood drain from her face as she took in her mentor's stern expression.

'Did you bring a weapon into the castle with you?'

Aldara's eyes remained on the small dagger. 'Yes,' she whispered.

'Yes?' Petra's eyes widened. 'You admit to this?'

'I can hardly deny it.'

Petra's gaze burned through her. 'Do you care to explain yourself to me before I call the guards, or would you rather explain directly to Prince Felipe?'

Aldara looked up at that. She could not tell the truth, but she also knew Petra would see through any lies. 'I did not know what I was coming into, and I did not want to be left vulnerable again.'

Petra's shoulders fell, just a little. 'And who did you plan on stabbing with this?'

'Hopefully nobody,' she answered honestly. 'I just wanted to be able to protect myself if the need arose. My experience is that not all men can be trusted.'

Petra lowered the dagger. 'You are admitting to me that you would use this on King Nilos's men, or on a family member perhaps, if you felt threatened?'

Aldara glanced again at the dagger. 'It does not matter who the men are loyal to or whether they are of noble birth. They are still men.'

'Your words are treasonous.' Petra shook her head. 'I am required to report this to King Nilos.'

Aldara watched the conflict play out on her face, hopeful her mentor would sympathise with her need to feel safe. 'I understand that you have obligations. I certainly never intended to make trouble for you. Rest assured, the dagger has not moved from that spot since I arrived here.'

Petra looked down at the weapon in her hand. 'You are lucky it was me who took the linen off your bed.'

Aldara was also thankful she had chosen to hide the poisons in the dressing room. 'I am sorry to have put you in this situation, my lady.'

'Companions do not carry weapons, Medea.' Her voice was soft.

Aldara swallowed. 'Why does every man in this castle carry a sword and women carry only their skirts?'

Petra turned the dagger over in her hand, studying it, before walking over to the bed and dropping it on the mattress. 'Get rid of it.' She looked at Aldara. 'If I find it again, I will take it straight to Prince Felipe.' She left the room without another word.

Aldara let out a shaky breath and picked up the weapon, stashing it in the basket before Nyla walked in and saw it. She pressed her hands against her pounding chest.

She needed to get Tyron out before it all fell apart.

CHAPTER 24

*J*ust when Tyron thought he could not be angrier at Aldara, she put herself at risk by bringing him food. When the bread roll landed in the middle of the floor, he had no choice but to eat it or risk the guards discovering it later when they brought their own version of food. He tore off pieces of the bread, surprised to discover meat stuffed inside. As much as he wanted to hold on to that anger, it fell away as he chewed, the salty meat falling apart in his mouth, the thick crust of the bread making his eyes close.

After he finished eating, he had to admit that it was the closest he had felt to satisfied in weeks. He had no idea what Aldara's plan was, but he knew it was going to require more strength than what the gruel provided. Whatever crazy plan she was concocting, he wanted to be ready.

He was preparing himself for exercise when he recognised the sound of the crossbar being lifted from the door at the end of the corridor. He could tell by the light in his cell that it was too early for food to be brought in. He stilled and listened as footsteps marched in his direction. Two guards stopped outside of his cell. One sifted through the ring of keys while the other stared at Tyron, a warning in his eyes and shackles in his hand.

'His Majesty wants to speak with you. No funny business now.'

Tyron said nothing as they entered his cell and grabbed him, securing the shackles around his wrists. Holding one arm each, they shoved him along the corridor, through the door and up the narrow stairs in single file. Tyron was relieved when they stepped out into the wide corridor with open windows and clean air. He took greedy breaths, like a dog trying to pick up a scent.

Where was she? It did not matter because he could not reach her.

He walked between the men, compliant and quietly observing his surroundings, his hands chinking with each movement. Maids and servants scattered like mice in front of them. He wondered how threatening he looked in his current state, certain that if a mirror were held in front of him, he would not recognise the man reflected.

'Keep moving,' said one guard, pushing him forwards.

Apparently he had slowed. Perhaps he was dragging his feet because he wanted so badly to see her. But then what? No, he did not want to see her.

He did not trust his reaction.

PETRA APPEARED in the doorway of the bedchamber. 'Come with me.'

Aldara stood up from the bed where she had been reading and followed her into the dressing room. Petra picked up a gown laid out on the armchair and held it up. It was orange silk with a plunging neckline and lace sleeves.

'Put this on,' Petra said. 'And then we are going to paint your face.'

Aldara stared at the dress. 'Where am I going?'

The mentor lay the dress back over the chair and stepped closer to Aldara, unbuttoning her dress as if she were a child. 'Prince Felipe has requested an audience with you and King Nilos.'

Aldara stared at her. 'Why?'

Petra's gaze remained on the buttons. 'There are some important guests arriving in a few days, and Prince Felipe wants you with him while he is entertaining. He requires the king's approval, so we need to prove that you are ready.'

Aldara took hold of Petra's hands. 'But it has not been three months.'

The mentor pulled her hands free and stared at Aldara with empty eyes. 'In case you have not figured it out yet, they make the rules up as they go.' Her gaze fell and returned to the buttons.

'I'm not ready,' Aldara whispered, trying to keep the plea from her voice. 'I can barely write a sentence.'

Petra glanced up. 'Prince Felipe does not care about your handwriting. He wants to show you off. Your social skills are of a high standard for a new Companion, and that is all that matters for a woman on display.'

She had failed at appearing new and raw, her language too advanced for a farmer. Aldara took hold of Petra's hands again and waited for her to look up. 'He can parade me all he likes, but I am not ready to share his bed. I just need a bit more time before…' Her heart was racing at the thought of what all this meant.

Petra gestured for her to step out of the dress. 'And your undergarments.' She went to collect the other garment off the chair and held it open for her to step into.

Aldara balanced on weakening legs as the dress slid up

her bare skin. The cool evening air prickled the exposed areas as a purple belt was fastened beneath her breasts, a trick she remembered from Archdale, designed to give them a fuller appearance. She glanced down, noticing the neckline reached all the way to her navel.

'Sit down. I will paint your face.' Petra did not meet her eyes.

Aldara sat and stared at the miserable image reflected back at her. She thought of Tyron caged beneath her, hungry and soon to freeze with the change in weather, while she lay with Prince Felipe in his warm bed. She had come to Corneo to free him. Where was that sharp mind and cunning plan everyone was relying on?

'Close your eyes,' Petra said.

Aldara was grateful for the instruction. She could no longer look at herself, instead thinking about Mako, safe and happy at home with his uncle and grandparents while his mother did unspeakable things.

'Open,' Petra said, thickening her lashes with a paste made from tea leaves. She finished with some colour on her cheeks and a thick coat of paint on her lips. 'Done.' She stood back to admire her work.

Aldara stared again at the mirror. Yes, there was beauty, but it was not her own.

'Come,' Petra said, gesturing for her to stand. 'They are waiting.'

She walked alongside her mentor down the long corridor towards the throne room. When they stopped outside the large doors, Petra raised her chin and said to the guard, 'Tell His Majesty and Prince Felipe that I have brought the new Companion to see them.'

'He is with someone,' the guard replied. 'Wait over there.' He pointed to the wall on the other side of the corridor.

The women stepped back to the wall and waited.

~

KING NILOS ASKED Tyron the same questions and made the same demands he always did, expecting a different response.

'We have been very patient with King Pandarus, giving him time to come to his senses as he is new to the role.'

'King Pandarus has been handling relations with neighbouring kingdoms for almost ten years. And as I have told you each time you have brought me here, my brother will not withdraw his men from the West for any man, blood-related or otherwise.'

The king glanced at his son, who stood beside his chair. 'It seems you are right. He does not value your life.'

Tyron was also looking at Prince Felipe, standing with his arms crossed in an overdecorated tunic. There was something about his smug expression that made Tyron want to wrap the shackles about his neck and squeeze. He was well aware of the fact that those thoughts had come about since seeing him with Aldara in the dungeon. 'King Pandarus will always put the needs of the kingdom before all else. That is what great kings do.'

King Nilos picked through a plate of preserved foods sitting on the table in front of him, selecting a black olive and tossing it into his mouth. He chewed it as though it were a fistful of toughened meat. 'He has been the king for five minutes and will soon lose the respect of his people when they learn of your death. It seems you are well liked in your kingdom.' He swallowed. 'I thought you would like to know that I am sending him a letter advising him of the date of your execution.'

Tyron watched as he reached for another olive. 'And what date is that?'

'Your king has one week.' He chewed for a moment. 'One week to get his men out of Corneo. If I discover so much as one Syrasan man in my kingdom at the end of the seven days, you die.'

'I understand that most of the region is loyal to Lord Belen. Even if you remove our men, your own people are prepared to fight against you.'

Prince Felipe spoke up at that. 'Our people in the West do not want to fight. What they want is food.'

'They have food. It is you who wants food. That is why you steal theirs.'

Felipe's eyes darkened and his jaw clenched. Tyron knew it was the wrong thing to say to the men who had all the power in that moment, and yet the satisfaction he felt was enormous.

King Nilos just laughed from his belly. 'And who told you that? Lord Belen? He's an old fool.' He picked up a small onion and popped it into his mouth. 'Let us wait and see what that brother of yours does now.'

Tyron shook his head. 'My brother will be saddened by my death, but he will not hand you the West to prevent it.'

Felipe shifted his weight and glared at Tyron. 'We are not playing games here. After we remove your head, we will take the land back anyway. Are you sure you do not wish to write to your brother and *beg* for your life?'

Another shake of his head. 'As I already said, it will do no good.'

King Nilos waved his hand. 'Take him away.'

The guards turned him round and pulled him towards the doors, which were already opening in front of them. Tyron looked through them and saw Aldara standing against the wall on the other side. She was staring off down the corridor, her thumb tapping on her other hand. It was a nervous habit of hers, one he remembered well.

She turned towards the open doors and stiffened at the sight of him. He should have looked away, but for a moment, the sight of her numbed every logical thought. Her dress reminded him of the one she had worn for him the night he had returned from the Zoelin border—sheer, revealing, and not for the eyes of another man. Especially not for Felipe. Her face was painted and her hair slicked into a prison-like knot, a far cry from the golden waves he had bathed in a few months earlier. He had not realised he had stopped walking until one of the guards yanked on his arm. Instinctively, he pulled himself free from the hand, his strength surprising the man. Aldara just watched, looking helpless and afraid for him.

'Is there a problem?' Felipe called from behind.

Tyron was not sure if he could walk away from her in that moment, but her expression was pleading with him.

The guards took a firmer hold of him, and when they tugged on him this time, he began to walk, his gaze dropping to the floor as he passed her. He did not trust himself to look up again, but he felt her eyes on him as he rounded the corner and walked away.

I am getting you out. Do nothing and trust me, she had written.

She had one week.

WHATEVER ALDARA HAD BEEN EXPECTING to see when those doors opened, it had not been Tyron. His unkempt appearance and wasting body made him barely recognisable. Only his eyes were familiar, finding her through the long hair that covered them. She had looked down at his filthy clothes and ghostly hands and felt panic rise inside of her at the realisation he would die in this place if she did not do something soon.

When he had pulled free of the guard, she had braced for

something brutal, something tragic. The encounter had caught them both by surprise, and she was afraid they would not be able to recover from the shock. But he had sensed what she needed from him and had found the strength to walk away.

'Medea,' Petra said next to her. 'Are you all right?'

Aldara needed to behave like the name belonged to her. 'Yes, I am fine,' she said, giving the puzzled mentor a reassuring smile. 'I just wasn't expecting to encounter a prisoner when the doors opened.'

'I apologise for that,' Prince Felipe said, walking out to meet them. His eyes swept down Aldara, drinking in the sight of her, slowing at each curve and inch of exposed flesh. 'Come in.'

They followed him into the throne room where King Nilos stood, eyes on Petra.

'Your Majesty,' said the women, curtsying in unison.

The king waited for them to rise before speaking. 'My son tells me the new Companion is ready for socialising,' he said, addressing Petra as if Aldara was not standing there.

'She has come a long way in the few months she has been here, Your Majesty.'

The king looked at Aldara for the first time, his expression sceptical. 'And what talents have you uncovered?'

'Not much so far as art forms, but socially she is doing splendidly. She is reading well and has picked up new languages with surprising ease.'

'Zoelin?'

'Yes, Your Majesty.'

King Nilos nodded, seemingly unimpressed. 'But she does not sing or dance?'

'She dances well enough for social purposes.'

'Which is all that would be required of her,' Felipe added.

His father turned to look at him. 'Well enough? Is that

what we are settling for nowadays? Our guests should be seeing the finest women in our kingdom, not the adequate ones.'

Felipe glanced at Aldara. 'I have spent enough time with her to know she is ready to entertain. We are going to need more than one Companion.'

'Petra will also join us.'

Judging by Petra's face, this was news to her. 'Your Majesty?'

'You heard my son. We are going to need more than one Companion.'

When Petra did not reply, the king's gaze returned to Aldara. She tried not to squirm beneath it.

'I suspect my son is keen to have you ready for more than simply entertaining our guests,' he said, making everyone uncomfortable. 'He convinced me to purchase you, and a few days later his own Companion vanishes from the castle— sent south, I believe.'

Felipe raised a hand. 'To a noble household in need of a governess, as was my plan for some time.'

No one believed him.

'She fetched a poor price,' King Nilos continued. 'Not long introduced and then gone. No wonder these women have no worth anymore.' He looked at Petra when he said that. 'If her mentor believes she is ready, then that is enough for me. She is the mentor, after all.'

Both Aldara and Felipe looked at Petra, each hoping for a different answer. The mentor's gaze was fixed on the king.

'She is ready for socialising, Your Majesty. However, we are yet to start her on the necessary herbs required for other aspects of her role, so I am afraid she will not be ready for anything beyond that for a few more weeks.'

'What do you mean?' Felipe snapped, comprehending perfectly. 'Why has she not started on the herbs?'

Petra turned her cool gaze to him. 'Because I have been instructed to have the women ready for introduction in three months. The herbs can sometimes make the women sick initially, so I tend to wait until they are settled in, sleeping well, and lessons underway before introducing them.'

Felipe shook his head, visibly disappointed. 'Well from now on all new Companions are to start the herbs the second they enter through that gate. Do you understand?' Then realising how that sounded, he added, 'I am referring of course to when my father selects a new Companion.'

'Of course,' Aldara replied, speaking up for the first time. When Petra glanced at her, she could have sworn there was amusement in her eyes.

'You heard her,' King Nilos said, laughter in his tone. 'Keep it in your pants for a few more weeks.' He looked at Aldara. 'I hope you are not weak-stomached.'

'In what sense, Your Majesty?'

'We have a public execution coming up, and my son will likely want you to attend.'

As soon as the king spoke the words, she knew he was talking about Tyron. 'Who is being executed?' She tried to keep her voice steady.

'King Pandarus has seven days to get his men out of Corneo before we execute Prince Tyron,' Felipe said, casting a disapproving stare at his father for bringing it up. 'You do not need to worry about Medea being weak-stomached. She is fearless.'

No. She was terrified.

'I am not sure that one horse race is an accurate indication of one's sensibilities,' Petra said.

The king nodded in agreement. 'In my experience, most women can handle a hanging, but not a beheading. It is too messy.'

Aldara's face went numb and her vision blurred for a

moment. She took in a breath and tried to focus on the conversation still going on around her. Then Petra curtsied because the conversation had ended. Aldara curtsied also, trying not to go all the way to the floor. 'Your Majesty. My lord,' she thought she said.

Felipe came into focus, still looking disappointed. She smiled at him before turning away. At least she hoped she did.

They walked through the open doors and listened as they closed behind them. As soon as they turned the corner, Aldara glanced across at Petra.

'Thank you,' she whispered.

Petra did not reply.

CHAPTER 25

*T*he next day, Aldara stood at the window in the corridor outside the Companions' quarters, staring out at the eastern wall. Always the same, men in pairs, gazes cast outwards, ready. No one thought to look behind them. Four guards on the eastern wall, plus guards below, moving between duties or simply sitting at the bottom of steps resting weary limbs. She guessed at the height of the wall. Thirty feet? She wondered how far a person could drop without hurting themselves. Ten feet? She had spent much of her youth climbing trees with Kadmus, and they had both jumped and fallen from heights of at least that without breaking anything. She closed her eyes, frustrated. Where was she supposed to get rope from?

Finished with the morning's lessons, she was free to go for a walk, read a book, or practice an instrument of her choice. But none of those things helped her get Tyron out. She thought about all the people back in Syrasan counting on her to save their prince from execution. She was failing, and the weight of that failure only rendered her more useless. Paralysed by fear, she had no viable plan, only fleeting ideas.

There was no Hali or Sapphira to conspire with, nowhere to draw strength.

Not true. There was Tyron, but she could not get to him. If she could just be alone with him for a moment, he would centre her, allow her to take what she needed from him.

She wondered how she might lure the guard on duty away long enough to get to him, then remembered the jar of water that sat on the ledge near the keys. Was she brave enough to poison a man just to see Tyron for a few minutes?

Heart beating faster, she walked back into the rooms. Nyla was taking a lie down and Petra had gone to meet with the king. She went to the dressing room and found the bag of poisons stashed inside a boot that had belonged to Calista. Aldara had heard Petra mention the former Companion's unusually small feet and had hidden the poisons there after her departure, knowing they would not be worn by anyone else.

Checking her surroundings, she removed the bag and took out the atropa belladonna, slipping it up her sleeve before shoving the bag deep into the boot. She glanced at the mirror, catching her wild expression. Just a few drops to make him sick. She did not want to kill anyone.

Once she had collected herself, she grabbed a book from the shelf in the main room and left, heading along the corridor towards the west wing of the castle where the dungeon was. When she arrived, she looked down the narrow stairs at the guard sitting on a stool at the bottom, scratching dried mud from the bottom of his boot with his dagger. She descended the steps towards him.

Hearing her approach, he looked up and got to his feet, narrowing his eyes. 'You cannot be down here, miss.'

She saw that it was a different guard from her previous visit. 'Forgive the interruption,' she said, smiling up at him as she arrived at the bottom. 'Prince Felipe brought me for a tour of the dungeon a few weeks back, and I suspect I dropped a rather expensive gold pin inside.' She glanced at the locked door.

'Prince Felipe took you on a tour of the dungeon?' he asked, his tone thick with scepticism.

'Yes, it was fascinating.' She touched her collarbone as she spoke. 'I have a newfound appreciation for what the king's guards do to keep us safe from criminals.'

He straightened, despite his own lowly contribution. 'No one has found a pin.'

'I am not surprised,' she said, stepping closer. 'There is barely any light down there, and it is the smallest of pins.'

He exhaled. 'Then assume it lost, as I can't let you in there.'

She laughed. 'I have no intention of going in there a second time. I thought you might check on my behalf.' When he did not move, she added, 'Prince Felipe would be so grateful if you could assist me.'

He studied her. 'Does Prince Felipe know you are here?'

She looked down. 'No. The pin was a gift from his lordship, and I was hoping to retrieve it without him discovering I had lost such an expensive item.'

The guard shook his head. 'A gold pin, you say?'

'Yes, half the length of my little finger.' She held her hand out to him, palm up.

He glanced down at the open hand and swallowed before stepping back from it. 'Do not move from that spot,' he said, pointing at her feet.

A smile spread across her face. 'I will wait right here for you.'

He lifted the crossbar, took the lantern from the ledge, and pulled the door open before stepping inside. He walked slowly along the corridor, holding the lantern close to the ground as he searched. She shook the poison from her sleeve, holding it behind her back as she tried to open it while keeping hold of her book. With her eyes on the guard, she stepped up to the ledge and carefully tipped a few drops straight into the cup, fearing the water in the jar would be shared with the prisoners.

She stepped back to her original position, hands behind her back, trying to put the cork in place. The book fell from her hand and the guard spun around to look at her. She stuffed the cork into the small jar and slipped it back up her sleeve before reaching down to get it. Only after she held the book up to show him the source of the noise did the guard turn and resume his search. A few minutes later, he marched back towards her, ignoring a prisoner who shouted as he passed.

'No luck?' she asked as he stepped out and closed the door behind him.

He returned the lamp to the ledge and shook his head. 'If you dropped it in there, it's not there anymore.'

She lowered her head, feigning disappointment. 'I see. Thank you so much for checking.' She turned and walked back up the steps, aware of his eyes on her as she walked. Only once she had reached the top did she hear him slump back down on to the stool.

As she headed along the corridor, it occurred to her that it could be some time until the guard had a drink, or maybe he would not drink at all—perhaps none of them did.

She passed the laundry and stepped out into the sun, making her way to her usual spot beneath the oak where she also happened to have a line of sight to the outhouse used by the guards. For two hours she sat pretending to read, watching the casual comings and goings of men in uniform, none of them familiar or in a rush. Finally, she was forced to give up. She knew if she did not return soon, Petra would come looking for her, and she could not risk losing the small amount of freedom she had.

Disappointed, she stood and brushed the grass off her dress before walking back across the lawn. As she stepped inside, the guard from earlier almost collided with her in the doorway. His pale face was covered in sweat and he all but pushed past her. She paused in the doorway and looked over her shoulder as he leaned on his knees and vomited on the grass. She waited for a moment to see what he would do. With a hand over his mouth, he continued towards the outhouse.

Aldara turned and headed for the dungeon, the book pressed against her chest, trying not to rush despite the strong urge to do so. When she arrived at the narrow steps, she peered down to ensure the guard had not been replaced, then checked the corridor. If she was caught, she would say that she came to look for her brooch and no one had been there to help. It was not a great story, but it was something.

Her breathing was shallow as she descended the stairs. When she reached the bottom, she saw that the guard had taken the keys with him. Glancing once up the stairwell, she placed the book on the stool and lifted the crossbar, surprised by the weight of it. She stood it up in the corner as she had seen the guard do earlier and pulled the door open, remembering to grab the book before stepping into the dark and tugging the door behind her so it would appear closed from above.

She rushed straight past the first five cells, not giving the other prisoners a chance to see her properly. When she reached the sixth, her eyes searched for him through the darkness. She found him standing with his back against the wall, his eyes on the window above.

'Tyron,' she whispered. The book fell to her feet and she gripped the iron bars.

His head snapped in her direction, eyes wide. She reached through the gaps for him. In a few strides he stood just out of arm's reach, his eyes searching for the guard.

'We don't have much time,' she said, needing to touch him.

Once he realised that she was alone, he stepped up to her, reaching through the bars and taking hold of her face. He bent to her height. 'I am so angry at you,' he whispered, his voice breaking with emotion. 'You need to get out of here.'

Tears spilled down her face, and she could not find any words.

'Did you hear me?'

He was telling her he was angry, and yet his hands told another story. She leaned into his palm, letting her tears fall on him.

'What were you thinking coming here?' He drew in a breath, his thumb wiping at her tears.

'I need your help,' she whispered, a sob escaping her.

His hands went around her, pulling her as close as he could with iron separating them. 'What is it?' His lips pressed against her hair. 'Tell me.'

She wrapped her small hands around his large ones. 'It was all planned, everything. Pandarus, your mother, Stamitos, Leksi—they all helped.'

He pulled back so he could look at her while he digested the words.

'I thought getting in here was the hard part, but now I don't know how to get you out.'

His hand went into her hair and he brought her close enough to kiss her again. 'Can you get yourself out?'

She reached through the bars and fisted his filthy shirt. 'Three months. Everyone agreed on three months. I was supposed to have another month.' Another sob came, and she let go of him and stifled it with both hands. The last thing they needed was for the other prisoners to hear them.

'Listen to me. If there is a way for you to leave, then you need to go *now*.' He shook his head. 'We don't have another month.'

She nodded. 'We have six days.'

His face filled with pity at the realisation that she knew. 'Where is the guard?' he asked, growing nervous.

She looked back down the corridor. 'I poisoned him.'

'You poisoned him?'

She drew a long breath, wanting to explain but not having time. 'I came prepared.'

He brushed at the new tears. 'You need to get out of here before someone arrives. Then you need to make a plan to leave, without me.'

'No,' she whispered, taking his hands again. 'We have six days. I'm not leaving without you. Help me,' she pleaded.

He shook his head, thinking.

Another glance down the corridor. 'Tell me what to do and I'll do it. I am in contact with Leksi. He will organise horses to get us back to Wripis whenever we need them.'

He swallowed. 'Write to him and tell him to have horses waiting in five days. Will the letter reach him in time?'

She nodded. 'How will we get out?'

'Do you have any weapons?'

She pulled the dagger from her pocket and held it out. He let go of her and took the weapon, tucking it into his pants beneath his shirt. 'I thought we could go over the wall.'

He stared at her. 'The walls are at least forty feet high.'

That was higher than she had guessed. 'And they are guarded at all times.'

'I can get us past the guards. Can you leave your rooms at night?'

'Only if requested by Prince Felipe.'

That statement tripped him for a moment, but he recovered quickly.

'We have a better chance in the dark. In five days, when the guard brings food in the evening, I need you watching and ready. A tray will arrive from the kitchen.' He pointed at the empty one by his bed. 'I don't know who delivers it. A kitchen maid, perhaps. When the guard delivers the food to me, I will take care of him. Wait a few minutes to ensure he does not return, and then get the keys and bring them to me.'

'Does the guard not take the keys when he delivers the food?'

'No. They only open the door when they empty the chamber pots, and that's a two-guard job.'

She nodded, feeling calmer.

'Now you need to go.'

She stared at him, not wanting to leave but knowing the consequences if they were caught. 'Five days.'

'Five days.' He pulled her close so her face was against the bars and bent to kiss her tear-streaked face. 'Go,' he whispered.

She let go of his hands and grabbed the book, glancing once at him before fleeing. When she reached the door, she peered through the crack to make sure no one was there. Satisfied, she pushed it open and stepped through, laying the book down while she put the crossbar in place. Snatching up the book once more, she walked up the stairs, wiping away the remaining tears.

A few steps from the top, she heard the scuff of boots headed in her direction. She froze, mind racing. Dropping down onto the second step, she leaned her back against the wall in a casual manner.

The sick guard from earlier rounded the corner, stopping abruptly when he saw her. 'What are you doing here?'

She looked up at him and a smile spread across her face.

'There you are.' She stood and fixed the skirt of her dress. 'I just wanted to let you know that we found the pin.'

He stared down at her, face clammy, before stepping around her.

'Are you all right?' she called after him. 'You look a little pale.'

He waved a hand, continuing down the steps. 'I'm glad you found your jewellery. Now leave.'

She did not need to be told twice. Stepping up into the corridor, hands wet and heart pounding, she walked away.

CHAPTER 26

When Aldara arrived at the Companions' quarters, she found Petra standing in front of the fire, staring at the flames. The women were slowly surrendering to the cloud cover and frosty mornings, wearing long sleeves during the day and huddling beneath their wool blankets at nights. Aldara watched as Petra brushed tears from her face and glanced down at her hands as if wondering what the foreign liquid was.

'Are you all right?' Aldara asked, stopping in the middle of the room.

'Yes.' She shook her head dismissively. 'My mind was a long way from here.' She looked around at the darkening room. 'Where have you been?'

Aldara held up the book. 'Far away also, on the battlefield in the South.'

Petra read the title of the book. 'Ah, back when Braul had lands worth defending.'

Aldara lowered it and watched her for a moment. 'And where were you, my lady?'

She sniffed and straightened, turning back to the flames.

She reminded Aldara of Fedora in some ways, her unhealthy need to appear strong at all times even though no one possessed that ability. Yet in other ways she was different—quieter, more resigned, sadder perhaps. And she belonged to a different king.

'Can I ask you something?'

Petra nodded.

Aldara came and stood next to her. 'Why does King Nilos hurt you?'

Petra stiffened, the flames of the fire reflected in her eyes. There was such a long silence that Aldara thought she might not answer the question. 'Because he is King Nilos of Corneo, and he can do and have whatever he wants. Except me.'

'So he hurts you because you refuse him?'

She shook her head, eyes shining. 'No, I never refuse him. He hurts me because he knows I submit out of obligation and that I feel nothing for him. He hurts me because my body is unresponsive, my mouth silent, my eyes diverted. He cannot possess me, so he punishes me instead.'

Aldara's eyes went to Petra's wrists, which were covered by her dress. 'He… he holds you down?'

The mentor glanced at her. 'He wants me to react, to feel, anything. My silence is the only power I hold.'

'And afterwards? Is he apologetic for hurting you?

She blinked. 'Afterwards he pushes me away, shouts at me. After is when he is most violent, because he hates himself in that moment.'

Aldara knew Petra's reasons for punishing the man with her indifference, but she could not let on. 'If you could pick a different life, any life you wanted, what would that life be?'

Petra wiped her eyes. 'That is enough of that talk. Neither of us should be thinking like that.'

'Why not? They do not own our thoughts.'

Petra looked at her properly for the first time. 'No good can come of it.' She watched Aldara for a moment. 'What life would you choose, since you clearly did not choose this one?'

'What do you mean? I came here by choice.'

Petra turned away. 'I have seen enough girls come through these walls to know which ones want to be here.'

Aldara continued to look at her. There were words rising, and she was not sure she could stop them from coming out. 'I have a son.' It was almost a whisper. 'He is with my family. I would choose a life with him every time.' Guilt pressed into her sides. She had left him behind because there was one other person she could not live without.

Petra's arms were wrapped around herself so tightly she looked like a frightened child. 'I have a son also,' she said, blinking back tears. 'He would be three years of age now.'

Aldara stared, her face filling with pity as she saw how much her mentor needed to say those words aloud. 'What is his name?'

'Xander.'

Aldara smiled. 'That's a beautiful name.'

'They may have changed it for all I know.' She turned back to the fire.

'They?'

'The family who have him. A distant relative of the king.'

Aldara swallowed. 'Where do they live?'

Petra shook her head. 'I don't know.'

Silence.

'Do you know anything about the family? Does the king get updates from them?'

'I do not know.' She thought for a moment. 'I know only what he chooses to tell me during moments of weakness, small moments when I hold some of the power. And they are probably lies.'

Aldara nodded. 'How long did you have him before he was given to the family?'

'He was not given. He was taken.' Her voice was raised slightly and her grip tightened. 'Four days. I fell asleep while nursing him, and when I woke up, he was gone.'

Aldara's insides felt heavy. 'You must have been devastated.'

'For a while, and then I got ill.' Her hands fell to her sides. 'Milk fever, quite bad. Or so I was told.'

'You do not remember?'

She shook her head. 'I was feverish. And I was grieving.'

'I'm sorry. It's a long life. There is every chance you will see him again.'

Petra watched the flames. 'Not while King Nilos is alive. He has promised me that.'

Aldara tried to smile. 'He certainly knows the way to a woman's heart.'

Petra looked across at her. 'You will say nothing of this conversation to anyone.'

It was like she was suddenly aware of the line she had crossed. 'Of course not.'

Petra hesitated. 'There is one more thing.'

She waited.

Petra was selecting her words carefully. 'Have you ever heard the saying "the apple does not fall far from the tree"?'

Aldara nodded. 'Yes.'

Before Petra could say anything more, Nyla walked through the door, yawning after having slept all day. 'Oh, I love a fire,' she said, stepping in between them and holding her hands out to the heat.

'Until the end of the cold season when we will be staring at it resentfully,' Petra said, straightening. 'Prince Kyril has invited you to eat in his chambers with him this evening.'

Nyla smiled. 'Excellent. He gets much nicer food than we do.'

'Yes, well don't let it sit in your teeth like last time.'

Aldara smiled.

'The potatoes were overcooked, and no one eats charcoal gracefully,' Nyla replied, her expression sulky. 'I am going to wash.' She went to leave and then stopped. 'Oh, do we know yet who the guests are that will be arriving in a few days?'

'Not yet. All I know is that they must be of some importance, as everyone inside these walls seems to be preparing for them.'

'Prince Kyril is being close-lipped about it. Why all the secrecy, do you suppose?'

'We will find out soon enough,' Petra replied. 'Medea, I suggest you go bathe also in case Prince Felipe calls on you later.'

Aldara eyed the paper and ink on the table. She needed to write to Leksi to let him know of the plan.

'Yes, my lady.'

She would do it when the others slept.

CHAPTER 27

The next day, after her lessons, when every other person in the castle seemed to be moving at a run, Aldara made her way downstairs. In one of her pockets was a letter for Leksi, and in the other an apple, a small piece of chicken and some barley bread.

First she went outside and walked a lap of the castle, slipping the food through Tyron's window as she passed. He needed to be strong if they were going to make it over that wall. They were also going to need some form of rope, and she still had no idea where she might get it.

Next she made her way to the laundry and found Velma, sweat pouring from her face as she ironed a shirt. The maid lay a piece of fabric over the top to protect it before running the hot iron over the top. She looked up when Aldara walked in and glanced about to ensure they were alone.

'Do you know anything about the guests coming tomorrow?' she asked Aldara, continuing her work.

'No. I think the secrecy is starting to make everyone mad with curiosity.'

Velma looked up, her eyes lit with adventure. 'There are

rumours of a ship arriving in the east. A king from lands no man has travelled.'

Aldara tried to guess at the girl's age. Fifteen, perhaps. Soon she would be old enough to marry her ditcher suitor if her parents approved of the union. 'We shall see tomorrow.'

'Will you meet him, do you think?'

Aldara tried not to smile. 'The king from lands that no man has travelled?' Velma's gaze returned to the shirt and Aldara felt bad for dampening her excitement. 'Perhaps he is searching for a Corneon bride.'

Velma suppressed a smile and looked up again. 'Do you have a letter, then?'

Aldara checked the door before pulling it from her pocket and handing it to her. She watched as the maid stuffed it into her apron. 'Thank you. I really do appreciate your help.'

Velma nodded and carried the iron back to the stove without saying a word.

After leaving the laundry, Aldara almost collided with a freshly shaven Prince Felipe, who was exiting the armoury. 'Oh, good morning, my lord,' she said, stepping back and curtsying. 'I almost knocked you over.'

That made him laugh. 'I can assure you that if we were to collide, I would be quite safe.'

'I think you underestimate my strength,' she replied, smiling. Her eyes went to the knight who came to a stop next him. Even with his head shaved, his receding hairline was visible. He looked down his long nose at her. She knew from the shape of it that it had been broken more than once. Her gaze returned to Felipe, waiting for an introduction.

'Medea, this is Sir Proteus,' Felipe said. 'Proteus has trained me since I was six years old.'

She curtsied and then looked up at him, trying to read his expression and body language. He was suspicious of her. 'Entrusted with the training of the Crown Prince. You must be very skilled, Sir Proteus.' Nothing changed in his posture or face. He was not one to be won over with compliments.

'Proteus is one of Corneo's best swordsmen,' Felipe said, taking the weapon being offered him.

Proteus neither confirmed nor denied the statement. 'And you are the latest Companion.' His choice of words made it clear he did not think she would be around long. He looked her up and down once and then turned to Felipe. 'Shall we?'

'My father insists that my brother and I train most days to keep our skills sharp,' Felipe explained.

She turned her attention back to him. 'Probably wise given what has taken place in the West.'

'We are a long way off from requiring me to fight.'

She looked up at him, puzzled. 'Oh?'

He frowned down at her as though he should not need to explain himself. 'I am the Crown Prince. It would not be sensible to put my life at risk. Our people expect me to rule, not fight.'

'Of course.' She could feel Proteus's eyes on her. 'You are lucky to have men like Sir Proteus to fight for you.'

'Yes. Proteus and his men are responsible for capturing Prince Tyron of Syrasan.'

Her eyes went to the man. 'Further proof of your skill, as I hear Prince Tyron is an excellent swordsman also.'

He was silent for a moment before replying. 'Is that what your mentor told you?'

'No, that is what history tells me.' She watched his expression harden.

'The Companions are taught history,' Felipe said, waving his hand as though the lessons were just a little fun had among the women.

Keeping her expression neutral, she asked, 'I wonder if I might come and watch you train for a little while.'

'Women are not permitted in the behourd,' Proteus said.

'She will not be training,' Felipe said, looking at him. 'Only watching.' He turned back to Aldara, a smile forming. 'I think we can relax the rules this once.'

Proteus bowed his head and stepped past her.

The three of them went outside and headed north until they reached a false wall. Behind it was a behourd. Archdale had also had one, but she had never seen inside it, as the men training there had the same views as the men in Corneo—it was no place for a woman. Even Tyron had not trained there, preferring the open space and green lawn of the butts.

Aldara looked about at the green plants climbing the stone walls and the straw-stuffed targets along the back. A battered pell stood in the middle and coarse sand covered the ground. She was not sure if it had been raked to smooth the surface or disguise the blood spills.

'Impressive, is it not?' Felipe said, his chest visibly puffing.

'Very.' She stood by the wall as the men stripped off their tunics before taking up their weapons again.

'Do not be afraid,' Felipe called to her. 'These are training swords, blunt so no one will be injured.'

She knew that a man who did not fight in battles would not train with a sharpened blade. 'That is good to know,' she called back.

The men moved away from her and began to circle one another. She watched as their swords came together in a clash of male ego. Felipe had been right, Proteus was an excellent swordsman, and judging by the fact that he did not even break a sweat during the exchange, she guessed he was holding back. Felipe, on the other hand, was pouring with sweat within minutes. Ten minutes in and his shirt clung to his back and neck. The fight ended with Proteus knocking Felipe's sword from his hand before wandering over to drink from the flask he had left on the ground next to the bow.

He watched her as he drank, and when he was done, he

said, 'A real fight would not last that long, at least not one I was involved in.'

She glanced at Felipe, who had collected his sword and was walking towards them. 'You are right, my lord. Sir Proteus is very good.'

'He is much fitter,' Felipe said, breathing hard. He dropped his sword at his feet and reached for his own flask.

'And how are you with a bow, Sir Proteus?'

He glanced at the targets behind him. 'You will see for yourself in just a moment.'

Both men were strong archers, handling the bow well over the long distance. She would have liked to see Felipe shoot a moving target on horseback.

'Do you want to have a try?' he called out, coming towards her.

She glanced down at the longbow in his hand.

'Look at her,' Proteus said. 'She will not even be able to hold it up without assistance.'

'Then I will help her,' Felipe replied, eyes on her. 'She handled the flag at the tournament without issue.'

Proteus shook his head. 'Yes, I remember. An embarrassing display.'

She held her tongue, following Felipe back to where Proteus waited. The prince stood behind her, positioning her legs and angling her hips in front of him. She made a point of holding the bow incorrectly, and then Felipe's arms wrapped around her, moulding her upper body as if it were made of clay. She fought the urge to shrug him off, to show him that she knew exactly what she was doing without being handled like a child.

Satisfied, Felipe took a step back from her. 'You are ready,' he said, crossing his arms and watching her.

She could have easily hit the target from that distance, but instead, she let her elbow drop on release and shortened her draw so she missed and fell short of the distance.

Proteus laughed at her, not in good humour like Stamitos and his friends had in earlier years but a harsh, superior laugh. 'Best stick to your sewing,' he said, taking the bow from her.

'Do not feel too badly,' Felipe said, suppressing his own laughter. 'Women are not built for archery.'

Aldara nodded. 'You are probably right. I will let you show me how it is done.' She stepped back from them so they could flex their muscles and polish one another's egos without her getting in the way.

Just before noon, the men grew tired and the three of them made their way back to the armoury.

'There are an awful lot of things to kill a person with in here,' she said, looking along the walls where the weapons hung. Some of them she did not recognise. 'What is that?' she said, pointing to a rounded blade attached to a pole.

'A scythe, used in battle.'

It looked similar to a farming tool they used during harvest back home.

'An impressive collection, but the number of weapons does not seem to match the number of men living within these walls.'

Felipe shook his head, smiling. 'This is not everything. There are additional armouries in the gatehouse and tower.'

'The turrets also hold supplies for the guards on the walls should the castle ever be attacked,' added Proteus. 'No enemy has ever made it inside these walls uninvited.'

That was very useful information. They could take what they needed before going over the wall. 'Well, I feel much safer. You are certainly well prepared, my lord.'

Felipe reached out and took hold of her face. He always grabbed her harder than was necessary for a gesture that was meant to be tender. 'When you are my Companion, you do not have to worry about your safety. No one is coming through or over that wall without my say-so.'

After seeing what had happened to his previous Companion, she disagreed entirely. 'How high is the wall?'

'Are you planning an attack?' asked Proteus, glancing at Felipe with his usual sarcastic expression.

She just smiled. 'I guessed around thirty feet, but Nyla thought it might be even higher.'

'Nyla is correct,' Felipe said. 'The wall is forty-four feet.'

Tyron had been right. She would need to find over thirty feet of rope for their plan to be viable.

'No one can fall or jump from that height without breaking their legs or back,' Proteus said.

'That's good to know,' Aldara replied. 'I will keep that in mind next time I leap from a tall wall.'

Felipe pulled her to him and kissed her hard on the lips. 'You have a bold sense of humour,' he said, releasing her.

'And it will get you into trouble one day,' Proteus added.

She looked across at him. 'Are jokes reserved for men also, Sir Proteus?'

His brown eyes flashed at her.

Felipe took Aldara's hand and placed it on his arm. 'Come, I will walk you back to your quarters. You do not want to provoke Proteus while standing in the armoury.'

She left with the prince, feeling the knight's penetrating gaze on her.

They would need to be prepared for him also.

CHAPTER 28

*T*he following morning, Aldara was shaken awake
by an overexcited Nyla.

'Time to get ready,' she said, pulling Aldara up into a
sitting position.

It was still dark and Aldara looked about confused, trying
to figure out why she had been woken. Then she remembered the guests were arriving that day, which meant it was
three days until she was leaving with Tyron. She could
survive three more days. 'Ready for what?'

'The guests, of course.' Nyla tugged on her arm. 'Are you
not dying to find out who it is?'

'Dying,' she replied, her tone flat. She gave up the fight
and got out of bed, glancing across at the other empty beds.
'Where is Petra?'

'Still with the king.'

Aldara was afraid of that. 'It's rather early for the princes
to be requesting us. Where are we going?'

Nyla led her into the dressing room and positioned her in
front of the mirror. 'They have not sent for us yet, silly, but it

is important that we are ready for when they do. It could be any time.'

Aldara took in her dishevelled nightdress and wild hair. 'With the way everyone is behaving, anyone would think King Nilos has never received guests before.'

'Oh, he receives plenty of guests, but not like this one.'

Aldara met Nyla's eyes in the mirror. 'You know who it is.'

Nyla immediately became flustered. 'I know no such thing.' She walked over to the dresses and began to sift through them.

Aldara joined her. 'Prince Kyril told you, didn't he?'

'He is not allowed to tell.' She kept her eyes on the dresses.

'Oh, I know, but he told you anyway. Swore you to secrecy, perhaps.'

Nyla's flawless skin flushed red. 'We have all heard the rumours.'

'Yes, but you know the truth.'

Nyla studied a green silk gown before eyeing the shoes beneath it to see which combination would work. 'I already know what I am wearing. What are you going to wear?'

'That depends on the occasion. Perhaps you know that also.'

Nyla turned to her. 'Sometimes I feel like the only Companion who treats this role with the respect it demands.' She let go of the dress and crossed her arms in front of her. 'We are Companions of Corneo's royal men. We represent the best of all women in this kingdom. It is a privilege I am honoured to have and will never take for granted. My entire life is devoted to Prince Kyril, so if he asks for confidentiality, he gets it.' She narrowed her eyes on Aldara. 'Prince Felipe is depending on you to make a good impression today. How you slept at all is beyond me, and you still do not know what you are wearing.' She turned back to the dresses, nostrils flaring after her speech.

Aldara had to admire her in that moment. She had almost forgotten that many women wanted this life. Hali had chosen it once—before she knew better.

She reached up and pulled down a light blue silk dress with sheer sleeves. 'I'll wear this. The colour will brighten my eyes, and it has long sleeves in case our guests prefer something more conservative.'

Nyla exhaled and took the dress from her. 'A smart choice.' She paused. 'I know you think I am too eager, but the fact is I love my life here, and I want to hold on to it for as long as possible.'

While Aldara could not relate, she understood. 'That's not surprising. Prince Kyril appears to treat you very well.'

'Prince Felipe will treat you well also if you simply follow the rules and do not provoke him.'

Aldara thought that was an odd thing to say. 'What do you mean, provoke him?'

'Make him jealous.'

She let the words sink in. 'Is he prone to jealousy?'

Nyla almost laughed. 'Everyone is prone to jealousy.' She walked over and laid the dress over the armchair next to her own. 'It is nothing for you to worry about. He never laid a hand on Calista.' She went still, thinking. 'Though I suppose that is because he did not care for her.'

Aldara frowned. 'What of his Companion before Calista?'

'Oh, there were a few incidents, but you really should not concern yourself with things of the past. Prince Felipe treats you well, does he not?'

'Yes.' Though she had noticed some possessive behaviours. Petra's words also came to mind, about the apple not falling far from the tree. 'Why don't you put the dress on and I'll paint your face.'

Nyla's eyes lit up. 'I knew when you arrived we would be good friends. Calista could not cope with the pressure of the role, not like us.'

Aldara looked down so all her lies were not on display.

'When I am mentor, the women under my instruction will live this life with the same passion we do,' Nyla said, her voice low. 'I pray you are still here to witness it.'

Aldara looked up and studied her sincere expression. 'Will you be all right seeing Prince Kyril with another Companion?'

Nyla scrunched her face up. 'Of course. The only difference is that I will be making him happy in a different way, ensuring his new Companion meets all of the needs his wife cannot.'

The sentiment was an uncomfortable one, and yet Nyla perfectly represented what the role was meant to be. 'You are an excellent Companion,' she said with sincerity. 'You really are. Not only do you understand the role, but you uphold every rule.'

Nyla seemed confused by that praise. 'We *all* uphold the rules.'

Aldara smiled. 'We all try to.'

'That is your nerves talking,' Nyla replied, assuming Aldara was lacking confidence. 'Remember everything you have been taught and you will be fine today.'

'At the mystery event with our mystery guests.'

Nyla began to undress. 'I will tell you this much: things are looking up for our kingdom. King Nilos is not about to sit back while Syrasan men occupy the west.' She collected her dress from the armchair. 'Long may he reign.'

The smile froze on Aldara's face. 'Long may he reign.'

❧

Petra returned to the Companions' quarters after the morning meal, eyes bloodshot and the previous day's paint long gone from her face, but no less beautiful. Her dark hair was swept up in a knot on top of her head. The girls had returned to the dressing room after their meal to fix the paint on their lips. Nyla was on the stool in front of the dressing table and Aldara was sitting on the armchair with her legs up, trying to keep warm in a dress that was too sheer for the cold morning.

'Good.' She appraised them through tired eyes. 'Lovely.' She touched a finger to her raw lips before speaking. 'King Nilos will send word once our guests have arrived and settled in. We shall all be joining them for a feast.' She wrung her hands together as she spoke. 'There are a number of noble guests attending: Lord Rouvin, Lord Paulos, Lord Gregor. Obviously no Lord Belen.'

Aldara kept her expression blank.

'Will the queen be attending?' Nyla asked.

'Unlikely.'

Aldara had noticed that she had not seen the queen in the entire time she had been at Masville. She assumed it was planned that way, similar to how Fedora had tried to keep the Companions away from Cora. 'Is it unusual for her to miss such an important occasion?'

'No,' Nyla said. 'Her Majesty is prone to headaches and often takes to her bed for days.'

Aldara also suspected the headaches came at convenient times, like when her husband ignored propriety and invited the mentor he was besotted with to attend an event.

'Now,' Petra said, regaining their attention. 'There is a reason for all the secrecy over the past few days, and you will understand why when I tell you who we are receiving. The king's guest is King Jayr of Zoelin.'

It was one of those moments where Aldara was sure she

had misheard, that the name spoken just sounded like King Jayr of Zoelin.

'King Jayr has travelled here with two of his advisors to discuss the possibility of a trade agreement between Zoelin and Corneo.'

There was no mistaking his name that time. Aldara felt her insides turn cold. She was thankful for the fact that she was already sitting or she may have dropped to the floor. 'King Jayr?' She shook her head, not wanting to accept what she was hearing. 'I thought... I thought Zoelin was considered a threat? What of the alliance with Syrasan?'

Petra did not seem particularly interested in the politics. 'The king is well aware of what has taken place between the two kingdoms, Medea. I suspect with the trade agreement annulled and Prince Tyron of Syrasan unable to fulfil his obligations, King Jayr may be looking elsewhere for allies.'

That explained King Jayr's refusal to join the fight against Corneo.

Nyla's eyes widened. 'Oh, I had forgotten about Princess Tasia's betrothal to Prince Tyron. Perhaps King Jayr is here to negotiate his release?'

Jayr was not there to negotiate Tyron's release; he would more likely be looking forward to attending his execution. After all, he could just marry Princess Tasia off to Felipe instead, further securing the trade agreement.

Petra held out her hands. 'Let us remember our roles and leave business to King Nilos and the princes, shall we?' She clasped her hands in front of her. 'We represent the women who will be sold into the trade, so it is crucial that we make a good impression. As this is the first time the two men have met as kings, we need to ensure our guests feel welcome and comfortable liaising with the royal family and noble guests.'

'I have never even seen a Zoelin man before,' Nyla said, placing her hand on her chest. 'What about you, Medea? Oh, of course you have. They were just across the river from your village.'

'Yes, I have seen Zoelin men before,' she replied absently.

'Are they really that much taller than Corneon men?'

She nodded. 'Much taller.'

Petra observed Aldara for a moment. 'King Jayr is supposedly very charming, so there is no cause for panic.'

There was every cause for panic. Aldara felt it surging through every vein in her body. King Jayr would soon be arriving at Masville, and she was about to be thrown into a room with him. It did not matter how much paint was on her face—he would recognise her immediately.

'Medea!'

Aldara jumped and looked at Petra. Why was she shouting?

'I called your name three times with no response. Is something the matter?'

Medea. Yes, her name was Medea. 'I'm sorry, my lady.'

'Are you all right?'

Aldara's thoughts pounded against the front of her head. *Answer the question.* 'I am not feeling very well.'

'It is just nerves,' Nyla laughed. 'Most new Companions are nervous before their first introduction. The fact that King Jayr will be present for yours is probably making it worse.'

Aldara stared at Nyla's moving lips, trying to guess at the words.

'Are you nervous?' Petra asked, suddenly next to her.

Again, Aldara jumped. 'I feel sick.'

'Nyla, get the chamber pot,' Petra said.

When Nyla stood, Aldara did also, holding up a hand to stop her. 'It's all right. I think I just need some air.' She had no idea how she was standing upright, but her legs held up.

Petra seemed unsure. 'Nyla will go with you.'

'No,' Aldara said much too fast. 'If I am going to be sick, I would rather not have an audience.'

Petra studied her for a moment before nodding. 'All right. Do what you need to, but make sure you are ready when Prince Felipe requests you. Do you understand?'

She could not go to that feast. 'What if I am too ill to attend?'

Petra stepped closer and took hold of her arms. 'You do not get to be sick. Prince Felipe wants you introduced today, so you will be introduced today. This is not my decision. Do you understand?'

'You will be fine,' Nyla said. 'Go empty your stomach and do not eat anything else before the feast. Trust me, this is normal.'

Aldara nodded, knowing that bringing up her meal would do little to fix her problems. 'Of course. You are right. I will be fine after some air.'

She felt their eyes on her as she left the dressing room. When she got to the main room, she snatched the quill from the table and scribbled a short note to Tyron. She could not afford to wait for the ink to dry. Folding it with trembling hands until it could not get any smaller, she slipped it inside her dress beneath the belt. Taking a final look around to ensure no one had seen her, she stepped out into the corridor, thankful to discover it empty.

She tried to walk slowly, she really tried, but with King Jayr due to arrive at any moment, her legs moved at their own pace. Some passing maids glanced at her with mild interest as she burst out of the small door near the laundry. It was unusual for a made-up Companion to be wandering around outdoors unescorted, and even more unusual for one to be moving almost at a run.

Rounding the corner to the west wall, she checked her surroundings before looking up at the glass windows high above, hopeful no one could see down at such a sharp angle. Her gaze fell to the windows along the bottom, counting. One, two, three, four, five, six. She stopped next to the final window, though instead of slipping the note through it and continuing, she crouched next to it, unable to leave. She should have stood up and kept walking, but the comfort she felt at having him close anchored her.

After a long moment she realised it was not comfort that held her there—it was fear.

~

TYRON HAD BEEN WATCHING the window when he saw the letter come through it. It fell by his feet and he immediately bent to pick it up, glancing once at the corridor before unfolding it.

KING JAYR ARRIVES at Masville today. Be ready.
  A

HE READ IT AGAIN. And then he read it again.

He could tell by the smudged ink that the note had been written in a hurry. Folding the paper back up, he buried it deep in the pocket of his tunic. Why was King Jayr coming to Masville? But even as he thought the question, answers formed in his mind. He was a man who liked to be on the winning side, and he had been biding his time to see how it would all play out. It was likely he would have heard of Tyron's upcoming execution, and with him dead, there was nothing tying Zoelin to Syrasan except bad blood.

His eyes went to the small window above him and he held his breath, listening. Complete silence—but he did not trust it. His gaze fell to the corner wall and he ran at it, his right leg pushing off the ground, launching his body so his left foot landed against the wall beneath the window. He sprang off it, climbing with a foot on each wall until his left hand reached the bars. He grabbed hold, his body slamming against the stone. He pulled himself up while his feet felt for uneven crevices to use as steps. There she was, a magnetic force, crouched in front of him, paralysed by fear.

'Aldara,' he whispered, making her to jump.

She turned, surprised by the sight of him and eyes already welling over. She reached out, wrapping her hands over his. The warmth of them almost made him lose his grip.

'What are you doing?' she asked, blinking away tears. 'You'll fall.'

He had just a few moments to read her, fix her, and get her to leave. 'You cannot sit there. If you are seen, we will both die in this place.'

Her eyes were searching his, needing something from him.

'I am to feast with King Jayr in a few hours. And likely Grandor Pollux. They will recognise me at once.'

Her hands gripped his tighter, and he wanted to tear the bars from the window and pull her through the hole. 'You need to find a way to get out of it. We will leave tonight.'

She shook her head. 'We can't go tonight. We won't have any horses—'

'We will steal them somewhere.' Watching her in such a state of panic was too much. 'Bring me the keys and let me worry about the rest.' Her grip did not ease. 'It will be all right, but you need to go.'

She blinked and more tears fell. 'I have to attend the feast. You know how this works… I have to attend.'

'No. Pretend you are ill.'

She brought her face closer to his. 'Prince Felipe is not you!' Her fingers dug into his, eyes pleading.

'All right, I understand. It will be all right.' He had no choice but to remain calm.

'I have to attend,' she said again, softer this time.

Tyron's arms were beginning to cramp. 'Listen to me. You find a way to hide yourself from them, wear a mask if you have to. Our son is waiting for you.' He knew it was harsh to bring Mako up at that time, but he needed her to find strength.

She nodded, black paint streaking her cheeks. 'All right, I'll find a way.'

'You know these men. Be smart around them.' Her fingers relaxed a little. 'Now go. You cannot be seen here.'

She brought her forehead to his hands, pressing against him.

'Go!' he said, harsher this time. When she did not let go, he lowered his body and released his grip on the bars, her hands slipping from his as he dropped to the ground below, landing in a crouch.

Silence above him as his head slumped forwards.

God, give her strength.

CHAPTER 29

*P*rince Felipe was waiting outside when Aldara arrived at the Companions' quarters. She stopped at the sight of him, wiping at the paint on her cheeks, trying to clean herself up. Only when she was close did he look up, visibly relieved to see her.

'Where have you been? I have people looking for you.' He took in her smeared face. 'It will not do for you to meet our guests looking like this.'

'I apologise, my lord. I just needed some air.'

'Petra suggested you were anxious. I could not picture it.'

He cupped her face and kissed her deeply, his body invading hers in a way that stifled her breathing. She struggled to keep soft beneath him, wanting only to push him away and take in air.

He pulled back but kept hold of her. 'I do not want you outside dressed like this unless you are with me. What did I tell you about the guards?'

She took his hands, trying to ease his grip on her. 'I understand. I apologise for making you worry.'

He released her and smiled as if he had conjured a

different person entirely. 'Go and get yourself ready. I am afraid I cannot wait for you, so I will have to send Petra to collect you.' He stepped back from her.

'Of course, my lord.' She curtsied.

His eyes moved over her. 'When King Jayr sees you, I want him to envy me. Give me the girl from the tournament, bold and mysterious.'

'And controversial?'

A smile grew on his face. 'If you like. Just remember who you belong to.'

He turned and walked off down the corridor.

As soon as he was out of sight, Aldara went inside to get ready once again. She scrubbed her face clean and then looked down at her dress, its hem filthy from her earlier walk across frosted grass. Taking it off, she selected the green silk dress Nyla had been considering that morning. She sat at the dressing table and got to work, using the colours in front of her to change the appearance of her face—higher cheekbones, fuller lips, thicker brows above smouldering eyes.

She took a moment to marvel at the strange creature staring back at her before going off in search of the lace shawl Petra had told her was beyond mending. It was on top of a pile of older garments tucked behind the shoes. She walked over to the drawer inside the open cupboard and rummaged around for the scissors and ribbon. Returning to the stool, she carefully cut a section out of it and attached a piece of ribbon at each end. She positioned it over her eyes, marking it with a dot of paint before cutting some holes. Satisfied, she tucked her hair into a low knot and tied the cream lace around her head like a mask. She looked in the mirror, studying her reflection, and applied one more layer of bronze paint to her lips. There was absolutely no way King Jayr or his men would recognise her. *She* did not recognise her.

Petra entered the room and her neutral expression dissolved. She shook her head. 'I do not understand. Explain to me what I am seeing here.'

Aldara looked at her in the mirror. 'Prince Felipe said he wanted the bold and mysterious girl from the tournament.'

Petra stared at her. 'Medea, you look… breathtaking, actually. But you also look like someone else entirely.'

Aldara stood up. 'There is a reason Prince Felipe does not keep a Companion longer than a few months. He is easily bored.'

Petra glanced behind her, aware of the passing time. 'Very well, but be prepared for the possibility of returning here to change once again.'

'Yes, my lady.'

Petra turned and walked back through the door. Aldara hesitated, glancing down at her chest, which pulsed with each fierce beat of her heart.

THE WOMEN WALKED into the great hall and looked about. Aldara's eyes went to King Jayr, who stood a full head above everyone else, his deep blue vest and dark skin contrasting the pastel shades and ghostly complexions of the Corneon guests. His hair and beard were trimmed short, and his watchful eyes moved about the room, stopping briefly on her. She kept still beneath his curious gaze, waiting to see if he would recognise her. Nothing showed on his face beyond a playful smile.

Near the refreshments table, two more Zoelin heads poked out from the guests—an advisor Aldara did not recognise, and Lord Pollux. She stiffened at the sight of him. The man who had introduced her to the life of a Companion was still in favour with the king and always managed to surprise her.

'First I will take you to Prince Felipe,' Petra said. 'We shall see what he has to say about the woman I am presenting before I make any further introductions.'

Aldara looked over to where Prince Felipe was speaking with his father, nodding in agreement while keeping his eyes on the room. 'After you, my lady.'

She was aware of the men turning to look at her. Every gaze felt like additional weight pressing down on her, and she struggled to keep her chin up and shoulders squared as she stepped between them.

From the moment Prince Felipe caught sight of her, she knew he liked what he saw. He excused himself, eyes moving over her as he walked towards them.

'And who do we have here?' he asked, a smile spreading.

Relief washed over Aldara. She even managed to return the smile.

'Medea is full of surprises, my lord.' Petra said, also relaxing. 'She looks lovely, does she not?'

Felipe brought his lips to Aldara's right cheek. 'She looks majestic,' he hummed. 'Come. I will introduce you to our guests.' He glanced again at Petra. 'My father is waiting for you.'

Petra's smile was strained. 'Thank you, my lord. I shall go to him now.'

Felipe reached for Aldara's hand and placed it on his arm. All she had to do was get through the next few hours. Only a few more hours of leaning and smiling and touching and laughing and lying and pushing through her fears. Just hours.

'Forgive the interruption,' Felipe said, stopping in front of King Jayr. The man he had been speaking to bowed and excused himself. Jayr's eyes moved over Aldara before returning to Felipe. 'I wanted to introduce my Companion, Medea. This is King Jayr of Zoelin.'

'I am very pleased to meet you, Your Majesty,' Aldara said in Zoelin.

Jayr took her hand and studied it before releasing it. 'Your Zoelin is impressive.'

'I have an excellent mentor. She is a true master of languages.'

'Perhaps we should speak Corneon, as Prince Felipe may struggle to keep up.'

Aldara could tell by the look on Felipe's face that he had comprehended that perfectly. She had not had time to imagine how they would be with one another. They were alike in many ways, and she could see their egos had potential to clash.

'I understand the language better than I speak it,' Felipe said.

Jayr's eyes remained on him longer than was polite.

'How long are you in Corneo, Your Majesty?' Aldara asked, moving the conversation along.

Jayr's gaze returned to her. 'Just a few days.'

'It is your first time in Corneo, is it not?'

'Yes.' He studied her for a moment. 'Where are you from, Medea?'

She could see his mind at work. 'Thovaria, in the North.'

'Perhaps that is why your accent is different.'

She took hold of Felipe's arm. 'Is it? I have never been told that before.' Felipe's hand went over hers. 'And what brings you to Corneo, Your Majesty?' She wanted to change the subject.

'We invited King Jayr to Masville to see how our kingdoms might work together,' Felipe said, answering for him. 'And perhaps see if we can find a new suitor for the princess,' he added, laughing.

Aldara forced a smile. 'Your sister was betrothed to Prince Tyron of Syrasan, was she not?'

'She was. The political climate changes things somewhat.' He held up his empty cup and shook it, looking about for a servant.

'Allow me to get you another, Your Majesty,' Aldara said, reaching for his cup.

He glanced at Felipe. 'She is very well-trained.'

Felipe patted her hand like one did a dog who had followed a command. She smiled up at him before withdrawing her arm.

'I shall be back in a moment.' She walked off towards the refreshment table, cup in hand, weaving through the noble men with their big laughs and lingering eyes, past the unsmiling Zoelin advisor who did not appear to speak Corneon, and into the shadow cast by Grandor Pollux, who turned to the table the same time she arrived.

Hidden beneath a veil of paint and lace, drawing strength from the crowded hall, she met his inquisitive gaze and curtsied. Rising, she reached for the jar of wine. 'Would you care for a refill?' she asked in Zoelin, glancing at his cup.

He held it out for her, watching her as she poured. When she was done, she refilled King Jayr's cup and placed the jar back on the table. Her mind went to the poisons tucked away in the Companion dressing room, wondering if she would have the courage to use them if they were strapped to her thigh instead. She did not wish Pollux dead, but seeing him rush from the room before retiring to his bedchamber for the rest of his visit would have been satisfying.

King Jayr, on the other hand... Would she have the nerve to take the life of man who killed, sold, threatened, abused so many of her people? For weeks she had sat in her cell in the tower at Drake Castle wishing him dead.

'I thought there was no food in Corneo,' he said, looking

down the table at the cured meats, fruits, cheeses, breads and sweets.

She had hoped to avoid a conversation. 'Those who control the food rarely go without.' It was the worst response she could have given, and she knew her mentor would be horrified to hear her say such a thing.

He was watching her again. 'Have we met before?'

That was not good. 'No, I have not had the honour. My name is Medea, Companion to Prince Felipe.'

'Grandor Pollux, Advisor to King Jayr.' He put his cup down and then took King Jayr's from her, placing it on the table. He opened her palm and studied it. 'I never forget a woman's hands. There is something familiar in yours.'

She withdrew her hand but her expression remained relaxed. 'Advisor to the king? He must value you very much if your marks are any indication.' She gestured to the ink that marked his skin like a sleeve, climbing up his arm, neck and scalp. The cut of his vest revealed markings on his chest as well.

He looked down at his arm. 'Has your prince explained their meaning?'

'Our mentor is responsible for such teachings. She has explained that the marks are made by men above you, recognising acts of wisdom, bravery and loyalty.'

'Women can be marked also.'

She remembered the marks on Princess Tasia's hand when she had met her briefly at Drake Castle. 'By women above them?'

'By the men they please.'

Of course. She smiled and glanced across at Felipe who was watching her. 'I should return with His Majesty's drink. He is probably parched by now.'

Pollux followed her gaze. 'Your prince looks anxious to have you back also.'

Another glance at Felipe. Pollux was right, there was something in his eyes. 'I pray you enjoy your visit, my grandor.'

As she turned to leave, he caught her hand. She looked down at the full cup in her other hand, its contents swishing, then up at him. After studying her palm again, he looked up at her.

'You are a perfect example of what Corneo has to offer.' He let go of her hand and reached up, touching her face. He traced a finger up her cheek, stopping at the lace. 'I feel certain we have met before.' His eyes stared into hers.

She froze beneath his touch, paralysed by memories of being trapped beneath the very hand on her now. Perhaps he did recognise her. She was certain she would know him anywhere, mask or no mask.

'There you are,' Prince Felipe said, coming up next her.

Aldara jumped, almost spilling the wine.

Pollux's hand fell away and he straightened. 'Your Companion is a fine example of the goods you have to offer.'

Felipe smiled, but it was a strange sort of smile. His eyes were too wide and he was showing more teeth than normal.

'Yes, she is a real prize. My apologies, but you will have to excuse us.' He looked at Aldara. 'Let us give King Jayr his drink.' He glanced again at Pollux before leading her away, his smile gone. Gripping her wrist too tight, he tugged her towards King Jayr while she struggled not to spill the contents of the cup as they stepped around guests.

'My lord,' she whispered, her arm beginning to hurt.

He ignored her.

When they reached King Jayr, Felipe pulled Aldara up next to him so she could hand him the cup. She took in his clenched jaw and drawn brows before handing the cup to King Jayr.

'Apologies for the delay, Your Majesty. I was speaking with Grandor Pollux.'

Jayr was looking at Felipe's grip on his Companion. The man was finely tuned to conflict and missed nothing. He nodded at her, eyes amused.

'We were just going to take some air,' Felipe said, still gripping her as though she might run off. 'Please excuse us, Your Majesty.' As he dragged Aldara away, he looked over to where his brother stood talking with Nyla. Felipe gestured with his head for the young prince to go to King Jayr. Kyril immediately excused himself and made his way towards the Zoelin king.

Beginning to feel uneasy, Aldara searched about for Petra and found her watching them from across the room where she stood with King Nilos. They just looked at one another, equally helpless, until Aldara disappeared into the corridor. The prince did not slow, continuing to drag her farther away from the open doors.

'My lord,' Aldara said, placing her free hand on his arm. 'Can you please stop and talk to me for a moment?'

He spun around, slapping her. She stumbled sideways, her shoulder slamming into the wall. Her hand went to her face and she raised her eyes to him, knowing better than to speak before he had communicated everything he wanted to say.

'You were meant to be getting King Jayr a drink, not whoring yourself off to guests.'

Only when he spoke did she notice the ringing in her ear. Her wrist throbbed where he continued to keep a hold of it.

One of the first lessons a Companion learned was how to handle jealousy. Do not argue, do not defend your actions— just apologise.

'I am sorry. I have upset you, and for that I apologise.' Her jaw ached when she spoke.

His shoulders dropped and his grip loosened, but only a little. He stepped towards her, a gesture of intimidation. 'Have you forgotten who you belong to?'

She shook her head. 'I am yours. I belong to you.'

He pulled her arm so she fell towards him. 'And should you let other men touch you?'

Another shake of her head. 'No.' He let go of her wrist and she remained where she was, knowing better than to move away. 'I am sorry,' she said again.

His hands went on her then, drawing her close so her head pressed against his chest. Everything about it felt wrong. She closed her eyes, trying to block out the feel of his lips on her hair.

'Show me your face,' he said, pulling back and removing the lace mask for a better view. 'Look at you. What were you thinking behaving that way? I could have hurt you.'

He did hurt her. As she was looking up at him, she thought she saw something resembling remorse, but then she realised it was more likely disappointment at having left a mark on the face he wanted displayed.

His eyes travelled to her nose. 'You are bleeding.' He stepped back from her as though it were contagious before taking a handkerchief from his pocket and offering it to her.

She took it from him and dabbed it against her nose. 'Thank you.'

He watched her for a moment. 'Go clean yourself up and wait in your quarters. I need to tend to our guests for a few hours, and then I am going to send for you.'

'To entertain your guests?'

'No, to entertain *me*. No veil, no paint.' He began lifting the skirt of her dress. 'And no garment.' His fingers found her bare leg, and his eyes closed as he stroked her skin.

She closed hers also, so she would not have to look at

him. 'We need to wait a few more days for the herbs to be effective,' she whispered.

He covered her mouth with his, silencing her. She knew his lust was fuelled by the possibility of another man desiring her. And she also knew he would not be talked out of it.

'Go,' he said. 'Before we cannot stop ourselves.'

She could stop herself.

'I will send for you in a few hours.' He went to leave and then paused. 'Do you need me to send Petra to you?'

She smiled reassuringly. 'No. You are already a Companion down. I can organise myself.'

Happy with her response, he bowed his head and walked back inside.

Aldara curtsied, rising only when he was out of sight. The smile fell from her face and she exhaled, her breath uneven. She touched the handkerchief to her nose again and looked at the blood. In a few hours he was going to send for her, lay with her, do whatever he wanted with her. The realisation did nothing to help the ringing in her ear.

She turned and walked away from the guests and the noise, a plan already forming in her mind.

She would not stay at Masville and submit to that man.

When she arrived at the Companions' quarters, she went straight to the bathing room and filled a basin with cold water. She winced as her fingers moved around her right eye, already swelling, removing the layers of paint.

Once she was cleaned up, she ran to the dressing room and changed into a long-sleeve cotton dress that was slightly too big, enabling her to move more easily in it. Walking over to the pile of folded shawls in the cupboard, she pulled them off the shelf, holding each one up to gauge their length. There were eight shawls, each around four feet on the longer side. She joined them at the corners using a knot her father had taught her, knowing it would hold their combined weight, and hoping the knitted wool would also. Each knot cost her a foot of length, leaving her with a twenty-five-foot rope. She knew the linen from the bed would give her more length, but she also knew Petra would be immediately suspicious if she was to return and find the beds bare one day after they had been changed.

She snatched the remaining poisons from their hiding spot and slipped them into the pillow cover before gathering the shawls and stuffing them in also. There was no reminiscing as she rushed through the main room and stepped out into the corridor without a backwards glance. She made a conscious effort to slow down so as not to draw attention, hugging the pillow cover to her chest. She rounded the corner, bracing to run into someone she knew or hear someone call her name. They would stop her, question her, instruct her away from Tyron. She was thankful for every step she gained in his direction.

Finally making it outside, she hid the pillow cover in a dark nook outside of the laundry, straightened, and with her mind racing and lips numb from fear, she made her way to the west wall.

CHAPTER 30

*T*yron was pacing the walls of his cell, counting the steps between each corner for no other purpose than to distract himself, when he heard her whisper his name. His eyes shot up to the window. She did not have to say it twice. In a few leaps he was on the wall and pulling himself up to her once again. The sight of her face almost made him lose his grip. Her right eye was slightly swollen and her cheek coloured. A fire lit inside of him.

'What happened to your face?'

She wrapped her warm hands around his and said, 'We have to go, now.'

He stared at her, wanting answers but realising there was no time for them. 'It will be too dangerous during daylight. And even if it wasn't, I cannot get the guard to come earlier.'

She brought her face closer to his. 'I want you to start making a lot of noise. Shout, kick the bars, whatever you need to do to be heard by the guard.'

He shook his head. 'I've been here long enough to know the guards do not respond to noisy prisoners. They won't care.'

She squeezed his hands. 'Let me worry about the guard. Just make as much noise as you can.'

She went to move back but he held her in place with two fingers. 'Are you absolutely sure about this? We only get one chance.'

Her sad expression answered his question. 'In a few hours I will not be able to go anywhere.'

He held her gaze for a long moment and then released her hand. 'Then we go now.'

She nodded, eyes welling up.

'Don't cry. We're leaving this place.'

She wiped her cheeks, and touching her fingers to her lips, she reached through the bars and pressed them to his. 'Whatever happens, I love you. I had to try. You know I had to try.'

'I know. Shh. It will be all right.'

She nodded again, trying to be brave. 'Make noise. The guard will come.'

He remained hanging there as she got to her feet and checked her surroundings. Only once she was walking away did he drop to the ground below. Walking over to the bars, he took a lungful of air.

Here we go.

ALDARA MADE her way back along the wall, past the servants and maids who were too busy to notice her. She stepped inside and headed towards the dungeon, listening for him as she walked but not hearing what she needed to. When she reached the narrow steps, she glanced down at the guard who was on his feet, ear to the door, listening. Only then did Tyron's voice reach her through the cracks in the heavy door.

The guard was young, and when he looked up and saw her standing there, he returned upright. She did not wait for him to come to her before she descended the steps, an air of importance in her manner.

'What are you doing?' he called out.

She came to a stop at the bottom and looked at him, disapproval on her face. She folded her arms, the way a mother does when she is cross at her child. 'The king is entertaining royal guests. You need to get your prisoners in check before he takes them for a tour of the grounds.'

The young man's eyes widened. 'I can't stop them making noise.'

The fact that he had not even asked who she was and what authority she had was a good sign. 'Of course you can,' she said, gesturing towards the door. 'Tell them to be quiet or they will be shackled.'

'You want me to shackle them?'

She glared. 'I want you to silence them before Prince Felipe arrives and takes the matter into hand.' She looked behind her as if he might arrive any moment. When she turned back to him, she said, 'I should warn you, he is not in a good mood today.' Her hand went to her cheek and his eyes widened when he noticed the fresh bruise.

'I'm not meant to go in. I just watch the door until the next guard comes.'

'I am afraid you do not have a choice.'

He glanced again at her bruise before turning and lifting the crossbar.

'Can I trust you to handle this?' Aldara said, turning to leave.

He nodded. 'I'll take care of it.'

'Thank you,' she said, her tone cold. She walked back up the steps, eyes closing as she heard the heavy door swing open behind her.

～

WHEN TYRON HEARD the door open, he pressed his forehead against the wall and continued to shout incoherently about anything that came to mind. The sound of the guard's mace hitting the iron bars silenced him.

'Quieten down!' the guard shouted. 'Any more noise and it'll be the shackles for you.'

He was young, inexperienced. From the corner of his eye, Tyron could see him standing a safe distance from the bars.

'King Nilos cannot be trusted!' Tyron shouted, his forehead remaining against the cool wall.

The guard stepped closer and slipped an arm through the bars, ready to strike him with the mace. Tyron reached out and caught hold of the weapon mid-air. He turned to see the guard's eyes widen in surprise. The man tried to pull his weapon free, but it was too late. In one fast motion, Tyron grabbed hold of his arm with his free hand and pulled, making his head collide with the bars. The dazed man blinked, and a trickle of blood ran from a split above his eye. The dagger slid from Tyron's sleeve and he drove it into the guard's neck. The man collapsed, his hands going to the wound in a vain attempt to stop the bleeding.

Tyron returned the dagger to its sheath and tucked it into the waist of his trousers. Crouching, he reached through the bars and took the guard's sword and scabbard before standing and fitting it on himself. The tinkle of keys made him look up. Aldara stood in the corridor, staring down at the man who was now still.

'Aldara,' Tyron said, keeping his voice calm and quiet. 'Pass me the keys.' She did not move. Perhaps the realisation that he could do that to another man was too much for her. 'Aldara,' he said again, reaching through the bars and gesturing for her to come closer.

She looked at the outstretched hand and followed it up to his face. As she went to take a step towards him, another arm reached out from the cell next to Tyron's and tried to snatch the keys from her hand. Failing, he grabbed hold of her arm and pulled her out of Tyron's reach.

'Let her go!'

Propelling her elbow forwards, Aldara forced the man's arm at an unnatural angle. He cried out, releasing his grip on her. She threw the keys into Tyron's outstretched hand, but as she went to move away, the angry prisoner grabbed her with both hands and began to shake her. She put a knee up to stop him and made contact with the bar instead, crying out. Tyron leapt over the growing pool of blood at his feet and tried the first key in the lock. Nothing moved. The next key did not work either. He cursed and glanced across just as Aldara wound her arms through the man's and pulled herself free. She really had come prepared.

Aldara stepped around the dead guard and took the keys from Tyron, fiddling with them until the cell door opened. 'Let's go,' Aldara whispered, looking up at him.

How long had he dreamt of putting his hands on her without iron bars between them? He stepped out into the corridor and pulled her to him, feeling the warmth of her through his clothes, knowing his state would be repulsive. She held on to him, pressing her face into his chest, saying nothing.

'Walk in front of me,' he whispered, pulling away.

The other prisoners had become aware of what was happening and were now shouting for their cell doors to be unlocked also. He watched them as they walked down the corridor, keeping as close to the wall as possible. When they reached the end, he closed the door behind him to contain the noise that followed them out, replacing the crossbar so as not to raise suspicion if another guard wandered down.

He followed Aldara up the steps. When they reached the top, she stopped and turned to him.

'Give me the dagger.'

He frowned. 'Why?'

'Because you have a sword and I need a weapon.'

He hesitated before pushing it into the pocket of her dress. 'You cannot freeze up. I need you moving when I say move and listening for the next instruction. Understand?'

She nodded.

'All right, where are we going?'

'The east wall. There is tree cover on the other side.'

'Rope?'

'I have around twenty-five feet.'

'And how tall is the wall?'

'Forty-four feet.'

He shook his head. 'We are going to drop nineteen feet?'

'Minus your height with arms extended.'

He thought for a moment. 'Do you have any other weapons?'

'There are bows in the turrets, but we need to get to them first.'

He nodded. 'I'll follow you to the wall, but if we encounter anyone, I need you to get behind me and stay there. Make sure I am always between you and them. Can you do that?'

'Yes.'

He ran a finger down her swollen cheek. 'Get me to the wall, and I will get you home.'

She nodded and stepped into the corridor. Tyron followed and collided with her back, as she was still and was staring ahead. He moved in front of her, drawing his sword. A woman stood watching them. He remembered her from the day he had left the throne room and discovered Aldara waiting outside. The mentor.

'Medea,' the woman whispered, looking at the sword in Tyron's hand. 'What are you doing?'

Aldara stepped around Tyron, holding a hand up so he would remain where he was. 'Petra, you need to leave and pretend you never saw us.'

Petra's eyes moved from the sword to Tyron. He waited to see if Aldara could contain the situation without anyone getting hurt.

'Medea, what are you doing?' Petra said again, her expression falling. 'Prince Felipe is waiting for you. Tell me this is not what I think it is.' She shook her head as the pieces came together.

'Please. If you walk away, you will have nothing to do with any of this?'

Petra stared back at her. 'Who are you? The truth.'

Aldara swallowed, her other hand going up in an attempt to keep everyone calm. 'I cannot tell you who I am.' She glanced at Tyron. 'But I came here to get Prince Tyron out. And we need to go.'

Petra shook her head, overwhelmed. 'You lied to me.'

'Yes.'

She stepped towards Aldara. 'I told you about my son, and you lied to me.'

'Most of what I told you was the truth.'

'We need to go,' Tyron said, voice low.

Petra's eyes locked on him. 'You have cost her her life. She will be hanged for her part in this.'

In a few moments, the hilt of his sword was going to come down on her head, and it did not sit well with him. 'No she won't, because I'm getting her out.'

'How? You will never get out of here. There are guards everywhere.' She looked at Aldara. 'What were you thinking? Prince Felipe is never going to let you escape. Perhaps he will not hang you, instead keeping you as his Companion, beating you every day to remind you to be grateful for this life.' She was panting then.

Tyron went to step towards her but Aldara grabbed his arm.

'There is a maid. Her name is Velma,' Aldara said. 'She has been delivering letters to me. She has no idea that I am not who I say I am.'

Petra looked broken. 'Why are you telling me this?'

Aldara walked over to her, and to Tyron's surprise, she did not step back or call out for the guards.

'Because I am going to find your son, and when I do, I will send you a letter telling you everything I know.'

Petra blinked and tears fell. 'You are lying. You are a liar.'

'I swear to you,' Aldara said, taking Petra's hands. 'I did not lie about having a son. I know your pain is unimaginable, and I swear to you, I will search for Xander and get word to you somehow.'

Petra shook her head, conflicted. 'In thirty minutes I am going to go to Prince Felipe and tell him that I saw the two of you. Keeping this from him might cost me my life.' She withdrew her hands from Aldara's.

'I understand. Thank you.'

Petra was not finished. 'When the prince catches you, I will not be able to protect you.'

Aldara nodded. 'I know.'

Petra looked at Tyron. 'I hope you know what you are up against.'

He did not reply as he stepped up and took hold of Aldara's hand. 'Time to go.'

Aldara let him lead her past Petra. 'I'm sorry,' she called as they walked away.

Tyron glanced back, hoping he had done the right thing in trusting the mentor.

THEY STOOD IN THE SHADOWS, Aldara hugging the pillow cover containing their only supplies, watching Tyron put on the gold tunic, minus a button. It was too big for him but it would do.

'Thirty minutes is not much of a head start,' he said.

'I know, but I suspect she will walk slowly.'

He was counting the guards—there were two on the east wall, and two more talking at the base of the narrow steps that they would climb.

'There will be men in the turrets.' She bit down on her lip. 'This really would have been better at night.' Glancing up, she added, 'We might be spotted from the windows above.'

He took hold of her arms, trying to focus her. 'Walk in front of me until we get to the wall—'

'And then stay behind you,' she finished. He was looking at her, needing to know she was ready.

'We are going to play soldiers, just like when you were a child,' he said. 'And I really need you to win.'

'All right.'

'Promise me that if anything happens to me, you will keep going. Use those survival instincts, the ones that outsmarted all those Zoelin guards. Promise me.'

Her eyes moved between his. 'I promise.'

'You get to Leksi and you go home to our son.'

She nodded. 'I promise.' Her eyes remained on his for a moment, and then she stepped out from the shadows, the sun's scrutiny burning holes in her back. Body clenched, her eyes swept every shadow, waiting for death.

The guards turned to them as they approached. Their eyes narrowed on Aldara before travelling to Tyron, whose bearded face immediately raised suspicion. They reached for their swords the same time he did. She stopped walking so Tyron could step past her into a clash of swords that she feared would be heard by the men above them. Tyron should have been disadvantaged fighting two men, but he moved with such precision and ease that the fight was over in seconds, the wounded men collapsing before being dragged out of sight.

Aldara looked around to make sure no one had seen them.

'I'll go first,' Tyron said, coming up next to her. He now had two swords and his own dagger.

'Where is the other sword?' she asked.

'I only have two hands.'

'So do I.'

He pulled her towards the steps. 'You are not fighting trained guards after a few lessons with Stamitos,' he whispered.

His boots barely made a noise against the stone as they climbed, while her slippers seemed to slap against it.

'So you would rather me be defenceless?'

He glanced back at her. 'You are not defenceless. You have me.' He raised a finger to his lips, silencing her.

She was glad to stop talking, as she was out of breath trying to keep up with him. How he managed to be fitter than her after being locked in a cell for months she had no idea, but he did not let go of her hand until they reached the top.

Tyron stepped onto the wall, a bloodied sword in one hand, the other raised towards Aldara, telling her to remain where she was. He disappeared out of sight, and Aldara heard a groan that did not belong to him. She placed the pillow cover at her feet and retrieved the dagger from her pocket, waiting with the small blade in her shaking hand.

There was another clash of swords, lasting longer this time. Perhaps he had met his match.

Footsteps came at a run and Aldara checked behind her, peering down the steps they had just climbed. No, these were already on the wall. She turned back, listening. Two men, arriving from the right, and Tyron was not done with the guard on her left.

As the footsteps came closer, she gripped the dagger tightly, the way Stamitos had shown her. She remained hidden until the men came into view, then emerged, driving the weapon through the side of the guard closest to her. He stopped, clutching his side and turning to her in surprise. The other continued at a run towards Tyron, his sword joining the chorus of noise to her left.

The man she had wounded was still able to fight. He stepped towards her, sword ready. Aldara watched his feet, and when he lunged at her, trying to knock the dagger from her hand, she ducked around him. Tyron came into view then, one guard dead on the ground, two more swinging their swords at him. His eyes went to her and then to the guard who was preparing to strike.

'You stupid girl,' the guard said, one hand over his wound, the other swinging his sword, no longer aiming for her weapon but for whatever he could make contact with. She ducked beneath his blade and sliced his leg. He cried out and raised his sword, bringing it down. She did not have enough time to get out of his way.

She braced for pain, but instead there was a deafening clang above her head. She scurried out of the way and watched as Tyron pushed the man's sword upwards before driving it through his chest. His other fight had not even finished before the last guard came at him, sweat pouring from his face as he gave everything in order to be the one standing at the end. Aldara stayed out of the way, checking behind her for more men. When she turned back, the final guard was sinking to his knees, blood pouring from his stomach.

Tyron grabbed her hand and dragged her towards the turret. When they entered, they saw a man sitting on a stool, head leaning against the wall, asleep. Tyron walked over and cut his throat without a moment of hesitation. Aldara's hands went over her mouth to stop from gasping. She watched as Tyron selected two bows and quivers filled with arrows and came towards her.

'Do you still know how to use a bow?' he asked, putting one of the quivers over her head. 'I'll give you the bow when we get to the bottom.'

She nodded, eyes focused on his face so she would not look back at the sleeping dead man.

'Where is the rope?'

She looked behind her. 'I left it at the top of the steps.'

'Let's go,' he said, pulling her outside again.

They moved at a run, Aldara stumbling and Tyron pulling her upright. She wondered how much time it had taken to kill all those men. Perhaps Prince Felipe was already on his way. Tyron grabbed the pillow cover and turned it upside down, shaking its contents out. Aldara grabbed the poisons and stuffed them into her pocket with the dagger. Tyron picked up the rope of shawls and looked at her.

'*This* is your rope?'

She glanced down. 'I had to improvise.'

He stepped up to the outer wall and secured one end around a protruding iron spike. She looked around before moving up next to him, watching him tie an expert knot in record time.

'I am going to climb over first so I am beneath you if you lose your grip.' He turned to her, face serious. 'When we reach the bottom of the rope, you are going to climb down my body until you are hanging from my feet. This will close some of the distance between you and the ground.'

She nodded. She would do whatever he asked of her.

'You told me you used to climb trees when you were a child. Do you remember how to get down? Bend your legs when your feet hit the ground. Roll if you have to. Tell me you remember.'

'Yes, I remember.'

He gripped her arms. 'We are still playing soldiers.'

She nodded.

He kissed her forehead and climbed on top of the stone ledge, lowering himself over the edge. She climbed up after him, heart pounding like a drum beneath her ribs. Gripping the rope and positioning the quiver hanging from her back so the arrows would not spill, she followed him down, certain her fingers were going to give out at any moment. Her feet struggled to grip the wall despite angling her body against it. She was sweating as she tried not to look down at how far she had to go.

'How are you doing?' Tyron called up, sensing her distress.

'Fine,' she breathed, but in the same moment, her foot slipped from the wall and she felt her hands burn as they slid down the wool.

Tyron reached up and caught her foot just as it was hurtling towards his face. They hung there for a moment, Aldara trying to get her hands to work and Tyron holding her weight while supporting himself with one trembling hand.

'I've got you,' he said.

Of course he did. 'Are you all right?' she asked, lifting her foot from his hand so he could take hold of the rope again.

'I shouldn't have doubted you,' he said, looking up. 'The shawls are sturdy and the knots strong.'

She gave a weak smile.

'Just a few more feet, and then you are going to climb down my back, all right?'

'All right.'

Tyron was around fifteen feet from the ground when he stopped.

'Hurry now,' he said. 'We need to move.'

He needed two hands on the rope to hold the weight of them both. Thankfully, Aldara found gripping him much easier than the shawls. She lowered herself down him, murmuring an apology every time he winced because she had become tangled in the bows.

'I want you dangling from my feet before you even consider letting go. Understand?'

'Yes.'

She slid down his legs until her hands were gripping the tops of his boots. She was at least eight feet closer to the ground than he would be. Staring at the rocky surface below, aware that Tyron was holding both of their weight, she let go and dropped towards the ground, landing in a crouch before falling onto her side. Small, sharp rocks bit into her skin. She stood up, testing that her limbs were all working, and looked up to find Tyron watching her, wanting to know she was all right. She nodded to let him know she was fine and held a hand up, telling him to wait a moment. Moving quickly, she picked up as many of the sharper rocks as she could and threw them to the side. She looked again, waiting.

Holding on with one hand, Tyron pulled the bows over his head and dropped them one at a time so she could catch them. Once she had moved out of the way, he let go of the rope and fell. She heard the air leave his lungs as he landed, body folding into a ball and tumbling past her a few times before stopping. She ran to him, helping him to his feet.

'Nothing broken?'

'Nothing yet.' He looked at her. 'They are going to come for us. Are you ready to run for your life?'

She swallowed. 'I'm ready.'

CHAPTER 31

They ran east towards the trees, Aldara moving at twice the speed to match Tyron's longer strides. They needed to move west, but the east wall was the only one not guarded—until it was.

They were about twenty yards from cover when the first arrow hissed past them. Tyron slowed so he was behind Aldara like a shield. Four more arrows flew past, barely missing them. She sped up, listening for the sounds of him; as long as he was behind her, she could keep going.

Soon, the arrows could no longer make the distance from the wall. They slowed a little, stopping only when they reached the trees. They stood panting, looking at one another, knowing they could not outrun the men who would soon follow on horseback.

Aldara reached into her pocket and pulled out the bag of poisons.

'What is that?' Tyron asked, still out of breath.

'Poison for the arrows.'

He said nothing as he grabbed the entire contents of his quiver in one hand and held them out for her. She uncorked one jar and carefully poured the small amount over the tips of the arrows. Tyron returned them to his quiver and they used the other full jar on her arrows.

'That should make up for your bad aim,' he said.

It was an entirely inappropriate time for jokes, but the comment helped to still her hands which were shaking violently. He steadied them in his own, not saying anything, making promises he could not keep, or comforting her with lies. He just kept hold of her hands for a moment, reminding her that he was there, no matter what happened next.

'Ready?' he asked.

She nodded and they ran north, the castle flashing through the trees to their left. Tyron led them into dense trees with ageing trunks and thirsty branches, setting a pace and adjusting it when she fell too far behind. They stopped when they heard the horses, neither surprised by the sound, only trying to determine how many men were in pursuit.

'Eight,' Aldara whispered. 'Maybe fewer.'

He nodded. 'The others will have gone south just in case. We need to kill as many as we can before they reach us or we won't stand a chance.' He gestured to her and began walking. 'And we want a horse.'

She did not answer as she was too out of breath, and could not respond with an equally casual tone when it came to taking the lives of the men.

They continued north at a jog, the thunder of hooves ever closer. Voices seeped through the trees, causing Aldara to jump at each noise. Tyron slowed to a walk and removed the longbows from his back, handing one of them to her and placing a finger over his mouth. She pulled five arrows from the quiver, careful not to make contact with the poisoned tip, holding them in her draw hand. Tyron turned to her, his gaze falling to the arrows before raising his eyebrows in question.

'A little something Sapphira taught me,' she whispered.

Tyron shook his head, the string of his bow already taut. A horse flashed to their left and Tyron swung and released the arrow before Aldara even had a chance to raise her bow. A groan sounded, followed by the thud of a body hitting the ground. The horse cantered off, giving them no chance of catching it.

An arrow hissed past Tyron's head and he reached back for Aldara, pulling her behind the thick trunk of an oak. He peered around the side, arrow aimed, waiting. Aldara's back was pressed against the tree. She raised her bow, her gaze sweeping the trees in case others came from that direction. She watched the shifting leaves down her arrow. The heavy breathing of a horse reached her just before it burst through the trees, its rider clutching a bow pointed at Tyron's back. Aldara released the first arrow, hitting the man's shoulder. A moment later, the bow was reloaded and she released a second arrow into his chest, knocking him from his horse.

Tyron kept his eyes forwards, trusting that she was up to the task. One moment of distraction would cost them their lives, and he could not be everywhere. Aldara stepped in front of the gelding that was preparing to flee, forcing him to stop, his front legs lifting off the ground for a moment.

'Easy,' she whispered, reaching for the hanging rein. The horse pulled away from her, snorting with defiance, but she kept a hold of him.

'Down!' Tyron shouted.

Aldara dropped to her stomach, pressing her body flat against the ground while keeping hold of the rein. Her eyes pressed shut and the smell of forest debris filled her lungs. A painful cry came from the gelding as an arrow pierced his chest. She turned her head and watched as the horse's legs folded beneath him and he collapsed onto his side, breathing rapidly as he lay helpless. The bending of wood and release of the string came over and over as Tyron fought for both of them while the gelding's breaths grew slower and slower. Then she was pulled to her feet, the bow returned to her hands, her remaining arrows thrust at her.

'Eyes on our right and behind,' Tyron said, almost shaking her.

He was trying to keep her alive. She looked at him and then down at the bow before nodding.

He walked in front, bow swinging gently side to side. She followed behind, twitching and nervous, seeing men in every shadow, watching the horse die over and over again in her mind. Then the sound of hooves. The sound of Tyron's bow. The sound of her heart pounding in her ears.

She was no soldier.

Another horse came from the left and Tyron swung in that direction, stepping around Aldara who felt as though she were cowering in his shadow.

Thud.

'Get the horse,' Tyron said, his bow taut and ready. Only a few arrows remained.

She moved out from behind him and stepped in front of the horse, expecting it to die. A low whinny came from it as it danced sideways, away from Tyron's threatening presence. She took hold of the rein, hope creeping in, only to be suffocated by the sound of Prince Felipe's voice calling to them.

'Well done,' said Felipe, sounding almost genuinely pleased. 'You made it a few yards farther than I expected.'

Aldara's eyes went to a still Tyron, outwardly calm as he tried to the find the prince amid the trees. She lifted her bow and watched the trees on the other side, trying to decide if she should let go of the horse to have better control over her aim if needed. The bow jolted in her hands as an arrow hit it. She gasped and Tyron turned to take aim at the shooter.

'I wouldn't do that if I were you,' Prince Felipe said,

emerging from the trees on horseback, an arrow pointed at Tyron.

Tyron turned and aimed at the prince, but two more guards appeared on horseback, bows ready. Lastly, Sir Proteus emerged, poised amid the conflict.

'We must stop meeting like this,' he said to Tyron.

Tyron glanced once over his shoulder before returning his gaze to Felipe, who was still approaching.

Proteus looked at Aldara. 'I told him you were trouble,' he said, head shaking. 'He never listens.'

Aldara's breaths were coming in sharp rasps. She pointed her arrow at Proteus, knowing that even if she and Tyron had the opportunity, they would be shot down in an instant by the other waiting guards.

'Medea,' Felipe called, an eerie calmness in his voice. 'Your mentor tells me you had a change of heart about coming to my bed. I almost didn't believe her as I had seen your willingness, felt it with my own hands.'

'That's far enough,' Tyron called to the prince.

Prince Felipe stopped and smiled. 'I heard you were crazy, but I never could have imagined how deep the infestation would filter.' He tilted his head and looked at Aldara. 'What has he done to you, my majestic impostor?'

Aldara's eyes went to him then, terror in them. The man looking back at her would kill Tyron and take her back to Masville to be suitably punished. Perhaps he would keep Tyron alive to witness it.

She stepped closer to Tyron, whose gaze was fixed on Felipe.

'Get the girl,' Felipe called to Proteus. 'I'll deal with her later.'

Aldara shook her head, finding her voice. 'I'm not going back there.'

Felipe laughed. 'You know I love your tenacity, but you do not have a choice here.'

'The lady said she does not want to go with you,' Tyron said.

Felipe ignored him, looking past him to Aldara. 'Come now, Medea. We both know you cannot even use that thing.'

Proteus sat smiling in the saddle. 'What are your orders, my lord?'

Felipe exhaled. 'I'm thinking, I'm thinking,' he said before lowering his bow, climbing off his horse, and walking towards them. 'It seems Prince Tyron wants to make a display of his masculinity in front of the lady. Don't you, Prince Tyron?'

'You are a brave man putting your bow down,' Tyron replied.

Felipe drew his sword and his eyes darkened. 'Come on. Let's see if all the stories about you are true.'

Aldara turned to see Tyron drop his bow and draw his sword.

'What are you doing?' Tyron asked. 'You want to fight when you have already won?'

Felipe stopped a few feet from him, readying himself. 'Actually, I'm going to cut off your head. And *she* is going to watch.'

Proteus dismounted and slipped his bow over his head. He walked towards Aldara, confident that she would not attempt to shoot him while a guard kept an arrow pointed at her.

'Right,' Tyron whispered to Aldara, so only she would hear him.

It took her a moment, but the second the word registered, Aldara swung right and shot the guard through the chest. He had been unprepared and surprised by her ability to use the bow. His wide eyes remained on her as he slipped from the saddle. She closed her eyes so she would not have to see what she had done.

At the same time, Tyron had turned to the guard opposite and, gripping his sword like a spear, hurled it at him, stabbing him through the stomach.

Proteus's eyes widened as he realised his vulnerability at that moment. He broke into a run towards Aldara, dark eyes fixed on her as he drew his sword. She raised her bow again and pointed it at him, not wanting to release it, not wanting the blood of another on her hands. But what would he do to her when he reached her? What nature of death would Tyron face at his hands?

She released her final arrow, piercing his neck. He continued to run a few paces before falling forwards, coughing and spluttering a few feet from her. She watched him, trembling and fighting the urge to go to him and beg his forgiveness for taking his life for the one she valued more.

Anger erupted from Felipe in the form of a roar. Aldara turned around, all out of arrows, all out of tricks. Tyron bent in preparation of a fight with no weapon to defend himself.

'What's your plan now?' Felipe shouted, gripping his sword. Spit flew from his mouth with each word. 'You can die now knowing she will spend the rest of her life paying for your crimes.' His face was twisted with the grief of losing his mentor, or perhaps just losing.

Aldara watched from behind Tyron, her mind returning from numb. Remembering the dagger still in her pocket, she slid it from its sheath and stepped towards Tyron to slip it into his hand. His fingers wrapped around it while his eyes remained on Felipe, whose sword was raised above him. Tyron blocked the first blow with the small blade, surprising the prince, his eyes falling to the dagger in Tyron's hand.

Aldara stepped back from them, tripping over Proteus's body as she did so. She looked down at the sword sitting loosely in his hand and reached for it, tossing it at Tyron's feet, but it was no good. Felipe's blows were relentless, coming down quickly on Tyron, who was barely able to defend himself, let alone reach down to pick up another weapon. Felipe forced him farther and farther away from the sword.

'Run!' Tyron called to her. 'Go!'

Aldara staggered back, terrified of staying and yet unable to leave. She turned and ran towards Proteus's tall black mare still waiting behind her. When she reached the saddle, she saw the quiver of arrows and looked down at the bow she was still clutching. She loaded it one more time, and with shaking hands, aimed it at Felipe. Nothing happened. Her hand refused to let go of the string, refused to take the life of the Crown Prince of Corneo.

Only when she heard a cry from Tyron did she find the courage to act. Aiming at Felipe's leg, she released the arrow, piercing his thigh. He cried out, dropping his sword and clutching the arrow with both hands.

Taking advantage of the distraction, Tyron stepped towards him, blade ready.

'Tyron, no!'

He stopped and looked at her.

'We have a horse. We are free to go.'

Tyron bent down and picked up Felipe's sword. The bow fell from Aldara's hands and she pulled herself into the saddle, kicking the mare into a canter towards them. He stood over the prince, sword in hand, eyes dark.

'You better kill me,' Felipe hissed through clenched teeth, 'or I will come for you. Both of you,' he added, looking at her.

Aldara held out her hand to Tyron. 'Come.' When he did not move, she said it again. 'Come.'

Slowly, he looked up, his restraint spent.

Her eyes pleaded. 'If you kill the Crown Prince of Corneo, it will be a very different war.'

Tyron's eyes returned to Felipe. 'You owe her your life.' He stepped back from the prince, eyes remaining on him until he reached Aldara. Taking her hand, he pulled himself up behind the saddle.

'You will not get far!' Felipe yelled.

Aldara looked down at him, but no words came.

His crazed eyes watched her as she swung the horse around and rode away.

Tyron said nothing, remaining completely silent as they headed north. She thought he needed some time to calm down, but twenty minutes into their journey, she noticed he was leaning to one side. She turned in the saddle just as he slipped from the horse. Grabbing for him, she managed to slow his fall. Stopping the mare, she leapt off and ran the few paces back to him.

He was on his back, his gaze locked on hers. Only then did she notice his hand clutching his stomach, blood seeping through his fingers. A scream sounded in her mind. Perhaps not in her mind.

He said something, and she crouched to listen. What was he saying?

More whispers.

She pulled back from him and pressed her hand over the wound, willing it to close.

'Aldara, you need to go.'

She looked at him, trying to make sense of his words. 'What? What are you saying?'

'Ride north for an hour, keep to the trees. When there is no more cover, move east. But you must stay off the roads.'

'Stop. Stop.' She shook her head, repelling the words. 'You're coming with me. You'll be all right.' She thought for a moment. 'I need you to keep pressure on the wound for me.'

He nodded, visibly paling.

She removed her dress and chemise, then put the dress back on. Gripping his arms, she pulled him into a sitting position and lifted his shirt, trying not to appear shocked at the sight of the wound. She wrapped the chemise around his waist in hope of slowing the blood loss, tying it in place before returning his hand to the area for added pressure.

'One moment,' she said, running off to retrieve the horse. The mare was startled by her fast approach, but thankfully did not flee. Aldara led the mare to Tyron.

'Come. Let's go.'

He looked up at her, an apologetic expression on his face. 'You need to leave. I can't ride.'

She took hold of his arm and tried to pull him up. 'You don't need to ride—you just need to hold on.' When he did not move, she gripped him harder. 'Please! Get up!'

'Go,' he pleaded.

'No. We did not make it this far, take the lives of all these men, for one of us to be left behind.'

'I won't make it.'

'You will. Now get up!' She went behind him and, with strength she did not realise she had, began to lift him from the ground. Seeing her determination, Tyron cooperated as best he could, balancing on unsteady legs when she let him go. She got down on one knee next to the horse, making a step with her leg. 'Sit behind the saddle so you can hold on to me.'

He looked down at her proffered leg. 'Aldara, if I step on your leg, I will break it.'

She began to cry then, covering her eyes with bloodied hands for a moment before sucking in a breath. More than anything else, she needed him to try. Removing her hands, she looked at him, face set, and said, 'Then break it, because I'm not leaving here without you. We leave together or we die here together.' Tears spilled down her cheeks stained with his blood.

He watched her a moment, choked by his emotion. Slowly, he lifted his left foot and stepped onto hers.

She kept her face neutral as the full weight of him pressed down on her and pushed his right leg up over the horse's rump as best she could. Wrapping her arms around his left leg, she slowly stood, pushing him onto the horse where he gripped the back of the saddle with his free hand. She slipped her foot into the stirrup and pulled herself into the saddle in front of him. Reaching behind, she wrapped his free arm around her as she looked up to try and gauge direction. If King Nilos's men caught up with them now, they would not stand a chance.

She turned to look at Tyron. 'Hold on. Do not let go of me. Promise me.'

A slight nod from him, his eyes barely open.

Aldara turned and kicked the horse into a canter, leaving behind the graveyard they had made together.

CHAPTER 32

The sun drew them west. Every landmark was foreign, and the only directional guide she had would soon slip behind the hills. She pushed the mare hard, thankful for her fitness and tolerance of a second rider. Wripis was a three-hour ride at a hard pace, but that was for someone who knew where they were going. The exit strategy had included an escort to Lord Belen's manor, but nothing had gone to plan.

They had been riding for about an hour when they reached the end of the woods. Aldara slowed the mare and stared out at the blanched, open fields in front of them. She felt Tyron's head press down against her shoulder and turned, trying to look at him. His eyes were closed, but one arm still enveloped her, a hand gripping her dress. She glanced up at the sun, trying to figure out what direction to move in.

'Just a few more hours,' she said, trying to sound confident.

Tyron did not reply.

She clicked her tongue and the horse went forwards,

cantering across the brown field. They moved west while she looked in every direction, sure they would be caught, listening for signs of life from Tyron.

Half an hour later, they stopped at a boundary fence where a few grazing sheep stood watching, ready to disperse if necessary. Aldara walked the mare along the fence line, eventually coming to a dusty road. She turned onto it, then remembering what Tyron had said, she veered off it, riding parallel until she realised it was taking her too far south.

Her tongue moved in her mouth, recognising her thirst. She crossed back over the road and rode north alongside barren farmland where the fences seemed to have given up. There was nothing to keep in, no reason for people to enter. Until she saw the well.

She stopped and glanced at the farmhouse in the distance, a thick covering of dust making it blend into the landscape. Spotting a broken rail, she stepped the horse over it and headed for the well. When she stopped, she tried to wake Tyron with a gentle shake, but he did not respond. Reaching back and feeling for a pulse, she exhaled with relief when she felt the weak beat against the tips of her fingers.

'Tyron, I need to get us some water.'

No response.

She tried not to cry as she realised the only way to get off was to take him with her. She slipped out of the saddle, guiding his body down as she did so. He tipped towards her as her feet landed on the dirt, and she almost collapsed under the weight of him. He groaned as she lay him on the ground, his wound weeping with fresh blood. Crouching next to him, she lifted his tunic and shirt and tried to inspect the area. There was so much blood she was having difficulty seeing the wound.

Standing, she stepped over to the well and wound the handle round and round, waiting for the rope to go slack as it hit the water. When the rope was fully unwound, it swayed gently, taunting her. Her hands went over her face and a sob escaped her. Just a few seconds. She would let herself fall apart for a few seconds, and then she would get up and do the next thing.

'What's all this?' came a voice.

She gasped and looked up to see a man standing over Tyron. He crouched down, studying the bloodied Corneo uniform before turning his face to her.

'What happened?'

She took in his threadbare clothes and concerned expression before stepping over to Tyron and lifting his shirt to show the man the blood-soaked bandage wrapping his middle.

The man shook his head as he thought. 'Sword wound?' He glanced up at Tyron's heavily bearded face.

Aldara nodded. 'Yes. We need some water.'

The man looked at her. 'This man needs a physician.'

'I'm taking him to Wripis. There is a physician there.'

The man shook his head again. 'Wripis is an hour north of here. He won't last the journey.'

Aldara closed her eyes, trying to focus on the 'hour north of here' part of that statement. 'Can you... can you just help me get him back on the horse?'

He watched her with suspicion. 'Wripis is under Syrasan rule right now.'

She swallowed. 'I know. This soldier is a relative of Lord Belen,' she lied. 'King Nilos has labelled him a traitor because of the blood connection. It's the only place he will be safe.'

The man stood. 'If King Nilos's guards are looking for him, you cannot be stopping here. I have my family to consider.'

She nodded, getting to her feet also. 'I understand. Can you help me get him on the horse?' she asked again.

He looked down at Tyron, conflicted. 'Wait here. Give me a few minutes.' He walked away before she could respond.

Aldara had no idea if he could be trusted. For all she knew, he could be on his way to send word to King Nilos. She had no choice but to wait, because there was no way she could get Tyron onto the horse by herself, and there was no way she was leaving without him.

Ten minutes later, the man returned with a woman, assumedly his wife, a pail of water and some boiled linen. Aldara tried not to cry as she thanked them repeatedly. The woman said nothing as she knelt next to Tyron, untied the shirt and examined the wound.

'He has lost a lot of blood,' said the man behind her.

The woman nodded and looked at Aldara. 'Try to get him to drink,' she said, gesturing to the pail where a metal cup bobbed on the surface of the water.

Aldara sat with Tyron's head in her lap. 'Drink, please,' she whispered. Most of the water ran onto her skirt, but he swallowed a couple of times before tiring. Aldara drank the rest of the cup and watched as the man pushed the horse back from the bucket.

The woman washed the wound and bandaged it firmly, working with experienced hands and a blank face.

'Give the rest to the horse,' she said to her husband, gesturing to the pail. The mare drank greedily, emptying the pail in a few seconds. When the woman stood, she looked at Aldara and said, 'We cannot do any more. We have no food to offer you.'

'You have done more than you realise. I cannot thank you enough.'

The woman nodded before walking away, the empty pail in her hand, the blood-soaked shirt in the other.

'Come,' said the man. 'I'll help you get him on the horse, and then it's off with you.'

Aldara stood up, carefully laying Tyron's head on the warm ground. 'How should we do this?'

'Get on,' replied the man. 'Do the best you can from up there.'

Aldara mounted and watched as the man grabbed beneath Tyron's arms and lifted him off the ground with surprising strength. He leaned Tyron against the horse for a moment and adjusted his grip before lifting him. Aldara took hold of Tyron and pulled him up behind her, her back supporting the weight of his body.

'Thank you for your kindness,' she said, looking back at the stranger.

The man just nodded and pointed north. 'One hour north at a steady speed.' He hesitated. 'Corneon guards patrol the area.'

She blinked and dug her heels into the mare's sides.

HER BODY CRAMPED from the weight of him pressing down on her. She kept having to reach behind and straighten him, each effort draining her remaining strength. The worry about encountering Corneon guards together with the possibility of never seeing her son and family again was making her panic. She thought about the possibility that Tyron was already dead, a corpse against her. Then she was too afraid to check, so she reached behind and held on to him, hoping he could siphon life through her grip as they continued north.

When Aldara saw the woods in the distance, she moved towards them, reaching the first tree just as the sun abandoned them, leaving grey light in its place. It seemed like an hour had passed some time ago, and she feared she had gotten them lost. Moving at a walk, she weaved through the trees, losing sight of the road to her right which she had been following at a distance. She thought about stopping, resting, giving up, but knew if she laid Tyron down on the leafy ground, he would never get up again. So she walked, stopping occasionally at the sound of hooves in the distance, wondering if they would be found, resenting the darkness while feeling gratitude for the invisibility it offered.

And then she heard hooves, not on the road but in the trees around her. Again she stopped, her tired heart beating numbly, her eyes closed. Closer they came, and then they were in front of them, next to them. Surrounding them. Swords were drawn, maybe three. Her eyes remained closed as she thought of Mako, smiling and loved, but without her there to see it. She wondered if Tyron would be left amid the trees, given up on, as you do with the dead. And what of her? She would pay for their crimes against King Nilos, for the dead men left in their wake.

'Who are you?' a man asked.

She opened her eyes, looking at the guard who had spoken before shifting her gaze to the other two men blending with the shadows, their glinting swords bringing visibility. She had no lies left in her. Their end brought only truth. 'My name is Aldara. This is Prince Tyron of Syrasan, and he is dying.'

There was silence for a moment, and then the guard said, 'Check him.'

She did not want to let them touch him, but the fight had left her also. One of the men dismounted and walked over to them, eyeing her cautiously. Only once he was next to her did she notice the *S* on the sleeve of his uniform. Her eyes widened and her grip on Tyron loosened. 'Syrasan guards?'

'Yes,' said the man next to her, trying to get a better look at Tyron. 'And this man is wearing a Corneon uniform.'

Tyron's facial hair made him unrecognisable. She could not blame him for being suspicious. 'It was necessary to get out of Masville Castle, to get over the wall. This is Prince Tyron, I swear it. Sir Leksi is staying at Lord Belen's manor and will be able to verify both of our identities.' When he did not say anything, she added, 'Please, you can take us there as prisoners if you like. We have no weapons and pose no threat.'

'Where were you headed?' asked one of the mounted guards.

'To Lord Belen's in Wripis.'

He glanced at the other man. 'You were heading in the wrong direction.'

She nodded, swallowing. 'I lost my way when we lost light.'

He considered her explanation. 'Are you travelling alone?' 'Yes.'

He continued to study her through the dark, trying to gauge if she was telling the truth. 'We will take you to Sir Leksi.' He looked at the guard on the ground. 'Tie his hands.'

Aldara looked behind at Tyron. 'You don't need to tie them. He is not conscious. He cannot even stay upright without support.'

'The men will secure him to prevent a fall.' He looked at the other mounted guard. 'Check her for weapons and put her on your horse.'

The guard on the ground helped Aldara from the saddle, holding her up for a moment when her legs failed. Tyron was not aware of any of it, his face ghostly pale beneath his long beard. The other guard slipped from the saddle and walked over to Tyron, checking for a pulse. Aldara was relieved when the guard proceeded to bind his hands—it meant he was still alive.

CHAPTER 33

Soldiers stared as the horses made their way between the tents. Their eyes moved from Aldara to Tyron, who was bound and slumped behind one of the riders. They came to a stop outside a large tent, and one of the guards dismounted and spoke with a young boy who came out to meet him. The boy looked over at Tyron and then disappeared back inside. A moment later Leksi stepped out, eyes landing on Aldara.

'Get the physician,' he said to the boy before rushing towards Tyron. 'What happened?' Leksi asked, glancing back at her while he checked Tyron for a pulse.

'We had to leave earlier than expected. They caught up to us.' Her voice was hoarse and her throat ached.

Realising that the man was indeed Prince Tyron, the other guards dismounted and rushed to help.

'We could not identify him,' one of the men explained. 'We had to take precautions.'

Leksi realised as they lifted him down from the horse that his wrists were tied. He pulled a dagger from his right boot and cut the rope. 'Take him inside,' he said, gesturing to the tent.

The men carried an unresponsive Tyron inside while Aldara remained on her horse, watching until he was out of sight. Relief made room for exhaustion, and for the first time that day, she felt the full extent of her fatigue. She could not even get off the horse. She sat there, hands still tied, while everyone else moved about her with purpose. Torches came towards her in the darkness, the boy from earlier who had returned with a physician holding tight to his leather bag of medical supplies.

After they disappeared into the tent, Aldara saw Stamitos and Pero striding towards her, the flickering flame of Pero's torch lighting their worried faces. She was too tired to cry, too tired for anything. They did not go into the tent; they came to her.

'Are you injured?' Stamitos asked, holding the torch up.

She did not think so. 'No.' Her face collapsed, but she stifled the sob that threatened to escape her. 'But Tyron is badly injured.' She looked down at the blood on her dress, and on her hands.

Pero stepped forwards and cut her hands free before reaching up to help her down. He kept hold of her when he realised her legs were not taking any of her weight.

'Take her to my tent,' Stamitos said.

They walked along the row of tents, Stamitos in front providing light, Pero keeping hold of Aldara, not saying a word. Stamitos stopped and pulled the flap back for them. Pero walked her inside and lowered her onto the cot. He straightened and looked at Stamitos.

'I will go to Prince Tyron and see if I can assist in any way.'

Stamitos nodded and watched him leave.

Panic blew in with the breeze when the canvas parted. The men passing the tent seemed to be in a rush. Aldara glimpsed them before the heavy fabric dropped back into place, muffling the noise. She gripped the edge of the cot, listening and trying to process everything that had happened. If Tyron died, it would all have been for nothing. Months without her son. The Companion banished, her life upheaved with Aldara's arrival. And all the men whose lives they had taken.

'What do you need?' Stamitos asked, causing her to jump.

She shook her head, thinking. What did she need?

Stamitos grabbed a flask of water and handed it to her as he sat next to her. She took a few large gulps and handed it back to him.

'Thank you,' she whispered, not looking at him.

'Are you ready to tell me what happened?'

She glanced at him then, eyes already welling. 'I'm afraid it's a rather long story.'

Stamitos glanced in the direction of the noise. 'Luckily for you I think we have quite a wait ahead of us.'

They remained seated, eyes on the opening of the tent, waiting for news. The story came out of Aldara in fragments, broken by long silences. Stamitos did not ask questions, happy to wait for the information and piece it together.

When she was done, he made her drink some more water, asked if she was hungry, if she wanted to wash. She could not eat or wash. She could not do anything while Tyron was a few tents down fighting for his life.

Stamitos rested his elbows on his knees and watched the shadows move by their feet.

'I'm sorry,' Aldara said, eyes also on the ground. 'I wasn't the right person to save him after all.'

He looked at her then. 'I disagree. You have always been the one person who can bring him back to us.'

She tried to smile but did not have it in her. It was quieter outside now; everyone had performed their role and were now where they should be. At least she hoped that was what it meant.

She was about to say something to Stamitos when Leksi stepped into the tent, his expression just as serious as earlier. He looked between them, unsure who to address. His gaze settled on Stamitos who stood up, ready to act, while Aldara continue to sit, her legs not cooperating with her wishes.

'The physician has closed the wound.'

'Has he woken at all?' Stamitos asked.

Leksi shook his head. 'No, but you can go see him.'

Aldara pushed off the cot with strength she seemed to have reserved for that very moment and looked at Stamitos. 'I'm coming.'

They walked with Leksi back to the tent where Tyron lay on a cot, looking a lot like a corpse. His bloodied clothes had been cut off his body and sat in a pile in the corner. Pero passed them carrying a basin filled with filthy water. He had washed the blood and dirt off Tyron, who was now covered by a white sheet, reminding Aldara of how Idalia looked before men had arrived to take her away.

She walked over to him, blinking away thoughts of death and searching for signs of life within him. While Leksi and Stamitos spoke in whispers behind her, she rested a hand lightly on his chest. There was warmth beneath the sheet—and the gentle beat of his heart.

'Will he live?' she asked no one in particular. 'The physician must have some idea.'

Leksi looked over at Tyron. 'The physician was surprised to find him alive after first laying eyes on him.'

Stamitos grabbed a stool and placed it beneath Aldara. She sank down onto it.

'Thank you.'

Stamitos nodded and looked back at Leksi. 'So we just wait?'

Leksi rubbed his palms against his eyes. 'Wait and pray. That's all we can do.'

THE PHYSICIAN RETURNED in the dead of night to check on Tyron and change his bandages. Aldara, who had fallen asleep on the stool with her head pressed against Tyron's shoulder, was woken by the clearing of the man's throat. She startled awake, looked up at the man's disapproving face, and then stepped away from the prince, apologising as she did so. When the physician had finished, he dropped some liquid derived from herbs into a cup of water and signalled to Aldara to help him. She cradled Tyron's head, watching it run down his cheeks before he finally swallowed. Her thumb stroked the hair behind his ear.

The physician said he would check on Tyron in the morning and left them. Aldara returned to the stool, expecting him to open his eyes and smile. She ran her hand beneath the sheet so her fingers touched his and her fore-head returned to his shoulder, his skin still warm and smelling of clean cotton and pine needles.

She woke before the physician arrived. Keeping her eyes closed, she slid her hand up and placed it over Tyron's heart to check if it was beating. It was a habit she had formed years before, proving that the fear of losing him was not new. For a moment she pretended they were just sleeping next to each other, as they had done so many times in the past. The comfort and warmth that moment brought carried her back off to sleep.

The next time she woke, it was with a hand on her shoul-der. Her eyes sprang open and she turned her head to look at

Tyron. His eyes were still closed, and the hand on her shoulder belonged to Stamitos. She turned to him and looked up.

'Good morning,' he said, letting go of her. 'I see you kept him alive.'

She glanced back at Tyron. Was there more colour in his cheeks? Maybe she just hoped there was. She withdrew her hands from him, suddenly aware of the cold.

'You should eat something. Change your clothes. And please wash.'

She stared down at her dress and moved her hands, feeling the stiffness of her skin where Tyron's blood had dried. 'Yes,' she said, standing up and touching her face, remembering that it was likely stained with him also. It would not do to go home looking like that.

Mako flashed in her mind, and she closed her eyes at the sight of his beautiful face.

'What is it?' Stamitos asked. 'Are you dizzy? Come, we'll get you some food.'

Aldara opened her eyes. 'No, I'm fine.'

'What is it, then? What do you need?' His good hand seemed ready to catch her.

She turned to him and exhaled, eyes meeting his. 'I need to go home.'

Stamitos's eyebrows shot up. When she did not offer an explanation, he asked, 'Now?'

Her lips pressed together and she glanced down at Tyron. 'I went to Corneo to free him. He is free. Now it is time for me to return to my son.' She tried to smile. 'And I think the physician will be relieved to have me out of the way.'

Stamitos studied her face. 'You don't want to be here when he wakes? Speak to him?'

She blinked and look down. 'Of course I do, but I'm not sure either of us will survive another goodbye.' A smile flickered and faded. 'Mako has waited long enough for his mother to return.' Her eyes went to Tyron. 'I chose him. And now it's time to choose my son.'

Stamitos nodded. 'I understand.' He released a breath. 'All right. Eat, wash, and then I'll have Leksi escort you.'

She shook her head. 'That's not necessary. Leksi is needed here.'

Stamitos tilted his head, looking at her like she had lost her mind. 'When Tyron wakes, what do you suppose will be his first question?'

He would ask where she was, and when they told him she had returned home, he would want to know every precaution was taken to ensure she arrived there safely. And there were few people he trusted with that task.

'I'd take you myself, but…' He held up his arm.

She smiled. 'Don't play victim with me. I have seen what you can do with one hand.'

A grin spread across his face, and they were quiet for a moment.

'How will we ever thank you for risking so much to return him to us?'

She turned to look at Tyron. 'Your gratitude might be premature. Let's revisit the subject when, and if, he wakes.'

Some colour had returned to his lips, she was sure of it.

'He will live if you tell him to,' Stamitos said. 'You have been his reason for persisting at life for some time.' He shook her shoulder lightly. 'I believe we have your mare. I'll have her saddled and waiting.' He turned and slipped through the flap of the tent.

'Thank you,' she called to his back, watching the canvas sway gently for a moment. She turned back to Tyron as she sat down on the stool and brought her lips to his ear. 'Did you hear what your crazy brother said? He thinks if I tell you to live, you will live.' She pressed her lips against his hair and then rested her forehead against him. 'What say you, my lord?' she whispered.

Tears spilled down her cheeks when she blinked. 'Wake up.' She lifted her head and took in his slack face, then leaned close again. 'I love you. And I want you to live. Please, my prince. When you can, when you are able, get up and *live*.'

She brushed her lips on his head as she stood up, her fingers combing his hair as she turned from him and walked out of the tent.

CHAPTER 34

*A*ldara and Leksi were two hours north of Arelasa
when they lost light. They stopped at a house
belonging to Leksi's uncle, not quite a manor but a noble
household nonetheless. The small family included two sons,
not yet of age, who fussed over Leksi like nothing Aldara had
ever seen. The boys fought over who would take his horse
and then ran about fetching Leksi food and refilling his cup
before finally sitting down on either side of him to ask
endless questions about the war.

'Will you be staying the night?' one of them asked, his face
eager. The other held his breath, waiting.

Leksi looked to Aldara for an answer.

'How far is Roysten from here?' she asked.

'Three hours with fresh horses,' Leksi's uncle answered.
'But you cannot travel in darkness. I suggest you spend the
night here and leave at first light.'

Aldara and Leksi looked at each other, both needed
elsewhere.

'I would like to keep going,' she said.

Leksi looked relieved. He thanked his uncle for the hospitality and accepted the offer of a fresh horse. The boys ran alongside the horses, shouting farewells to their famous cousin until they could run no more.

The next part of the journey took longer than the expected three hours, as Loda was tired and Aldara had not had the option of a fresh horse since she would not be returning any time soon.

They had slowed to a walk when they reached the dirt track that led to the farm. Leksi stopped his horse and looked at her. She smiled at him, even though he could not see.

'I suppose offering you a bed is pointless?'

Leksi's horse was already turned around. 'I need to get back.'

'You should never have left.'

'And risk Tyron waking and telling me I am to be drawn and quartered? No, thank you.'

Artemus had wandered out of the house and was trotting down the track, barking at them.

'Can I request one more favour from you?' Aldara asked, peering at him in the darkness.

Leksi glanced in the direction of the barking dog. 'Of course.'

'Can someone write to me? If anything changes. If he…'

'Tyron will write to you himself.'

She watched his sincere expression for a moment.

'Until next time,' he said.

She nodded. 'Until next time, Sir Leksi.'

He turned and cantered away just as Artemus reached them. The dog watched the departing horse for a moment before looking back at Aldara and barking again. Aldara dismounted and waited for the dog to recognise her. When Artemus's tail began to wag, she cupped her head, keeping the dog's tongue just out of reach while they greeted one another.

When the dog had calmed, they walked in silence along the track to the house where Kadmus and Isadore were waiting outside. Isadore stood next to the chopping block where the axe was perched, wedged into its surface. Kadmus had walked forwards to get a better look, watching her quietly as she emerged from the dark, Artemus and Loda either side of her. His face collapsed with relief at the sight of her.

The men ran to her and wrapped their arms about her, laughing—crying, perhaps. Dahlia came out of the house to see what all the fuss was about. While she could not find it in her to embrace her daughter, she did let the men fuss over her, saying nothing as they kissed her, lifted her and swung her about.

Dahlia disappeared into the house and appeared a few moments later with a sleepy and bewildered Mako in her arms. The infant looked about, eyes wide as he tried to comprehend why he had been pulled from his bed.

'I have just got him used to sleeping in his own bed,' Dahlia warned as Aldara pulled the boy into her arms and wept into his hair.

Mako was still and unsure. When she covered his face with wet, salty kisses, he studied her with interest for a few moments before a coy smile spread across his face.

'Children do not forget their mothers,' Dahlia said, looking away from the emotional scene.

Aldara held him out to look at him properly. Even in a few short months he had grown so much.

'Your mama's back,' Kadmus said, encouraging the boy's excitement. 'And I imagine she has some exciting stories for us.'

Aldara hugged the boy to her again, and her father wrapped his arms around the both of them.

'Perhaps the stories can wait,' Isadore said.

She closed her eyes, trying to block the stories from her mind for a while longer.

'Inside with you,' Dahlia said, waving everybody towards the house. 'Have a wash before you do anything else.'

Isadore let go of Aldara and slipped an arm around his wife, pulling her into the pack. They walked into the house, Dahlia stiff beneath her husband's arm, Kadmus shaking his head and whistling for the dog to follow, and Aldara holding Mako with no intention of ever letting him go.

'I see those royals fattened you up again, just in time for the cold season,' Isadore said.

'Nothing a few extra chores won't fix,' Dahlia said.

Aldara had Mako on her hip and looked past her father at her mother. 'Was that a joke?' She turned to Kadmus. 'Is Mother making jokes now?'

Kadmus laughed and stopped walking so the others could enter the house ahead of him. 'Yes, Mother has been a bundle of laughter in your absence.'

'That is quite enough,' Dahlia said, unsmiling but her tone warm.

Aldara glanced once at the empty road where Leksi had left her, on his way to where he was needed most.

The first few nights back in her home, Aldara could barely sleep. She lay awake watching Mako sleep next to her, an arm draped over him, breathing in his soapy scent. She listened to the sounds of Kadmus's sleepy breaths in the next bed, replaying each day of the previous few months and practising Tyron's technique of finding room inside her for every painful memory. She thought of Tyron a lot whenever she watched Mako sleep, aware of how alike they were. She wondered if she closed her eyes and tried to listen for him, feel for him, if she might feel the moment he drew his last breath.

Live.

It was four days after her return when a messenger arrived with a letter for her. She held it with trembling hands as she watched the man ride away, a cloud of red dust between them. Mako ran through the dust squealing with laughter while Dahlia scolded him from the doorway.

'He's all right,' Aldara called back to her, wanting her son to enjoy his youth in whatever way pleased him, because years went by fast and she knew there was no returning to them.

She opened the letter, telling herself that if Tyron had passed away, someone would have come in person to tell her the news. Or would they? Who was she to expect such a thing?

The sight of Tyron's handwriting made her breath catch and her hand go over her mouth.

My dearest Aldara,

Where are you? Upon opening my eyes, it was my first thought, and upon opening my mouth, it was my first question. I was relieved to learn that you are exactly where you should be. You are with our son.

My next question? How in God's name did you get us to Wripis? I am in awe. What an impressive soldier you turned out to be. You win, you crazy, stubborn, beautiful girl. I sit here, alive yet feeling on the brink of death, because of you. I owe you my life, but this is not a new thing. I have been yours from the first time I heard you laugh.

Tomorrow I travel to Archdale, where I will remain until my health is restored. Given that I am exhausted by the simple act of holding a quill, I imagine it might be some time until I can come to Roysten and thank you in person.

Mako must have been pleased to see his mother. The memories I have of the two of you together will sustain me until I can make new ones.

I hope you know that you are the reason I am alive. You kind, funny and fierce girl. My love. My reason for believing in miracles. You are my life.

YOUR PRINCE,
   Tyron

SHE READ IT AGAIN, and then again, feeling him radiating from the words on the page. To know he was alive was one thing, but to read what was in his heart was quite another. She read it one more time, and then her hand fell to her side.

Still gripping the letter, she watched as Mako returned to her, face dirty and beaming. She crouched and opened her arms and he ran into them, almost causing her to lose balance. She pressed her lips against the top of his head, over and over until he wriggled free of her grip and was off at a run again.

THERE WAS no question that Otus was enjoying his retirement. The old war horse wandered the paddocks with the mares during the day, and in the evening, Mako sat on him while he ate his grain, enjoying the attention paid him.

'Hold on to his mane,' Aldara said as she stood next to them.

Kadmus walked into the barn and looked over at them. 'He is growing attached to the old gelding,' he said, grabbing the shovel and walking over to the stalls.

'I can see that.'

Kadmus stopped next to them, watching his nephew. 'Should I be worried that you have barely said a word about what happened in Corneo?'

It was true, she had not said much about it, perhaps because she was still processing her guilt and figuring out what it meant for Syrasan. She wondered what King Jayr would do now that another suitor for Princess Tasia had fallen through—been killed by them. Would Tyron be expected to fulfil his promise now that he was back at Archdale? And then there was Petra, holding her head high despite all that had happened. Aldara had meant what she said: she would make every effort to locate the mentor's son and tell her everything she herself would want to know as a mother separated from her child.

'Prince Tyron is alive. I suppose that is the important part,' she said, eyes on Mako.

Kadmus emitted a short laugh. 'You suppose? Sister, you sold yourself to a foreign king in order to get to him. There is no point in trying to play down your feelings now.' He walked into the first stall and began to shovel the manure.

'Did he miss me?' she asked, choked up. 'Was I wrong to have left him?'

Kadmus stopped and leaned on the shovel. 'He missed you most at night.'

She nodded. 'Yes, nights were hardest for me also.'

Kadmus studied her. 'I know it was a difficult choice to leave him. I know you feel guilty and that my reaction added to that guilt. I'm sorry.'

She glanced at him. 'I know why you did.' She pulled Mako from Otus's back and walked over to watch Kadmus work. 'Saying thank you doesn't seem adequate for how you stepped up in my absence.'

'It's what family does.'

Mako was wriggling to be put down. He always wanted to help Kadmus with his chores. She bent down and set him free. Kadmus stopped and waited for him to grip the shovel lower down.

'For what it is worth, thank you,' Aldara said. 'The only reason I could fathom going ahead with the plan was because I knew the rest of you would be here to love him the way he needs.'

Kadmus was about to respond when the sound of a wagon pulling up at the front of the house made them look at one another. He laid down the shovel and the three of them walked outside to see who it was.

The wagon door swung open and Lord Yuri stepped down before offering his hand. Hali reached out and took it, stepping down and thanking him before looking around. Aldara moved around Mako and broke into a run. When Hali spotted her, she did the same. They collided in an embrace in the middle, Aldara's eyes closed as she sucked in a breath.

'Dear God,' Hali said. 'I am so angry at you. You promised me you would not do anything stupid, and the next thing I hear, you have gone to Corneo to be sold as a Companion after promising me you would not. I told Yuri I shall never forgive you.'

Aldara squeezed her harder. 'Did you come here to tell me that in person?'

Hali pulled back, squinting at her. 'Yes!'

Aldara exhaled and took her friend's hands. 'I promised you I would not do anything stupid, so I made a plan with King Pandarus's approval, and the support of his family and his men.'

Hali leaned in and whispered, 'Were you really surprised that *he* was willing to sacrifice you? I thought you were smart.'

Aldara glanced back to watch Mako trying to catch up with them. 'Not at all. I'm sure he is devastated by my return.'

Hali pulled her hands free so she could crouch down as Mako approached. 'Hello there,' she said, beaming at the boy. She looked up at Aldara, smile vanishing. 'This does not mean you are forgiven.'

Aldara held up her hands. 'I would never assume such a thing.'

Mako let Hali pick him up and fuss over him. Kadmus walked past them, nodding at Hali before going to tend to Lord Yuri, who was waiting near the wagon. Dahlia and Isadore were yet to return from the village, and so it fell on them to play host. Hali and Aldara followed, Mako still in Hali's arms, pointing at the chickens that had taken advantage of the barn door being open and escaped.

'It is very good to see you safe and well,' Lord Yuri said to Aldara, bowing. 'Hali has spoken of nothing else. I almost regretted telling her of the situation.'

'Actually,' Hali said, 'you *immediately* regretted telling me, but it did not matter, because a few days later I received word from Princess Sapphira.'

'Don't let Sapphira hear you calling her that,' Aldara said.

Hali's eyes widened. 'Did you know she is with child?'

Aldara smiled. 'I had my suspicions.'

Hali looked at Lord Yuri. 'That translates to Prince Stamitos told her when he was not meant to.'

Lord Yuri and Kadmus laughed.

'And where are the two of you off to?' Aldara asked, changing the subject.

'Arelasa,' Lord Yuri replied. 'And yes, I am quite aware that this is not on the way. Hali can be rather convincing.' And he did not appear to mind in the slightest.

'It seems she was determined to tell me to my face that our friendship was at an end,' Aldara replied.

Everyone laughed, except for Hali.

'Would it kill you to beg for my forgiveness?' she said to Aldara.

Lord Yuri placed a calming hand on Hali. 'There is nothing to forgive. Prince Tyron is alive and regaining more strength every day.'

Aldara's smile faded at hearing his name. 'Have you seen him?'

'I do not think His Majesty would appreciate Lord Yuri showing up at Archdale with me,' Hali said.

Everyone fell quiet. Hali handed Mako to Kadmus and asked Aldara if she wanted to take a walk.

'Would you care to inspect our flock, Lord Yuri?' Kadmus asked.

Lord Yuri gave Hali a knowing smile. 'Yes. Let us leave the women to have the conversation they would rather not have in front of us.'

Hali smiled at him, and Aldara could see the same love between them she had witnessed years earlier.

The girls stopped to catch the few stray chickens that had wandered out, Aldara laughing as Hali darted about in her expensive dress, remembering the first time she had seen her walk out of that small, crowded house all those years back.

'You look just as ridiculous as me,' Hali quipped.

'No I don't,' Aldara replied, pushing the barn door closed and then looking at her. 'Your dress is beautiful, but not practical for any form of work.'

'Then it's a good thing I don't do any work.'

Aldara threaded her arm through Hali's, and they strolled away from the barn and the ears of the men.

'What do you do at the manor?' Aldara asked.

Hali shrugged. 'Whatever I like, really. I do a lot of cooking.'

'And what does the cook think of you taking over the kitchen?'

Hali glanced at her. 'Oh, she doesn't mind. I'm not sure if you remember, but most of the staff are so old they can barely perform their duties. Yuri is too kind for his own good.'

'Yes, I have always suspected that about him,' Aldara replied, smiling. 'There was one young maid by memory.'

Hali nodded. 'Yes, saviour of my sanity. I have been teaching her to read and write, hoping to improve her marriage prospects so she does not settle for the groom who seems to lose his tongue whenever she is present.'

'Goodness, what a snob you have become. We can't all be swept off our feet by widowed noblemen.'

Hali stopped walking and glanced back to ensure the others were out of earshot. 'All right,' she said, exhaling. 'Start at the beginning and do not stop until you get to the part where you are safely home and standing here with me.'

There was healing in speaking the story aloud, not just a summary of events but the parts she could only tell another Companion, and the parts she could only tell Hali. Her friend surprised her by not interrupting once, holding her pity and opinions until the end. Only when Aldara had finished did she let her brave expression fall.

'Don't look at me like that,' Aldara said, looking away. 'You endured far worse at the hands of King Jayr.'

'Yes, but our parting was rather civil in comparison. I did not have to kill anybody during my time there, as tempting as it was.'

Aldara lifted her gaze. 'Prince Felipe was not a particularly likeable man, but he did not deserve to die. I betrayed him—all of them. I never expected to feel guilty about that part. I suppose I never expected to make any sort of connections with people, imagining only a collective enemy.'

'You cannot feel guilty. You know as well as I do what would have happened if Prince Felipe had forced you to return to Masville Castle. He spelled it out for you.' Hali grabbed her hands. 'Someone had to lose. It was you or him, and I thank God it was him.'

Aldara's face softened. 'Does that mean I am forgiven?'

'Absolutely not.'

She exhaled, smiling. 'I miss you, but I am so glad to see you happy.'

They turned and began walking slowly back to the house.

'I am happy,' Hali said. 'I only hope Lord Yuri feels the same.'

'Of course he does. There is no hiding it.'

Hali bit down on her lip and looked over to where the men stood chatting. 'There are a few noble households who no longer call upon him. They'll happily receive him, as long as I remain at the manor.'

Aldara glanced across her. 'Yes, propriety always wins with those kinds of people. Lord Yuri is a smart man. He knew how it would be, and chose you anyway.'

'Why do you suppose he did?'

Aldara stopped and turned to her. 'Because he has lived long enough to realise that happiness is far more important. He loves you.'

Hali watched her for a moment. 'What do you suppose will happen when Tyron comes to see you?'

Aldara shrugged. 'I honestly don't know.'

'You cannot return to Archdale as his Companion, not with Mako.'

'No.'

'Would you return without him?'

Aldara shook her head. 'Never, and Tyron would never want me to.'

Hali resumed walking and Aldara fell into step with her.

'And even if by some miracle Mako was invited to live there with you, you swore you would never go back.'

'Not to live.'

Hali glanced over in the direction of Byrgus's farm. 'Does your special friend know of your return?'

'Leo?'

'Yes, *Leo*,' she said with a smile. 'Has he called on you?'

The awkward conversation between them came back to Aldara. 'Yes.'

'And?'

Aldara inhaled before speaking. 'And I told him there was no future for us.' When Hali did not respond, she added, 'I suppose you think I'm a fool for throwing away my one prospect.'

Hali's face was serious. 'But he is not your only prospect.' She pulled a face. 'He is just your easy prospect.'

'I cannot afford to think like that.'

'Like what? Optimistic?'

Aldara laughed. 'Hali, do you remember when we were at Archdale and you said to me, "We are so past fairy tales now"?'

Hali looked over at Lord Yuri for a moment, watching him crouched down, speaking with Mako. 'I was wrong.'

Aldara closed her eyes against the words. She could not let hope back in because it would destroy her. The best outcome she could ask for had already taken place.

Opening her eyes, she turned to her son. It was enough. Mako, her family, her free life, a living and breathing Tyron.

It had to be enough.

CHAPTER 35

*W*hile Tyron was grateful to be recovering at Archdale, with every comfort he could imagine, he also felt misplaced. Two weeks it took for him to gain enough strength to leave his bed and eat his meals by the window in his bedchamber. He would stare out at the servants moving about below, speaking and laughing as they passed one another.

As he watched, he reflected on the previous few weeks, going over everything that had happened, trying to make sense of it, find meaning in it. He was figuring a way forwards, his thoughts stealing entire afternoons.

Visitors came and went. His sister would sit quietly next to his bed, observing him in a way that was unusual for her. His mother would bring Princess Tai and make a fuss about her not jumping on the bed because his wound was still healing. He had no doubt that she wanted him well, but suspected she did not want him well enough to return to Corneo. One time she fell silent for a long time, and when he asked her if something was the matter, she spoke of her overwhelming gratitude. She wanted to write to Aldara but was struggling to put into words what she wanted to say to her. He had looked away, relating to the struggle.

Queen Salome gave birth to a son, and his mother brought the boy to him so he could meet the new Crown Prince of Syrasan. Aside from the usual feelings that came with holding new life, Tyron also felt a tremendous amount of relief knowing that if anything were to happen to Pandarus, he was no longer next in line to rule. Sapphira also came to visit, breaking the news that she was with child and asking that no fuss be made about it. She asked if he was planning to take a trip south when he was better.

Yes, he was.

Three weeks into his recovery, after his morning meal, he told Pero that he was going for a walk outdoors.

'I will come with you, my lord,' said the squire, looking up from his poems.

'I would prefer to go alone.'

Pero nodded and waited for him to leave before taking up his quill once more.

When Tyron stepped outside, he was surprised to discover the sun held no warmth, the air thick with coming rain. He stood in the cold, grieving the end of the warm season because he knew how much the sun sustained Aldara. Already tired from the long walk to get that far, he rested for a moment, surprised when Cora appeared in the doorway, squinting against the glare as though it were a form of torture.

'I'm surprised to find you up this early,' he teased.

She stepped outside and walked over to him. 'Well, I went to visit you in the pleasant darkness of your chambers, but you were not there.'

He inhaled deeply. 'I needed air.'

'Are you sure you should be out here alone? What if you fall?'

He watched her, amusement in his eyes. 'Careful, that is bordering on concern. Besides, I am not alone, am I?'

She maintained her scowl despite his smile, and they both looked out at the dry lawn of the bailey that would soon green up with the arrival of rain.

'There is something I wanted to tell you,' she said, her tone casual.

'Should I be worried?'

Her eyes went to him briefly. 'I met with Pandarus yesterday.'

'Now I am worried.'

'While you have been slowly clawing your way back from death,' she continued, ignoring him, 'the rest of the kingdom has been in a panic. We have men on the northern border, men on the eastern border. And everyone is waiting to see what comes of the mess left behind in Corneo.'

Tyron had been waiting also, wondering what King Jayr's next move would be after recent events. 'All right, I am curious. Why did you meet with Pandarus?'

She hesitated, which was very out of character for someone who never thought twice about what came out of her mouth. 'I have not been of much use during this war, or any war for that matter.'

He smiled. 'We have men to fight our wars because we prefer to keep you unarmed.'

She looked at him. 'There are other ways I can help.'

He waited for her to continue. 'I'm listening.'

Her gaze returned to the brown lawn. 'I am going to wed King Jayr and put an end to the uncertainty.'

He laughed, a short disbelieving sound. 'No you're not.'

'Yes I am. Pandarus has already sent a messenger to Zoelin with his offer. I will wed him as early as next week.'

Tyron's expression darkened. He would go straight to Pandarus and put an end to this madness. However, as he went to leave, she reached out and grabbed his arm. Physical gestures were so rare for his sister that he immediately stilled beneath her hand.

'It is done,' she said. 'And for once, the decision was mine.'

He stared at her. 'You cannot marry that man.'

'You think I cannot handle a man like Jayr?'

He pulled his arm free. 'I know you cannot. The man is a monster.'

'People say the same of me.' Her back straightened. 'You underestimate me.'

'You underestimate *him!*' She flinched but he continued. 'You cannot handle me raising my voice? He will take a hand to your face every time you displease him.'

She raised her chin. 'That might be true of other women, but not the queen. You forget that I spent years learning about Zoelin culture, preparing for this exact reason.'

'If this is about choosing your own husband, then choose someone else.'

'Tyron, we have run out of options. Even if you still were to marry Princess Tasia, it is not enough for us anymore. We need influence.'

'You speak as if *you* will have influence—'

'I will have influence.'

He shook his head, wanting there to be another answer. 'You will be at risk, forever looking over your shoulder.'

'I will also be the queen of Zoelin. You see it as a tragedy, but I see it as the first real decision I have ever made for myself.' She was silent for a moment. 'We are all capable of sacrifices. This is mine.'

He turned and walked away from her.

PANDARUS DID NOT SEEM SURPRISED to see Tyron. He was in

the throne room with one of his advisors when the guard announced his arrival. Pandarus told his advisor to leave them and shuffled the loose pieces of parchment spread across the table in front of him into a neat pile. He sat on the edge of the table, looking at his brother, as though he were waiting for something.

Tyron did not keep him waiting long. 'I just spoke with Cora.'

Pandarus nodded and folded his arms in front of him. 'I can see that by your face.' He frowned and looked about. 'Before you begin, I want you to know I had the same reaction as you initially.'

'I doubt that. I said no.'

A knowing smile spread across Pandarus's face. 'So did I, but contrary to what we might believe, Cora might actually know what she is doing.'

Tyron stared at him. 'King Jayr has proven time and time again that he cannot be trusted. And you want to hand him our sister?'

Pandarus stood. 'You think I *want* to hand Cora over to him? Do you realise the position we are in at the moment? If the trade agreement between Zoelin and Corneo goes ahead, we have nothing else to offer. Your betrothal to Princess Tasia ended when your execution date was set!' He calmed himself. 'You wanted the trade agreement gone, well this is the cost. We do not have the men to fight both the Zoelin and Corneon armies if they were to fight together. Lord Belen's dismal contribution is no match for an army that size.' Pandarus looked at his brother. 'I have already sent the offer.'

'What were your conditions?'

'No alliance with Corneo. No trade with Corneo.'

'And why would he accept? His attraction to Cora is not worth that much to him.'

'Because we have proven we are the stronger side. King Nilos is desperate, and a desperate king cannot be trusted.'

'I would say we are rather desperate right now.'

'We have Galen, we have food, and we have the West of Corneo. King Nilos has only starving people and spreading disease. I know what I would choose.'

Tyron shook his head. 'How can you trust him?'

'I can't. So I must trust our ferocious sister.' Seeing Tyron's doubt, he added, 'Historically, the queens of Zoelin have been treated with a great deal of respect.'

He linked his fingers behind his neck. It was the longest he had been out of his bed in some time, and he was bordering on exhaustion. 'What did our mother say?'

Pandarus exhaled. 'She does not know yet.'

He blinked. 'Are you prepared for that conversation?'

'No.'

They looked at one another, Tyron noticing a change in his brother. The arrogance that had been present since youth was slowly being replaced by something else—something that had been present in his father.

'I am certain King Jayr will accept our offer.' Pandarus unfolded his arms. 'And when you are well enough, I would like you to return east, manage the food supply there, and implement better farming practices. Lord Belen likes you. Let's keep it that way.'

Tyron nodded. 'The plan sounds rather long-term.'

'Is that a problem?'

'No.'

'I need someone I trust there. Stamitos will soon be wanting to return for the birth of his child.' He studied Tyron, trying to read his expression. 'Don't worry, I'll let you keep Leksi. The last thing I need is him brooding around here because he is lost without you.'

Tyron nodded and remained where he was.

'You want something,' Pandarus said, visibly enjoying the power he had in that moment. 'What is it?'

He was now so tired he was tempted to ask for a chair, but his pride stopped him. 'I am loyal to you, to our people. I am loyal until my death. Wherever you send me, I'll go. I will always fight in your name and give my life for the causes you see fit.'

'Yes, yes,' Pandarus said, moving him along. 'You have proven your loyalty enough times. What do you want?'

'Just one thing.'

Pandarus's gaze shifted to the wall and he emitted a long whistle. 'I am not going to like this, am I?'

'No.'

But he would ask it anyway.

CHAPTER 36

They were out front of the farmhouse, Aldara wrapped in a shawl against the cold afternoon air while Kadmus and Mako raced the length of the small house.

'Winner!' Mako squealed every time, even when he lost or gave up halfway.

Kadmus turned around, walked back to him, and lifted him high in the air. 'You're a cheat is what you are.'

'I wonder where he gets that from,' Aldara called out.

Dahlia stepped past her, a basket of washing on her hip. 'I did not realise we were done for the day. Your father is still out there working.'

Kadmus glanced at Aldara, a grin on his face. She inhaled and said nothing. Only when Dahlia had disappeared behind the house did she speak.

'Never mind that I was first up this morning and completed every chore with Mako attached to my leg.'

'When will you learn?' Kadmus laughed. 'Whatever you do, it will never be enough.'

Aldara rolled her bare feet on the wooden steps, her eyes going to the road. They always went to the road. It had been weeks since her return and she had not heard from Tyron since his letter—the letter she carried in her pocket. 'All right, one more race, Mako. Then we need to feed the horses.'

Kadmus lowered the boy next to him and bent down, ready to race his eager nephew, when Mako turned around and shouted, 'Horse!'

Aldara's eyes went to the road, the usually empty road, where a tall chestnut horse trotted along, turning onto the track and coming towards them. On top of the horse sat Tyron, his hair trimmed and beard short, wearing royal dress, a red tunic and brass buttons that caught the sun's reflection. There was colour in his face, and the weight had returned to him. His bright eyes locked on hers and a smile spread across his face. She wanted to get up, run to him, but she was enjoying the sight of him, healthy and happy to see her.

He stopped a short distance from Mako, who had wandered over to investigate the visitor. Tyron crouched and spoke to him in a soft voice while their son kept a wary distance, occasionally looking back to see if his mother approved of this man. She stood, walking over to stand by Kadmus. They watched as Mako crept closer to his father, trusting a little more with every word exchanged, until Tyron held out his hands and Mako stepped forwards to be lifted so he could pat the horse.

Only then did Aldara walk towards them, heart pounding and hands clammy. He turned his head and looked at her, eyes shiny at the sight of her.

'Up, up,' Mako squealed, pointing to the horse.

Tyron laughed. 'You might be a bit young.'

'You might be surprised,' Aldara said, smiling up at him.

Kadmus gave an awkward bow. 'My lord,' he said. 'Do you mind if Mako and I borrow your horse?'

Tyron glanced at him, nodded, and then handed Mako to him. They watched as Kadmus sat him in the saddle and told him to hold on to the mane like he had been taught. Kadmus then led the excited boy around at a slow walk, remaining by the shoulder of the horse in case he was needed.

Aldara sneaked a look at Tyron, whose pride was visible. 'He may have some of my vices,' she said, turning to him.

His eyes went to her, and he turned also. 'At least he uses a saddle.'

She had stopped at a polite distance, unsure of what he wanted, of his expectations. And not trusting herself close to him.

'Did you get my letter?' he asked.

She looked down at her pocket and pulled it out to show him the yellowing paper, read so many times it was wearing along the folds. They both stared at it for a moment. 'Yes,' she replied, looking back at him. She exhaled, her nerves visible. 'You look much better than the last time I saw you.'

'I imagine you do too.'

She suppressed a smile. 'I was fine after a bath or two.' She pushed the letter back into her pocket and they both glanced over at Mako, who was babbling words to Kadmus that only family could translate.

'How long are you staying?' Aldara asked. She seemed to be asking that question a lot to visitors.

'I have men waiting in the village,' he said. 'I return to Lord Belen's manor in the morning.'

She nodded. What else had she expected? Her hands kneaded the shawl that was pulled tightly around her.

'Are you cold?'

Her eyes returned to him. 'I don't know what I am. Nervous, perhaps.'

He smiled. 'Nervous? After everything?'

'Especially after everything.' Her gaze dropped to his elaborate brass buttons.

He stepped closer and placed his hands on her arms, the warmth from his hands immediate. She stopped breathing, still focused on those buttons.

'Look at me,' he said. When she hesitated, he added, 'Please.'

She looked up and told herself to breathe.

'I came here to thank you in person. I came here to see my son, to see you.' He reached up and brushed back her loose hair. 'And to ask one more thing of you.'

Anything. She swallowed. 'What is that?'

His eyes moved between hers as though wanting the answer before having asked the question. 'Will you come with me?'

Her eyes widened, but she said nothing.

'And Mako, of course.'

She looked at her son. 'And Mako,' she repeated.

'Yes.'

She turned back to him, unsure. 'You want me to come to Wripis… as your Companion?'

He shook his head, his hands moving down her arms. 'No.' He stepped closer, his legs brushing against the skirt of her dress. 'I want you to come to Wripis as my *wife*.'

Her breathing changed, and she suspected he was holding her up. 'As your… wife.' It was not a question; she was getting used to the sound of the word.

'Yes,' he said, pulling her to him, his hands sliding along her back. 'As my wife.'

She shook her head. 'You want to marry me?'

He laughed. 'I have wanted to marry you for a long time.'

She looked around, thinking of all the reasons they could not marry. 'But you are not allowed to marry me.'

He bent down to her, kissing her. 'Yes I am,' he whispered into her mouth.

'But Pandarus—' She kept her words to a minimum so his mouth would not leave hers. Her hands went to his face, just in case.

'Gave me his blessing,' he finished.

She was crying then, withdrawing from him and covering her eyes as her body shook beneath his grip.

He wrapped her until she could barely draw a breath. 'I really hope they are happy tears.'

She could not respond.

'Please look at me,' he said. 'Please look up and tell me yes. Tell me you will marry me and I will not have to leave here without my family.'

She lowered her hands and looked at him, her body trembling. 'Nobody is walking away this time.' She tried to smile but a sob came in its place.

He lifted her, pulling her legs around him, soothing her with words.

She buried her face in his neck and clung to him.

They remained that way, time slipping past them. He could not put her down, and she was unable to let go.

And for the first time neither of them had to.

EPILOGUE

*A*ldara bent and tore the long weeds from the earth, noting the improved quality of the soil. Their gardener, Miles, worked alongside her, stopping regularly to look at whatever latest bug Mako wanted to show him.

'It's a big one all right,' Miles said, crouching down to get a better look.

They had selected their own staff, keeping the household to one maid, a cook and a gardener. When it came time to select a governess, Aldara had found excuses, delaying the process until Tyron one day kissed her on the forehead and said, 'No governess.'

'What have you found, Mako?' Aldara called to him.

'A beetle,' he replied, walking over and showing her the black and purple insect.

She wrapped an arm about his chubby shoulders and kissed his dirty face. 'It's beautiful.' She straightened, placing her hands on her lower back and wincing as she stretched.

'Are you all right, my lady?' Miles asked, glancing across at her bulging stomach.

She turned and smiled at him. 'Yes.'

'Perhaps you should go inside,' he said, his face creased against the bright sun. 'Rest for a while.'

She shook her head. 'Soon the baby will be here, and the cold season. There will be plenty of time for rest when I am trapped indoors.'

He went to speak and thought better of it, returning to the weeds instead.

Aldara glanced about the garden. 'Mako, why don't you go check the tomatoes.' He turned and ran off. 'Only pick the red ones!' She exhaled and rubbed at her lower back, watching as Mako stepped between the rows of vines, searching for ripened fruit.

At the sound of a voice, Mako looked in the direction of the house. A smile lit up his face. 'Father!'

Aldara turned to see Tyron walking towards them. He bent and scooped their son into his arms, his eyes going to her, a soft smile forming. When he reached her, he put the boy down and placed a hand on her belly.

'Has my wife been resting in my absence, Miles?' he called to the gardener.

Miles continued to pull weeds. 'I haven't had much luck getting her out of the garden, my lord.'

'That sounds about right,' Tyron said, crouching down and kissing her belly. His forehead rested against it for a moment, and her hands went into his hair.

'How was your sister?' Aldara asked.

Tyron had gone to Zoelin for the sole purpose of checking on her, to ensure she was settled, coping with her new role as the queen of Zoelin, and most importantly, being treated well by her husband, King Jayr.

He stood up, bringing Mako with him. 'Seemingly enjoying her new status. But you know Cora. She is not one to admit defeat.'

'No, but you can normally tell how well she is coping by the amount she is drinking.'

'I would say moderate to excessive, so about normal. She has a surprising number of spies already at work.'

'How does she know she can trust them?'

'It's Cora—she trusts no one.'

Aldara looked him for a moment. 'What of Princess Tasia?'

'Rumoured to soon be betrothed to a suitor in Asigow.'

'Asigow?' She fell silent.

'What's the matter?'

'I'm trying to decide if that's better or worse than a marriage to Prince Felipe.'

'Better,' Tyron said without hesitation. 'Reports suggest his near-death experience has not improved his nature.' His expression softened. 'And what about you? Any luck finding Petra's son?'

Aldara bit down on her lip and turned her face away. 'No, nothing yet. It seems the boy is not with any of the king's extended family. Lord Belen is being very helpful. We have to locate him eventually.'

'Don't lose hope. Lord Belen has a lot of contacts outside of the West.'

'I am grateful he does.'

Tyron ran a finger down her face. 'We are all grateful. Most of our information is received via his contacts.'

Aldara looked at Mako. 'I saw him yesterday. He insists we are safe here.'

Tyron smiled and brought his forehead down against hers. 'I would never have gone to Zoelin if I thought for a moment there was any danger. King Nilos is too busy trying to win back favour with the few men still loyal to him to start another war.'

Mako, losing patience with their adult conversation,

began tugging on his father's tunic. 'Are they here?' he asked, bouncing with excitement in Tyron's arms.

Tyron turned to Aldara, eyes smiling. 'Yes, they are here.'

She looked past him. 'They are? Why didn't you say so?'

He rolled his eyes. 'Because I wanted to have a conversation with my wife who I have missed for the last six days.'

'And the priest?'

He kissed her hair and wrapped an arm about her. 'Any moment now.'

They walked slowly back to the house, the modest home Tyron had thought was too small and Aldara had thought was plenty. Out front stood Lord Yuri and Hali, eyes on the priest who had arrived on horseback, dressed in his finest robe. The old man dismounted with great effort before rummaging through his saddlebag, in search of the book of God from which he would read.

'Look at you!' Hali said, catching sight of Aldara. She moved towards her, arms outstretched. 'You look ready to burst.' She wrapped her arms about her before kissing her cheek.

'I feel ready to burst.' Aldara looked past her to Lord Yuri, who was watching them. 'My lord, how was your journey?'

Yuri walked over to them once he was sure he was not intruding. 'Uneventful, just the way we like it. You look lovely, my lady. Motherhood certainly agrees with you.'

'My back has a difference of opinion.'

Tyron, who had gone to help the priest, came over and stood with them. 'Is everyone ready?'

'Yes,' they all answered at the same time.

The old priest shuffled towards them, his head stooped and back hunched. 'Where is the chapel?' he asked, looking about through squinting eyes.

'There is no chapel as such,' Aldara said, turning to him. 'But I have just the spot.'

They strolled down to a small lake alive with water lilies and wild ducks, framed by overhanging trees. They stood in the shade, the priest with his back to the water, soon-to-be husband and wife standing in front of him, and two witnesses.

Aldara leaned against Tyron while Mako, immediately bored by the priest's dry tone, searched the grass for insects.

'Stretch out now also Thy hand from Thy holy dwelling place, and unite Thy servant and this handmaiden.'

The priest spoke loudly to compete with the sounds of nature.

'She looks beautiful,' Aldara whispered. 'And so happy.'

People had already formed their own views on the northern lord and the former Companion. The wedding was not to sway opinion—it was just for them.

Tyron kissed the top of Aldara's head and looked back at the couple in front of them, repeating vows of love and faithfulness. Hali began to cry, smiling with embarrassment as she wiped her cheeks. Lord Yuri reached up and wiped at them also, his own eyes shiny.

'Unite them in one mind, wed them into one flesh, granting to them the fruit of the body and the procreation of fair children.'

Tyron placed his hand on Aldara's stomach, his thumb rubbing gently. 'They deserve their own miracle,' he whispered into her hair.

She smiled and pressed against him. His arm tightened around her shoulder and he inhaled, breathing her in, the way he always did. Her eyes closed, holding on to the moment—another moment that was theirs to keep.

'Crown them with glory and honour.

'Crown them with glory and honour.

'Crown them with glory and honour.'

ACKNOWLEDGMENTS

I would like to express my gratitude to the many people who contributed to this book. What started as a pregnant dream, has now grown into a series.

My biggest thank you goes to my readers. Without readers I would not get to do what I love. Next, a huge thank you to my rock star husband who supports and encourages me even though my writing takes time away from him. A big thank you to Joanna Walsh from Saltwater Writers for your feedback and support. A shout out to Dr Timothy Blake for checking all the medical components of the story. Thank you to Kristin and the team at Hot Tree Editing for polishing the manuscript into something beautiful, and to my proofreader Rebecca Fletcher for catching everything I missed. Thanks to my beta readers for your honest (and entertaining) feedback and to the very talented Ben Kawala for another gorgeous cover. And finally, a huge thank you to my Launch Team for your encouragement, honest reviews and being the final set of eyes on my work. Your support is much appreciated.

ALSO BY TANYA BIRD

THE COMPANION SERIES:

The Royal Companion #1
The Common Girl #2
The Majestic Impostor #3

99855808R00214

Made in the USA
Columbia, SC
12 July 2018